naughty bits

AN ANTHOLOGY *of* SHORT EROTIC FICTION

3

naughty bits

AN ANTHOLOGY of SHORT EROTIC FICTION

3

LETTY JAMES

AMANDA MCINTYRE

KATE AUSTIN

MEGAN HART

JENNIFER DALE

EVA CASSEL

GRACE D'OTARE

ALISON RICHARDSON

ADELAIDE COLE

Spice

NAUGHTY BITS 3

ISBN-13: 978-0-373-60553-8

Copyright © 2011 by Spice Books.

The publisher acknowledges the copyright holders of the individual works as follows:

THE COUNTESS'S CLIENT
Copyright © 2009 by Alison Richardson

DEVOURED
Copyright © 2008 by Sherri Denora

DREAMER
Copyright © 2008 by Kate Austin

THE PIRATE'S TALE
Copyright © 2009 by Splendide Mendax, Inc.

ACTING THE PART
Copyright © 2009 by Eva Cassel

HER LORD AND MASTER
Copyright © 2009 by Jennifer Dale

MIRROR, MIRROR
Copyright © 2008 by Pamela Johnson

REASON ENOUGH
Copyright © 2008 by Megan Hart

THE FLOWER ARRANGEMENT
Copyright © 2009 by Adelaide Cole

For questions and comments about the quality of this book please contact us
at Customer_eCare@Harlequin.ca.

Spice and Colophon are trademarks used under license and registered in
Australia, New Zealand, Philippines, United States Patent and Trademark Office
and in other countries.

www.Spice-Books.com

Printed in U.S.A.

Recycling programs
for this product may
not exist in your area.

TABLE OF CONTENTS

THE COUNTESS'S CLIENT

Alison Richardson

THE PRACTICE OF GENUINE VIRTUE LEADS TO A life of odious boredom—of that there can be no question— and I cannot imagine that there is a woman alive who honestly aspires to the unhealthy ideal of true feminine chastity. The *appearance* of virtue, however, is a very useful thing. Scandal is a noblewoman's enemy; it robs her of her freedom and her place in society, and it ought to be avoided at all costs. As the only daughter of Frederick the Great's most famous general, I have always known what Prussian society expects of me, and given the constraints placed on young women like myself, I have never doubted that a certain amount of deception is essential to my personal happiness. To actually *be* as virtuous as narrow convention demands is far too high a sacrifice for any woman to make; to *appear* virtuous, however, requires only a small measure of ingenuity and a little luck.

Until the age of twenty, I could boast that I had lived a perfect life of apparent virtue, enjoying all the pleasures that are every woman's natural birthright without the slightest injury to either my status or my person. I have now, however, had one notable failure, and I feel compelled to record the story of this unhappy event, so that others might avoid the snares that caught me.

Let me first explain more clearly the general principles that have guided me since my youth.

It became evident to me at a young age that if a woman wishes for herself a degree of independence in her erotic pursuits, she must take care that the men in her life remain discreet and tractable. Achieving this state of affairs is no easy task, and the institution of marriage is, as the turbulent history of my own family attests, no solution to the problem. Accorded a greater degree of free movement than women, men are correspondingly more difficult to keep silent and still, and this fact introduces a great many complexities when you are seeking to gain some measure of control over them. The male's natural loquaciousness and desire for gratuitous self-display only adds to the problem. Secrecy is a woman's greatest boon, publicity a man's first desire, and in understanding that fact, you have understood the origins of the war that rages between the sexes.

Fear of death is, of course, an excellent inducement for a man to hold his tongue, and if you are lucky enough to find yourself in a situation in which the man would forfeit his life should he reveal his true relationship with you, then you find yourself well placed indeed. If you, like me, live in a garrison town, the ready availability of soldiers offers excellent possibilities in this regard. Everyone knows that fucking the general's daughter is a hanging offense in the Prussian army, and because of this wise policy, I have been entertained by countless recruits without the slightest harm to either my reputation or theirs.

This healthy and useful diversion, such a source of consistent enjoyment throughout my youth, was sadly no longer available to me when my family decided to send me to Paris to live with my aging aunt and my cousin Robert, and it was in this new city that I made my first misstep.

At this point in my life, I had been recently widowed, after a brief and uneventful marriage to a man much older than myself, and my father had decided that closer ties to my late mother's relatives in Paris would be useful both to me and to the family. When the roads cleared in the spring, I left Berlin with a small staff and my belongings, for an extended stay in the French capital, accompanied by my deaf and nearly blind aunt, who talked of nothing across all of Germany but her eagerness to see her son. My cousin Robert did his best to make his mother and me welcome in his Paris house when we arrived, and as a man of wide-ranging philosophical interests, he was a pleasant and diverting companion. I spent many fruitful hours watching him at his delicate experiments, and we discussed Bailly and Lavoisier over dinner every evening with great enthusiasm.

Unfortunately, I could find little else to do for amusement in my cousin's house, all of Robert's male servants being either old or ill-formed.

Robert had always been fond of me, and he was happy to have me and his mother with him. That I did not doubt. But during my early days in Paris, there was sometimes a certain tension about him that made me wonder if the sudden introduction of two women into his household had not altered his solitary habits in ways that he sometimes found straining.

I arrived home early one afternoon from my walk in the park to discover that that was indeed the case. My deaf old aunt was off taking chocolate with some other ancient countess, and our manservant opened the door with a look of unusual nervousness. I would have noticed his odd manner had my mind not been distracted by an injury my little dog had sustained during our walk. He had scraped his paw against a rough stone while playing in the grass, and given the calamity that had befallen my darling, I was deaf to the pressing suggestions of the loyal old man that I wait in the front room for a glass of wine to refresh me after my walk.

After ordering the man to send up hot water and some rags for my poodle, I ascended the stairs to my bedroom, but decided, halfway up, that I wanted a book to entertain me if I was to spend a quiet afternoon alone with my poor pet, and I returned to the library.

I entered the door to find Robert reclining on his new red velvet divan with his breeches around his ankles. A very strong and energetic girl was taking her pleasure across his lap, and he was holding her ass very tightly, his eyes focused with intense concentration on her generous bouncing breasts.

She was astonishingly well formed, the girl in my cousin's lap—plump, pretty and blonde, and also entirely naked, and she was riding his cock with great vigor, which spoke well of the seriousness with which she approached her chosen profession.

I complimented my cousin on his taste in whores and asked him if he knew where his librarian had put the copy of *Héloïse,* now that it was back from the binders.

Robert had been flustered by my precipitous entry, but when he noticed that I was not at all upset by the condition in which I had found him, he let out a hearty laugh and said he was pleased to discover that we shared a taste for more than philosophy.

He also revealed that the social appointment he kept with such insistent regularity every Thursday evening was in fact a visit to a local brothel, the place that Claudette (that was the name of the plump blonde in his lap) called home. He confessed himself relieved to know that despite having spent my early years in a desolate, hopeless backwater like Prussia (his words, not mine), I had not been quite as sheltered as he had assumed. Indeed, my cousin, in his kind and good-natured way, was so happy to be relieved of the unpleasantness of secrecy, which can be such an ugly source of discord in a home, that he gallantly suggested that if I had nothing better to do I should come along on his Thursday visits.

The brothel of Madame Barthez, my cousin's favorite house of pleasure, was equipped with an ingenious set of peepholes so that clients and their women might be watched with complete anonymity at any time, and through these little holes, placed discreetly through oil paintings or within the patterns of wallpaper, one could observe the favorite sport of the French aristocracy in all its vice-ridden variety. Unfortunately, despite its unquestionable visual interest, Madame Barthez's house could give me no actual *physical* pleasure, save what I could give myself. The brothel had no men on offer, and I have never been able to expand my tastes to girls, though I know that this is a damning mark of my provinciality (one for which Robert has often rebuked me).

Even with this additional source of diversion, my situation in Paris was still not what I would have wished for myself, and I was beginning to fear that I might well be confined to the modest pleasures of voyeurism for the foreseeable future. After all, there are only so many situations in which one can arrange to have fear of imminent death working to keep a man's lips sealed, and no such lucky occasion had presented itself to me in a while.

Then, on a slow Thursday at the brothel, an evening on which there happened to be very little for me to watch, I was sitting in the private room that the girls used when they were waiting for more clients to arrive, and a new opportunity arose.

The girls had gotten used to my visits over the weeks, and on this particular evening, they took little notice of me. Though I think that most of them had no real liking for me, they tolerated my presence amicably enough, mostly, I think, because my cousin was such a good customer—young, rich and full of harmlessly perverse desires that helped run up his tab. One might expect that these girls would have preferred easy, simple jobs, but that was far from the case. They had all the disdain of aristocrats for the men who came to the bordello wanting nothing more than a short, satisfying fuck. Such straightforward, uncomplicated sexual urges they considered a mark of bad taste, and they felt ill-treated when all a client asked of them was the use of their pussy for a quarter hour.

It was this fastidiousness that provided me with a solution to my difficulties. There was one man in particular who was the constant object of their scorn, a commoner of some unspecified trade who, like my cousin, was always there on Thursdays. When Madame Barthez came to say that this man had arrived, the girls always squabbled over who would be sent to him. (Madame never said his name; she only announced with a severe eye, "He's here. One of you has to go.") She usually had to choose someone herself in the end, and the unlucky girl always left grumbling.

When asked why they disliked this client so much, the girls talked about his appallingly bad French (the man was a foreigner—an Englishman or Irishman, probably Irish), and they mentioned the lack of ornament on his clothes; but the most common complaint was the simplicity and brevity of the services he required.

"He always arrives right after the theater lets out, so you're sure to miss a better client when you have to go to him, and then he takes his pathetic quarter hour and that is all you earn for the night."

"I think he's used to fucking cows on some English farm, the vulgar bastard."

"He doesn't even bother to undress, and when you walk in he hardly looks at you. He only tells you to get down on all fours on the bed, and then he just takes out that big horse's dick of his and rams it in, like some horny country boy."

"I tried loosening his breeches myself once, to see if I could get him to take a little more interest, but the stupid peasant just pushed my hand away and said that he wasn't paying extra for any theater."

"Cheap bastard."

"I moaned once, and he slapped me on the ass and told me to shut up."

"He's beneath us. Madame thinks so, too—he should just go and find a girl on the street. But he is a *client* of the Duke de Brecis, so Madame can't send him away."

These girls understood the web of social obligations that bound together the French aristocracy and their dependents better than most ladies-in-waiting.

It was a Thursday, and Madame Barthez had just ordered Claudette to go to this detested cheap client when the plan came to me, already fully formed, as if I had been considering it for weeks. A whole crowd of young Russian noblemen had just arrived in the foyer, and Claudette was complaining that she had been with the dreaded Irishman just two weeks ago, and arguing that it wasn't right to make her miss a chance at the Russians. The other girls were begging her to stop resisting, since none of them wanted to have to go themselves.

"How is he to look at, this foreigner?" I asked, speaking loudly in order to be heard over the bickering.

The girls all shrugged and said grudgingly (I could tell they hated to say anything nice about him) that he was not unappealing, if one did not mind the crudeness of his clothes.

"Does he have all his teeth?" They all gave little irritated sighs, vexed to have their argument interrupted by such a stupid question, and then told me that he did in fact still have all his teeth as far as they knew.

"I'll go, then," I said matter-of-factly, standing up from the lounge.

Madame Barthez laughed nervously. "Ah, *la jeune comtesse* is witty."

"I am not joking," I answered, pulling off my gloves and my jacket. "And I'll pay you for the time. Then you'll have double the fee for this Irishman, plus whatever Claudette can tease out of the Russians."

"But, Comtesse…" Madame was clearly worried about what my cousin might think of my allowing myself to be used in this manner.

"Someone get me a dress." My own gown, I knew, would betray me; no one, even the stupidest commoner, would mistake it for that of a prostitute.

The girls were staring at me with wide eyes—it is no small feat, I think, to shock a roomful of whores—all except Claudette, who pulled a garment out of the wardrobe and held it out toward me, smiling reassuringly, as if worried I might change my mind.

I had no intention of changing my mind. I could see no reason this unpopular client should not be made to provide me with some relief from my forced chastity. I do not know why this simple solution had not occurred to me before. Men flocked to this place every night, and not all of them traveled in elevated circles. I had no Irish aquaintances, and no English ones, at least not in Paris; this man would never know that I was not just another one of the many girls Madame Barthez had in supply. He would have no cause to tell anyone about our meeting, for no one boasts about sex with a whore. The girls would not begrudge me the satisfaction, and the man would never know he had done something about which it would be worthwhile to brag.

A few of the girls had recovered now from their surprise and rushed forward to help me dress, realizing that my strange inclination was to their advantage. Madame Barthez still did not look happy as she led me up the stairs, but when I whispered to her that I would pay her double for the time, her expression softened.

As my hand was on the doorknob to the room where this stranger waited for his hired company, I wondered what I would do if their account of him had been somehow misleading and I walked through the door and saw someone I knew.

To my relief, the man was in fact unknown to me, and the girls had, as it turned out, undersold his charm. The simple cut of his clothes was not a detraction. Plain linen looked well on him; his thick, muscled body would have looked awkward in a satin waistcoat. His jacket was off, and he had loosened his shirt at the throat; with his collar hanging open like that he looked like a gardener waiting in the kitchen for his supper. His wavy, red-blond hair had the same disheveled look as his clothing, tousled and disorderly, though short like an artisan's. There was indeed something gorgeously crude about him, a quality all the more striking given the affected and extravagant fixtures of the room.

I do not know if you have ever had such an experience yourself, but I can tell you that it is quite an interesting sensation to be so suddenly faced with an unknown man who expects you to give yourself to him without the slightest preparation.

The man had been standing at the window, staring out into the night. *"Tu es nouveau,"* he said brusquely after he had glanced over at me. The girls had been right; his French was appalling.

"Yes, sir, I'm new," I answered in English, not wanting to hear any more of his French, and he gave a small start of surprise.

"Are you English, lass?"

Not Irish, I noted. A Scot.

"No, I am German," I said truthfully, deciding selective honesty would be simpler than invention.

He looked away quickly when I met his eyes. "Take off your clothes and get on the bed," he said, brusque again now that his surprise had passed. My hands were trembling with excitement as I fumbled with the clasps of my borrowed gown. Luckily, prostitutes' dresses are meant to be easily shed, and I had left my undergarments downstairs. In a few moments I was naked. I walked over to the bed, still trembling, and then paused for a moment at the edge, unsure what to do next. It seemed comical to get on all fours right away, even though I knew that was what he would ask of me. I sat down on the bed instead, and tucked my legs over to one side. Since it seemed to make the man uncomfortable when I looked him in the eyes, I averted my gaze while I waited for him to join me.

I saw out of the corner of my eye that he was walking toward the bed, loosening his breeches as he approached. He told me to turn around, and now I got on my hands and knees, facing away from him. The bed sagged as he climbed onto it, and he settled right behind me, his knees on either side of my legs, his lowered pants falling over my bare calves. He reached between my thighs to open the folds of my pussy, and pushed his cock inside me just as the girls had said he would, shoving it in all at once, and it was so large it made me gasp. Grabbing hold of my hips with his large, callused hands, he started to fuck me.

I struggled to keep my breathing steady as I neared climax, knowing instinctively that the man would find it strange if he noticed that I was enjoying myself so much. But I think he must have felt my muscles contracting around him, because as soon as I came, he did, too, crying out as he thrust inside me one last time, pulling back on my thighs so that my bottom was cradled against his hips.

He stayed like that behind me, pressed tight against my ass, for almost a minute, but once he moved he stood up from the bed quickly, and when I turned around his back was to me and he was fastening his breeches. I was not entirely sure of the etiquette involved in leaving after this sort of assignation. Making my best guess, I stood up and said, rather like a lady's maid, "Will there be anything else, sir?"

That was evidently not the proper question to ask, because he laughed. "No, lass, nothing else."

He stepped back toward me and took my chin in his hand, turning my face first to one side and then the other, inspecting my profile rather as one might look over a horse. The gesture irritated me, and he must have seen the displeasure in my eyes, because he quickly took his hand away and said roughly, "Tell Madame Barthez you're to come to me again next week. I've had my fill of French girls."

The next week went almost exactly like the first, and our third meeting was not much different, either, up until our final exchange. This time when I asked him (in the same lady's-maid manner) if there was anything else he required, he gave me a long stare and asked me where I had learned to speak English like that. I was, I regret to say, flustered by the unexpected question, and I did not answer right away.

"What do you mean, sir?" I asked, stalling for time.

"How does a German whore learn to speak English like a bloody duchess?" he asked more bluntly.

Now I saw my mistake. Since I had learned English through congress with my relatives on that island, I sounded like them when I talked, and the speech of the English, I remembered, varied a great deal with their station, much like the Germans. Had I thought of this potential problem sooner, I might have spoken to him only in French. "My mother was in service to a family who had an English governess," I said quickly, offering the first story that came into my head, "and I learned by copying the way that she spoke."

"Then you're a good mimic," the man said. "Next week you'll have to talk to me some more, Duchess."

"Of course, sir," I said, and curtsied, which was a ridiculous thing to do, given that I was naked. I knew it did not quite strike the right note, this tendency of mine to imitate an English maidservant when I spoke to him, but I could not find any other plausible model, especially since it was clear that he had no particular love for French whores.

He laughed at my stilted answer, and I looked away, embarrassed and still flustered at my lie. I had not anticipated that this man would ever want to speak with me, or I would have thought out a better story in advance.

"What's your name, girl?" he asked me next.

"Anna." I said my real Christian name without thinking, hurrying now to step back into my dress.

I had just pulled the gown over my shoulders. To my disconcertment he reached out and fastened the front clasps for me. His large, thick fingers were surprisingly nimble, and there was an odd, unexpected intimacy in the gesture that I found unnerving.

"Very well, Anna," he said, stroking the side of my breast with his fingertips. "I'll see you next week."

"Yes, sir." I was still a lady's maid, despite my best efforts to refrain from curtsying, and I heard him chuckling as I left the room. I was half-certain as I left that day that he had somehow figured out my real identity, and I had half decided not to go back to him.

As the week passed, my fear faded, and the next Thursday when I entered the room where he was waiting, I did not find my client staring out the window, as I had before. He was seated on one of the couches. A carafe of wine was set next to him on a table, and he held a glass in his hand.

Surprised by that small, unexpected sign of extravagance, I stopped just a few steps inside the door.

"Take your clothes off and come over here," my client said. He spoke without smiling, but his voice was not as brusque as it had always been before.

This change in habit made me wary; I disrobed and walked toward him with my eyes cast down, looking, I am sure, every bit like a hesitant virgin.

I stopped about a foot away from him, expecting him to stand.

"Come closer," he said, and I could hear amusement in his voice.

He was watching me again with the same horse trainer's eye he had used before, looking up and down the length of me as if searching for some flaw. When I came within arm's reach, he reached out and grabbed hold of my hips. "How are you tonight, Anna?" he asked teasingly, pulling me closer so that my pussy was only inches from his face.

I was blushing furiously; it made me horribly nervous to have to speak with him. "I am well, sir— Oh!"

He had leaned forward and bitten me lightly on the thigh, and it had taken me by surprise. Now he was chuckling at my reaction. He turned me around now so that my back was

toward him, pulling me closer so that I was standing between
his knees. Though I could not see him, I suspected that he
was looking over my backside with the same farmer's gaze
he had just applied to my front, and I was both aroused and
indignant, finding myself so appraised.

He was fondling my buttocks as he looked at me, and when
he leaned in and nipped me on the bottom with his teeth, I
started like a nervous colt, which made him laugh once again.
It was a natural response to pull away, annoyed as I felt by his
amusement, but he did not let me go. He pulled me down
onto his lap and pinned me back against his chest. "Tell me
again how you are tonight, Duchess," he murmured against
my neck.

I realized that hearing my accent aroused him; it was not
hard to understand that a commoner would find it pleasing
to imagine that he was in bed with an aristocratic woman.

"I am well. Very well," I said, a bit breathless. "And how
are you, sir?"

"Exceedingly well," he said, his voice a low rumble against
my back. "I have been looking forward to having more of
that tight cunt of yours all week, Anna. And I got some good
news today, something you'll have to help me celebrate."

That made me wonder for the first time what profession
this man practiced.

"What sort of news have you had, sir?" I asked, turning to
look at him. I was curious to hear what merited celebration
in the life of an artisan (if that was indeed what he was).

"Do you know what a telescope is?" he asked, bringing
one hand down between my thighs to stroke my pussy.

I was distracted, or this first question would have surprised me more. I paused a moment before answering to ask
myself whether a prostitute might plausibly know what a

telescope was. I decided that in Paris anything was possible and answered, "Yes."

"I've been given a commission to build a new telescope for the king."

"Oh!" That startled exclamation escaped my mouth before I could stop myself.

This Scotsman, it seemed, might not be so far beyond my circle of acquaintance as I had thought. For my cousin had just been saying at breakfast that he hoped the favor of fitting out the new Royal Observatory would be granted to him, and he thought that the king's minister was leaning in his direction.

The man did not seem to think my reaction odd. I suppose he must have assumed that I was impressed to hear he had business with the Crown.

"That sounds like a fine honor, sir," I said, recovering from my surprise. "I am sure it is a great testament to your skill." My cousin and his Italian lensmaker would spit nails when they heard it. Who on earth was this man?

He was laughing at me again. "I believe you could be presented at court without incident, my dear, with the lovely English you speak," he said, which was rather ironic, since I had indeed been presented at the English court, entirely without incident.

"Anna?"

"Y–yes, sir?"

"I want you to suck on my cock for a while," he said. "Can you do that for me?"

I slid out of his lap to the floor and unfastened his breeches. I had never touched his penis before, and I must have made some small sound of admiration when I first took it in my hand, because he laughed and said, "Do I please you, Duchess?"

"Yes, sir," I whispered, and met his eyes, and this time he did not look away, as he always had before. He held my gaze as I leaned in to run my tongue along his cock.

I did my best to be a credit to my feigned profession; I used every trick I could think of to tease his prick until it was hard and straining. My client seemed to appreciate the effort. He leaned back against the sofa with his eyes closed, occasionally giving a low murmur of approval, and I was coming to realize that the smallest noise of pleasure from this man signified more than a shattering groan from another.

"Come here," he said finally, pulling at my arms. "Come up here and fuck me now." I straddled his lap on the sofa, and he yanked his shirt up over his head and then settled my hands on his chest. He seemed huge underneath me, his chest twice the width of my shoulders, the muscles in his arms flexing as he gripped hold of my thighs. When I started moving on top of him, it was hard not to let the great pleasure it gave me show on my face, but I struggled to keep my features as calm as possible.

A moment later he took my face roughly between his hands and said, "I'm tired of your modesty, Anna. I want you to moan this time when I make you come, do you understand?"

I sucked in a breath of surprise at the command, so at odds with what the other girls had said that he liked. I had no objections, of course; I much preferred giving myself over completely to the task of riding his cock, without having to divert my energies into pretense.

"Go on, then," he prompted.

He let me work his wide, hard prick in and out of my pussy at exactly the angle that I wanted, and soon I was half out of my head with pleasure.

"Yes, that's right, Duchess," he said with a low, thick laugh. "That's how I want you to fuck me."

I was close to orgasm, dripping with sweat, when he grabbed hold of me and flipped me onto my back on the sofa. He began thrusting into me now, pushing my knees back toward my shoulders to tighten my pussy around his cock.

"My name is James," he said, his voice rough and labored. "I want you to say it."

"James," I moaned, my climax beginning as I said his name. "Oh, James…"

He slumped onto me when he came, falling over to one side, his face pressed against my neck. For a moment I forgot that he was not really my lover, and I slipped out of character. I lifted one hand to smooth his hair back from his drenched forehead, and turned to press a kiss against his brow, but as soon as my lips touched his skin, I wondered whether such a caress might not be out of place between a prostitute and a client.

I pulled my hand away from his cheek, but James grabbed hold of it and kissed me on the wrist, grinning. "Go and tell Madame Barthez I want dinner," he said.

"Y-yes, sir," I said, blinking a little stupidly as I struggled to become a lady's maid again.

Madame Barthez was shocked when I told her he wanted dinner, and she had just said that she wanted to know what I kept in that cunt of mine when she remembered who I was, and began apologizing profusely. I laughed and told her it had nothing to do with my merits; the man had just gotten a big commission from the king.

On hearing that, one of the girls suggested a little testily that if this Irishman had recently come into money, perhaps he would want additional company, and I said I would ask, although I had no intention of doing so. I knew already that the answer would be no, and it was rather odd, the pride I felt at that conviction, considering it is in fact completely

inappropriate for a woman of my station to be pleased to
know that a commoner thinks her a capable whore.

So his name was James.

It occurred to me as I followed the dinner back upstairs
that if I wanted to know more about him, I could always just
ask.

"Take that dress off and come and sit in my lap," the man—
James—said to me as he sat down at the small table where the
serving boy had laid out the meal.

I smiled at him hesitantly as I settled across his knees, and
he smiled back. He could barely reach the table with me on
his lap, so I took up a piece of cold meat and offered it to
his lips. The food was all this sort, of a shape and kind easily
offered by fingers, without the bother of a knife and a fork
(I am sure by design), and I had had practice enough at this
sort of task that I could do it with grace and confidence.

The man was, I think I can say without undue arrogance,
thoroughly charmed at being fed in such a manner, catching
my fingers sometimes with his tongue or between his teeth,
as if he hoped to find that these, too, might be edible. When
he finally appeared much more interested in my fingers than
the food, I decided he must be sated.

It seemed to me that if I wanted to question him about
himself, it would be easiest to speak to him as if we had met in
normal company. For the purposes of convenience, I thought
it allowable to ignore the fact that I was naked.

"Have you been in Paris long, sir?"

He was preoccupied with gnawing gently on my index
finger when I asked him this, and he answered me with it
still between his teeth. "A few months now," he said.

"And do you enjoy yourself here?" The formulation of that
question was not exactly right, I suspected. German reflexive

pronouns had a habit of sneaking in where they did not belong in my English.

"*Here* I enjoy myself enormously," he answered, grinning up at me. "But you are one of the only things I have found in Paris that I like."

How can that be, I was about to joke, *when everyone says there is no better city for a man with philosophical tastes?* But I stopped myself just in time.

I found it murderously difficult, the most difficult thing I had had to do so far, to pretend to be ignorant as he talked to me. He was from Edinburgh (he told me that as if he did not expect me to know where it was), and he had been apprenticed to an apothecary who made instruments for professors at the university there. That was how he had gotten his start; now he was in Paris being paid to teach the Duke de Brecis experimental philosophy, which was the duke's latest passion. Once James began talking, it was clearly a relief to him to unburden all his frustrations to an almost-countrywoman. He seemed to think that, being German, I must find the French as irritating as he did, and he was not entirely wrong. He disliked aristocrats, too, most strongly, particularly ones who dabbled in natural philosophy, which meant that he especially disliked my cousin Robert, and was consequently very happy that he could now boast such a fine victory over him in the matter of the king's telescope.

Halfway through his account of how he had won over the king's minister through some particularly clever demonstration, he stopped abruptly and told me that he was tired of talking, and then picked me up and carried me over to the bed.

After his extended dalliance with my fingers, he was apparently eager to find out how the rest of my anatomy felt between his teeth. He had a rough, ardent way of touching me that was skillful without being mannered, and by the time he finally pushed his cock inside me again, I was as ready to be taken as a woman could be. He had me not once, but twice, and he fucked me with such slow extravagance that I could only think that the king's commission must have been quite a large one indeed.

I should admit that when I first left the room that night, I was being rather stupid about what had happened, thinking myself lucky that my scheme had gotten me not just a service-able weekly lay, but a lover of no little skill and enthusiasm.

Only when I entered the downstairs parlor did I start to reflect again on the potential difficulties that had also made themselves apparent over the course of the evening. My cousin was waiting for me, lying stretched out on a divan with a girl lying between his thighs licking his cock, and he looked up with a laugh when I walked into the room.

"You naughty girl. Madame Barthez told me what you have been up to these past few weeks."

I had not told Robert about my assignations on the preced-ing three Thursdays. By the time he had finished with his girls, my client had been long gone, and I had worried that the venture might be a little too bold even for his libertine tastes.

Luckily, he seemed amused. "This is marvelously daring of you, cousin," he said. "It's a shame that women aren't allowed to brag."

"I think I may have been less clever than I thought, cousin," I replied, sinking down into a nearby chair. "I believe you might know the man I've been servicing these past few weeks."

"Who is he, then?"

"A Scotsman named James who makes philosophical instru-ments."

"James McKirnan? That showman the Duke de Brecis brought back with him from Edinburgh to teach him how to use his new air pump?" Robert stood up, pushing aside the girl in his lap.

I shrugged and said I didn't consider it likely that Paris was home to more than one philosophical Scotsman with that particular Christian name.

"That man's no philosopher," Robert said derisively. "He's nothing but a clever mechanic. And he aims above his station, coming to a brothel like this one." This observation got a murmur of approval from the girls in the room.

"He likes it when I speak to him in genteel English," I told Robert with a smile, "and calls me Duchess while he's fucking me."

That information sparked a great deal of amusement; my cousin almost cried in his mirth.

"It's good that you told me about this," Robert said. "This Scotsman seems to be coming into fashion of late, and I was thinking of inviting him to visit me. It would have been awkward for you to run into him in the hall. You remember that commission I was speaking of this morning?"

I nodded, remembering the bad news I had for him.

He went on before I could speak. "I thought I might ask this McKirnan to join Ernesto in working on the glass, since he seems to have gained a few admirers for himself at court."

"Oh, cousin, you won't be happy," I said, sorry to have to tell Robert that he had lost out to this commoner. "He's already been given the commission on his own. That's why he kept me with him for so long tonight."

Robert's face dropped into a scowl, and he sent his brandy glass crashing against the wall with one smooth, sullen gesture. "Damn it, what would make them choose that charlatan over me?"

I told him everything that James had said to me about his demonstration before the minister. Robert flopped down into the nearest chair with a bitter laugh, and said, "As gullible as peasants, the French monarchy." He motioned to the girl who had been lying between his legs before. "Come here, you."

Robert leaned back in his chair and closed his eyes as the girl opened his breeches again. "Well, I hope he makes a mess of it," he said. "And I hope that you plan on seducing him to excess and ruin, cousin."

"That will be difficult," I said with a laugh. "All the girls say he's painfully frugal."

"How long did he stay with you tonight?" Robert asked, and I did not know the answer.

"Three and a half hours," one of the girls said sullenly. Now that this client had loosened his purse strings a bit, some of them were obviously perturbed at me for taking away his business.

"I hope you gave him his money's worth," Robert said. "How is our mechanic with his pants down?"

"Really in every way admirable," I said honestly.

I considered staying away the next week, but Robert thought there was no serious risk in seeing James again. "Some of the philosophers invite him now, when only men will be present, but you won't see him in a salon," he assured me. "Besides, who would believe his story if he told it?"

That was a good point. If a nobleman related such a tale, he might be believed, but who would listen to a commoner who said he had bedded a countess in a brothel? I decided there was no reason to deny myself.

My client was sitting on the couch again, and this time he smiled at me when I walked through the door.

"Good evening, sir," I said, smiling back, much less nervous than I had been before. I was sure now that he had no suspicions about me, and no small slip was likely to make him question my identity.

"Good evening, Duchess," he said, leaning back with his hands clasped behind his head to watch me undress.

"Take your hair down," he commanded as I put my gown on a chair, and he smiled at me again as my hair fell around my shoulders.

I crossed the room and settled between his feet, reaching up to stroke his penis through his breeches, mimicking a pose I had seen Claudette take with my cousin. "Shall I suck on your cock for a while, sir?" I asked, knowing that he would like hearing my genteel voice pose such a vulgar question.

"Yes, Duchess," he answered with a grin, leaning down and taking hold of my hair in one fist. "Suck on my cock for a while."

I opened his pants, and he held on to my hair with both hands as I bent over his lap. "That's good, lass," he murmured as my mouth closed around his prick. "Take it all the way in, just like you did the last time."

After a while he said, "Anna, you must like sucking my dick, to do it so well."

"I do, sir," I answered. "I'm happy to know that I please you." Truth be told, I was beginning to enjoy playing my role, now that I had worked through the first awkwardness of it. I had never been so deferential to a man before, and I took the same pleasure in this novel behavior that another woman might have felt at being demanding.

"You please me very much." He pulled me up into his lap and laid me out across his knees. "What do you do to keep this pussy of yours so wet?" he asked with a smile, plunging two fingers inside me. "You're dripping whenever I touch you."

I gasped in surprise at both the question and the intrusion. "It's not artifice, sir."

He worked his fingers in and out of my cunt until I moaned and arched up against his hand.

"Don't lie to me, lass," he said, chuckling. "I know a great deal about chemistry."

"I promise, sir," I said breathlessly. "It's not artifice that makes my pussy so wet for you."

He smelled his fingers and then licked them, and laughed, realizing I was telling the truth. "You like it when I fuck you, don't you, Anna?"

I nodded, and he pulled me closer to his chest.

"Tell me," he commanded in a low voice.

"I like it when you fuck me, James," I said, and he kissed me, full on the mouth, the first time he had done so. It shocked me at first, but the feel of his greedy mouth wasn't unpleasant, so I kissed him back.

He took hold of my hair again, winding it around his palm, and pulled my head back so that he could kiss my throat. His other hand was working again inside my pussy, and as I leaned back while he bit into my neck and my shoulders and then bent down to suckle at my breasts, I thought that being a whore was really not such a bad life, when your clients took such trouble over you.

This time he fucked me standing up while I lay on my back at the edge of the bed, and he looked magnificent doing it. Without any conscious intention to flatter him, I heard myself telling him how handsome he was, and he answered back that I was a very pretty girl and that it made his cock hard just to look at me. When he finished he lay down next to me on the bed and took me in his arms, kissing me on the mouth again, and on my cheeks and my neck.

"You know, Anna," he said after a while, running his

fingertips over my stomach, "I could feed you for a week for what it costs me to spend two hours here."

That almost made me laugh out loud, wondering what he would think if he knew what I spent weekly on wine alone.

Had I actually been a woman of the trade, I would have anticipated what was coming next, but as it was, it took me completely by surprise.

"Come and live with me, Anna," he said. "I'll take good care of you—I make a decent living with my work."

I was stunned. I was also, strangely enough, vaguely insulted that he had begun such a conversation with a reference to economy. So he thought it would be cheaper to feed and board me himself, did he, rather than to pay for me by the hour?

What does one say to such an offer?

"I am sorry, sir, but I couldn't—"

He held his fingers up to my lips, frowning. "Don't think that I can't provide for you just because I don't walk around in satin breeches like these ridiculous Frenchmen. I'm not without resources."

"It's not that, sir. It's just…" What on earth could I say? "I'm not allowed to leave, sir. I owe Madame Barthez for my clothes and my board, and I have to stay until I've worked off the debt." That was a good, prostitute-worthy excuse, I thought as I said it.

It did not work.

"I'll pay your debts with Madame Barthez, Anna. You needn't worry about that. Come and live with me. Let me take care of you."

Pushing away from him in my discomfort, I stammered that I was sorry, but I couldn't come and live with him, and

I couldn't explain, but it simply wasn't possible, and after a frozen moment of shock, he stood up from the bed.

What he did next didn't surprise me at all—he called me a vile slut and said he hoped I died in a gutter, and then stormed out with his breeches half tied and his shirt in his hand.

I waited a few minutes, and then went downstairs to tell Madame Barthez I would not be returning the next Thursday. Robert found the story amusing when he met me an hour later, but I must admit that I was irritated to have had my convenient arrangement spoiled by James's ridiculous histrionics.

"You know, dearest, if you were in fact a whore," Robert pointed out as we rode through the quiet Paris night toward home, "it would have been a fine compliment. You ought to feel flattered."

I said I supposed he was right.

"Really, you've had an impressive career. It's what all those girls are hoping for, to become someone's kept woman, and you got an offer when you'd only been at it a month. Of course," he added, "I believe that one usually aims to become the mistress of some dissolute younger son of the nobility, but since you were new to the trade, you can be excused for your bad judgment in seducing a mechanic instead."

I was not finding all this witty banter nearly as entertaining as he was.

"Of course, your mechanic might have had his advantages," Robert said. "Unlike a nobleman, a commoner might have married you in the end if you played your cards right, and made an honest woman of you."

At that, I threw my gloves across the carriage, but unfortunately missed his face.

"Cheer up, darling," Robert said. "Just think how tormented your poor Scotsman has been these past few weeks, imagining all the countless other men who were also paying you to spread your thighs for them."

At least that thought was amusing.

After that night I thought the only unpleasantness that awaited me was a return to my earlier boredom. I was, unfortunately, mistaken.

A few weeks after my last meeting with James, my cousin and I attended the theater with one of Robert's aging uncles, the Duke de Thouen. I was watching the floor as we moved through the foyer, taking care not to tread on anyone's gown, when someone grabbed me by the wrist. A second later I was yanked flush against a wide, hard chest; I looked up and saw to my horror that the man who was accosting me was my mechanic from the brothel, James.

"I see you took a better offer, Duchess. Wise of you. I couldn't have bought you such a fine necklace," he said through clenched teeth.

I recovered my composure almost at once. My face was a mirror of startled, confused surprise, and I said in French, "You mistake me for someone else, sir. I am not a duchess."

My feigned ignorance seemed to enrage him even more, and he shoved me roughly away. "I know you're not a duchess. You're nothing but a common whore." He glared over at the elderly duke, who fortunately did not understand English, and said, "I'd say you made a poor trade in one respect—I can't believe he fucks you as well as I have."

My companions, who had been momentarily startled into silence, were now roused to indignant protest. Robert, always useful at such moments, leaped forward and struck the man across the face with the blunt head of his walking stick. "Go stumble into a gutter with the rest of your drunken friends," he said as James slumped against the wall, surprised by the sudden blow. "My cousin does not know you, and if you speak to her again, you'll be dead before morning."

There was blood trickling from the corner of his mouth when James looked up again, a hand pressed to his injured jaw. He blinked at Robert, realizing for the first time who he was. "Your cousin?" he repeated.

"Yes, my cousin, you pathetic charlatan," Robert said. "The Countess von Esslin, a woman I'm very sure you have never met. Now make your apologies and get out of our way." Robert's pompous fury was really masterfully convincing. I could have cheered.

Our elderly companion leaned forward now to take my hand in concern. "Are you all right, Anna, my dear?"

Until that moment, I believe that James was beginning to think himself genuinely mistaken. On hearing my Christian name, however, he let out a short laugh and said, "Your family has strange habits, Duke," and then pushed through the crowd, away from us.

Robert and I were deeply troubled by this exchange, and we talked of nothing for the next few weeks but how to deal with this unruly commoner we had both unwittingly enraged. Given his antipathy toward Robert, it seemed likely that James might try to use the information he now possessed to harm us both in some way, and we tried in vain to come up with some simple plan to silence him. Bribery seemed an option, but approaching James with an offer, we knew, would be fraught with danger, and neither Robert nor I wanted to risk additional unpleasantness by propositioning the brute ourselves.

We decided that we would do nothing for the time being, feeling that we could reasonably hope that the inherent implausibility of his story would lead James to hold his tongue a little longer.

In the meantime his fortunes in Paris continued to grow, and we discovered with great alarm that he had been asked to perform some of his recent electrical experiments before the Thursday salon of the famous Marquise de Comté, a weekly social and literary gathering of considerable reputation. This was dangerous news indeed, for this salon, a hotbed of philosophical radicalism, was famous for its open disregard for the conventions of ordinary morality (and hence was one of my cousin's favorite haunts), and it was just the sort of place in which James's fantastic story might be told to great advantage, and possibly, given its erotic potential, willingly believed.

Robert and I decided that we should attend the salon that night ourselves and meet the danger directly. It is always harder to insult someone to his face, we reasoned, than behind his back, and once the entire salon had seen me treat James publicly with cold and distant indifference, they would be less likely to believe that there had been some previous connection between us.

The marquise was standing with her new Scottish favorite to greet us as we entered, and I wondered if James had placed himself in the aging beauty's good graces through more than just his scientific prowess. He was wearing, I noticed, silk breeches and a much more elaborate cravat than had been his previous custom, and he stared at me quite blatantly, his eyes half angry and half expectant.

"Have you met Mr. McKirnan?" the marquise asked once we had exchanged our initial warm greetings with our hostess.

"No," I said coldly, resting my eyes on his face only briefly and refraining from giving him my hand. "Is it true that Luc Valont will be reading his poetry tonight? *That* we did not want to miss."

My cousin smiled behind his gloves.

This promising start to the evening was followed by disaster.

As soon as most of the guests had assembled, there was a belated fanfare from the front door, and a messenger from Versailles hurried into the room. Robert's presence, the courier reported, was urgently needed at court; some delicate problem with the Prussian ambassador had emerged, and because of my cousin's family connections in Berlin, the king had ordered that Robert be brought to him without delay.

Once the marquise had promised that she would see I was safely returned home, Robert had no choice but to comply with the messenger's orders and leave me alone, bereft of my greatest ally.

Nervous to see him go, I followed him out onto the front steps. We dismissed the servant waiting at the door and stood for a few moments together, taking each other's counsel privately. After a few last whispered words of reassurance and comfort, he said goodbye.

I had just crossed the threshold when I noticed that James was descending the stairs from the second floor. He was alone, and the hall was entirely deserted.

With swift, rough force, he grabbed me around the waist with both hands and dragged me unceremoniously into a sheltered corner behind the bend in the stairs.

I struggled in his arms and ordered him to let me go.

He did not obey.

"Why are you now too high to speak to me, Countess?" he hissed in my ear, both arms clamped firmly around my waist. "You used to disrobe at my command."

I ground the heel of my shoe into his foot in hopes of securing my release, but I might as well have thrown feathers at a giant. My assault evoked no reaction at all. (I have heard it said that the lower classes are less sensible to pain than we are, and advance this event as further evidence of that.)

"Tell me, Countess," he said. "How many other clients did it take to keep you satisfied?"

I drew a deep breath. "I met no one but you," I answered, trying now to speak obligingly, hoping that since he did not obey orders, and force was useless, persuasion might work instead. I did not want anyone to find us in our current pose, nestled behind the stairs.

"And how did I earn that honor?" he asked sharply. "To be asked to pay good money for a woman who wasn't a whore?"

I found this complaint unfathomable. To this day, I do not understand why a man should be so angry to learn that his favorite prostitute was actually a countess, and I am always left to reflect on the fact that they have minds that are limited and strange, these bourgeois.

"You were a man of no social standing," I explained, hoping that my reasonable tone would placate him. "I thought it unlikely we would meet in public."

"I should have known you weren't a whore," he muttered, tightening his arm around my waist. "No one screws with that much enthusiasm just for money."

"I can't see that you have any cause for complaint," I said stiffly. "You seemed satisfied at the time that you'd been well served."

"Well served indeed," he answered roughly. "But no more so than you."

Under the circumstances, I had no desire to flatter his vanity.

"I paid as well," I told him. "Double the usual rate." I assumed that this additional information would help him see that no one had attempted to cheat him, but it seemed to only rouse his anger further.

"You little bitch," he said furiously, his mouth pressing behind my ear. "What right did you have to play such games with me?"

I was suddenly very afraid that he would reveal his story to the assembled salon as soon as he returned upstairs, only to spite me. He seemed angry beyond all reason, and utterly unpredictable.

"What do you want from me?" I asked, hoping that perhaps his silence could be bought. He must have had some end in mind, I assumed, when he grabbed me and dragged me into that back corner.

He slid one large hand down over my hip and gathered up the fabric of my skirt in his fist. "You know what I want, Anna."

He was wrong; I was not at all sure what he wanted. Revenge? My public humiliation? A return to our previous arrangement?

I seized on the last of these as the least objectionable possibility, and said hesitantly, "We…we could meet again, the way we used to."

I felt his arms slacken around my waist, and I thought for a moment that he was going to release me. Instead, he spun me around and pressed my back against the wall, both hands gripping hold of my waist.

"Oh, Anna, my love," he groaned huskily, his lips very close to my own, "I thought you were lost to me."

Then he kissed me fervently, crushing my body back against the wall with such force that it was difficult to breathe.

"I knew you couldn't really be cold to me," he said, taking my cheek against his palm and leaning his forehead against mine. "Not for long. You were just cross with me, weren't you, darling, because of the way I left you."

I was beginning to suspect that he had misunderstood the terms of my offer. I was perfectly willing to let him fuck me again, seeing as he did it so well, but I did not envision any relationship between us that would involve him calling me darling.

"Come home with me tonight," he whispered.

I told him that I had no intention of going with him to whatever boardinghouse he called home. I had meant to suggest that we could meet again at the brothel.

"At—at the..." he stuttered stupidly. "Why there?" Then he frowned. "I won't have you as my mistress by half measures again, Anna. I want to have you in my own bed."

"I was never your mistress!" I snapped, irritated by the liberties the man was taking, behaving as if we had been true intimates rather than merely passing acquaintances. We were hardly well hidden, there behind the stairs, and I knew that this interview needed to end soon. "Let me go. If you don't want to meet me at Madame Barthez's, there's nothing more for us to discuss."

For some reason he let out a low laugh. "Did you like it there," he asked with a slow smile, "pretending to be a whore?" He leaned down to kiss my neck, holding me so tightly that my efforts to push him away were futile. "We can play any game you like, my darling Anna, once we're together in my chambers. You can be anything you want for me."

James was without question the most irritatingly thick-skulled man I had ever met in my life. He nudged my thighs apart with his knee and pushed his silk-covered cock against the curve of my lap. "Four long weeks it's been since I've taken you, Anna. I won't go that long without you again. You're coming home with me tonight, my love."

"Who do you think you are to dictate terms to me?" I sniffed. The soldiers back in Potsdam had known their place; I didn't know what to make of this man who had the temerity to keep speaking of me as his love, when to do so clearly violated all the rules of social decency.

"Don't be so proud, little one," he said with another laugh.

"I am not proud," I told him, frustrated. "Are you too stupid to know when you are in the company of your betters?"

That comment he did not seem to find amusing.

"Do you mean to let me into that little aristocratic cunt of yours again, or don't you?" he asked bluntly.

He was clearly too dim-witted to understand the distinction I had tried to impress upon him. I explained once more that I had no objection to fucking him on occasion—secretly, discreetly and at times of my choosing—but I had not yet reached such a stage of wanton disregard for propriety that I would become the permanent mistress of some lowborn Scottish mechanic.

He did not like that answer. "I'm not for hire, Countess," he said coldly.

Since I had not offered to pay him, I am not sure what he meant by that retort.

"Come upstairs with me now," he demanded harshly, taking hold of my elbows. "With your hand on my arm."

Appearing in public with him in such a way was absolutely out of the question. He was being an unreasonable idiot, and I told him so in no uncertain terms.

His face hardened. "Why should you care if those powdered courtiers know you are giving yourself to me?"

I told him that the answer to that question should have been obvious, if he had any brains in his head.

His face had now lost all hint of the boyish earnestness it

had so recently displayed. "What good does it do me to bed a noblewoman," he challenged, "if no one knows of it?" He grabbed hold of my wrist and placed a threatening kiss against my palm. "What would all those fops upstairs think if I told them how easily and how often you came for me?"

"No one would believe you," I replied haughtily.

"Maybe not," he said, dropping my hand. "But the story would be a pleasure to tell."

"My cousin will have you beaten within an inch of your life if you breathe one word about what we did together," I threatened, frightened now that he really might speak. "You haven't risen so high that you're beyond his reach."

James glared at me, and after consigning me and my foul cousin to the ninth circle of hell, he turned and stomped abruptly back up the stairs to the salon.

After taking a few minutes to collect my wits and straighten my clothes, I followed him. I entered the salon to find that James had already begun his demonstrations. He was standing behind a large table crowded with instruments of his own invention, which, when properly manipulated, produced all sorts of wondrous effects. Under other circumstances, I would have deigned to find his experiments interesting, but in this case, my only reaction was a certain wry amusement at the awkward explanations he was offering in his execrable French.

"I say," said a young viscount standing to my left, when James had finished his demonstration. "That was marvelous."

"Yes, marvelous indeed," I said, speaking loudly and clearly to be sure that everyone within hearing range would not miss what I was about to say. "Such skill in the lower classes is just like the ingenuity of the bees, isn't it? Manual cleverness must be akin to the elaborate habits of animals. They also construct quite complicated things without the benefit of real intelligence or understanding."

James's French was better than I had thought, because he glared at me as if he had understood the insult clearly. He mastered his anger quickly, however, and asked if the assembled ladies and gentlemen would like to see a demonstration of mesmerism now that he was finishing showing them the wonders of electricity.

The techniques of Dr. Mesmer had recently been all the rage in Paris, but my cousin assured me that the claim of mesmerism—that a person could be brought under the power of another through the manipulation of their bodily magnetism—was nothing more than the grossest kind of fraud. Since Robert was not there to expose James for the empty showman he was, I decided to take my cousin's place as the voice of reason.

"Have you brought some fellow charlatan here tonight," I asked derisively, "to help you perform your little magic tricks?"

"Don't you believe in mesmerism, Countess?" James asked with false deference.

I told him that of course I did not.

"Perhaps you would like to serve as my first subject," he answered with a little bow, "so that you will be more easily convinced of its power."

I had no desire to put myself forward in this way, but the entire salon was so intrigued by this attractive challenge that they all insisted I comply.

James had me sit down in a chair, and taking his place across from me, he grasped my thumbs and looked deeply into my eyes. I remember thinking the posture patently ridiculous; after a few moments, he began running his hands around the outlines of my figure, keeping them some little distance from my body.

That was the last thing I remembered for about a quarter of an hour.

Some months later, a letter came into my hands that described the incident that followed, and though I myself cannot confirm its accuracy, I offer it to you as the best account of the event that I possess:

Paris, 17 Mai, 1785

I recently enjoyed a spectacle in the salon of the Marquise de Comté that I must share with you, though it goes against our common custom to do so. It is a shame that you were not here to see this delightful entertainment in the flesh. Once you have read my account of it, I am sure that you will think so, too.

You know, of course, the Countess von Esslin, who is as famous in Paris for her tiresome virtue as she is for her beauty. Though she has unnaturally little taste for male company, she does seem fond of literature, and she has been, these past three months, a periodic guest in the salon of the marquise, and it is said that they have become great friends (though one wonders at the pairing).

[The duke now relates the circumstances of James's challenge; since these details are already known to you, I will skip ahead to the part of the letter that contains news you have not yet heard.]

The countess was visibly agitated, almost angry, when the ministrations began, but after this artisan-philosopher had spoken for some time, running his hands at a little distance from her body, the lady sat calmly, staring straight ahead without blinking.

Would that I had learned the art from watching! Our friend
the mechanic stepped away from the countess now and said,
"You are to listen to me very carefully, do you understand?"
And the countess nodded, pliant as a child.

You can imagine that there was no little expectation in
the room. "You feel a great constriction around your chest,
and it is hard for you to breathe," was the first thing he said,
and the lady did indeed begin to shift in her chair, gasping
for breath, her hand fluttering to her bosom.

"Loosen your dress, and the feeling will be gone," he told
her, and she took her hands to her bodice and obediantly
unfastened the clasps of her gown, breathing more easily as
she loosened each bond.

"Keep your hands there," he said sharply as she began to
lower her hands again to her lap. "Push the fabric aside and
show me your breasts."

A slight mumur went through the small audience at the
boldness of this command, but as the countess obeyed it immediately, there was no time left for anticipation.

Her breasts were lovely, by the way—pouting, and full
enough to fill a hand but no more.

Now he told her to get down on her knees, and at that some
of the ladies protested, but the marquise quickly waved away
their objections, as eager as the men, I think, to see her pious
friend put to such uses. The artisan-philosopher only stood
there smiling throughout the entire exchange, as if he had
no concern for its outcome, and when the issue was decided,
he turned back to his subject and instructed her to open his
breeches.

Like the rest of us, too, he was already hard, and his member
stood up like a post when it was free. He told her to take it in
her hand, and to our delight, she did that obediently, looking
up at him with docile eyes for further direction. He told her

to kiss the tip of it, and then to lick it, and she pressed her lips against the crown of his cock, and then ran her pretty little tongue along the shaft, without so much as a murmur.

Next he told her to take it into her mouth. I should say, before going on, that this mechanic of ours had an exceedingly fine cock, one of the largest I have ever seen, but in her altered state that seemed to cause the countess no trouble. She closed her mouth at first just around the crown, and he spoke to her again sharply, saying, "No, take it in farther." She opened her mouth more, taking in his stiff cock halfway, and again he said, "Farther, Countess. All the way in." And to our amazement, the entirety of that enormous phallus disappeared into her mouth until her lips were pressing against his groin.

He kept giving her instructions, and we all had the pleasure of watching that delicate little mouth work this artisan's huge cock with all the skill of a whore, sucking on it and laving it with her tongue as she took it in and out of her mouth. Indeed, the sight gave us all pause to wonder if the countess was indeed as innocent as we all believed—I do not quite think that mesmerism could create such skill de novo (though perhaps she learned the art chastely, during her brief marriage?). The mesmerist kept his hand on the lady's head as she sucked on his cock, stroking her hair with his fingers, saying low words of encouragement when she did something that particularly pleased him.

Before he had taken his pleasure, he ordered her to stop, and she pulled away, her face upturned again, waiting for instruction. The man sat down now in the chair where the countess had been seated before, his pants open and his stiff red prick standing up in his lap, still glistening with the moisture of her mouth. He told her to come to him, and she got to her feet and took the several steps to the chair, stopping just at his knees. The countess was wearing a very simple gown, in the new classical style, and it was no hindrance at all for the mechanic's talented hands; he reached up underneath her skirts and in a moment had undone her undergarments and taken them down around her ankles. At his command, the lady stepped gracefully out of the linen underclothes, and stood waiting before the knees of her master.

The mechanic pushed her thighs apart and pulled her forward until she was straddling his lap. Then he reached underneath her skirts again and grabbed hold of her hips.

The lady let out only a small gasp as he pushed his cock inside her, but the other women in the room were quickly growing indignant.

The artisan, showing more self-restraint than I would have under similar conditions, told them that if they would be quiet, he would bring the countess out of her trance.

The look on her face as she came to her senses and felt this commoner's hard cock between her thighs was one of sublimely comical horror, and I believe that it was this reaction that had been the man's entire aim, though I am not sure I completely understand his motives. He must have been very proud, our mechanic, and very vexed over her insult, to prefer this moment of revenge over the pleasures of orgasm.

His hands were still under her skirts, and he gripped her hips and held her down on his lap as she struggled to rise, saying in a taunting tone, "It is unkind of you, Countess, to leave before the gentleman is finished," and in response she shoved away from him with surprising force. She tipped over backward onto the floor, sprawling on her bottom with one hand clutching the bodice of her open dress. She was a delectable sight, so disheveled.

From here I can tell the story myself, and it was not, I must confess, one of my finer moments. I spat back, "You are no gentleman," but the insult carried little force under the circumstances, and the arrogant bastard only laughed and said that he was sure I had known that the moment I first saw him.

I was angry to find myself bested by a mere artisan, but there was little I could do to save face. My first desire upon realizing my position was to flee, but I have never liked to leave a roomful of people when I suspect that I will become the topic of conversation as soon as my footsteps fade in the hall, so I did not leave the gathering at once. I thought perhaps I would see some way to salvage the situation if I stayed—to pick myself up, as it were, from the floor.

The muscians had begun to play again, now that our little spectacle had ended. The couples in the room had all turned their attentions to each other—whatever had happened in those minutes I had lost had left the men in a state. They were all of them amorous now, urging their mistresses' hands to their laps, none of them in the mood for conversation. With no other choice left to me, I settled into a chair some little distance away from James.

When I had regained enough composure to be disdainful, I looked over at him and asked with a raised eyebrow if he did not also need to relieve his discomfort. He answered that some pleasures were sweeter than lovemaking, and that tonight he had been completely satisfied.

We sat there like two antagonistic diplomats, eyeing each other across the short distance between our chairs while the room around us filled with moans and murmured pleadings.

I would have to go, I realized after a few moments more of reflection. Everyone needed to think me devastated and scandalized. It was, after all, better to leave and let them talk.

In recalling this evening now, I am moved to reflect, just

as I was then, on the volatile and unpredictable nature of the lower orders. A young woman of position may often find it necessary to seek entertainment in the arms of some attractive, lowborn brute, but such promiscuous socializing with ill-bred men has distinct dangers, as I learned all too well myself.

In the end, my decision to flee the salon was a good one. I left Paris for an extended stay on my cousin's country estate, and though the rumors that circulated after that dreadful evening were not pleasant, I was not nearly as compromised as I had feared. My sucking on a commoner's cock for an audience had the odd effect of making me appear more virtuous in the eyes of *le monde,* not less, since my supposed innocence enhanced the erotic interest of the story and made the virility and power of the mesmerist even more marvelous. As the story was repeated, James's influence stretched out from those few lost minutes until it occupied the entire evening. The Comtesse d'Esslin, they said, had been mesmerized when she accepted the dare; the mesmerist had lured the famously virtuous beauty into the performance by using the powers of animal magnetism. This specter of showmen inducing innocent, defenseless women to perform scandalous acts caused no little anxiety, I am told, among the more conventional members of polite society.

★ ★ ★ ★ ★

DEVOURED

LETTY JAMES

CHAPTER ONE

MARCO RINADI SAT DOWN NEXT TO ME, SMOKE curling from his nose like a dragon in heat. He leaned closer and the pungent smell of freshly chopped parsley mixed with the bitter smell of cigarette smoke made my knees weak—and I was sitting down.

"I heard about you," he said, his voice a raspy baritone that made me want to pour honey down his throat—and maybe lick it off his tonsils. He propped his elbow next to mine on the table and stubbed out his cigarette in the ashtray he'd brought with him to the nonsmoking section. He was so close, I could feel the heat of his dark olive skin.

I can imagine what he'd heard from Alex, the ex, who was his sous-chef. There were no secrets in the kitchen. I cleared my throat wishing I knew which way this was going. Finally, I got it out. "What did you hear?"

"I heard—" he gave me a smile that made me want to crawl into his lap and give him something to really smile about "—I heard you're called the Queen of Darkness."

I laughed. "That's a new one. It's usually Bitch from Hell or Ball Breaker. Alex tell you that one?"

He didn't answer, but looked me over as if scrutinizing my ball-breaking capabilities. Either that or he was imagining me naked. I had done my own share of fantasizing since he'd called. To make his job easier, I shrugged out of my suit jacket and rolled up my sleeves. I could feel my nipples tighten in the cool air off the water. It felt refreshing after a day spent in a sun-heated car. The corners of his mouth curved up and he unbuttoned the flap of his chef's jacket. I could picture us dropping articles of clothing on the way to the bedroom. I cleared my throat, and then didn't know what to say. He reached into his pants pocket and pulled out a gold cigarette case embossed with his initials. A gift from a lover, I was sure. He offered me one.

"No, thanks. I don't smoke."

"Pity." He took a cigarette out and let it hang between his lips. He tucked the case back in his pocket and pulled out a small silver lighter, also embossed, and covered with scratches. Older gift, I surmised. He cupped the flame against the slight breeze. "Do you mind?"

"Would you put it out if I did?"

He laughed. "I'd think about it."

I enjoyed watching him smoke, watching his hands and mouth move in harmony, watching his eyes crinkle up. Maybe it just went with the bad-boy persona that he had managed to perfect, but it worked for me. Too well, probably. I took a sip of my iced tea. He looked at it with distaste.

"They couldn't do any better than that for you?"

"That's what I ordered."

"Honey, you're here at The Alley. My restaurant. I think I can treat you to something better than an iced tea."

"I don't drink when I work."

"You should. It makes things a lot simpler." He motioned to one of the waiters, who practically ran over to do the master's bidding. "Frank, bring us two Grey tonics."

I glanced at my watch even though I knew what time it was. We had a five o'clock appointment. He had kept me waiting for fifteen minutes. It had been a pleasurable wait as I watched tanned boat jockeys glide their motorboats up and down Ego Alley, and listened to the squeaking of fiberglass hulls against rubber-wrapped pilings.

We'd met at a charity function two years ago. It was right after Alex got the job as Marco's sous-chef and dumped me for Rachine Hines, a waitress who fancied herself a foodie, but didn't even know how foie gras was made. But Alex didn't want smarts, just willing pussy.

I'd helped organize the function, so my attendance was required. I saw little of Alex, with Rachine wrapped around him like a boa in heat. I'd stopped at Marco's table to thank him for his contribution. A group of model-gorgeous women were clustered around, as if he was giving something out for free. Maybe he was later. I shook his hand, loving the way his was firm against mine, not some wimpy you're-a-woman-I-don't-want-to-hurt-you limp shake. It made my smile broader.

He'd stopped the chatter around him for a moment by leaning forward and giving me a kiss on the cheek. Five o'clock shadow, smoke and musky cologne.

"Good work, kid. Alex is a fool." Then the chatter had started again, and I'd moved on to thank other contributors.

I'd fantasized about that compliment for three days, and about how I could get Alex and Rachine fired, and Marco would create a new dish named after me called 'Revenge Is Sweet.' Ha! Dream on, girl. That didn't happen, but we did keep running into each other at various functions, where some

woman was always hanging on his arm. I had him all to myself
on Tuesday nights, watching reruns of his reality show, where
he traveled to exotic locales and ate with the natives. There
were rumors he was going to do a new show, which was why
I was here—Superagent, my best friend, Claire, calls me. I'd
rather be a spy, but real estate agent is as close as I've gotten.
It can have some pretty thrilling aspects, though, such as sitting next to this hunk of man and getting his full attention.
That's what happens when you're a Realtor and money is at
stake. People tend to pay more attention. I've always enjoyed
that part of the job. I slid my high heels off under the table,
wiggled my toes and checked my watch again.

"You got a date?" Marco asked.

"What?" He startled me, the way he was scowling. "No.
I just didn't put enough money in the meter to stay and have
a drink. I'll need to go move the car soon."

"What did you think we were going to do? You think I'm
some kind of wham-bam guy?"

Were we planning on having sex, and had I missed that part
of the conversation? I hadn't even received my drink yet.

"You're a busy man, Mr. Rinadi. Isn't it dinner rush
soon?"

"Call me Marco." He leaned back in his chair and put his
arm around the back of mine. "Don't worry, sweetie. Alex is
in charge of the kitchen tonight. I'm just here to schmoose.
Now relax. I'll have Frank put your car in the hotel parking
lot."

"But the hotel lot is just for guests." I didn't want to have
a fight with any of the hotel staff.

"You're my guest. Frank will move your car," Marco said
firmly. Which is exactly what he told Frank when the young
man showed up with our drinks. Frank took it in stride, as if

it were an everyday occurrence. I could use an unflappable Frank in my life.

Marco called another waiter over to get us some appetizers. Finally we got down to business and talked about his house. It would have made much more sense to meet at his place, but he'd been insistent over the phone about meeting at the restaurant. We argued a bit over the possible price, but I was able to convince him of what the market could bear based on the comps I'd done early in the day. I also let him know nothing was final until I saw the house. He nodded his head over the papers, then pushed them back to me.

"Everything looks good. Come out tomorrow night."

I sighed inwardly. Here was another client who didn't understand the basics of real estate.

"I need to come out during the day in order to look around. See what might need to be done to the property, possible problems we could run into."

"Fine. Come at six. You'll have plenty of daylight to check things out. I'll make you dinner."

"That's not necessary." I did not need to be in a house alone at night with this man. I needed a client, not a lover. Not that he was offering anything, but I could see myself doing something stupid.

"I know it's not necessary, Queen Christine. We're going to get to know each other pretty well over the next few months, because I suspect there aren't too many buyers in my price range. Plus I want to try out some new dishes and you can be my guinea pig. You're not a picky eater, are you?"

"Absolutely not," I replied, and took a sip of my vodka tonic. Then wondered how I was going to swallow one of those slimy snot balls, otherwise known as oysters, which Frank had set before us. Marco pushed the platter toward me, offering me first choice. I couldn't do it, even for a multimillion-dollar possible client.

"Sorry, Marco. I can't eat oysters." I hoped he would infer that I had an allergy. No such luck.

"Can't or won't?" He lifted an eyebrow. That's probably how he kept control in the kitchen—all he had to do was lift that eyebrow. But I wasn't backing down.

"Sorry. Won't. Bad experience when I was young."

"Too bad. You know they are considered the classic aphrodisiac."

"Chocolate is more my speed."

He smiled and slid the oyster into his mouth, swallowing it whole, the brine washing down his chin. Now that part I liked, imagining him licking me with a saltwater tongue. He must have seen the lust in my eyes. He wiped his mouth and leaned close, his arm encircling my shoulders this time instead of the chair. "You watch me eat oysters and I'll watch you eat chocolate."

"Deal," I said, looking into his bright green eyes. Flecked with blue and gray they reminded me of my favorite moss agate fertility stone that Claire had bought me for my birthday the year Alex and I decided to have a baby. The problem was whenever Alex saw that hard stone he went limp. It made an excellent dildo after he left.

The vodka was making my head fuzzy, so I broke my cardinal rule and took a roll from the napkin-covered bread basket. It was rich brown pumpernickel, still warm. I smeared it with some butter from the provided ramekin. Ah, what bliss. I closed my eyes, savoring the sweet, chewy ecstasy of buttered carbs.

"Honey, you really need to get out more," Marco whispered in my ear, making my arms break out in goose bumps as I swallowed. I opened my eyes and found he was still close enough to kiss. I resisted and leaned back in my chair, lifting my glass so there would be some solid object between us.

"If I got out much more I'd be big as a house." The minute I said it I could have smacked myself. Never talk fat with a chef. One thing I'd learned from Alex. The other was never get married again, but that didn't apply here. Frank saved me by bringing an appetizer of grilled shrimp with a mango dipping sauce. I promptly pulled a curled pink morsel off the skewer and dunked it into the sauce, licking my fingers afterward.

"That's better," said Marco. Apparently I'd been putting on a show and didn't realize it.

The show was interrupted by a tall heavy man who had the jowls of a bulldog. He reached a meaty paw across the table as Marco stood up. Marco was a big man, but he looked like a beanpole next to this guy.

"Chef." The big man nodded in greeting.

"Don. So glad you could come. Have you met Christine Monford? She's my real estate agent." Marco turned to me and winked. The Jowl man shook my hand, and I swear it disappeared in his sweaty one. I wiped my palm against my skirt under the table. "Christine, this is Don Franco—he's my banker." Marco motioned to one of the staff to bring Don a chair. "Christine's somebody you need on your contact list, Don. She could bring you lots of customers."

Don grunted my way and I wondered what kind of banking he handled. I'd been in this town a long time and knew almost all the mortgage people. He didn't look familiar and he was somebody I wouldn't forget meeting. While Don hadn't impressed me, Marco had. He was continually combining business and pleasure. A man after my own heart.

I pushed my feet back into my pumps and stood up to go. The party was over as far as I was concerned. Marco jumped up beside me. Don just looked at me with sad eyes that literally perked up when Frank placed a beer in front of him.

I put my jacket back on, watching Marco watch me. His eyes seemed to caress the skin under my jacket, leaving me much too warm.

"I'll see you out," he said.

"That's not necessary," I said. It was high time I hotfooted it home before I got myself in trouble and started playing footsie. I picked up my briefcase and purse. "Nice meeting you, Don." We nodded at each other, since his hands were busy, with a beer in one and fried calamari in the other. Marco took my elbow and held it gently all the way through the restaurant and hotel lobby. I turned to him at the foyer doors to thank him and remind him of our meeting the next day. His hand was still possessively on my elbow when Alex walked through the lobby. He stopped right in front of us.

"Chef, we've got a problem with the customer at table five. Says he talked to you about a special case of wine for his party tonight." Alex shifted from one foot to the other.

Marco sighed and ran his hand up and down the back of my arm, an automatic caress. I smiled brightly at Alex just for the sheer evil fun of it.

"Tell him I'll be right there," Marco said, effectively shooing Alex away. Then he turned to me and gave me a kiss on the cheek, holding his face against mine for just a moment. "Umm, you smell good, but duty calls. I'll see you tomorrow night." He gave me a salute, then was gone.

Alex appeared again. What did he do, just go around the revolving door?

"What do you think you're doing?" he practically spat at me.

"Waiting for my car. Is there a problem?" I gripped the handle of my bag in case I had to throw it at him. Here was the man who'd always lectured me on networking but once I had started networking for my own career instead of his, suddenly it was considered bothering people.

"You know there's a problem. Keep your paws off Marco."

"Oh?" I raised my eyebrow. "I didn't know he was yours to claim. I thought you were into girls, Alex."

"Very funny, Christine. Just because the man has had the hots for you since day one doesn't mean you have to sleep with him. You're being very immature to retaliate that way."

I was so mad I didn't know what to say. Fortunately, the valet swung my car up to the curb just then. I had splurged last year after a big sale and bought a black Mercedes sedan. It was slightly used, but nobody needed to know that. I looked at the car which to me symbolized my independence from Alex, and suddenly wasn't so mad anymore. Alex might have the love of a bimbo, but I had a Mercedes and the ever appreciative glances of hot men. I gave the valet a generous tip, then turned to Alex, who was still skulking there.

"I hadn't planned on sleeping with Marco. I am simply selling his house. It's what I do very well, and he knows that. I don't need to retaliate, Alex. I'm very happy with the way things worked out. If you'll excuse me, I have another appointment."

I turned and climbed into my luxury automobile, sparing only one glance at his still scowling face. He'd got what he wanted. Now I was going to grab what I wanted.

CHAPTER TWO

THE NEXT EVENING, AFTER CHANGING CLOTHES twice and shoes three times, I settled on a basic black wrap dress and strappy black sandals. More party attire than business but I was willing to risk it if he was. I pulled into Marco's driveway and surveyed the property as I pushed the button to slide the sunroof closed. I'd never been inside this house although I was familiar with the neighborhood. I'd done my research, though, and pulled the tax records. Five bedrooms, five baths, five million dollars. It was hidden in a neighborhood full of twists and turns that took full advantage of the waterside location. I knew he had bought the property after giving up a condo in town. Apparently too many parties at the condo were upsetting the neighbors.

He greeted me at the door with a kiss on each cheek. He smelled even better than yesterday. He had an apron on that said Kiss the Cook. I laughed.

"You like? My niece gave it to me for a Christmas present. She didn't want me to ruin my nice clothes when I was at home. It does come in handy occasionally."

"Is it like the cobbler's children sometimes, that you don't cook at home since you do so much at the restaurant?" I was used to making my own fare, because Alex would usually settle for a bowl of cereal when he was home. The food honeymoon had lasted about as long as the real one.

"I always cook at home, even if it's just a simple pasta. Cooking is my life. I live it. Now come eat. We need to fatten you up."

I liked the fattening up part. I could go along with that. He took my hand and pulled me into the foyer.

"I heard you're not planning on sleeping with me." He still held my hand. His was warm, but a chill went up my arm.

"No," I replied, smiling. "Sleeping is not what I had in mind."

He laughed and pulled me closer, taking my chin in his other hand, rubbing the tender skin underneath. His fingers were rough, covered with calluses and burns, old and new, but they gently teased my neck, trailing down to my collarbone. I met him eye to eye and tried not to giggle. It would have been seductive if it hadn't tickled so much. He burst out laughing, hugging me to him and kissing the top of my head.

He stepped back to hold me at arm's length. "You, my dear, are going to be the death of me. Come on, let me show you the house and then we'll eat. Would you like a drink?"

I declined until all the paperwork was done. It was the usual tour of a gorgeous waterfront home with five bedrooms, five baths, gourmet kitchen, finished basement with in-law suite possibilities, the works. I thought we would get flirty in the bedroom, but Marco was all business until we were standing out at the poolside railing looking over the Severn River.

"I would never get tired of this view," I said. From the back of the house was an Annapolis dreamscape view of the Severn River, the Naval Academy with its familiar green, copper-domed chapel, the Naval Academy Bridge upriver, then farther up, the Route 50 bridge. "I bet you have a great view of the Blue Angels during Commissioning Week."

"Spectacular," he replied. I turned and found he was looking at me, not gazing upriver as I had just moments before. A warm glow settled in my chest, and it wasn't from the late summer heat. He reached out and gathered me in his arms, crushing my notepad between us. He kissed me and I opened my mouth, inviting him in. He tasted of honey with a back note of smoke. I hoped he appreciated the half box of Mentos I had chewed on the way here. He seemed to as he tugged my notepad away from me and tossed it on the patio, where it landed with a muffled thump. Padded leather is so much sexier than a hard clipboard. Speaking of hard, Marco was hardening and lengthening against my belly as we clung to one another. He bent me over slightly, tearing his mouth from mine, kissing my neck, which no longer tickled, running his hand down my back to cup my ass, then pulling my leg around his thigh. I was clinging to his shoulders, biting his neck—I wound my leg around his, thinking I would come in an instant if he made the slightest thrusting movement. But he didn't.

He stopped kissing me, held me hard and still against him, panting into my neck, his hot breath against my pulse calming us both. I unwound my leg from his and loosened my passionate grip, running my hands down the sheer cotton of his shirt then onto the rough muslin of the apron. I stepped back and he let me go. He was bent over a bit, as if I was still in his arms. I nervously smoothed my skirt as he watched me. He finally straightened and stretched his whole body. He rolled his shoulders and flexed his neck. What was he warming up for? I thought we had already started.

He took my hand and kissed it gently, then, still holding my hand, he said, "Forgive me. I got a little carried away."

I gave his palm a slight squeeze and pulled away. "I wasn't having any problem with it."

He laughed that deep rumbling laugh that always filled a room with contentment. Today it seemed to boomerang around the river, making me happy just to be here for this moment in time. He cranked open a canvas umbrella over the glass dining table and motioned for me to take a seat on one of the wrought-iron chairs, the blue-and-white-striped ticking cushion at least four inches thick. I picked my notepad from where Marco had dropped it, and sank down in the chair.

"I'll be right back." He walked past the hibiscus-bordered hot tub, waterfall and pool combination and through the patio French doors. Before I had a chance to miss him he reappeared sans apron, bearing a tray with a bottle of champagne, two flutes and my personal, although according to Alex hokey, favorite appetizer of jumbo shrimp cocktail. There was also a small two-sided bowl, one half filled with assorted olives, the other left empty for the pits, and a small plate of fresh mozzarella and tomato slices drizzled with basil olive oil. As he placed the dishes on the table, he said, "The lamb is in the oven. I didn't want you to get hungry."

He must have been serious about fattening me up.

He reached for the champagne bottle and tore off the foil. I thought surely he would open it as Alex had instructed me long ago—twisting the bottle, not the cork, and loosening slowly, allowing just a small, discreet popping sound. No, Marco stood with both thumbs against the mushroom-shaped plug, the bottle poised over his groin, and let the cork fly into the air. Champagne gushed out, and he pushed it to my mouth, so I could suck it from the bottle. The frothing liquid

spilled down my chin and onto my chest. Marco knelt before
me and pushed my hands away to lick the sweet wine from
my skin. One hand still held the bottle, while the other was
at my knee, massaging my leg under my skirt.

I plunged my fingers into his black-and-silver mane, holding his head between my breasts, then running my palms
down his back, feeling every muscle. He released the wine
bottle to grip under my bottom and pull me forward so I
was at the edge of the chair, my legs now wrapped around
his torso, my skirt up to my thighs. His hands roamed up my
spine as we kissed, not content with just lips to lips but lips to
tongue, to cheeks, to eyes, to ears. He tasted of sunshine and
earth and smoke. I pushed myself harder against him, squeezing my legs around his wide chest. His rough fingers pushed
down the straps of my dress and bra, making my breasts spill
out. Marco took what I offered, his fingers running across my
nipples like fine sandpaper, then his tongue soothing, then
teasing, then sucking. I bucked against his chest, longing to
feel him inside me. Hard and deep and now.

"Now, Marco, now," I gasped in his ear. He stopped, simply
stopped, rocking back on his heels, releasing my legs wrapped
around his middle. He ran his hands down the backs of my
legs, gently setting my heels on the sun-warmed concrete. I
wanted to hurl myself at him, thrust my breast in his mouth,
demand that he suckle. Instead I reached to cover myself, but
he took both my hands in one of his.

"Do you know why the man usually takes the champagne
in his mouth?" he whispered, nuzzling at my breast with his
Roman nose.

"No," I croaked. My whole body was throbbing for his
touch.

"Because men are greedy. They do not realize how one
small thing can make a world of difference. Like the taste

buds not only receiving pleasure, but giving pleasure. You taste of sweet honest sweat, an aphrodisiac to me. My tasting it gives you pleasure. Heighten that pleasure with one small thing." He reached out and dipped a finger in the olive oil, smearing it over my puckered nipple with his rough fingertip. I groaned when the smell of basil perfumed the air as the oil heated. He pushed my hands between my legs, hard against my pussy as he pinched my nipple, once, twice, three times. I came in a moaning rush, falling against his shoulder as he kept caressing my breast, kissing my neck.

He sat back on his heels again, tucking my breasts back into my bra, pulling up the straps, caressing my shoulders. I pulled my skirt down to my knees.

"I will never look at basil the same way."

He laughed and kissed me on the mouth, lingering. I had to grip the arms of my chair to keep from clutching at him.

"Who needs oysters?" he said, his voice husky with need. I reached for him, but he stood quickly, taking my hand in his. He gave it a gentle squeeze. "First course." Then he turned to pour the champagne while I watched the muscles in his forearm move with the grace of a well-trained chef. I didn't know food could be quite so entertaining.

He handed me a full champagne flute, then picked up his own.

"A toast," he said. "To pleasure—in all its forms."

"To pleasure," I said as we gently clinked the crystal glasses together. I took a sip. It was smooth, barely sweet, with bubbles that foamed across my tongue. I blushed to think of them foaming across my chest.

I reached for my notepad and flipped it open. He simply shook his head, so I closed it and pushed it aside. It could wait. At least until after the appetizers.

CHAPTER THREE

WE ATE THE SHRIMP AND TALKED OF THE CITY.
How we had both arrived by accident and fallen in love with
its historical waterside charm. We nibbled at the cheese and
tomatoes. I followed his lead and rolled mine up, dipping it
into the basil oil.

"I suppose I should have brought out utensils," he said,
smiling as he licked his fingers.

"This is much more fun."

My breasts felt full and heavy, peaking again with desire
every time he looked at me. Surely he wouldn't send me home
without letting me reciprocate, but I didn't want to get greedy.
Every word he spoke with his husky, smoke-laden voice was
like a stroke against my skin, petting me into languorous
submission. I wanted to roll over like a dog and have him
stroke my belly.

He took his cigarette case and lighter out of his pocket.

"Do you mind?" he said.

"I suppose that's become an automatic question for you,
hasn't it?"

"I guess it has." He smiled, then lit up, blowing the smoke upriver, away from me. "It's something that has become a habit, like so many other things in my life. It's very hard to change because it brings me pleasure. What are your pleasurable habits?"

I twirled the empty champagne flute in my hands, not sure how to answer his question. He motioned for me to put it down so he could refill it.

"I brush my teeth every night."

He raised his eyebrow, making me smile. "How very Girl Scout of you."

"I like that fresh minty taste," I said.

"Ah, I thought I detected a hint of mint before."

I blushed. The man had brought me to orgasm and I was blushing over my teeth-brushing habit.

"Come on, darling, there has to be something else that's a little more wicked." He leaned forward, egging me on.

"I eat something chocolate every day."

He snorted. A very manly noise that made me laugh. "Doesn't every woman do that, since they declared chocolate is good for you?"

"I masturbate every Saturday night."

That got his attention. He sat up straight and peered at me through narrowed eyes. He took a drag from his cigarette and did the smoke-through-the-nose trick that he'd done yesterday. It made him look like a wonderfully dangerous fuck. I was wet now and it wasn't from the champagne.

"So…" He drew the word out for about five seconds. "Every Saturday night?"

"Yep." My throat was starting to tighten. I took a sip of champagne to ease it a bit.

He knocked the ash from his cigarette over the railing into the grass. "Alone or does somebody watch?"

"Alone, of course."

"That's not a bad habit. It doesn't harm you in any way. Rather boring, actually, if you're making a date with yourself to avoid a man. Playing it safe."

"I don't play it safe." I could feel my back tensing up. That's what I was trying to get away from this year. I had played it safe with Alex and it had gotten me nowhere. I had told myself this year that I was going to take a chance with men. Marco had nailed it and it made me mad. "I'm not playing it safe with you. This is rather unethical professionally, and probably pretty stupid personally."

"Christine, you're merely playing footsie with me. We've been dancing around each other for two years now. How many charity events have we both attended? You've always thanked me for my contribution and moved on. I was starting to think you were the Ice Queen, not the Queen of Darkness."

"And now I'm here. And I do believe what we were doing ten minutes ago could have me qualified as the Queen of Sin." I stood up. I was starting to feel insulted.

"You're leaving?"

"I think that might be best." I picked up my notepad.

Marco leaned back and took a drag off his cigarette. "You're running scared."

"I am not scared." I could feel a blush overtaking my whole body. He was damned right I was scared. This man brought out something in me that was totally heathen. With Alex it had been light and breezy and fun, at least in the beginning. I had felt like I was marrying my best friend. The problem was I felt as if I outgrew him years ago.

This man was there and beyond. This man had seen and done things that I never had and didn't know if I'd ever have the courage to do. He had traveled the world, immersing himself in all sorts of cultures, having adventures, while I was here in small-town America learning about amortization rates and contract clauses regarding mold removal. Yeah, real exciting life.

But I wanted to climb this man's frame. I should have restrained myself before. Okay, small mistake. I needed to regroup. I wanted Marco's respect, and I probably wasn't going to get it by letting him ravish me. He struck me as the unrestrained ravishing kind, the type that was friends with all his ex-lovers. The type that received gifts of engraved lighters and cigarette holders from satisfied ladies. I could be one of those satisfied ladies. I wanted to stamp my foot with frustration.

"Having second thoughts, Christine?"

"No." I straightened my spine and lowered the notepad clutched to my chest. It had simply drawn his attention to my breasts. I took advantage of his distraction.

"Why don't we meet tomorrow at my office before you go to the restaurant? I'll have all the information in the computer, and I can get all that downloaded into the system once you sign the papers."

"No." His eyes narrowed. They weren't focused on my breasts anymore, but staring at me with the glint of a challenge.

"All right." I took a deep breath. The man was maddening. "Where do you want to meet?"

"I'm not giving you the listing, Christine."

"I see." Yes, I had probably made a huge mistake. A pleasurable one certainly, but still a mistake. Never, ever, mix business with pleasure. What was I thinking? For the second time in two days, I mentally smacked myself upside the head. "Well, thank you for the appetizers, and the stimulating company." I turned on my heel and took three steps.

"I have a proposition for you," Marco called out. Probably

something like *Battle of the Network Stars,* I thought. Except this time it would be *Battle of the Real Estate Agents.* Had his friends in reality TV given him tips on how to sell a house, or seduce an agent? I couldn't resist. I had to know. This would make a wonderful watercooler story.

Marco stood and stubbed out his cigarette on his plate. He walked over and ran his fingers lightly down my bare arm. I shivered and he grinned.

"Do you like this house, Christine?"

"Of course. It's beautiful."

"Would you like to live here?" He crossed his arms over his expansive chest, one large, scarred hand rubbing his chin.

"With you? I don't believe in moving in on the first date."

He chuckled. "It doesn't have to be with me. I will give you this house. Give it to you free and clear, all paid for, if you will spend the night with me and do anything I ask."

Surely he was joking. "I can't pay the taxes on this place, much less the utilities."

"I'll throw in all expenses for five years." He waved his hand as if this were some minor detail.

"What's the catch?" I said. "You can have any woman you want."

"Ah," he said, "you've already heard the catch. One night. Anything. You."

"Deal," I said. "Put it in writing." Then I promptly dropped my notepad into the pool.

CHAPTER FOUR

AS I WATCHED MY LEVENGER LEATHER SYMBOL of success sink to the bottom with little swaying motions as if it were dancing, I figured I had finally lost my mind. I tried to remember what had happened in that Robert Redford movie when he offered Demi Moore a million dollars for one night, then realized I hadn't seen the film, just the trailers. How did it end? Was I doomed? No, probably just stupid.

Marco handed me a linen napkin with something written on it. I read it out loud. "I, Marco Rinadi, being of sound mind and body—" I looked up at him. "Are you sure about the sound mind part?"

He laughed. "Keep reading, Christine."

I swallowed and licked my lips. "—do promise to give Christine Monford my house at 428 Severn Court and five years of expenses for its upkeep. In return Christine Monford promises to agree to any action I deem required for the night of Monday, May 7, 2007. Signed, Marco Rinadi." I looked up at him, trying to stall, but not sure why, just knowing the whole thing scared the hell out of me. "Should we have our signatures witnessed?"

He called my bluff. "Certainly. Whom shall I call? My attorney? Yours? Both?"

I thought about phoning Sean McGavich, my divorce attorney. This deal would be the talk of the bar association meetings for months to come. Sean was good and never named names, but in a small town like Annapolis a person in the know could always figure it out. Did I trust Marco? I could trust him to satisfy every single fantasy I had, but that wasn't at stake here—it was *his* fantasies that were to be fulfilled. What if that involved whips and chains? I could probably do that for a little bit. Golden showers? *Ew.* I flinched at the thought. I studied him standing there with the open cell phone and the raised eyebrow. I hadn't heard anything bad about the man except he loved to have loud parties and loved the ladies. As far as I knew all the ladies had loved him back. Even if he was lying, did it really matter? One night with Marco was worth it. I motioned with my hand for him to shut the cell phone.

"Just answer one question, Marco. Why?"

"Do you agree to the terms?"

"I'm not sure. You could have any woman do this for free, Marco. What is going on?"

"Would you do anything for free?"

"It depends. Making love to you, certainly."

"Really? No meal, no agent contract, no promises of phone calls, no future favors, nothing?" He ran his finger from my collarbone to between my breasts, then back up again. "Think about it, sweetheart, while I'm getting the lamb ready." He gave me a quick kiss on the lips, then went inside. I stared down at my notepad, which was now at the bottom of the pool. Would that be me, ruined forever after taking the plunge? I had come here knowing it was a good possibility I would have sex with Marco, even preparing for it with my special black lace matching bra and panties set. So why was I so unsettled over the offer?

It brought up the whole matter of trust. I trusted that I could be a big girl over a one-night stand, but for Marco to put so much on the line made me wonder what was truly at stake. What did he really want? Some kind of odd control over me? Some kind of creepy head game that he would film and post on the internet? I could always say no if the cameras came out, but what if he had them mounted around the property and I didn't even know it? I scanned the corners of the house, where security cameras were usually mounted, and saw nothing. I knew the place had an alarm system. They could be hidden in those. I ran my hands up and down my arms, trying to warm up from the sudden chill.

I jumped when Marco came up behind me and wrapped his large hands around my biceps. He nuzzled my neck, then released my hair from its loose bun, running his hands over it, petting it. He gently turned me around and kissed me, our bodies sliding against each other like butter on lobster. He whispered against my lips, "Still scared?"

"No," I whispered back, and meant it, for when he held me it seemed nothing else in the world mattered except feeling him, smelling him, tasting him. If he had drugged my wine, I didn't care.

He picked me up and held me against his chest. I nibbled at his earlobe as he carried me inside and laid me on the wide brown suede sectional couch. He kicked off his boat shoes, then stretched out next to me, his head propped up on one hand, the other hand under my skirt, caressing my thigh.

I boldly began unbuttoning his shirt and pulling the tail from his waistband. He shrugged out of the garment, leaving me to admire his smooth wide shoulders, which I couldn't resist running my hands over, feeling the corded muscles underneath the warm tan skin. I pulled at his undershirt, silently demanding that he shed that, too. Reaching behind his back, he pulled it over his head, revealing a chiseled, hairless chest with dark nipples. Oh my, what a treat. I ran my nails across a nipple, making him groan.

He pulled me hard against him and his cock twitched, full and demanding, against my bush. I opened my legs wide to cradle him between my thighs. Three thin pieces of fabric to go before ecstasy. I reached for his belt buckle, but his hand enfolded mine.

"It's Saturday night, Christine."

"Uh-huh." Who cared? I figured it was my night to get lucky, and this time he wasn't going to stop me. I pulled the end of his belt loose. He pushed himself off the couch, grabbing both my hands in his. The man must do yoga, the way he bent away from me. My dress was up to my waist, my legs sprawled open in invitation. "Why do you keep stopping?" I almost wailed in frustration. He crouched beside the couch, still holding my hands still.

"You're a greedy wench, aren't you?" he said, smiling. "Now tell me about your Saturday nights, Christine." The sun was setting across the river behind Marco. It was as if there was a shadow man in front of me, a dream man holding my hands tight, demanding my secrets before he would release me. "You weren't lying were you, darling?" He put his head down and I was blinded by the sun's last light full on my face. I closed my eyes against the glare. At the same time he slowly licked my palm, running his tongue between each finger, mimicking how I wanted his cock inside me.

"Jesus, Marco." I reached for his belt again with my other hand, but he just held it tighter.

"Talk, Christine. No, better yet, show me." He released

my hands and stood up just enough to sit back on the coffee table. The sun hit my face full on again. "Oh, that's perfect," said Marco. He shifted a bit so the sun was illuminating my whole body. "Do you need anything? A vibrator?"

"Do you have one?" I couldn't resist asking.

"Several. What kind?" He stood up, ready to do my bidding.

"Actually, I don't need one." I closed my eyes, debating whether to be truthful. A blush spread across my body. Maybe as a chef he would understand. Maybe as a chef, he had done this before. I pushed that thought out of my mind. I was here, now, for mutual pleasure only. "I need a pickle, or a cucumber, or a squash." I put my hands over my still closed eyes.

"Kosher dill, sweet, or bread and butter?" I could hear the laughter in his voice.

"Doesn't matter as long as it's big and whole. Don't you dare laugh. This was your idea. I'd be happy with a nice friendly man fuck."

He did laugh then and I could hear him opening a jar, then pouring something. He padded over and set down a plain white china plate with a huge dill pickle on it, and next to the plate he put a glass of red wine. He leaned over and kissed me as if this were a simple date and he had brought me an hors d'oeuvre. He picked up a remote from an end table and pushed some buttons. Van Morrison's husky voice flooded the room.

"How did you know?" I asked him as he sat down again on the end of the coffee table, letting the light fall on me.

"I take notes," his shadowy self said. Then he took a sip of wine and waited.

It was my turn now to get him all hot and bothered. I, too, could play that leave-them-wanting-more game. I stood up and pulled my dress over my head. I tossed it in Marco's direction. It hit his head and slid down his back. He sat up straighter as I sipped the wine in turn. I kicked off my shoes and stacked two pillows on the couch, then straddled them. I faced the sun and closed my eyes. I let Marco fade back into shadow and Van's voice rumble through me until it was just me, with the sun, the music and my fingers making love. I released my breasts from their bra cups, letting the lacy material hold them high from underneath. I wet my thumbs and rubbed and pulled my nipples into straining, puckered peaks. I rocked back and forth on the pillows, the nubby fabric caressing my clit through my panties.

I was throbbing and wet within minutes, knowing Marco was watching me, imagining his fingers, tongue, cock deep inside me. I opened my eyes, focusing on the horizon, the blue and pink and gold streaking across the sky. I stood up and eased my black lace panties down, tossing them in Marco's direction. I heard him groan, and wondered if he was naked, touching himself.

I picked up the pickle. It was still cold and wet. I sat back against the couch and closed my eyes again. I spread my legs and rested my feet on the coffee table. I rubbed the pickle back and forth across my clit. Bumpy and wet. I imaged it was Marco teasing me. I was ready, swollen and juicy. I pushed the pickle in slowly with one hand as I massaged my clit with the other. A moan escaped and I heard a deep one rumbling in return.

There were never enough hands when I did this on my own. As if Marco could read my mind, he was suddenly there between my thighs. He pushed the coffee table aside, resting my legs on his shoulders. He pushed my hands away and fucked me with the pickle, rhythmically, as he licked and sucked my clit. I pounded on his back with my heels as I pinched my tits and came with a yell that echoed off the high ceiling.

I was empty and spent for mere seconds when Marco filled me with his cock, oh so much larger than the pickle. Larger, harder, fiercer. I clung to him as he pounded into me, making me scream over and over, losing myself against the slick hammering muscle of Marco. He came into me with shouts nearly as loud as my own, his back and buttocks rock hard with the strain. He flipped us over on the couch, still deep inside me, and nipped my breast lightly, making my cunt clench against him.

"I could eat you up, woman," he growled, pulling me down on his sweat-slicked chest.

"Anytime," was all I could get out.

His hands danced down my back, rubbing, stroking. He unsnapped my bra and tossed it aside, letting my breasts swing free. He captured one orb and suckled gently as the sensation traveled through my body down to my cunt, wetting again around his cock. He was once more thickening deep inside me. He rubbed his other hand lightly down my spine, one finger trailing along my crack to push ever so slightly against my anus. He didn't enter but simply pressed, the action tilting my clit against his groin. His coarse hair against my tender clit made me almost weep with pleasure. He pulled out just a fraction, then back, then out, back and forth, slowly, gently sucking, pushing, fucking. I came hard against him, my teeth clenched. A sob caught in my throat. I hid my face against his neck to hide my tears of release.

He sat up, bringing me with him. He pushed the hair off my face and kissed the tears away.

"You okay?" he asked. I nodded, not trusting my voice. He held me tight against him and stood up. I shrieked and he laughed, the rumble rolling through our bodies like a wave.

Holding my bottom, with my legs locked tight around his waist, he carried me outside. It was full dark now, stars blinking in the sky, the pool lights shimmering across the water. He stepped onto the diving board and walked to the end, which bent low with our combined weight.

"What are you doing?" I foolishly asked.

"Going for a swim. We've had our appetizers and our vegetables. Think of this as cleansing the palate." With that he jumped into the water, holding me tight. We went deep into the pool, where we floated apart, only to come to the surface and join again with a kiss that held the promise of many, many more.

CHAPTER FIVE

HE WRAPPED US IN THICK WHITE TOWELS WHEN
we climbed out of the pool. We went inside and sat at the
island counter and ate slices of lamb with a squash casserole
that tasted like something a grandmother would make—filling, comforting and probably full of fat. Marco warmed up
crusty bread just for me and we finished off the bottle of red
wine. By the end of the meal I was languid with well-being.
I rubbed Marco's bare calf with my foot.

"Tonight you get to chose what we do. When is it my
turn?" Yes, I was being greedy, when we'd barely started.

Marco swung his balloon-shaped wineglass between his
fingers. "I've had a grand time being in charge so far. Why
should I give my power over to you? Wouldn't that be negat-
ing our agreement?"

"Oh, come on, Marco. I know what you're playing at. I'm
not that naive. I don't get the house. I don't want it. I have
a career, and someday I'll be able to buy a place like this for
myself. I don't need someone to give me a house, especially

not one in return for sex. You wouldn't have really done it, anyway."

He swiveled toward me, his chest bronze and beckoning in the candlelight. I longed to touch him, but kept my hand in my lap.

"You're not a very trusting soul, are you?"

"Let's just say I've learned my lessons."

"I tell you what." He stood up and ran his hand down my bare shoulder, raising goose bumps. "I'm going to now do what every woman dreams a man will do for her."

He'd already cooked me a wonderful dinner, so that left that out. I thought about a foot massage, or maybe him painting my toenails, or hmm, maybe dressing up as a pirate. The possibilities were endless. "I can't imagine," I said.

"I'm going to wash the dishes," he announced.

"Oooh, that's a good one. Naked?" I asked hopefully.

"Sorry. Too much hot water involved."

I did get to watch him clean up wearing only a towel around his waist and that was almost as exciting, waiting for the towel to drop at any moment.

I knew it was supposed to be his night, but I couldn't wait any longer. He had finished washing the dishes and was making coffee when I got off the stool and hugged him from behind. It was a risk, making the first move. Would he chastise me? Oooh, maybe spanking would be involved. I hadn't tried that before. Was it in the plan? The man had seriously corrupted me by now.

All I got out of him as I pressed against his back was a low "umm" like the purring of a cat. I divested him of his towel and stroked his butt. High and tight. I let my own towel drop to the floor, and leaned against him again, rubbing my nipples across his back, standing on tiptoe to rub my bush against his ass. The purring had escalated to short moans.

The cappuccino machine started to hiss. Marco stepped back and spread his legs. I knew an invitation when I saw one. I reached up between his legs and cradled his balls. They puckered and rose under my hand. I reached around his waist and grabbed his cock with my other hand. He was full and ready, the head already weeping for me. I spread his wetness over the head and his cock danced in my hand.

"Haven't you had enough?" he growled.

"Never," I teased. I turned him around, using his cock as a handle. He moved willingly, bracing his back on the counter, his feet still spread, offering himself to me. I got on my knees and took him in my mouth. I wanted to give him as much as he'd given me. I wanted him as crazed with desire as I had been out on the patio when he had rubbed my nipples with oil. I licked and sucked and nibbled. Each time he tried to pump into me, I pulled my head away and pushed him against the counter. He took my head in his hands and I pushed those back too. When his whole body went rigid, ready to explode, I took him as deep in my mouth as I could, wanting to take that small part of him, but he pulled me roughly up by my armpits and slammed me against him as he spurted between my breasts. We sprawled awkwardly to the floor, both of us panting.

"Not on the first date," he rasped.

I closed my eyes and savored the sensations around me. The hard floor, the warmth of Marco's thigh against mine, the now cold, wet cum against my chest. I could have fallen asleep right there. I jumped when a hot, wet dish towel rubbed across my torso. It was Marco leaning over me, cleaning me off. He helped me up and handed me a mug of coffee.

"Come on," he said, and motioned with his head toward the stairs. He waved for me to precede him up the steps. I simply waved back. We smiled at each other. I had laid my body completely open for this man, but I didn't want to climb the stairwell naked before him. He seemed to read my mind, and reached for my hand so we could ascend the soft, carpeted stairs side by side.

CHAPTER SIX

MARCO'S BEDROOM WAS THE EPITOME OF masculine luxury. The walls were painted a deep blue with white trim. As well as a king-size, padded leather sleigh bed with a wrought-iron lion holding a ring in its mouth at each corner, there were two large walnut nightstands, each stacked with books. Across from the bed was an entertainment center that included a flat-screen TV and a stereo. I had noticed during the house tour that the view from the floor-to-ceiling windows was of the Chesapeake Bay, which now twinkled with boat lights.

Marco put his coffee on a coaster on the left nightstand. He opened the top drawer and tossed me a coaster, which I placed under my mug on the right nightstand. He flipped down the tan-and-blue down comforter. *"Entrez, mademoiselle."*

He didn't have to ask me twice. I slid between the cool, soft sheets, thinking I should have showered first, but Marco was already in. He pulled me against his side and kissed the top of my head.

"Are you hungry? I didn't give you any dessert," he said.

"I am perfectly satiated," I replied, kissing his neck.

"Why do I have the feeling that won't last?" He rolled on top of me, pinning me to the mattress. I studied his face in the lamplight, as he studied mine. Over the years my heart had leaped every time I saw that face in a crowd. It was as if I knew how dear it could become to me, and I didn't want to risk it. I didn't want him to become just another failed memory, but here he was already dear to me, ingrained in my skin, my body, my mind forever. I reached out and ran my hand over his crow's-feet, the skin soft above his emerging nighttime stubble. He pulled me into a bear hug, hiding his face against my neck.

"So what do you do on Sunday nights?"

I laughed and ran my fingers through his hair. He was so damned comfortable, just as I knew he would be. It was time for me to leave, but I'd promised him the whole night. "Let's see. Read. Watch TV. Paint my nails. Dream about exotic chefs fucking me."

He chuckled into my neck and ran his hand down my side. "Where were you when I was a teenager?"

"My God." I pushed him back in mock terror. "You mean you were even randier than you are now?"

He smiled and rose to a sitting position. "We would have killed each other, Christine. That or had ten kids by now. Jesus—" He covered his face with his hands, then peeked out. "You are on the pill, right? I didn't even think to ask. Shit, I've never done that before."

"Yes, not to worry." I patted his knee as I leaned back against the headboard. I pulled the comforter over my breasts. I'd started taking the pill again two months ago, looking forward to getting back in the dating game. I hadn't planned on entering it with such a virtual bang. I took a sip of cappuccino. It was strong and hot and perfect.

After I put my mug down, Marco motioned for me to slide down, and began massaging my shoulders.

"Your talents know no bounds," I said. If I wasn't already putty in his hands, I would be soon. I rolled over onto my stomach to give him full access to my back. His hands could have been insured.

"Did you and Alex ever want kids?"

I opened my eyes and peered up at Marco. He was now lying on his side, his head propped on his hand. His eyes were hooded, sleepy.

"In the beginning, when I saw a family as a very romantic existence, I did. Then I realized I would essentially be a single mom, with Alex being gone six days a week. It was more work than I was ready for. I want a partnership when I finally have a family. How about you? Do you regret not having children?" It felt odd to be talking of children after we had wasted copious amounts of Marco's sperm this evening.

"Yes." His fingers trailed up and down my spine in a mindless caress. "Annette never wanted any. Then when the show came along we just got too busy. Now the show's over and it's just me and the restaurant." He pinched my butt cheek, making me jump. "Don't listen to this old fool. Midlife crisis talk."

I scooted over to take him in my arms, but he gently pushed me onto my back and settled between my thighs. "How would you make love if you were making a baby?" he asked.

I pulled his face to mine and kissed him, and between each kiss I told him. "Slow. Deep. Often." With that, we made love exploring each other's bodies as new lovers, the completeness of Marco entering me, sinking into my body like a ship into the fog. I wanted to surround him with the essence of me as I wrapped my arms around his back, my legs around his, holding him as we fell into each other's eyes as we came, our orgasms a joining, rather than a release. Afterward, I closed my eyes against the emotion, not wanting to hope for anything beyond the moment. We fell asleep still joined together.

When I awoke I was empty, alone, and tied spread-eagled on the mattress. The room was gray with moonlight. Marco sat on a chair at the foot of the bed. I could see the yellow glow of his cigarette. The windows were open, and a breeze blew the linen curtains into curls of cloth. It also swirled over my body, making my nipples pucker and my skin pebble with goose bumps.

"It's almost morning," Marco announced.

"So it is." I said it calmly, though my mind was screaming with the doubts from last night. I tugged at my bonds. Silk scarves, not leather. Possibly breakable.

"You promised me a whole night."

"I did." I took a deep breath, running the night through my mind. There was no hint of craziness. Did I miss a sign somewhere? Had he used the kitchen knives too menacingly? My upper lip broke out in a sweat.

Marco came and sat on the bed next to me, a large dark shadow once again. He stubbed his cigarette out in a small ashtray I hadn't seen him holding.

"You like being in control, don't you, Christine?"

I nodded, then didn't know if he could see the small movement in the dark. I tried to speak but just croaked, so I had to clear my throat before I could say simply, "Yes."

"I do, too. That could be a problem for us."

I didn't know what to say to the "us" remark, so I kept silent.

"Do you want me to untie you, Christine?"

"Yes. Please." Then I'd be out of here as fast as my little legs could carry me.

"Do you want to tie me up?"

"I didn't realize that was an option."

"It could be if you wanted it to be. You know, I've never used these rings before." I remembered the lion heads mounted on the bed. Nothing like having an aha moment. "A friend of mine installed them as a joke when I got the new bed. I didn't mean to scare you. I thought it could be a wonderful surprise. Guess it was more surprise than wonderful, huh?"

"You could say that."

"Want to give it a go?"

"I'm not into pain, Marco."

"I'm not really, either, although in certain contexts it could be quite pleasurable. For instance…" He reached over and tweaked my nipple. I gasped at the slight pinch. My traitorous cunt immediately lathered up. "Or spanking. That could be fun to try."

"What did you have in mind, Marco?"

"I'm not sure. I just thought this would be an exciting way to end the evening of bliss you promised me."

"That's right. The exchange. How could I forget? Do the furnishings come with the house?"

"But, Christine, you said you would make love for free." I could see the flash of his smile and I instantly relaxed. The man wasn't sinister; he was just too damned exciting for me.

"This isn't making love, Marco. This is sex."

He tapped his forefinger against his lips, then pointed it at me. "I do believe I wrote, 'any action deemed required.'"

"Well, in that case. Action away."

He laughed. "It all seems so calculated now. I'm afraid it's lost its bit of fun."

"What's the matter? Can't get it up after coming three times in one night?"

"You wench," he said, and reached for something on the

nightstand. The silver blade of a knife glinted in the moonlight. My body jumped back as Marco leaned toward me, only to cut the scarf that held my left hand. Then he reached over to slice the scarf off my right wrist. I sat up and he cut both bonds off my feet. "You're a very naughty girl to question my sexual prowess."

I giggled with relief, then shrieked with surprise as he pulled me over his lap and spanked my bare bottom hard. "Ow." He spanked again, more gently this time, but with a sting. I wiggled against him, noticing the growth of his cock as it pushed against my belly. He smacked again and I wiggled some more. He pushed a finger into my wet cunt and we moaned together. I twisted away from his finger and mounted his now fully stiff cock. I rode him hard and fast, pushing my breasts into his mouth, demanding to be suckled, which he did, hard and wet. The sound of our bodies slapping wetly against each other drove us both to a frenzy and we came quickly, yelling into the darkness.

The next time I awoke I was alone again, but this time the hot sun was shining onto the bright white sheets and I could hear Marco singing Italian opera in the shower.

I have never been a girl who likes to spend the night. The morning after is just too awkward, with lying promises and bad-breath kisses. I got out of bed and promptly had to sit down again. I was sore and achy, my legs limp noodles. I took a deep breath and tried once more, holding on to the nightstand. I remembered that every article of my clothing was downstairs.

I made it down holding on to the banister and praying that I wouldn't run into a housekeeper. Not that she would be shocked by a naked woman appearing in her boss's house. I suspected I wasn't the first. I got dressed, and as I went to pick up my purse I saw the linen napkin on which Marco had written the night's contract. I tucked it into my purse for posterity.

I left my notepad at the bottom of the pool. I wrote Marco a thank-you note on real paper that I found next to the phone, and let myself out of the house just as I heard the shower turn off.

I called Claire at her coffee shop and she brought a plain black coffee and strawberry scone to my car.

"Didn't want to do the walk of shame, huh?" She eyed my disheveled hair and obvious evening attire.

"Shut up, Claire," I said as I handed over my money.

"Anybody I know?"

"Probably," I said. "That's why I'm not telling you."

"Oh, come on. Just a hint."

"He's rich and a control freak," I blurted. Don't ask me why. It must have been the lack of sleep.

"Oooh, sounds perfect for you."

Then I blushed like I've never blushed before and just about ran over Claire's toes, trying to get away. He was perfect for me and I hated it. I could never have him. He was independent, cocksure—yeah, that was a good word for him—and scary as hell, the way he could read me. Nope, didn't need him. Just when I'd discovered my own independence from Alex, I didn't need another man mucking up my life. Maybe we could have another "contract" night, but long term he was nothing but trouble.

I thought back to our discussion about babies. He clearly just wanted to practice making them. No, I needed to find myself a nice, reliable, predictable man.

My Marco fantasies had come true. I couldn't ask for any more. It would only bring about disappointment. I gave my thoughts a little mental hug as I pulled into my parking space. Memories of last night would keep me warm for a long time.

CHAPTER SEVEN

I TOOK A LONG HOT SHOWER, THE WATER EASING the soreness outside. My brain was as swollen as all my womanly tissues. Last night was how I'd imagined my wedding night would have been with Alex. Instead, we'd had greasy hamburgers from room service and an obligatory fuck while Alex had one eye on a football game on TV. I should have known then I wouldn't ever have his full attention.

The doorbell was ringing as I got out of the shower. I twisted my hair up in a towel and threw on my Hello Kitty terry-cloth robe. It was probably Molly from next door, wanting to know how things had gone with Marco. I debated telling her what had happened. I wanted to keep the memories to myself for a while. Who would believe me, anyway?

I threw open the door with a smile, expecting Molly's freckled face. It was Marco lounging against the iron railing, smoking a cigarette.

"Do you always kiss and run?"

"Goodbyes aren't my thing, Marco. I left a note."

He fished a crumpled piece of paper out of his front pocket.

He smoothed it open and read it aloud. "Thanks for a lovely evening. I can refer you to another agent about the house. See you around town. Christine." He balled it up again and tossed it behind his shoulder. "What kind of crap is that?"

I leaned against the door for support and pushed my toes into the foyer's cold tile. I felt like a schoolkid being reprimanded by a teacher. "It's polite crap."

"Jesus, woman. What do I have to do to get through to you?" He ran his hand through his hair, clutching it at the top of his skull. I had seen him do that at a cooking exhibition one time when the portable burners wouldn't work. "May I come in?" His tone was rather surly.

"You can't smoke in here."

"Fine." He chopped the word out as he dropped the cigarette on the concrete and stubbed it out with his snakeskin boot. Then, to my surprise, he leaned down and picked up the butt and brought it inside with him. I waved him into the kitchen and over to the garbage can. He ran the butt under the faucet, then disposed of it.

"Don't look so surprised. Just because I'm a smoker doesn't mean I'm not responsible."

I didn't know what to say to that, so I just said, "Juice?" and waved the cranberry juice container toward him.

He shook his head, then turned one of the kitchen chairs around and straddled it. I sat down across from him, holding my paper cup of coffee with both hands. He looked as if he wanted to strangle me.

"I'm leaving for France this afternoon. We're doing a pilot taping for a possible new show. Food history."

"That sounds fun."

"I hope so. I don't believe in doing it if it isn't fun. We could have had fun this morning, Christine. I was planning to make you breakfast. Hoping we could talk some more."

I took a sip of my coffee. It was lukewarm now but a welcome diversion. "Sorry. I just thought it would be more comfortable for both of us if I just left. I won't tell anyone, if that's what you're worried about."

"Why would I be worried about that?"

I shrugged. "Working with Alex, or why you have to find another real estate agent."

Marco leaned forward and rapped his knuckles on the table. "I'm not selling the house, so I don't need another agent. And I don't give a rat's ass about any loyalty to Alex. You do know he's going to La Grange? I found out yesterday that he tried to poach half my staff."

"Yesterday. I see. So this was more like a revenge fuck? Hmm?" I got up and threw my coffee into the sink, wishing I had the guts to throw it at Marco. I kept staring out the window across Spa Creek, where I could see the top of the hotel where all this started, two days ago. How soon had Marco called me after Alex resigned? The scene blurred and I blinked away tears. I knew the night had been too good to be true.

"Christine, stop it." His finger stroked the back of my neck. I shivered and stepped away, but he pulled me into his arms and held me tight like he had last night. His deep voice rumbled against my chest as he spoke. "I've wanted to be with you for two years, Christine. You know that. You can't deny the attraction we had—do have—for each other. But I didn't want to barge in when you separated. And I wanted to give you time after the divorce. Give you time to get back on your feet. I didn't want to be the fallback guy. Yeah, there might have been some feelings of revenge going on yesterday."

I tried to pull away from him but he wouldn't let me go. "But you know what, Christine? It was revenge that I'm the smarter man. I don't know how he let you go. He's a damn fool. I've told you that before and I will say it a thousand times over. Any man would be a fool to let you go." He tilted my chin up, so I would look into his agate-green eyes. "Will you give me a chance, Christine? When I get back, will you give me a chance to show you how smart I'm going to be?"

I smiled against his mouth and kissed his love-bruised lips. "Yes," I said. "And I'll show you how I'm even smarter." He squeezed me even tighter and lifted my feet off the floor.

"That's my girl. Now give me something to take with me." With that he opened my robe and ran his fingers down my belly to cup between my legs. He stroked a finger over my soreness and I gasped. "Ah. I'll give you a month to heal up." He knelt down and pushed my thighs open. I grabbed the edge of the sink above his head. He licked and sucked and drove his tongue into me until I came against his mouth, keening with pleasure. He stood up and I fell against him, clinging to his waist. He kissed me and I tasted myself on him, musky and salty. He set me back down on the kitchen chair, knowing I would fall over if he let me go. Then he was gone, leaving only a hint of smoke.

Work was busy for three weeks. Marco and I talked every day about the new show, my business, the restaurant changes, everything. I never knew when he would call and he was adamant that I call back. He needed a partnership, not a power struggle, he insisted. It was hard for me. Alex and I had always had very traditional roles. He talked, I listened, he earned money, I spent it, he was on top, I was on bottom. Marco asked for my opinions, reveled in my work successes and gossiped just like a girl about people on the set.

Two days after he left, I found the linen contract napkin in my purse and bought a frame for it. I hung it across from my bed to remind me of that treasured night. I still hadn't told Claire or Molly anything except that I thought we were dating—at least phone dating, if that counted.

By the third week, I was ready for Marco to be home so we could go out on a real date. I got a call from Don Franco telling me he had some papers for me to sign.

"What is this about, Don?" I asked. "Marco told me you were his banker."

"Banker, lawyer, Indian chief. Just come on over. I think you'll be pleased."

Everybody's a comedian. Bursting with curiosity, I picked up Don's lunch order from The Alley and made my way through lunchtime traffic to his office. The restaurant had packed enough food for a dozen people. Don, his secretary, Myra, and I sat on their waterside balcony to eat. Myra kept giving me little smiles and Don was much more attentive than he had been the night I met him. We were spooning up the panna cotta pudding when Don had Myra bring in the file. It was the deed to Marco's house. He was signing it over to me free and clear, with a provision of five years of maintenance expenses.

"He must love you very much," said Myra as she handed me a ballpoint pen. I felt as if I was going to throw up.

"I don't want it," I said to Don. Myra looked crushed; her pert little face crumpled as if I had just stomped on a Christmas present.

"You have three days to change your mind." He pushed the papers a fraction closer to me. "Why don't you just give it a look–see, and if you change your mind you can come see me tomorrow." He put a gold key ring with a large round gold disk and a gold key on the polished teak table next to the papers.

I signed in a daze next to each little paper arrow sticky. Myra picked up the key ring and put it in my hand. The shiny disk had a C engraved on it. I looked at Myra, wondering what she must think of me, what Marco had told them. She closed my fingers over the key ring.

"Enjoy it, honey. It's a true gift."

I could only nod, and left their office as I had Marco's that morning, with wobbly legs. I drove over to his house—my house?—slowly, thinking I would get a call any minute telling me this was a joke. I glided down the driveway, surprised to see landscape workers mowing the lawn and trimming the bushes. The doorbell echoed through the empty house when I rang. No housekeeper came, no maid, no Marco. I let myself in. The key worked perfectly. I drifted through the house, up to the bedroom, where the bed was neatly made as if we had never been there, down to the kitchen, which was as clean as a model home. On the island was a huge bouquet of mixed flowers, spilling over the vase in their lushness. There was an envelope propped against it with my name on it.

I opened it.

"Christine—As promised. Love, Marco. P.S. Something in the fridge to keep you occupied until I get home. Love again, M."

I opened the refrigerator and there was a whole shelf full of kosher dills.

I closed the fridge, slid to the floor and burst into tears. This wasn't a partnership. This was a buyout. I had a good long cry, then wiped my tears. I stood up and looked at Marco's card. Love. Twice. Jesus, the man was scaring the shit out of me. I locked the house and drove home still in a daze.

CHAPTER EIGHT

WHEN I GOT BACK TO THE COMPLEX, I WENT directly to Molly's and pounded on her door. I poured out the whole story as we drank white wine and ate chocolate covered shortbread.

"Are you insane?" Molly yelled when I told her I wasn't accepting Marco's gift. She tugged on her two braids in a way that reminded me of Marco pulling his hair. "He wants to give this to you. He thinks he's in love. Take it and run."

"That's just it, Molly. *Thinks*. He *thinks* he's in love. How can he possibly love me after one night?"

"Christine, haven't you been gaga over him for two years? Didn't you tell me how all he had to do was smile in your direction and it would cheer you up for a day? Stop doubting yourself and enjoy what the two of you have for now."

"And what do I do when it crashes and burns?"

"You sell the damned house and make a nice profit. Come on. You care about him, right?"

"Right." Molly was right. I had gone into that meeting with Marco planning to seduce him in some way, longing for his attention beyond a chat in a corner at some charity function or sponsor party. I was half in love with him before I had kissed him for the first time. Now I was scared silly that it was too good to be true.

"Molly, ya know when your parents told you to beware of something that sounds too good to be true, it's because it usually is."

"Yes, Christine, and you've hit the jackpot here. But what are the consequences for accepting this? Do you have to have sex with him?"

"I'll feel guilty if I don't."

"Oh. A pity fuck." It sounded so ridiculous coming out of Molly's mouth even I had to laugh.

"Okay, okay. I'd screw him anytime, anywhere. There, I admit it."

"So what's the problem?"

"This little thing called love."

"Oh, deal with it, you idiot. Give it time. If it doesn't work out, you can always give the house back. Or hey, give it to me." We clinked our glasses in agreement. I went upstairs to my place after we'd finished the bottle and I'd told her three more times about the pickle incident. Molly had a way of making me laugh until I wasn't embarrassed anymore. We agreed to meet for breakfast and I would take her over to the house.

I fell asleep on the couch and dreamed of Marco holding me tight. I woke up to the doorbell's constant chiming.

"I'm coming, I'm coming!" I yelled, thinking it was Molly.

It was Marco in leather jeans, biker boots and a ripped T-shirt. A leather jacket was slung over his shoulder. His greeting was a scowl.

"What are you doing here?" he demanded.

"I live here."

He pushed his way inside. "Why aren't you at the house?"

I flopped on the couch, suddenly conscious of my wrinkled clothes and morning breath. I had wanted to meet him feeling sexy, confident, worthy of grand gifts.

"You're insane. You know that? Nobody gives anybody a five million dollar house."

"Sure they do." He tossed his jacket on the couch next to me. I could smell the leather and smoke. "It's not about the house, is it?"

"You said you wanted a partnership, Marco. This feels decidedly uneven."

"Bullshit. You just can't accept something you don't think you're worth. It's not a one-upmanship, Christine. It's a gift. And you are so very worth it. What do you want?"

I looked at him, his wild hair, his craggy face, his burned hands, his leather armor. "Just you," I said. "I just want you."

He sat down on the couch next to me and pulled me onto his lap to straddle him and look him in the eye. My longing for him made me hide my eyes against his neck. He smelled of spicy sweat and sweet smoke. He held me tight and I could feel us melting into each other.

"You've got me, Christine. All of me. Now let's go home."

But home was here in my arms.

★ ★ ★ ★ ★

DREAMER

KATE AUSTIN

CHAPTER ONE

THE DREAM COMES, AS IT HAS FOR AS LONG AS she cares to remember, rolling over her like a tsunami. It comes despite everything she's tried to stop it. Meditation, medication, fornication.

Nothing works.

Since the night he came into her life, the night he changed everything and then disappeared, the dream has haunted her.

Her body weeps for him, damp and hot with the aftermath of the dream. She never comes in the dream, but her body aches for release, her nipples pebbling with desire for his lips.

She wakes each time on the edge, her back arched, her arms reaching, screaming for it, for him, for the orgasm she's done without for almost three years.

Waking up hurts.

She's tried sex—well, of course she has. She's tried deep-down dirty sex, sex with strangers, sex with friends, sex with toys, sex with almost anyone or anything. But like the dream, she gets so far and no further.

She can hang on the edge for what seems like forever, her body dripping and reaching for more. *Please, please, more,* she hears herself sobbing, feeling more than a little like Oliver Twist and wishing—even with all the hell she'll have to go through to get to it—for his happy ending.

On the edge as she is, her legs shake, her teeth score her lips until they bleed. She looks down at her body, at her rose-red, painfully hard nipples, her blush-pink skin, her legs sprawled as far open as she can get them, and more often than not, a head she doesn't recognize between them.

No matter how talented the tongue—and she's become a connoisseur since him—she can't come.

Now she understands the agony represented by the term "blue balls"—three fucking years' worth of it.

"No medical reason for it," more than a dozen doctors have told her. GPs, gynecologists, psychiatrists—they do the tests, they hem and haw, and then they say, "Sorry, nothing we can do."

Except, of course, for the psychiatrists, who would love more than anything to put her through the therapy wringer until she bleeds her childhood, her extremely active and sometimes dangerous sex life, her dreams and desires.

But Miri will not submit herself to that invasion. She's full to the brim with self-knowledge.

Yes, her childhood was shit—wasn't everyone's? Yes, it made her the woman she is today. No surprise there.

Yes, she's had a varied, mostly entertaining, occasionally frightening sex life for almost thirty years. And she wouldn't trade it for anything. There were a few encounters—if she had it to do over—she might decide not to indulge in again. She might tamp down her darker side just a little bit, but having lived through them, she is more than content to keep the memories.

As for dreams and desires? Only one of each.

Not enough, she tells herself, for a psychiatrist to enjoy, though she's fooling herself. They'd *love* them.

The dream and the desire to get off the fucking edge, to fall—as she used to on a more-than-regular basis—deep into the full-body pleasure of orgasm.

God, she misses it with the intensity of an addict. She's jonesing for it, for the way her entire body heats up as she climbs toward the peak, the way she can never stop herself—if he, whoever he is, hasn't already taken care of it—from reaching for her straining nipples with dampened fingertips.

She loves the first touch of her fingers on them: a gentle stroking of the areola, though that gentleness never lasts long. She rolls her lengthening nipples in her fingers, then pinches, softly at first, one and then the other—a sharp squeeze—hard enough to sting, to send a quiver of heat right through her.

The slide of tongue in her mouth, on her belly, her thighs. She's open for it, for him, wet and hot and fragrant. She's panting, but forces herself to take deep breaths when she can—the scent of her own arousal, the strongest aphrodisiac she knows.

She's shaking, writhing with an ecstasy that's almost pain. So close, so ready. She needs him inside her, needs that final thrust, but she's almost there. Miri knows if she reaches down with a saliva-moistened fingertip, she can push herself over. But she doesn't do it. She waits for him, for that added sensation of fullness.

She remembers so clearly the rush of blood to her clitoris, the buzzing at her pulse points as her heart beats harder, the anticipation of the delicious soreness she'll feel in a few hours, a reminder of her body's disregard for posture when in this place.

She sighs as she remembers the sweet arch of her back, the strain as she tries to prolong the moment.

Because before *him,* before the dream, she'd wanted the edge, craved the thrill of it—knowing the longer she held out, the better the orgasms would be, the longer they'd last—until the pleasure overwhelmed it.

Now all she craves is the fall.

CHAPTER TWO

THE DREAM BEGINS AS IT ALWAYS DOES—IN HER favourite bar, the place where she feels safe, her home away from home, where the waiters and the owners are her friends, where they watch over her.

She never brings a date to Lily's, never takes anyone home from here. Don and Sam and Lily steer men on the make away from her, making it clear before she has to that she's one of theirs, that she's not interested. They steer over people—men and women—who might interest her, who want what she wants. A nice evening out, interesting conversation, nothing more.

It might be the only rule she has about sex—*this* place is *her* place, the one place she doesn't use to troll for men.

Not that it isn't a good place for that purpose. It's in the middle of midtown, a haunt of single men and women, full of construction sites and office buildings—and Miri likes variety—but she's never been tempted enough to break the rule.

Not until the night *he* shows up.

He's not much of anything, really. Not tall, not handsome, not charming. She doesn't give him more than a quick glance, but then he sits down next to her and he smells like sex. Like amazing, sweaty, three-day weekend and maybe calling-in-sick-on-Tuesday sex.

She can't—even now—figure out what the smell is. It's not aftershave, which she, purely on principle, despises. It's not the sweet smell of the urban male: minty toothpaste and expensive, spicy deodorant. Not that tangy smell of the construction guy: sweat and beer and the faint remnants of Irish Spring from his morning shower.

It's an aroma, a flavor, a combination all his own, and Miri, though she still tries to define it, never gets any closer than that first impression. *He smells of sex.*

When she turns, against her will, to look at him, she sees the fine details she missed when he entered the bar. That *not much of anything* Miri first thought quickly turns into a desperate mental grab for her "never in Lily's" rule.

He has thick dark lashes guarding amber eyes. Miri reads enough romances to know just how much of a cliché those amber eyes are, but he has them. She's not imagining them. His skin, though she guesses his age to be somewhere between forty and fifty, is so fine-grained it appears to have been airbrushed.

He has her favorite kind of lips: a slightly pouting lower lip—perfect for nibbling—and a beautifully shaped upper one—perfect for tracing with her tongue. They have her licking her own in response.

His body is broad across the shoulders, trim at the waist, his worn jeans tight over his thighs and molding his perfect ass. And yes, she noticed *that* as he walked across the room.

His ears are small and tucked tight into his head, completely exposed by his buzz cut. Difficult, she thinks at the time, to tell what color his hair might be. She'll have to wait—no longer even trying to stop herself from breaking the rule—until she has him naked to find that out.

It has to be tonight.

Because she's never felt this way before, never been this hot and impatient without a touch or a word.

She can't even be sure he'll be interested. Until he turns to her, his knees—no mistake there—meeting hers between the stools. They're warm, the heat transferring even through the denim. And his hands, when he carefully lays them on her bare knees, are as hot as she feels.

"Another drink?" he asks, his eyes asking more of her than those two words could possibly imply.

"Uh," she says, feeling like an idiot for having to glance down at the bar to see what she's drinking. "A Scotch." She looks at Lily behind the bar. "She knows what I drink."

He follows her gaze and nods at Lily, holding up two fingers. "Scotch is good. Gets a nice buzz on. But only one more, okay?"

She doesn't pretend not to know what he's saying. They're far beyond that. The Scotch is a lubricant, just the way the heat of his hands is, the way the feel of the rough denim on her skin is.

She smiles to herself. Lubricant may be the last thing she needs; she's dripping with need, her panties moist with it. She watches his nostrils flare and knows he's caught the scent of her arousal.

"Jack," he says, lifting one of his hands from her knee.

She places hers in it and the arousal intensifies. She suspects that the combination of desire, impatience and astonishment on his face are reflected on hers.

"Miri," she says. "Pay for the drinks."

She shrugs her jacket over her shoulders, slides off the

stool—careful to give him just a flash of thigh—and struts over to the door to wait for him. She wants to watch him walk across the room, this time with the added knowledge of having him naked soon.

He drops a bill onto the bar and turns toward her. It's only because she's watching so closely that she notices the slight grimace of pain as he adjusts to the tightening of fabric around his cock. Even from here, in the relatively dim light of the bar, she can see the size of him, can imagine the sweet taste of ejaculate on the head of his cock. She licks her lips and wonders whether she's imagining the groan she hears as he touches a perfect tongue to those perfect lips.

"The hotel across the street," he says, his hand steady on her arm. "Okay? Because I don't think I can wait any longer than that."

She brushes her breasts against his arm in reply. Another groan, this one needing none of her imagination.

"Come on," he growls, tugging at her arm. "Hurry."

He's tall, much taller than Miri, and she's almost running to keep up with him as he strides across the street. But she'd run if she had to, do almost anything to get them past the check-in and up the elevator into a room, any room.

The lobby is quiet and they have the elevator to themselves. Her nipples are pressed tight against the silk of her bra, echoing the stretch of his jeans around his cock.

"I can't touch you," he says, leaning against the opposite side of the elevator. "Not yet."

"If you touch me…" She pauses. "If you touch me now, we'll be fucking before we reach the next floor."

His wolfish smile should frighten her, Miri thinks, but it doesn't. It only increases her anticipation.

The elevator dings one more time and the doors open. They

walk sedately, with a carefully calculated distance between them, to the room at the end of the corridor.

"There's no one on either side of us," he says, shoving the key card into the slot.

"Good."

The room is cool and dark, the faint pink of the setting sun barely visible through the sheer curtains. The king-size bed beckons, but they restrain themselves, hanging their jackets in the closet, using the facilities. Miri includes a quick swirl of mouthwash and forces herself to stop before giving herself the sponge bath she'd normally indulge in under these circumstances.

She smiles. She's *never* been in these circumstances, never been so sure of herself, of his awareness of her. She knows he'll notice if she washes, knows he'll notice if she doesn't. She also knows which he'll appreciate more.

So she stops herself and revels in the scent, in the dampness between her legs, in the surety of knowing he wants her as much as she wants him.

She wants him naked. She wants to taste him, to nuzzle into the hair at his groin, to smell him the way she knows he does her.

Miri hesitates. Should she undress here? Before she steps through that door and he's there, ready and waiting for her? Will it make things easier? Yes. Faster? Yes. Will it make things better? She doesn't know the answer to that question. In the end, she changes nothing.

A deep breath, a shaking hand on the doorknob, a step through and there he is, silhouetted against the flames of the setting sun, the curtains ripped back to expose the city wrapped in the colors of twilight.

She can't really see him, only the shape of his body, and

she hesitates again. What if she's been wrong about the whole thing? About the way he wants her?

She waits, her hand on the cool wood of the door, her heart pounding with anticipation and the slight touch of fear. He turns toward her, his silhouette growing broader as he moves away from the window.

When she sees his face, she relaxes. As much, she thinks, as she can while she's on this seemingly uncontrollable roller coaster of arousal.

"Sit," he commands. "Right there."

CHAPTER THREE

MIRI TRIES NOT TO THINK ABOUT *THAT* NIGHT while she's awake, leaving that painful pleasure for her dream. But there are times—and this is obviously one of them—when she can't help herself.

There is only one solution, one way to get Jack out of her waking head. Two ways, really, though they both end up the same way. A man or masturbation. Walking the edge, stretching for the fall.

The desperation keeps her focused on the possibility. The anticipation keeps her focused on her body. Neither leave her room for Jack.

But the few men she could call for this service aren't what she wants this day. She doesn't want any distractions. She doesn't want to have to consider what he wants, where he's at in the cycle.

What she wants is twofold: get Jack out of her head, and an orgasm. She'll be happy to manage the first.

Because during that drive for release is the only time Miri's body isn't overwhelmed by her racing mind, the one time in her life when she can concentrate on something other than whatever's in her head. When she can focus on the pounding of her heart, the soft bump-bump of her pulse, the ache between her thighs.

She remembers, even now, the first time.

It happened by accident the first time, though never again that way. Because Miri had never been slow, and once she discovered *it,* she figured out how to achieve it all on her own.

She wasn't very old, maybe eleven or twelve, and for once she was in the bathtub alone, her baby sister somewhere else. The door was closed, the water warm, and she, as ordered, was scrubbing the grime from her knees. The washcloth, old, faded and soft, tracked between her thighs and she felt something, a tiny tug, a warmth swelling in *that* place.

Her mother had never ordered not to touch that place; in fact, she'd never spoken about it at all. All Miri knew was the tiny bit she'd learned in school, and that tiny bit, she understood, was myth.

But once discovered, like the heart of Africa, she never lost it. Even the first time, Miri knew exactly what she wanted. She added soap to the washcloth, making it softer and slicker, and she slowly, ever so slowly, rubbed and rubbed and rubbed until her mouth formed an O and so did her body.

She pulls open the blinds in her bedroom, leaving it bathed in a soft reflection of the summer light. It's just warm enough, the air conditioner blowing a soft breeze of cool air right over her bed, as she prefers.

Her nipples pebble, aching for the first touch of that cool air. Miri moves slowly, savoring the anticipation. She'll make this last.

Might as well make it last, because there will be no end, no explosion, no climax. Being on the edge is like going to an endless movie—she gets to the big chase scene and it goes on forever. The hero never wins the fight, never gets the girl. The music never swells up to the final crescendo.

She goes to her toy drawer, filled now to the brim with items bought in the hopes that *this* one, this particular vibrator, this gel, this toy will push her over the edge.

None have, none will.

So she chooses her old favorites. Pleasure gel for her clit. The small pink vibrator she's had since before *he* ruined it for her. A duo of vibrating eggs. A small, black leather crop. A bottle of warming massage oil.

She places them all on the bed and then adjusts the pillows. Two for under her ass, two for behind her neck. She's learned to be careful about this, knowing how long she'll be arched like a bow, knowing the ache she'll suffer in her back and neck unless she pays attention now—before it's too late, before she's too far along.

She pulls off her T-shirt, slithers out of her jeans, then walks barefoot to the kitchen and fills a small bowl with ice cubes. She pulls out Yo-Yo Ma's *Soul of the Tango* and puts it in the CD player.

The preparation entices her, begins the swell of her labia, the throbbing of her clit. Her nipples harden, her breath becomes uneven.

Each step is important, each move choreographed, enjoyed, taken slowly and thoughtfully. All she has is the anticipation, and she will draw it out as much as she can, push it until the pleasure becomes pain, and then she'll push it further until she can't stand it anymore.

And then she'll give it up, hope once again banished by the memory of Jack.

Miri lies down on the bed, still in her bra and panties, their removal another essential step in the dance, a step that comes later. She closes her eyes and reaches out to ensure the toys are within reach.

She begins.

She heats the massage oil in her hands. Starting at her feet, she massages with the oil, slowly, sensuously, licking her lips at each touch of the warm, wet fingers on her skin. Calves are next, then she lingers at the backs of her knees.

She is intent on the sensation, slowing even further. The combination of heat and slide and almost tickle at the back of her knees translates heat and slide and almost tickle to her center. She feels the first faint tug, the first tightening of the inside muscles, and slows even further.

Not yet, she whispers, *not yet.*

Her thighs—the top and back and outside first, caressing the soft skin and avoiding the growing heat, the pulsating part of her that can't stop saying *touch me, touch me now.*

She leaves the insides of her thighs untouched, moving to her stomach, allowing only the very tips of her fingers to venture inside the elastic of her panties, a gentle tease and more tightening.

Miri slaps down the part of her mind that is thinking *maybe today's the day,* knowing that way lies despair.

Her arms are next, her shoulders, her upper chest, once again allowing her fingers to linger only just inside the lace of her bra, her nipples straining, desperate for a touch.

She sits up, the cool cotton almost unbearably delicious against her heated skin. She leaves the oil for a moment and picks up the crop.

She rolls over, the pillows under her hips, her thighs and ass exposed. A light tap on her right thigh, a matching one on the left. Another pair, harder this time, the skin on her thighs heating as she strikes them. A curl of sensation deep in her cunt echoes each strike, dampening her panties.

She wriggles against the pillows, trying to reach the right place. She rubs, the motion faster and faster, but the pillows have too much give, are too soft and yielding. She starts to reach for the vibrator and stops herself.

"No, Miri, no cheating," she says, then pulls the back edges of her panties up her ass, leaving the two cheeks exposed, pulling tight enough that now, when she rubs against the pillows, the silk against her anus, the pulled-tight silk against her cunt, adds an extra layer of heat.

The skin tingles as she smacks the crop lightly against her exposed cheeks. Craving more, she whips it hard and fast and the tingling turns harder and sharper, and she knows, if it weren't for him, if he hadn't ruined her, she'd be coming right now.

The heat radiates from her ass and she soothes it with the oil, cheating just a little by tugging at the panties. She rolls back over, the cotton abrasive against the now-sensitive skin of her thighs and butt.

She wiggles down in the bed, her hips once again on the pillows, and finally touches her fingers to her inner thighs. The muscles jump; she can feel them as she massages the oil high on the thighs.

She is dripping with anticipation, the scent as luscious as late summer strawberries just before they turn too ripe to eat. She squirms, each sensation—the oil on her skin, the tingle of pain on the back of her thighs and her ass, the aching nipples, the throbbing in her cunt—heightened by the aroma.

She takes a cube of ice from the bowl, the cold water dripping through her fingers. She is panting now, the anticipation almost overwhelming. She touches the ice to her right nipple through the lace and arches into the sensation. She rubs the coldness around and around until she can hardly bear it, then moves to the left one. She alternates, rubbing each nipple until the ice has vanished and her cold fingers have replaced it.

She pinches first one and then the other, pulling the lace down, pushing up her breasts until she can see the rose-red nipples ripe and ready.

And then she leaves them standing stiffly, craving more, and reaches for another piece of ice. This once melts even more quickly against the heat of her labia. Even through the silk, the heat is so intense the ice melts in a moment. She reaches, again and again, for more ice until the silk is dripping wet and the cold has completely lost the battle with the heat.

Now, she thinks, and removes her bra and panties, sprawling naked on the bed, her ass on the pillows, her pussy throbbing. She reaches for the stimulating gel and loads a drop on her forefinger. Miri takes a deep breath and touches, slowly, gently, tenderly, her swollen labia. The sensation is exquisite, almost unbearable, and she spreads the drop over her lips, each movement a delight. The hard bud of her clitoris is next and she can feel the spiral beginning, feel the burn and the ache.

She rubs, gently at first, then harder. Harder again. Her inner muscles clench and Miri smiles. Finally. Her mind has stopped working and only her body is paying attention.

With her other hand, she reaches for the eggs and places them, one after the other, inside. She turns the dial to high, never once stopping the massage.

She is close, so close. Almost there, almost flying. Her legs are trembling, her arms shaking, her inner muscles clenching at the eggs, drawing them deeper, holding them in.

Twenty minutes later, Miri stops the massage and pulls out the eggs.

She smiles, this time sadly. She has gained an hour of distraction. She has forgotten Jack for that small period of time. It is almost enough.

CHAPTER FOUR

SHE NEVER SAW HIM AGAIN AFTER THAT FIRST time. They didn't exchange phone numbers or last names; he's never again showed up in Lily's. Not when she's been there and no other time, either. Don or Sam or Lily would have told her.

Instead, she has spent the ensuing years dreaming about him, dreaming about that night. She's walked the streets of her neighborhood hoping to run into him, though for all she knows, he could have been from anywhere, from a city halfway or all the way across the country. He might live in some small town or in the wilderness. Despite the hours they had spent together, Miri doesn't know where he might live. If she did, she might pursue it, so she feels lucky she doesn't know.

If she thought he lived in a big city, what would she do? Travel to all the big cities in the country and spend hours wandering the streets, looking for his face, his body? What if she thought he lived in a small town? Or somewhere in the wilderness? After three years, she knows she might be crazy enough to try anything, so she's glad she doesn't have any idea, glad she can't even guess where he's from.

Instead, she does what the masturbation was supposed to do, what she's promised herself she won't do. She relives, again, the night he ruined her.

He commands her to sit, and she doesn't hesitate, simply steps forward and sits down in the chair. She rests her arms on the wooden armrests, places her feet together flat on the floor and settles in.

"Close your eyes." His voice is husky and deep and she tries to decide whether seeing him is more important than listening to that voice. She chooses obedience and closes her eyes.

She listens as he walks across the room and leans over her, his scent lush and ripe and intoxicating. He whispers, so close that she feels the words as much as hears them, "Don't open them. No matter what, don't open your eyes."

Miri nods and scrunches her eyes tight. "Remind me," she says, "because I might forget."

"I have a better idea."

She hears a ripping of cloth, and soft cotton, imbued with his scent, fall over her eyes. He must have ripped his T-shirt, she thinks as he ties it at the back of her head.

"Tight enough?"

She nods again.

"I'm not sure I'll be in any condition to remind you of anything," he says, "and I want to focus. Is this okay?" He touches the blindfold.

"Yes," she says. "I think I like it."

His voice moves away, lowers itself closer to the floor and she feels his hands, big and warm and callused, on her ankles. And then she feels his tongue, right there on her ankle bone, wet and supple. He circles the bone, lifting one leg to his mouth, pushing the other aside so he can settle between them.

Miri reaches for his hair but he stops her. "I'll tell you what to do," he says. "Just enjoy."

She pulls her arm back and enjoys.

Enjoys the feel of his tongue on her anklebones, the warmth of his body between her legs, the sound of her breathing, his breathing. She can feel her heart beating and imagines she hears his, pumping in time with hers.

He stretches his hands around her foot and pulls off her sandal. His tongue follows his hands, a firm rasp against her sole, a quick nip at the base of her big toe, a damp tip sliding slowly between each toe.

He takes a deep breath and leans into her for a moment, and she knows he's smelling her, the spiraling intensity of her arousal. It's everywhere, filling the room with salt and strawberries, swirling with his own aroma, converting the very air they breathe into sex.

He removes her other shoe, arousing that foot, then pulls her legs farther apart. Another rip and her ankles are tied to the base of the chair, her legs far enough apart that he can rest his body between them.

"Okay?" he asks, his hands on the backs of her knees, pulling them parallel to the legs of the chair.

"Perfect." A whisper is all she can manage.

He ties her knees to the chair and her skirt pulls up to her thighs. She is exposed beneath it, the crotch of her panties soaked and pungent. He ties her wrists to the armrests, her elbows to the bend of the arms.

Miri doesn't move, simply waits for instructions, every inch of her body desperate for his touch. She doesn't know where she wants him to touch, and she's careful not to indicate any preference. He knows what she wants.

He runs his fingers up her thighs, stopping when he reaches the hem of her skirt. "What's in your bag?" he asks, rattling the shopping bag she had carried into Lily's.

"A dress. A sundress."

"Good," he says, before he rips her skirt down the front seam, pulling it from beneath her. He shifts his hands under her hips and lifts her up as far as she can go tied as she is. She hears him take a deep breath, then another. In, a slight moan. Out, hot breath on her panties. In, another moan. Out, more heat.

His hands clench on her hips, then lower her back onto the chair. His tongue settles on her belly, a swirl of dampness across her heated skin. When he moves to another spot—on her hip, across her ribs, underneath her arm—the wetness left behind cools her enough to bear the pleasure for one more moment without moaning.

She forces herself to sit without moving, without consciously clenching her inner muscles. She allows it to happen to her. She allows *him* to happen to her.

Miri has never done this before.

She has always been the actor, never acted upon. She has always been in charge of her own pleasure, of her partner's pleasure. From that very first time, Miri has known how to get what she wants, how to get to the edge, to stay there until she can bear it no longer.

She has always known exactly what to do and when to do it, and she has done it. Always.

This time, in this hotel room, Miri is acted upon and she understands, suddenly, that there is undeniable pleasure in being pleasured. That passion can be given rather than taken.

And she doesn't know how she will live with that knowledge.

Jack's tongue slides down the inside of her arm, slowing, stopping at the crook of her elbow. A light nip. He doesn't need her voice to tell him what she likes. Her body responds more quickly than she could speak the words.

Please. More.

He takes note of each shudder, each quick breath, each time her skin reddens, each time her nipples swell, her scent intensifies. It's as if they're linked together in some unfathomable way, as if her body is connected to his mouth, his hands.

He tears her T-shirt from bodice to hem, then from her shoulders. The air-conditioning feels good on her skin, allows her to relax even further into the chair, to loosen the muscles that had begun to tighten into the final spiral.

She never wants this to end.

AND IT HASN'T.

Her best friend, Heather, has Gypsy blood, and one of the things she's told Miri over the years is to be careful what you wish for. Miri laughs. She's lived a perfect life, she tells Heather, and has nothing to wish for.

How ironic that the one thing she wishes for, she gets.

How ironic that Miri's one wish—for her night with Jack never to end—turned out to be right out of a Grimm's fairy tale, a dark wish that changes her life forever. She doesn't become a princess; she doesn't find a goose laying golden eggs; she doesn't even find out that her family is the royalty of the land and that she is wealthy and famous beyond her imagining.

What she ends up with is the opposite of what she wants. What she gets is a life she couldn't have bargained for.

Miri thinks now that she'd give up sex completely if it were possible, if she could figure out a way to live without the dreams, if the psychiatrists might give her drugs that would rid her, once and for all, of that night. Of Jack.

Her occasionally dangerous sex life has become even more so and yet no matter how many risks she takes, she stays safe. Irony again.

The sex club in the suburbs. Definitely not her best idea, but when she sees the ad in the back of the alternative paper she can't help herself. One word sells her on it—*bondage*.

She emails the address listed in the ad and waits by her computer for an answer. She goes through the screening process, provides him—a man is doing the screening, obvious from his questions—with everything he asks for.

Age. Height. Weight. Measurements. Hair color and length. Preferences.

He asks about tattoos and piercings, and though he doesn't say so, she knows she will have better luck if she has them. Luckily, she has a single tattoo and a pierced navel. He grudgingly accepts this.

Her job, her marital status, her sexual experience—and here she thinks he gets much more than he bargained for because he goes offline for almost twenty-four hours. When he comes back, he asks for pictures. Lots of them.

Pictures of her dressed. Pictures showing her tattoo and piercings. Pictures of her scantily clad—his words, not hers—and naked.

Naked and sprawled, completely exposed, on her bed, though she is at least careful enough to hide anything that might signal her location. She does wonder, at one point, whether every sex club goes through this lengthy screening, but she ignores the warning voice and continues on.

She is desperate by this point, almost two years without an orgasm, almost two years after *the* night.

Finally, he asks for a phone number. She gives him a cell number for a phone she has purchased for this purpose, just as she has given him an email address created especially for this exchange. Foolish Miri, thinking this will keep her safe, when she has no sense of safety.

He invites her to what he coyly calls their next get-together. "Just a few of us, my dear," he says in his smarmy, slimy, trying-to-be-sexy voice. "Just so we can meet each other before we go any further."

Miri once again shakes off her misgivings and follows his directions. She drives out of the city, into the dark unlit streets, her hands tight on the wheel of Heather's borrowed car. She drives for what seems like forever before she arrives at a house deep in the country, surrounded by nothingness. There are no streetlights, no neighbors, no apartment buildings or convenience stores.

There is only darkness.

She pulls into the driveway, stops her car in front of a sprawling bungalow and gets out. She ignores the four or five trucks parked haphazardly in front of the house. She ignores the curdling in the pit of her stomach. She ignores the warnings echoing in her mind. She ignores the stench of cows. She ignores everything except her body's craving.

A tall, thin man steps onto the porch. Her contact had not reciprocated with pictures of himself, but Miri knows who he is. She recognizes his laugh.

"Miri." He laughs. "Come on in and meet the gang."

She expects couples. She finds four men and one woman. One very big woman. She is bigger than any of them, scarier than any of them. Because she is in charge, and Miri can tell right away that this woman has been waiting for years for another woman to show up at this club.

And yet Miri still doesn't walk, doesn't get back into her car and drive away while she still can.

If she had this story to make up, she would make it worse than it is. She would make it more violent, more evil, more

dangerous. She would make the men less tawdry, the woman
more demanding, the sex… Well, she'd make the sex more interesting. And she'd certainly make herself have an orgasm.

Because that would definitely be ironic. The worst sexual
experience of her life would be the one that gave her what
she needed, what she wanted more than anything. Instead,
mostly, Miri is bored by it all.

She realizes it isn't safe; after all, there are five of them
and only one of her, and she is the new meat. And in this
crowd she is grade A meat, prime rib when they are used to
hamburger. But she is still bored. Bored practically to tears.

The woman, Faye, pours her a drink, and Miri knows
without even tasting it that it is drugged. GHB, she guesses,
and she wonders where these suburbanites got it, wonders
what connections they have. She refuses it, saying she doesn't
drink, that she likes to be alert, winking at Faye and then at
the men.

Faye hesitates, wanting to force her to drink, but the men
overrule her. They know she won't run and they'd rather
she be aware. And Miri still thinks this might work, that
the danger might give her the edge she needs to get over the
edge.

She's wrong.

For a short time she does think it's a possibility, when Faye
takes charge and orders the men around her. Miri waits while
Faye wraps ties around her wrists, her knees, her ankles. She
tests the cheap fabric and knows freedom is only one sharp
tug away.

Faye directs tongues everywhere, hands everywhere, rough
and hot on Miri's body. She hears them panting, feels them
touching her, hears Faye's voice directing them. One to her
right breast, one to her left. One to her belly. One to her anus.
One to her clit.

Faye chooses her mouth. It's almost enough. It would be enough, she thinks, if they weren't all so excited by her appearance, by having some woman other than Faye in the room with them.

For a moment, a very short moment, Miri feels a sense of possibility. It lasts only as long as they do.

And that's not long enough. Their excitement at seeing her naked body sets them off. They grab their cocks, she feels the shudders of a few short strokes and then it's over.

The danger of this encounter lies in her boredom, not in their numbers.

She says thank you politely, ignoring the pleading in their eyes, and drives home. She throws the newly purchased cell phone into the river as she passes over it, and deletes the email address she has given the man.

And Miri falls back into her memories of *him*.

CHAPTER SIX

JACK RESTS HIS ALMOST-NAKED CHEST BETWEEN her legs. He has removed no clothing, only the strips that he has torn from his shirt. The gaps leave a warm patch of skin roughened with his body hair to rub against her thighs, her belly, to tease her through the silk of her panties.

His jeans chafe her legs, the fabric almost harsh in contrast to that small patch of warm skin. His hands never stop moving, circling her skin until every inch of it—except those that crave it the most—screams in voluptuous sensuality. Nothing has ever felt this good.

Nothing ever will. Miri knows this even now, before Jack has removed the rest of her clothes, before he has removed any of his. Before she has touched his skin. Before, she realizes, he has even kissed her.

The moment she has this realization, she can think of nothing else except his lips. She can't see them but she remembers them perfectly. The lovely bow of his top lip, the strong line of the bottom. She can't stop her tongue from reaching out and touching her own lips.

Jack's head pulls away from her belly with what seems to her like reluctance. His body follows until all she feels is the aftermath of heat. She can tell he hasn't moved far, that he is standing in front of the chair, that he is considering something.

"I shouldn't do this," he mutters. "If I do, it will be too much."

Miri doesn't speak. She *wants* the "too much"—whatever it is. She wants anything and everything he wants to give her.

She waits, hears footsteps as he walks over to the window. He stands there, looking out. She doesn't know how she knows this, but she does.

What is odder than the knowing is that the heat he has built in her, one touch at a time, does not dispel when he leaves her waiting. The opposite is true. It's as if he's left her simmering on a stove, the bubbles roiling in her body. The heat may be set on low, but that doesn't stop the bubbles.

She hears the moment he makes up his mind. He turns—sharply, she thinks—and strides across the room to her, his footsteps firmer and quicker and more adamant than before.

She catches her breath, and it's a good thing she does.

Because he leans down and, without touching her anywhere else, captures her lips with his. Softly at first, they explore her mouth, gently rubbing against her bottom lip and then her top.

She'd been right about his lips. They are perfect.

She feels his arms trembling against the chair, and opens her mouth to him, wanting to give him something in return for what he's given her. He doesn't move, though the trembling increases.

She touches the tip of her tongue to that perfect upper lip, follows it with her teeth. A slight groan rewards her. She swirls her tongue across his bottom lip, then into his mouth, deep into his mouth, dueling with his tongue.

Finally, she thinks, when he groans and takes charge of the kiss the way he's taken charge of her body. And again she is transported. He kisses the way he touches her, with all his attention, with every inch of his body involved.

She feels him settle against her, his weight warm and heavy against her skin, each inch of which craves him. He rubs against her like a cat: slowly, subtly, silkily. And all the while he is kissing her. He never stops kissing her, never gives her a moment to breathe, and she doesn't want one.

She doesn't want to breathe if it means giving up the weight of his body against her, the feel of his tongue in her mouth, the press of his cock against her. She squirms against him— reaching, striving for that perfect spot.

She feels his lips grin against her before he pulls away. "I knew this wasn't a good idea," he says, and leans in to kiss her once more. "But it was worth it."

His tongue takes a quick swipe at the sensitive skin behind her left ear and he whispers, "Later," and moves away. She listens to the sound of his zipper, the thud of his shoes on the floor, the erotically soft sound of cotton sliding down his legs. She imagines the body beneath the clothes, the long, lean muscles, the hair arrowing down his chest to his cock.

His cock.

She doesn't need to see it to know that it's standing straight out from his loins, doesn't need to touch it to know that it's hot and silky smooth, doesn't need to taste it to know that it tastes of sex, doesn't need to smell it to know that it smells of hunger.

He walks back toward her, his footsteps light and sure, feet bare on the carpet. Dampness pools again, her scent stronger and richer as she imagines his naked body touching hers.

He can read her mind; she's sure of it now.

Because he leans over her and whispers again. "If I untie you, will you promise not to move?"

"Yes," she whispers back. "Anything."

She feels his skin touch her as he unties the bands from her elbows, her wrists. She moans as he unties her knees and her ankles, but she doesn't move. She'll do nothing to endanger this evening.

"Stand up," he says. "I'll help you."

Miri is shaking as she places her hands on the arms of the chair and levers herself out of it. Jack lifts her into his arms and carries her to the bed, placing her on her back in the middle.

"Don't move," he says again.

He settles onto the bed beside her, the warmth of his body, knowing he's naked next to her, arousing both comfort and raging desire. He runs his hand from her shoulder across her chest, then down the middle of her body, stopping just above her pantie line.

"You're so beautiful, Miri. So beautiful I want to devour you. Roll over."

He waits while she rolls onto her belly, and she waits to see what delights he has for her. He unsnaps the fastenings of her bra and pulls it from her. Her nipples pucker and rub, against her conscious will, against the linen. He tears her panties from her and then he begins.

He starts again with her feet, his tongue wet and silky against her soles, her ankles, her calves and thighs. He spreads her legs and settles between them, his warmth turning to heat as he moves up her body.

He runs his tongue up the crease of her ass, teasing her anus until she has to fight not to squirm against him. He grasps her hips, curling his big hands around until they're mere inches from where she wants them, teasing her curls, the crease of her thigh.

He shifts her upward and nips at the curve of her ass, then licks his way up her spine, his body following his tongue until finally, finally, she feels his cock against her, thick and heavy and burning hot. It nestles against her ass and once again she fights not to move.

He nips at her shoulder blades, her neck, her ears, and then lies over her, covers her with his body, his cock hard against her ass, his arms stretched above her head, her hands in his.

"God, Miri, if I move, if you move, it's all over."

She nods in understanding. She knows at this moment that if she shifts, even an inch, if he touches her clit, her cunt, even her nipples, she will go over. If his cock moves, even an inch, he will go over. So she waits while he takes a few deep breaths.

He takes another deep breath and moves away. "Roll over," he says again, his voice so deep and gravelly she can barely distinguish the words.

She settles again in the middle of the bed.

Jack's body hovers above hers. Miri senses his indecision, his anticipation, his fever. But he's much stronger than she and he pulls back. Again.

He grabs two pillows from the bed, lifts her hips and places the pillows beneath her. He spreads her legs, and she imagines him licking his lips as a starving man might before a feast. She imagines this because she knows this is what she would do if she had him lying naked before her, his cock waiting for her mouth.

He carefully arranges himself over her, his cock touching only the pillows, his weight on his arms rather than on her.

And then, and then, oh, God. He takes her nipple into his

mouth and she explodes. A single touch and she can't stop herself.

"Don't move," he says. "I know," he whispers, his tongue moist and gentle on her nipple, drawing out the orgasm until all she can do is moan against his hair.

When she is—finally—silent and still, her breathing relaxed, he moves again, and Miri realizes that coming hasn't changed a thing. She is still on the edge and one more touch will put her back over it.

He moves down her body, and this time he doesn't stop at her pantie line. He nuzzles into the lush hair and then slides farther. She imagines the feel of the linen on his cock and knows he can hardly bear it. That if he willed it, he might come without another touch.

She clenches her hands at her sides to stop them from reaching for his shoulders, for his hair, for his face and mouth and hands. For his cock. Her mouth waters to taste him. To lick her way around his body as he has done, is still doing, to hers.

He presses the pads of his thumbs to her labia, gently, carefully. Presses the lips apart and then touches, lightly, his tongue to her. She quivers and fights not to move.

He slides his tongue between the folds, up and down, slowly, the lightest of touches, avoiding her clitoris, but stroking deeper into her with each slide.

She is lulled into sensation, like slipping into a warm bath, the orgasm sneaking up on her like an earthquake, an unanticipated explosion coursing through her body.

Jack smiles against her and continues to tongue her, harder this time, more insistent, and the sensation continues. She can't stop shaking, can't stop the waves of feeling rolling over her. Here, now, is the tsunami, wave after wave of it.

When he stops, she allows herself to reach for him, allows herself to pull the blindfold from her eyes.

She pulls him up the bed and pushes him onto his back. "Don't move," she says, as she leans forward and fastens the blindfold over his eyes. "Don't move."

"Don't hurry," he says in return. She watches his hands clench tight at his sides and the muscles in his thighs shift as he tries to relax into the bed.

She begins, as he did, at his feet, echoing his touch, his movements. She is careful to avoid his cock, though when she reaches his thighs the scent is almost too much for her. She wants it in her mouth, in her cunt, so badly that she begins to sweat at the nearness of it.

She forces herself to move on to his belly, to his nipples—he's very sensitive, and when she nips one of them between her teeth, she feels the warmth of pre-ejaculate on her thigh. She slows when she reaches his neck and ears, loving the sound of his groan when she licks behind his ears, when she nips the lobe, when she slides her tongue inside.

"Turn over," she says. "Carefully."

She moves the pillows to the center of the bed so they'll fit under his hips. She adjusts him so his cock is not pressed too tightly against them. His hold on himself is precarious. Shudders course through his back, his thighs, his chest. He is on the edge, walking the tightrope in a high wind.

She begins this time at his shoulders, moving slowly and lightly. She avoids the base of his spine and the backs of his knees, knowing what touch will be too much.

She can't resist one quick swipe of her tongue over his ass, one nip on each cheek, a quick lunge into his anus. But she stops when he shivers.

She pulls away the pillows and tells him to roll onto his back. She lays her body over him, her mouth at his right ear and whispers, "What do you want? Do you want me to suck your cock? Do you want me to fuck you?"

She pulls the blindfold from his eyes and waits for his response.

"I want everything."

Miri smiles.

She slides down his body, savoring every motion, every groan, every shiver. She takes his balls into her mouth and he groans. She touches her tongue to the damp tip of his cock and he shakes.

She slides her tongue around the sensitive head. It's too much; she knows it is as he grabs and pulls her up and under him. His cock thrusts, hard, deep into the heart of her, and she screams, her cunt convulsing around him.

Three strokes and he joins her, his rough voice chanting, "Miri. Miri. Miri."

The weight of him, on her and in her, relaxes her into a puddle of warmth, and she sighs. Then sighs again when he resumes stroking, his cock hardening with each movement. The pressure is almost pain, and positively too much pleasure.

"Again," he says. "Come with me. One more time."

And she does.

When she wakes in the morning, her sundress is draped on the bed beside her. A glass of freshly squeezed orange juice and a pot of coffee rest on the bedside table, a single red rose on her pillow.

And no Jack.

CHAPTER SEVEN

MIRI WAITS FOR HIM AT LILY'S. IT'S ALL SHE can do.

She gives up sex with strangers. She gives up sex with friends. She tries, but fails, to give up masturbation, though she *has* given up the elaborate scenarios. She uses masturbation now as comfort rather than sex.

She gives up fighting it. She has tried everything, and nothing works. It's a waste of her time and energy, and it's unfair to use others—though she knows they enjoy it—for her drive to release.

She still has the dream most nights, but now she savors it, knowing it is all she has of him, of that perfect night. She stops worrying about the release and enjoys the anticipation, as he'd planned for her to do. As he'd so carefully arranged for her to do.

She spends most nights at Lily's. She drinks a single glass of wine—white or rosé on the warmer days, a deep rich Italian red when it's cold or rainy.

It has been six months and she is almost ready to give up

Lily's, as well. It is a hot summer night, four years almost to the day since...

She no longer stares at the door, trying to conjure him up. She's sure he's gone. Gone home to somewhere else, gone home to a wife and children, gone in an accident or a mugging. Because there is no way that he wouldn't have come back, no way he didn't experience what she did.

No experience could be so perfect if it was one-sided. Knowing that, finally figuring that out, has allowed Miri to contemplate giving up her vigil. She's not quite ready, but she will be.

Soon, she thinks.

She hears the door open behind her. She smells sex. She smiles and turns toward him.

★ ★ ★ ★ ★

THE PIRATE'S TALE

Grace D'Otare

"HELLO?" MAEVE DROPPED HER BAGS IN THE HALL. *Peering across the foyer, she could just make out her husband's shape slumped in his favorite old leather chair. She shrugged off her coat and tossed it. It landed over the banister. "Why are you sitting in the dark?"*

"Why are you so far away?"

Her heels clicked on the parquet. "Bad day, darling?"

Devlin watched her cross the room, swirling his drink. "You're wearing those boots again," he said.

"I am."

He turned away to concentrate on a long swallow from his glass. "Not all bad, then."

She smiled at that, and brushed a hand over his hair, feeling his forehead as a nurse might check for fever. He twitched, meaning don't fuss, *and patted his knee.*

Maeve arranged herself in his lap, her knees swinging over the rolled arm of the chair, and wondered what to do.

They both had bad days now and then, with all they'd been through. Dev usually went off alone and came back when he'd healed himself. Or close enough to healed himself. Rarely did he let her see the suffering, much less offer what small comfort she could.

He set his glass on the floor. His palm skimmed beneath the hem of her skirt. The skirt was a favorite of Maeve's, a great sweep of charcoal silk velvet. Despite the steady rise of his hand, the skirt veiled boots, legs and his intent. Beginning at her ankle, he traced the fit of her boot as it climbed her leg.

"Jesus. Where does it stop?"

The smoke of aged, oaked whiskey on his breath, and leather in the air, whetted Maeve's appetite. Dark and chilly as Dev's spirits ran tonight, she felt the tingle of warmth they made between them spark, and begin to burn.

"Ahhh, there's a good man." She wiggled deliberately, settling more comfortably in his lap, and he pinched the tender skin above the boot's cuff. "I knew you'd find your way."

"What's this you're barely wearing?" Blunt fingertips tickled the edge of her lacy thong.

"Layers are the secret to a well-dressed woman," Maeve replied with an invitational tip of her hips.

"Thinly spread layer."

"Mille feuille cake," she teased, hoping for another pinch.

"Naughty girl."

"Think of it as a visual aid."

"A visual aid? When you're hip-high in these…" he whispered across her ear "…pirate boots," making her shiver, another little retaliation.

"Pirates. Now, that reminds me of a story." She shifted her butt in his lap deliberately, achieving precisely the result she'd hoped for.

"Do tell," her husband answered, with enough growl in his voice to really make it worth her while.

The Pirate's Tale

The only life Gertrude had ever known was the convent.
"The convent? I thought this was a lusty pirate tale?"

"Fine. Skip the convent. Straight to the bedroom."

"That's more like it."

It was a cold, dark bedroom.

Gertrude wrapped the coverlet tighter around her and poked the fire. Two months at sea, two days in port and two hours in a carriage traveling streets that were worse than those on the island of Santa Ava, only to be deposited at the door of a respectable house and deserted.

She eyed the bed suspiciously. It was huge; big enough to sleep six orphans. Who else would be sleeping in there tonight?

The door banged open and in clomped a pair of dirty boys, a large brass tub and the housekeeper, Mrs. Allworthy.

"Right here." The woman pointed to the space in front of the fire. "Carefully! Don't slosh all over the Captain's India rug."

The water in the tub was so hot that steam rose into the air.

"Mrs. Allworthy?"

"A moment," she answered, with a glance at Gertrude. "Back downstairs, you two, quick step! Bring up the other pails of boiling water from the kitchen. Run!" From her apron pocket she pulled a glass bottle and dumped the contents into the water. The room bloomed with the scents of rose and rosemary. "You had a question, missus?"

Gertrude tried to sound merely inquisitive. "Who is planning on bathing in my room?"

"You, dear."

"I've already washed," she said. "Thank you."

"The Captain ordered you a bath."

"He hasn't seen me since we made port. How would he know I need a bath?" she grumbled. "Please don't go to any more trouble. I prefer to bathe…standing. Thank you."

"Standing? You mean a spit bath? With your clothes on?" An odd expression flickered over the older woman's face. She arched her back and rubbed her distended belly. From where Gertrude stood, it appeared the baby might come before Mrs. Allworthy left the room. "Ever sat in a bathtub, my dear?"

"Why does that matter?"

"You haven't! Ha! I'll be a ripe tomato." She barked a laugh that colored her face as red as the fruit, then she started to hiccup. "Pardon me. Where does he find 'em? *Uuurp,* there I go again!"

"Find who?"

"Well now, the Captain's been married before, I'm sure you've heard?" The woman narrowed her eyes. "Don't believe one word of the rumors. Captain wouldn't harm a fly, much less his wives."

"That's a...relief," Gertrude said. *Wives?*

"Don't wait too long, poppet. Water's best when it's hot enough to turn you pink all over." Mrs. Allworthy winked and rubbed her belly again. "I'm away. I've my own chicks and a husband to settle in for the night. Good luck, my girl." She chuckled and burped her way out the door. "Never sat in a bath! Going to be a long night for both of them...."

Gertrude slumped. Long night? The Captain must be going out again this evening. Nothing was proceeding according to plan. She'd gambled on love, new experiences and a world beyond the locked doors of Santa Ava's convent orphanage.

She'd lost. The Captain had been too busy to do more than stare at her across the deck during the crossing. Alone, confined to the ship, she'd found seasickness her only notable new experience.

Steam from the bath fogged the mirror over the mantel. Her reflection blurred. She dipped her hand in the tub's water. The sweet-spice scent of rose and rosemary swirled around her. The water appeared clean enough. She'd been told baths were dirty. It smelled lovely.

Maybe she should try it? Many things she'd been told at the convent had turned out to be untrue. That certain private behavior caused spots, for instance. Or that women who were not virgins would never find a husband. Also—clearly—false.

Here she sat in a fine house, married. For the most part.

What sort of pirate was this husband of hers, two months at sea and all he did was watch her across the deck, staring with those intent blue eyes, as if she were the dangerous one?

She sat down on the rug, unhooked her stockings and carefully rolled them down her legs, one by one. Absent husband or not, she was capable of creating a new experience for herself. She wiggled her toes in the carpet. Carpet in a bedroom! A luxury right under her feet.

Shrugging off the coverlet, she reached beneath her dress to untie her drawers.

Why had Mrs. Allworthy asked about her clothes? Who dared to take off all their clothes to bathe? Gertrude unfastened the buttons down the front of her gown and lifted it over her head, leaving her shift in place. The last time she had taken off everything...well, she couldn't remember the last time she'd taken off all her clothes at the same time. Not with fifty women and children watching every move.

The door banged open.

The Captain, her new husband, entered the bedroom carrying a bucket of hot water in each hand. His shirtsleeves were folded up, revealing cords of muscles straining from the weight of water and pail.

For once, his look wasn't full of apprehension. Admiration, perhaps? Appetite, most definitely. She was, after all, practically naked, the sheerness of her shift hiding all her flaws but none of her charms.

Gertrude panicked. She grabbed the coverlet off the floor and wrapped it around her shoulders like a tent.

The first time they'd met, she'd known immediately he was a captain of men in both form and function. Deep blue eyes and blue-black hair. A straight, sharp nose, unbroken, unlike many of his shipmates. Tall, but wiry. He could use a few good meals.

And that commanding voice. "I've brought more water."

Several questions occurred to her. *Don't you knock?* was the first. *Will you stay?* was the last.

The Captain stepped farther into the room and dumped one bucket of steaming water into the tub. The other he set by the fire.

"Nothing to say?"

His shirt was open. He had dark hair on his chest also. The room seemed smaller.

"Gertrude is a mouthful. Do you have another name?"

Old Gertrude. "No," she told him.

"I thought I might find you in the bath already, Gertrude." He pointed. "Water's hot."

She shuffled backward until her calves hit the bed. The convenience of her shipboard seasickness returned to her. New experiences were all well and good when you were in control of them.

She did not feel that the man standing in front of her was quite under her control.

"Actually, there are three other Gertrudes residing at the convent," she babbled. "Gertie, who is fifteen and quiet. Trudy is seven and never quiet, but she wets the bed when she has a nightmare. The youngest is called Baby Gertrude. I'll miss her."

The first time they'd met, in the Mother Superior's office,

he'd looked at her exactly this way, as if he were gazing at a ghost.

A slow smile now curved his mouth with hints of fear and wonder.

She blushed everywhere. Thank heaven, all he could see was the red in her cheeks. How could anyone as ordinary as she was inspire such a look?

"An abundance of Gertrudes."

"Tradition. All the baby girls left at the orphanage..." Gertrude stopped. Her nerves tingled in alarm. "What are you doing?"

"Can't let a hot bath go to waste," he answered, as he finished unbuttoning his shirt. "Go on."

She turned toward the wall, as if suddenly fascinated by an etching of a sloop. "Girls are always christened Gertrude, after the patron saint of the West Indies."

There was a snap of leather and the clink of a buckle. He was taking off his pants.

"Perhaps...I'll wait outside."

"I'd prefer you didn't."

Water sloshed and the Captain exhaled an indecent sound.

She peeked over her shoulder. His head lolled against the back of the tub. His arms rested along the brass rim in one long line of flesh that stretched from earlobe to fingertip. Beads of water on his skin sparkled in the fire's light.

His abandoned clothes lay beside the empty water bucket in a pile. Shirt. Pants. It was the white linen of his drawers that gave Gertrude her first palpitation. He was naked in that bathtub.

"Tell me. How did the sainted Gertrude make her name?" he asked, as if they were conversing over dinner.

"Virgin." The word was impossible to say without

squeaking. "In 1306. Educated in the convent, lived a life of great mental activity."

"Great mental activity. You can be sainted for that?" He pointed to a small table without opening his eyes. "Pass me the soap, if you please."

Pass me the salt, he might have said. Gertrude sidled over to where Mrs. Allworthy had left a pair of apothecary jars and a rough sea sponge.

"The sponge also, if you don't mind."

Gertrude angled her way toward the tub.

"How old are you?"

"Here's your soap."

"Put a little on the sponge for me? You didn't answer my question."

"It's not a polite question. I'm giving you time to recon-sider." She dripped a little of the fancy liquid soap on the dry sponge. "It's not soaking in very well."

"Come closer. Dip the sponge in the water." He didn't move a muscle. His eyes remained shut, eyelashes curled on his cheek. She'd never noticed how pretty a man's eyelashes could be.

Was he watching her through the curtain of those lashes?

Gertrude dunked her hand in the extra bucket of hot water. She squished the sponge until it bubbled. "Here you are."

"If you wouldn't mind—" the Captain sloshed forward in the tub, bracing his arms on his lifted knees "—washing my back, please? Piracy is not a trade that rewards politesse."

Wash his back? Gertrude had to think for a moment. What was he talking about? What should she do?

The moment surrounded them, tingling with opportu-nity.

New experiences. She stepped behind him. With him leaning forward, the front of his body was hidden from her sight. But the view of his tender nape trailed all the way down his back to the shadowed split of his buttocks. Muscles arched across his shoulder blades and tensed along the valley of his spine.

Water everywhere, and all Gertrude could think was how dry her mouth felt.

"How old did you say you were?" he asked again.

Keeping the sponge as a barrier between her hand and his skin, she buffed his shoulder.

"More than twenty." She scrubbed with broader strokes. "Quite a bit more. Closer to thirty, if you must know."

He gave a snort. "I thought so. They told me you were nineteen. And married before."

She nearly dropped the sponge. "Who told you that?"

"The old woman with the bad teeth," he said. "The age was an obvious lie. No way to tell about the rest."

No way to tell? Gertrude coughed. Hardly a subtle hint. "I was not married. Precisely. More like…betrothed. At least, I thought so. He seemed to think…well, never mind."

Distracted by the conversation, and getting more comfortable in his company, she scrubbed lower. A corner of the coverlet dropped into the water.

"Bother." Reasoning that he couldn't see behind his back, she shook the blanket off her shoulders and onto the floor. Without the quilt she was able to move more freely. Scrubbing lower, she admitted, "I think perhaps the Sisters meant to warn you off."

"Warn me?"

"I am not young and not…inexperienced." Gertrude offered an honorable retreat. "It appears you've been misled, sir. Considering that we haven't yet…" She had no idea what word to use, so she skipped it entirely. "I'm sure we can arrange for a proper annulment."

He turned and glanced over his shoulder. "So eager to leave already? I heard you had a problem with locked doors."

"They told you *that?*" She dropped the sponge. "Oh dear."

"Allow me."

Twisting to retrieve the sponge, he deliberately exposed the front of his body to her. Gertrude looked away almost immediately.

He offered her the sponge on his hand. Water ran between his fingers, dripping onto the rug. Dark hair created unexpected shadows and textures all down his body, even more so between his legs. She wanted to look again.

"You don't know me." Gripping the edge of the tub until her knuckles whitened gave a focus to all the nervous energy building inside. "I'm not who you thought. I'll...leave in the morning."

"Think you will simply walk out of here?" he asked, in a tone that rang skeptical.

"I've supervised the care of fifty orphans, sir," she said. "I'm certain I can manage myself alone."

In fact, she'd planned this moment for ages, ever since her last disastrous escape. Now, her trunk held a folio of carefully forged letters of recommendation on convent stationary. She had a change of clothing. Enough coin saved for lodging and food. She could manage.

"I went to the convent for help." The Captain slowly squeezed the sponge with his fist. Gertrude began to sense... something was making him angry.

"For your soul?"

"No. Not that kind of help. I wanted a servant. And I was offered—you."

Gertrude felt her throat close. "They told me you were a widower in search of a healthy wife. They told me I would

be free to run your household, while you traveled at sea."
Finally she asked, "Who?"

"The one in charge, your Mother Superior. The one who
insisted we marry." He dropped the sponge into the water.
"Whose soul do you suppose she was protecting, mine or
yours?"

Neither, Gertrude guessed. *Devious old witch. Couldn't keep
me locked in the convent, so she locked me in a marriage vow.*

In one swift motion, the Captain emerged from the bathtub, steam rising off his skin, water splashing everywhere.

Showered in the drops off his body, Gertrude was treated
to a shocking view of his privates, right in front of her face.
"Good Lord!" she yelped.

She meant to close her eyes. And she would. Eventually.

The whole area looked nothing like what she'd expected.
Everything appeared heavier, darker, redder, all softly secreted
in black curly hair. Contrasted to his muscled thighs and the
flat strength of his abdomen, here, he was vulnerable. At first.
Even as she stared, a change began. His skin darkened in the
very masculine opposite of a blush. No shame, no retreat
implied by this rush of blood. He stretched and swelled as if
his cock were reaching out for her, pointing at her, choosing
her.

The Captain took full advantage of her inspection. He
was out of the water and reaching for her even as she turned
away. Pulling her to his chest, he caught her in his arms. His
dripping body soaked the back of her shift.

Leaning over, he spoke into her ear. "Piracy taught me
three lessons."

She felt too much at once. Warm. Wet. The weight of him.
The low rumble of his voice.

"One. To be a pirate is to take without asking."

Each of his arms dampened an area across the front of her

gown, hot where their skin touched, cool along the edges, where the air met bathwater. The contrast made her shiver. She lifted her chin and swallowed.

His finger traced a line down her throat to the tip of her breast. "Two."

She jolted. Too fast for any objection, his palm cupped her breast completely. Hot. Hard.

"A wise pirate takes where there is excess, where something of value is wasted."

Gertrude felt her heart pumping under his hand.

"Three." His words whispered through her hair. "A good pirate *never* gives anything back."

He released her so quickly she wobbled, eyes tightly shut.

"I may not know who you are, or how you came to be here, but this time—you will stay."

This time?

The expression on his face led her to glance down at herself. Her gown hung, almost as wet as if she'd gotten into the tub. It clung to her skin, raising goose bumps. But worst of all, the sodden fabric was completely translucent. Without thinking, she cupped her breasts to hide the burning peaks.

He grabbed his clothes from the floor and pounded toward the door. At the threshold, he stopped. He fumbled for a moment, then pulled a ring of keys from the pocket of his trousers. They jingled, softly as a church bell. "I'm going to close the house for the night. Stay here."

The sight of the keys made Gertrude tremble. "Do you think to lock me in?"

His back stiffened, as if he had some horrible decision to make. She tried not to stare. His naked torso made her think of statues—Greek statues. Ancient gods. Pagan rituals.

"For better or worse, you are my wife. These are the keys to my household," he said softly. With thumb and forefinger, he singled out a small gold key, shinier than all the rest. "Use all but this one. This key is mine alone. Is that clear?"

"Yes." She felt relieved and edgy at once.

He dropped the ring onto the credenza by the door.

"You *will* wait here."

The door shut with a snap.

Gertrude hurried over to where she'd dropped her gown. Quickly, she switched her cold, wet shift for the dry dress in her satchel, but her skin continued to prickle, her heart continued to flutter.

Pacing the room, window to door, fireplace to bed, she stepped into a damp patch on the rug. Everything came to a halt as she recalled the sensation of water from his naked body dripping over her. Her nipples tightened again.

The keys gleamed in the firelight.

Why get angry when she offered to release him from a forced marriage? Why expose himself to her like that, and then...walk out?

Her hands reached to comfort her breasts. Tentatively, she squeezed. Her palm was smaller, cooler. It soothed where the memory of his hand burned. She squeezed herself tighter, harder. It wasn't the same. It wasn't enough.

What was taking him so long? It was completely irrational to think he'd left her for good, as the boy who delivered bread to the convent had done. This was the Captain's home, after all.

She stared at the keys. Was it some sort of test? Ordering her to stay in her room, waiting for him? Clearly, this man did not know her.

Gertrude's inability to follow the rule of confinement was Mother Superior's greatest distress. As a girl, her tendency to cross forbidden thresholds was mostly curiosity; running away with the baker's delivery boy had been her first outright attempt at freedom. His seduction was only disappointing, but his abandonment had infuriated her. Disgraced, disobedient, she'd spent two months locked in routines of penance.

Never again.

This wasn't the convent. Keys to the household meant nothing if she was required to stay in her room. With careful fingers, she took up the ring.

Ting-a-ling. Again, the soft sounds of a bell.

The patron saint of the West Indies was welcome to remain in her room, with her mental activities. Gertrude had doors to open. Questions to answer. And a naked husband to find.

Room by room, floor by floor, she searched. The house seemed quiet as a grave.

How many wives had lived here? she couldn't stop herself from thinking. *And how many had died?*

The dark wood floors creaked as she traveled the halls. No one took notice. None of the servants appeared to live in. Where could they have gone? Even the kitchen fire had been smothered. Moonlight over the transom windows was the only light in the house.

Most rooms held only a few spare bits of furnishing—a wooden chair, a candle on a table, a locked trunk. The house reminded Gertrude of her time on the ship, as if the Captain never really left the sea. No signs of children or guests or even servants' lives. It was a lonely house.

Methodically, Gertrude opened every door, tried every key.

Except one.

There was one remaining door off the front hall. And one remaining key. The jitter of excitement pushed her forward.

The door appeared to lead to a parlor, or perhaps the

Captain's study. She pressed her ear to the door. *Silence.* Slowly, she turned the knob. *Locked.*

The Captain must have gone out, back to his ship, or perhaps the tavern. He had ordered her to stay in the room and then left the house? Infuriating man.

She twisted the knob hard.

What could he possibly have to hide in a parlor? Visitors waiting in the hall would be able to see right into this room when the door was open, for heaven's sake.

The ring of keys jingled nervously.

This one is mine alone. Is that clear?

Gertrude held her breath. What was the worst that could happen? What was the worst thing he could have hidden in the parlor? She sorted the forbidden key from the rest. Was it her imagination, or did it burn as she took it between her fingers and slipped it into the lock?

The bolt shifted with a soft click.

Easing the door open, Gertrude was surprised to see the glow of a fire. She hadn't noticed any light around the edge of the door when she'd stood in the hall. Even more surprising was her view of the Captain, completely dry and dressed in fresh clothing. *Strange.* Gertrude tucked a lock of her own wet hair behind her ear and leaned farther into the door's gap.

The Captain sat in a chair by the hearth, his legs spread wide as if he was bracing himself for trouble. The firelight emphasized shadows under his eyes and gaunt cheeks Gertrude hadn't noticed earlier. He didn't look at all like the healthy man who'd carried two heavy water buckets into her room.

Nudging the door a bit wider, Gertrude saw Mrs. Allworthy setting a tray on the desk nearby. There was a bowl of broth, a big spoon and a small biscuit. Sick-room food.

Gertrude blinked in confusion. Mrs. Allworthy appeared slender and straight as a girl.

What? How?

"Here now, Captain," the woman said. "Eat to keep your strength."

"Leave it, Anne. Leave me." He looked past her to the portrait on the wall. The face of a pretty, soft-featured girl, haloed by a prim white bonnet, made a gloomy contrast to the black-crepe drape of mourning.

"You know I'll not do that, sir." With a generous sigh, Mrs. Allworthy tugged at the laces on her bodice. Dipping her shoulders, left then right, she let her shift slip down to her waist.

Gertrude's mouth dropped open.

The Captain's did not. "Anne. No."

"Too many months alone, you are. It's a widower's comfort you need, sir. And I mean to give it to you."

The woman's breasts spilled over her bodice, practically bouncing with relief at their freedom. Her nipples, the size of sovereigns, dark as her eyes, popped to attention.

The Captain spoke directly to her décolletage. "I don't think—"

"I do think. You'll take your medicine without complaining." Mrs. Allworthy's arms scooped beneath her skirts. Gertrude watched her fingers fiddling under the cloth, as the woman leaned forward, offering her bosom to the Captain's face.

"And your husband?" the Captain asked. "Mr. Allworthy?"

"Not married yet." She winked.

The woman had introduced herself as Mrs. Allworthy, mother of three boys. She'd rubbed her belly and claimed to wish for a girl next.

What magic was happening here?

"My George has a generous heart. He'd hate to see you suffering, sir, when you've done so much for us. He knows

I'm no blushing bride." She straightened her back, wiggled her hips. Ties undone, her white ruffled drawers dropped to the floor. "After the vows are said, I imagine he'll see it different. But tonight is tonight and tomorrow will take care of itself."

Even Gertrude could see the Captain's face was fully alert. His chest rose and fell with a steady rhythm that Gertrude realized her body was mimicking.

"Life goes on for the living, sir. You'll feel joy again, when the memory of her leaving is less sharp." Turning her back fully to Gertrude, Mrs. Allworthy hoisted her skirts and stepped close to the chair.

As if to be polite, the Captain shifted in his seat.

The woman climbed into the chair, one knee to either side of his lap. She dumped her skirts forward, flashing the white moons of her buttocks at Gertrude.

Her bottom was…astonishing. Plump and dimpled, Gertrude had the urge to pinch that muscled flesh and confirm it was entirely real.

The Captain must have had the same urge. He took each side in one hand, spread his fingers and squeezed. And squeezed again.

Gertrude clenched her own bottom cheeks at the sight. Goodness. What would it feel like to have a pirate's hands squeezing her?

"Ahh. That's it." Mrs. Allworthy's voice went from practical to a purr. She pushed forward, lifting her bosom. "I'm here tonight to remind you of the little joys."

"Not that little," the Captain mumbled.

"Pooh, you flatter me," she said as the Captain opened his mouth for the breast served up before him.

His eyes closed. Mrs. Allworthy wrapped a hand around his head, threading her fingers into his hair as she cupped him to her. Gertrude thought her expression as gentle as a midwife with a new babe.

"There now. That's right."

Their bodies began to rock in a rhythm, with Mrs. Allworthy pressing forward, humming a low sweet note, and then rolling back on her haunches. The Captain spread his legs wider, as if they needed stabilizing.

His face was mesmerizing. His cheeks hollowed, he sucked the woman's breast vigorously. His tongue must be licking her, wetting her nipple, making it tingle and harden, just as Gertrude's had hardened in the bath. And still he sucked.

Gertrude clasped her hands beneath her chin, firmly pressing her wrists to her own burning breasts.

"Good lord," she prayed. "What next?"

Mrs. Allworthy answered with glee. She wiggled one hand, then the other, beneath her skirts. Then she rose high on her knees, forcing the Captain to relinquish his hold with a sloppy, smacking kiss.

He moaned. Mrs. Allworthy's hands, beneath the curtain of her skirts, were making the man moan. The rhythm of their bodies quickened.

Gertrude's grip on the keys tightened. She wanted to see. She wanted to know what was going on under those skirts.

It was as if Mrs. Allworthy heard her plea.

"Let's get these out of the way, shall we?"

The Captain groaned happily.

Skirt, apron and petticoat were suddenly hauled over the crook of her arm like the train on a rich lady's dress. Mrs. Allworthy's bottom was once again bare for all the world—or at least Gertrude—to see. One knee was planted on either side of the Captain's lap and something new was visible.

The Captain's pants had been opened. He still gripped one

cheek of Mrs. Allworthy's buttocks with his long fingers, but his other hand was gripping something else entirely.

The shadows of Mrs. Allworthy's thighs made it difficult to see, but what Gertrude *could* see was huge. Definitely larger than what she remembered prodding into her on that one other sad occasion. And much larger than it had looked in the bath upstairs. How could he possibly...?

"Help a lady to her seat, if you please, sir?" Mrs. Allworthy crooned.

The Captain smiled for the first time since Gertrude had peeked through the open door. It was a reluctant smile, slightly stiff with lack of use, but heartfelt. Of all the things she'd seen so far, it was the smile that twanged a jealous string in her soul.

Mrs. Allworthy could make the Captain smile.

"With pleasure," he replied. His grip on Mrs. Allworthy's buttock tightened as his other hand tilted.

Ever so slowly, Mrs. Allworthy found her seat. She appeared...relieved, grateful, perhaps even pleased by the whole experience. Gertrude watched closely, growing more and more certain. Mrs. Allworthy was enjoying herself just as much as the Captain! She wasn't wincing; she was moaning. She wasn't rigid, either. She was the lush, curling opposite of rigid.

It was difficult to say which bothered Gertrude more at that moment, the Captain's dangerously blissful expression, or Mrs. Allworthy's.

Would Gertrude feel that same bliss with the Captain? She leaned on the door frame. Her fingers clutched the fluted wood as Mrs. Allworthy began to undulate, forward and up, rising off the Captain's lap and slowly pressing down. The Captain's head lolled back against the chair, his eyelids heavy. Breathy gasps filled the room. Sweat began to shine on the

Captain's brow and in the valley of those bouncing breasts. Their breathing matched, flowing out with every downstroke of Mrs. Allworthy's curvy bottom.

It shocked Gertrude to realize she was breathing exactly the same way.

Mrs. Allworthy moaned loudly, prompting a change in their rhythm. She angled her body forward, grabbing the back of the chair with white-knuckle strength. The Captain's heels began to pop off the floor, tapping a beat in syncopation to the lady's quickening pace. Tipped forward, Gertrude had a clear view of the deep red flesh of man and woman coming together. It shone in the firelight, slick with moisture. Rising and falling together, they made the sound of something juicy, of someone licking their lips…. Gertrude swallowed. She was the one licking her lips.

Awareness of her own body traveled head to toe before she could stop it. She was damp with sweat everywhere, but worse than that, she was melting, slick and hot, in the shadowy folds between her legs.

What Gertrude saw was nothing like what she'd experienced. She couldn't stop wondering what it might feel like… sliding down around a man's—*that* man's—thick flesh…rising and falling, faster, faster….

Mrs. Allworthy parted her lips and gave an open-throated cry, pausing midstroke with a sort of shocked expression on her face. Flushed, panting, she let her eyes drift shut as a smile curved her mouth. Her spine softened and she relaxed her grip on the chair.

"Goodness, sir. I believe I have arrived at our destination prematurely." She nuzzled her cheek against his hair, his thighs still bumping an insistent pattern against her.

"Perhaps I can encourage you to visit again?" The Captain's

hands became fully occupied with the woman's rear, lifting her as he rose from the chair, while still attached.

The woman squealed with the glee of a child being tickled, and wrapped her legs round his waist. Two giant steps landed them at the parlor game table, with Mrs. Allworthy on her back, her ankles in the air and petticoats flopping.

"It's a gentleman you are, sir, and the world's a better place for it," Mrs. Allworthy said, her voice catching as the Captain adjusted himself firmly to the new position. "Any woman would be lucky to have you. For a night, or a lifetime."

Pushing away her kind words, the Captain squeezed his eyes shut and pumped his hips in a hard thrust.

…a night, or a lifetime.

Gertrude gasped. She couldn't help herself. It was as if the Captain had pressed himself into her, driving all the air from her lungs.

She slapped her hand over her mouth. She wasn't entirely sure she wasn't seeing some kind of ghost, a spirit of the past perhaps, but it seemed prudent to remain silent.

Too late.

The Captain's eyes opened wide, his face taut with aware-ness. He looked directly at her.

That piercing glare shook Gertrude to the bone. She spun around, grabbed handfuls of her gown and ran up the stairs, two at a time. Her footsteps echoed in the oddly empty house.

With the bedroom door shut and braced behind her, she held her breath, waiting for heavy footsteps coming after her. Nothing.

After a long moment, she admitted to a small quantity of frustration. Relief, of course, but also, quite definitely…in the strangest way…disappointment.

Why didn't he follow her? How could he look at her that way and not follow her?

She opened the door a crack. Silence. No creak of wood. No whistle of air across a chimney.

Gertrude shivered. At the orphanage she'd heard many tales of island magic and saints with visions. She'd never believed such things could be true.

Stepping into the hallway, she strained her ears for the tick of the cabinet clock. The motion caused a jingling in her pocket, the same bell-like sound she'd heard when the Captain had first laid temptation on the table.

The key.

Her hand scrambled in her pocket.

"No. Oh, no."

She'd left the door unlocked.

He would know. There'd be no hiding the fact that she'd used the forbidden key.

Unless…she crept back downstairs and locked it, ever so quietly. Her mouth went dry at the thought, but her feet shuffled forward. Quickly; she must do it quickly, while the Captain was still…busy.

She crept back down the stairs. In the gloomy silence of the house, it was impossible to ignore her pounding heart. From the bottom stair, she could clearly see she'd left the door open. A sliver of light broke through, brighter than firelight. Had they lit more lamps?

Gertrude hardly hesitated. Instead of pulling the door shut, she pushed it open just far enough to see inside. She squinted against the dramatic change of light.

Sunshine?

The curtained windows of the Captain's study filtered the cheerful midday sun. Gertrude looked back over her shoulder at the transom above the front door, not even ten feet from where she stood.

Midnight dark.

How was it possible?

Blinking quickly to adjust her eyes, she turned back to the study. Voices. Had someone else joined the Captain and Mrs. Allworthy? With a steady fingertip, she eased the door open wider.

"Piss-sakes, Captain, let her go. And good riddance! She was an infant. I doubt she even knew the word *cock,* much less how to use one."

The man Gertrude knew as One-eyed Jack, the Captain's first mate and friend, stood beside the desk. He'd been kind to her on the long voyage, repeatedly asking if she needed another blanket or something to warm the bed on cold nights. Gertrude had been wary of him at first. The scar that creased his face had taken his right eye and left him with a fierce expression. During the crossing, Gertrude had heard one story that he'd fed the eye to a shark, another that he'd fallen under the sword of a Queen's Dragoon and a third in which a storm had dropped a burning spar on the poor man. The Captain had figured prominently as Jack's savior in each version, which left Gertrude convinced that much of the tale was true.

The Jack standing in this sunlit study could not be called one-eyed. Hale and unscarred, dressed in a loose shirt and riding trousers, he was the picture of health. More than that, Gertrude realized, he was beautiful. His hair had soaked in the sunlight, and gleamed with gold. His skin glowed with vigor.

What strange thoughts these visions brought. Watching Jack, Gertrude wondered was it a life of piracy or merely life itself that scarred a man?

"The bakery boy would disagree," the Captain answered.

"A boy. Doubtful he knows how to use one, either."

Gertrude leaned in. Did she hear that right? *Bakery boy?* Had she… She searched her memory. No, she had never said… Who'd told him?

The Captain kept his head down, focusing on the piles of stationery, maps and ledger books that covered his desk. Jack turned his attention to a painting on the wall. In this room, Gertrude noticed, the black drape had been removed from the pretty portrait, which now hung near the window. The place of honor over the mantel held a different picture, of a wide-eyed shepherdess in a standard pastoral setting.

Posing beside the painting, Jack imitated the girl's bovine expression. The Captain ignored him, until he grabbed a long breakfast bun off the tea tray and held it to his cheek, stroking the bread with his fingers.

"Admit it," Jack said. "They're perfect for each other."

"Do you mean to comfort me—" The Captain's voice started softly. "—for the loss of a second wife—" Gradually, its edge sharpened. "—by congratulating her on her good sense—" And finally became something lethal. "—at leaving me?"

He fixed Jack with the glare that gave Gertrude palpitations.

Jack bit off a hearty chunk of bun, then perched himself on the corner of the Captain's desk. He smiled. "I can think of better ways to comfort you."

And the strangest thing happened.

The Captain blushed.

Gertrude thought at first he'd become volcanically angry. The color rose up his neck into his cheeks, as though he were about to explode. But no. Instead, he looked away, flustering over some papers on his desk.

"Go home, Jack."

"I've no home at port. You know that."

"Go back to the ship, then. Go find a pub and get drunk. Go find a woman and get—"

"Not in the mood."

"Fine. I have work to do here."

"How long till the ship is repaired?"

"They can't say yet. I've another ten men to bribe before I can even start the repairs." Gertrude heard the tension singing in his voice, and her palpitations beat harder.

"It's not your fault, you know. The damage to the ship, that dim-witted, unfaithful little wife—"

The Captain cut him off with a slam of his hand on the desk. "Then whose fault is it?"

"No one's, you bloody idiot!" Jack jumped up. He was a seaman with arms like muscled logs. He shoved the heavy desk sideways like a pocket door. Momentum cleared the top, scattering paper everywhere.

Without the barrier of his desk, the Captain stood.

Gertrude sucked in a breath. A spicy scent prickled the air.

Jack didn't back away. He stepped in closer, closer, and growled, "Fate happens to us all, my friend. Good and bad."

When he butted his chest against the other man's, Jack's open shirt slipped off his shoulder. Gertrude could see the glowing curves of pectoral muscles and arms. Poised before the Captain, he reminded her of an old painting she had seen copied in a Bible. David and Goliath.

"I'm sick of standing by and watching you mope about." He raised both hands and grabbed the Captain by his shirt. Gertrude heard the sound of cloth ripping. Chest to chest, eye to eye, Jack shouted, "It's enough, you hear me?"

It lasted all of a heartbeat.

Gertrude bit her lip this time before she gasped.

The fight was on.

The Captain swung. Jack ducked. With a shoulder to the Captain's middle, Jack knocked the other man flat to the rug. Grunts and thumps followed. She glanced away. Rolling, twisting bodies forced both men's shirts to fall away. She looked back. They were both dressed in the close-fitting pants preferred by horsemen. Gertrude could see every muscle of their thighs and bottoms outlined as they wrestled.

She ought to turn away. But she didn't.

The men's upper bodies grew shiny with sweat. Jack groaned loudly, although the Captain maintained a silent, grim-faced determination.

With a sudden thump, he managed to lock Jack beneath the full stretch of his body. He held him facedown with one arm tight around his throat, the other pressing his wrist to the floor.

The Captain was breathing hard, his body rocking with each sharp exhalation. Jack bucked against him, but the Captain would have none of it. He slammed the man back into the rug with a thrust of his pelvis.

Jack groaned again, low and long, as the Captain punished him with several more pushes—again, and again, and again. Gertrude stared without blinking, watching as his buttocks hollowed every time he clenched them and pressed Jack deeper into the carpet.

A hot blush rose to Gertrude's cheeks when she realized she'd let it happen again. She was clenching her own buttocks in time with the Captain's, unconsciously mimicking his body's motion. With a shaking inhalation, she forced herself to relax.

Jack keened a wail of surrender. His face grimaced with resistance before he dropped his forehead to the floor. All the tension released from his muscles at once.

The Captain fell onto the other man, panting heavily. They lay pressed together for a long moment.

"Sorry, I—"

"I'm not," Jack responded clearly. With a laugh, he easily pushed the other man off him and rolled to his side. His face was flushed, his lovely sunlit hair tousled, and Gertrude noticed with a reverberating shock that the front of his trousers appeared darkly stained.

"Clears the humors, doesn't it? Oh dear, you still appear to be a bit blocked," he added.

The Captain braced his back against the desk, spreading his legs wide. Gertrude thought he seemed to be moving rather stiffly parts that only moments ago had appeared quite athletic. She blinked and looked more closely. The placket of his own trousers bulged, as though he'd stuffed a fist in his pocket.

"Well now." Jack propped himself up on one arm and smiled winningly. "Whatever shall we do about that?"

"Enough, Jack." Weariness still frayed the Captain's voice, but Gertrude heard the edge of something else, as well. Something a little rueful. Amused. "Give it up, my friend. You can't fuck my troubles off my mind."

"Actually, I was considering another course of action."

Jack's words held both Gertrude and the Captain bespelled for a moment, long enough for the golden-haired man to lean forward and rub his face against the other man's swollen crotch.

This time, the groaning sound came from the Captain. His hand rose and hovered inches away from Jack's golden head. Gertrude couldn't tell if he meant to push him away or clasp him tighter. Jack opened his mouth and hummed a hot breath Gertrude could almost feel. Then he dragged his tongue over the swelling beneath the cloth.

The Captain hissed.

"Like that?" Jack laughed. "Wait until I get you bare...."

Bare.

The word alone made Gertrude shiver.

Everything she'd seen this night was a heady mix of the perverse and the sublime. How easy they all were with their bodies. Fierce and gentle, they gave and received, fighting for what they wanted. She wanted to feel that strength. Ride the power of the moment. Sweat until every muscle was slick. Lick bare skin. Make him cry out....

She must have made some sound despite every good intention, because suddenly, the Captain's eyes were once again staring into hers.

Frozen. Time froze, as did she, right where she stood.

The look on her Captain's face flashed like lightning, changing from astonished to avid. Desire galvanized his hovering hand. He clasped Jack's head firmly to him and, rocking hard against that busy mouth and tongue, he never took his eyes off her.

Encouraged, Jack reached to free the buttons in his way.

No. She couldn't watch another moment.

Gertrude grabbed the doorknob and jerked the door shut with a bang. Breathing fast, she fumbled in her pocket.

"The key. The key, I must..."

Trembling fingers made it harder to fit the key into the lock.

It wouldn't turn!

"Please, no!" She crouched to the height of the lock and jiggled the key from side to side. That sweet, bell-like ting-a-ling rang in the metal opening. "Please, please turn!"

The door swung wide. With her hand braced on the knob, Gertrude fell forward, landing on her knees.

"What are you doing?" the Captain boomed in his on-deck voice.

This was the same Captain who had helped himself to her bath. His feet were bare. His shirt was damp, his blue-black hair dripping in wet curls over his collar. The room was dim, lit only by a small fire in the hearth.

"The fire...you...I..." She looked up at him, key in hand.

His expression was incredulous. "I told you not to use that key."

She sat back on her heels. "Sorry?"

"Hardly good enough," he said. He grabbed her by the arm and jerked her to her feet.

Gertrude's palpitations amplified. This was a grown man, used to being obeyed. Her heart, her stomach, and lower, between her legs, fluttered with anticipation. After everything she had seen this night, she should have been horrified, terrified, humiliated.

Maybe she was, a little. But...she liked the feeling.

"I also told you to wait upstairs for me." His hand was gripping her arm so tightly it hurt. She pulled and he released her, only to back her against the wall, caging her with his arms.

"Why?" Gertrude tilted her chin.

"Why? Why what?"

"Why give me that key if you didn't want me to use it?" It wasn't easy to meet his burning stare without spontaneously combusting. Her eyes obliged with cooling tears. "It made me wonder, were you setting a cruel trap, or merely mistaken?"

"Mistaken?" He sounded incredulous. The Captain was never mistaken. He was only obeyed. He pressed toward her; she could feel the warmth of his body through her dress. "You are the one who is mistaken if you think you can disobey me without consequences."

Whatever he planned he had to step back to maneuver. Gertrude immediately ducked under his arm and jerked the knob of the front door.

"Oh, no, you don't," he growled, obviously insulted. Who dares to run from the Captain? But his tone implied something else, as well—that he was game.

He slapped one hand against the door, preventing Gertrude from opening it more than an inch before it banged shut again. He cocked an eyebrow, as if to say *care to try again?*

Gertrude wasn't sure whether to scream or...giggle. This was a battle, like the one he'd had with Jack. That thought made it hard to concentrate. She ducked under his arm once more and dashed toward the chair by the fireplace, thinking to put a large piece of furniture between them.

She got as far as the tea table. The painting of the shepherdess was gone. In its place was a pencil sketch of a young woman with dark hair and round eyes, standing at the threshold of the parlor. Stock-still with embarrassment, Gertrude recognized herself, as she might have looked only moments ago, her expression focused, yearning...and full of desire.

The Captain took full advantage of her hesitation. Catching her from behind, he wrapped his arms around her and carried her flat to the floor, pinning her beneath him. Crushed against the carpet, slightly breathless, she found that the weight and heat of a grown man's body on hers made it difficult to sense many particulars.

Except one. The long line of his—Gertrude was not afraid to use the word *cock*—was pillowed against her bottom.

"Ready to accept your punishment?" He nuzzled her temple, the threatening words drifting softly across her cheek.

Gertrude squirmed. "No."

"Oh, good." He chuckled while his fingers danced a come-hither tickle beside her knee, rucking up the hem of her gown, inch by inch.

When she felt cool air hit her thighs, she began to wiggle in earnest. She'd tossed the dress over herself without a chemise, or an apron or even drawers, for goodness' sake. The farther up he pulled the dress, the harder she squirmed to keep it down. The more she struggled, the more tightly tangled the dress became.

His hands began to touch her everywhere—her hair, her neck, her waist, her hips. The carpet abraded her breasts. His body trapped hers in a cave of warmth, but allowed her to move. The more she wiggled, the more he enjoyed it. The moment her dress twisted over her waist, exposing her bottom, Gertrude gasped. Time stopped.

The moment bubbled through her, intoxicating as wine. *What next?*

It was the essence of every forbidden door she'd ever opened. Vulnerable and curious, she couldn't stop the moan of feeling that spilled over.

"At last," he murmured.

Smack! His hand slapped against her bottom. She spluttered with shock. It didn't hurt, but the sound was so loud it mortified her. Someone might hear them!

"Stop! What—?"

His hand interrupted with another *smack!*

This time, heat bloomed. Stretched alongside her, he restrained her with nothing more than the arch of his foot curved against the back of her calf. Gertrude pushed herself up to her hands and knees, resisting for the sake of pride.

"I won't—"

"Ahh. Better and better." His voice oozed every satisfaction of the conqueror.

This time she knew what was coming, and that little moment before it happened was...just as good. The sound and feel of his hand landing smartly on her rear made her head snap up. Desire and embarrassment seemed to complement each other, the feelings winding more tightly inside her. Her skin was burning with awareness.

Too much. It had to... "Stop," she moaned. Even Gertrude could admit it wasn't a very clear statement of her wishes.

She glanced over her shoulder at him, wondering what emotion she'd see in his face. Frustration? Determination?

Wonder. Longing.

Meeting her gaze, he raised his hand to the curve of her bottom and gently caressed her with his palm, stroking, soothing, squeezing. His hand seem to change temperature, warm on her back, cool where he'd spanked her bottom, warm again as he explored the softness of her thighs. Gertrude relaxed, first lowering herself to her elbows, and then her knees slid back, her bottom coming to rest last of all on the carpet.

"You will not leave me," he said, his words direct but his tone concerned.

"Can you make me want to stay?"

Gertrude matched his glare and the Captain ruefully shook his head. "What a fierce thing you are." The complaints didn't affect his hands-on enjoyment of the view. "I should have seen that."

She rolled away, mirroring him, shifting her dress to modesty. There were too many feelings inside to speak.

"I see why the old woman wanted you gone."

"Wanted me gone?" Gertrude repeated indignantly. She studied the hollow of his elbow. "Maybe." She licked her lips and the truth slipped out. "I planned to leave. I think the Reverend Mother found out. You were her last chance."

"So which am I, mistaken or cruel?" His hand reached for the hem she'd adjusted, skimming the fabric, pulling it up, one finger at a time, giving her plenty of time to object.

Her bottom tingling, her heart thumping again, Gertrude could hardly speak. "The paintings near the window. Are those your wives?"

"How did you...?" His hand stopped.

"Is that why you didn't want me in here?" she asked, knowing the answer. "You cared for them. You still do."

"Maybe."

Her dress was fully above her waist, but he did not look down until a silent understanding flowed between them. She would not judge his past, if he did not judge hers.

When he reached for her again, Gertrude blushed. What a picture she made—completely clothed above the waist and bare skin below.

"A cruel man would give me the key as an excuse for punishment," she reasoned as steadily as she could. "A mistaken man might think I was not ready to know his past."

A wicked smile spread over his face. "So I must be..." skimming a hand up her leg, he pressed inward "...both."

Gertrude felt that little whirl of anticipation.

He would know. He would feel her. Wet.

No door to hide behind here. At the last moment, she grabbed his wrist and swallowed so hard it hurt. He kissed her throat, his hand thwarted in the act of reaching for her.

"I must know," Gertrude said. "Why did you marry me? Why agree to her demand?"

"You'll never believe me." His lips to her ear, he trusted her with his confession. "I knew you. The moment I saw you in the convent."

Startled, Gertrude released his arm. He took hold of her hip in a solid grip.

"Visions and dreams," he whispered, pulling her close. "I've seen you a hundred times. You saw the picture above the mantel. I drew it months ago."

"In this room? Did you see me...here?"

There was a flicker of alarm in his eyes when he answered. "Yes."

"Tell me," she whispered, impossibilities weaving together in her mind. "What did you see?"

"You watching, so beautiful, so curious." His hand resumed its journey toward her center. "Your face...you were glad to see me happy. I thought you were an angel."

Her spine curled to meet him. Slipping her hand around his nape, she guided him into a kiss, her mouth as wet and open as the rest of her. They kissed as his fingers began to play in the slippery mess she'd made of herself.

What strange magic had brought them together?

"Mother Superior warned me I'd be sorry if I didn't change my ways." Gertrude closed her eyes to better enjoy the sensation of hands where they didn't belong.

"And are you sorry?" He slid one finger, then another, inside.

"No, I don't..." She found it difficult to think in words. "Oh...my...heavens."

This felt better and worse than being touched on the outside. It was somehow exactly what she craved, but quickly insufficient. The intimacy, the fullness of his fingers was more than anything she'd ever felt, but less than enough. She rocked against his wrist asking for more. His thumb waved in answer, again, and again.

Sorry? How could she be sorry to have used the key?

"I'm...not at all...sorry."

He pulled his hand away. Nearly drunk on new sensations as she was, it took Gertrude a moment to understand. He'd lifted his glistening fingers to his mouth and was licking them clean.

"Salty, sweet. L'eau de Gertrude," he said with a grin. "Don't be sorry. Be yourself."

Everything she'd seen that night—Mrs. Allworthy's generosity and Jack's fierce affection, every door she'd ever opened—made her ready for this, for him.

"I will." She reached down and popped the button covering the rise in his trousers. "And you will be my pirate."

He lifted so she might ease his pants over his hips.

"I've heard a pirate takes without asking." She wrapped a hand around his cock, and experimented. A squeeze here, a tug there, the upward brush of her fingertips…it felt as strangely wonderful as she'd imagined. "Something of value."

Half choking, half laughing, he pressed her onto her back and opened her thighs with the spread of his knees. "And a good pirate?"

Now she was the one making odd sounds, as he pushed in deep. "Never gives anything back."

Pressing farther, locking them together, he answered, "Take it. Keep it." His voice dropped to a rasp. "Tell me what you want. I'll give you anything."

Visions of memories flashed through her mind.

"Bare. Let me see all of you."

"Yes." He reared up, pulling her hips into him, and she inhaled sharply. He stripped off his shirt and tossed it aside. "Right here in this room, where you've haunted my dreams."

He leaned over and kissed her, his lips softer than ever. Would every kiss warm her this way? Would every touch melt her?

"Now you," he demanded.

He tugged and twisted at her dress until, finally, they were skin to skin. Gertrude basked in the warmth of his body so close to hers.

Gliding together was another kind of magic. The Captain's eyes drifted shut and then suddenly flew open. The light of the fire made his body shine, damp everywhere with exertion. Their rhythm insisted, like a knock at the door. He pushed harder to be let in, to be welcomed. Gertrude arched her back, rising into the moment, opening to the gripping blissful moment of *what next?*

Afterward, they lay wrapped together in quiet. But Gertrude could not rest. "That key. Where did you get it?"

For a long moment, there was no reply. "Your Mother Superior gave it to me."

"What?"

"She told me it was the key to happiness." He pulled Gertrude closer, and rubbed his chin across the top of her head. "And I must forbid you to use it. When you spoke of leaving, I remembered her words. You'd made me a little desperate, and she knew you better than I."

Indeed she did.

"But...I opened your door with that key."

"Impossible," he told her. "The study has a dead bolt. It locks from the inside, when I don't wish to be disturbed."

She pushed herself up and turned to look at him.

"I opened the door," he insisted, "when I heard you jabbing away at the keyhole."

Gertrude considered the possibilities. In a very careful voice she asked, "How many times have you seen me in this room?"

His fingers played with the curtain of her hair, falling toward his face. "Many. So many..."

Many?

The ring of keys lay abandoned near the fire, the smallest one shining brighter than ever. Gertrude tried to look away, but couldn't. "And am I still forbidden from using that key?"

"She did say it was the key to happiness," the Captain said as innocently as a man might with a hand lurking over a lady's behind.

"Well, then." She smiled like the saint she would never be. "Be sure to lock your door."

"Dreaming of two handsome men, are you?" Devlin asked.

"If one is good, two are—" Maeve yelped, then sighed, conveniently forgetting her next words.

"Better?" he snarled, nipping lower, loosening her shirt.

"Never better, my love."

Maybe they would start in the chair? It was convenient. Maybe later, he would let her play the part of One-eyed Jack.

"There's none better." Maeve shifted, and lifted, and both of them moaned. "Moods and all, you're the key to my heart."

"Moods? What have I got to be moody about, with a practically pantieless pirate in my lap?"

"My thoughts exactly."

"You'll be leaving the boots on."

"Absolutely."

"And I'll be locking the door."

★ ★ ★ ★ ★

ACTING THE PART

Eva Cassel

WE'D BEEN FILMING IN THE SOUTH OF FRANCE
for only two weeks when rumors of a real-life romance between Mikhail and me spread through the British tabloids like
mold on warm mayonnaise. All completely—semi—false, of
course. But try arguing *that* when there are pictures of Britain's
"most eligible bachelor" spreading sunscreen all over your
American ass. "Friends can spread sunscreen on each other
on their day off at the beach," I told my publicist.

She laughed. "Is that your official statement?"

I'd been warned about working with both Mikhail Sommerville and Derek Jackson, the director. The unlikely prog-
eny of a beautiful, dark-haired Russian actress and a British
physicist, Mikhail had an international reputation as a heart-
breaker. He had a literature degree from Oxford and would
occasionally moonlight as a playwright for the Royal Theatre
in London. I'd never worked with anyone like him before,
actors generally being rather blank in all the ways that matter.
My agent told me he had ridiculously high standards and a
knack for making actresses cry.

The first time we actually met was in a tiny Parisian café near the Musée d'Orsay. Derek led me over to Mikhail—who was sipping a noisette and reading a French newspaper, dressed all in black, dark brown hair raked back off his face—and made the introductions.

"Lydia Castle, I'd like you to meet the infamous Mikhail Sommerville, your costar."

"Infamous, eh?" Mikhail stood up, looking a little embarrassed, and held out his hand. At least six foot two, he towered over me.

His cheeks dimpled slightly as he smiled. I squeezed his hand. He held on to it a second longer than necessary, lowering his chin and staring into my eyes—as though we were in on the same joke. I have to admit, I swooned a little.

I'd seen enough pictures of him to know that he was gorgeous, but I hadn't expected the effect he would have on me. Unlike most of the pretty Hollywood boys, Mikhail was reported to have something rarer than good looks—character. He actually looked as if he was thinking, lots, about everything. I could see that he was sizing me up.

Perhaps it was just my insecurities, but I thought he appeared unconvinced that I was the right woman to play a moody, passionate medieval writer named Sandrine Farot—feisty enough to dare to write when few women could read, with a sexual appetite to match the perverted king's. I'd been dying for a role like this ever since I knew I wanted to act.

The three of us sat down. The midmorning sun streaked through the floor-to-ceiling café windows. Derek slapped Mikhail on the shoulder. "I'm glad you didn't greet Lydia the way you did Juliette Binoche."

Mikhail burst out laughing. His broad, easy smile was mesmerizing. I glanced from one to the other for an explanation. Mikhail sighed, still looking rather pleased with himself.

"When we were filming *Sun into Midnight,* and I met Juliette for the first time, rather than shaking her hand, like I just did yours, I laid a wet one on her."

"What?" I exclaimed, looking at Derek for confirmation; he nodded and shook his head in amusement and exasperation. "Why would you do that?"

Mikhail shrugged nonchalantly. "It was an intense film. I needed to make sure we had the right kind of chemistry to pull it off."

"So what did she do?" I had to know.

"What do you think?" He exchanged a look with Derek. "She slapped me."

"And do *we* have the right kind of chemistry?" I heard myself asking.

"I don't know, let me see," he said, darting a hand behind my head and pressing his mouth against mine. Fair enough, I'd asked for it—and was glad I had. His lips felt soft and solid at the same time. My mouth was slightly open, as was his. I felt the tip of his tongue just barely touching my bottom lip. I got shivers on top of my goose bumps.

When he finally let go—just as abruptly—and sat back in his seat, sipping his noisette as though nothing had happened, I felt drunk. *I* had no doubt that we had the right kind of chemistry for a Derek Jackson film. I couldn't wait to start.

We didn't see each other again until a month later, when filming began. At the time, Mikhail was in the throes of a vicious divorce with wife number two, a French songbird named Maxine. His cell phone was constantly ringing off the hook and it was understood that he might be scarce around the set.

This time, we bumped into each other over the lavish breakfast buffet at the Cassis Hotel, located in the heart of the fortressed French town of Carcassonne, where most of the main crew was staying for the duration of filming.

"I recommend the banana pancakes," he said with a grin, slapping his cell phone shut. He was dressed more casually that day, in a white T-shirt and frazzled jeans. There was a hint of a British accent, but his *R*s and *S*s were hardened by having Russian as a second language—a real European mutt. He also looked a lot younger that morning than he had at the café, more like his thirty-five years. His light brown eyes, almost the color of desert sand, danced mischievously as he continued to stare at me.

"If we're going to be having sex in front of twelve people in a month, we should probably have breakfast together," he said. "What do you think?"

My stomach dropped to my shoes like a broken elevator. "Why is Derek waiting that long to do the scene?" I asked, delicately selecting fruit for my plate as though I wasn't sweating like a teenager.

The scene we were both referring to was an intense, emotionally fraught collision between our two characters. The sex was supposed to be the "shred each other to pieces" kind. From watching Derek's previous three films, I knew he was capable of making it happen. My knees had quivered just reading the scene. I'd been desperately trying to shed my tame, good-girl image since my breakaway role in a generic romantic comedy; if a Derek Jackson film didn't do it, then nothing would!

"He always does this," Mikhail answered. "He wants the tension to build. The scene won't work unless we're actually dying to fuck each other for real." He said this so nonchalantly you'd think we were talking about the history of steam engine design. Meanwhile, every time he made any kind of reference to us having sex, my clit would pulse against my silk underwear. If he was trying "to build tension," it was working beautifully. I already wanted him.

Over the next week Mikhail "let himself go" at Derek's instance. His character was supposed to slowly descend into madness. His facial hair, carefully monitored by the makeup crew, was beginning to cast just the right five o'clock shadow. It made him look more handsome than ever.

"Tomorrow I get to touch your breasts," he whispered into my ear a week and a half into filming—again, over the breakfast buffet. I almost dropped my *pain au chocolat* into my coffee. He'd walked a few paces ahead of me by this point. He stopped at the fruit platter and turned around to gauge my reaction, his mouth twitching into a playful smile.

I'd argued a long time with my agent about whether to do the nude scenes. Once you do them, there's no turning back. We squeezed an extra million dollars out of the deal. I'd already known at that point that Mikhail would be my costar and thought nothing of it—one giant, masculine mitt on your breast was bound to be the same as another. Wow, was I ever wrong! I was a wreck just thinking about it; Mikhail had a knack for making me feel like a nervous twit, even though he was only six years older.

The next morning, I thought I was going to throw up. This was by far the sexiest scene I'd ever done—and it was just the beginning. This had to go well; Derek was taking a huge chance on me.

I skipped breakfast. I didn't want anyone to know how nervous I was, and I knew Mikhail would see right through me. The last thing I wanted him to think was that I was a twittering, insipid American who squirmed at the mention of "boob."

Wardrobe fussed with my bodice for nearly an hour, opening and closing the front to make sure Mikhail wouldn't have problems. I tried to concentrate on something else, but every time Lisa from wardrobe grabbed the front laces with her hand to check if the tension was right, I pictured Mikhail doing the same. *How on earth had I agreed to this?* I debated calling my agent up and saying I hadn't been in my right mind when I'd signed the contract.

I looked at myself in the mirror one last time before making the five-minute trek to the set. My long, light brown hair was arranged in a messy updo, tendrils hanging haphazardly around my face. There was a distinct blush on my cheeks, and my lips looked abnormally moist. Normally, the makeup and costuming put me into character, made me forget myself; I became my character. But all I could think about was Mikhail, and not Marcel and Sandrine.

All the narrow streets were made of cobblestones; I walked onto the set in running shoes, with my billowy, multilayered gown bunched and balanced in my arms.

The set had been constructed in the actual castle, completely transformed to look as authentic as possible. The scene was to take place at the entrance to a tight, spiral staircase. Every eye turned in my direction as I bent down to replace my shoes. When I stood up again my gaze instantly found Mikhail's.

He was standing near the entrance to the staircase, wearing a long, tailored black overcoat, trim black pants with high boots, and a loose white shirt. He grinned. I readjusted the massive pile of fabric in my arms and walked over to him as confidently as I could.

"Wardrobe fixed the bodice issue?" Derek asked.

"Uh, yup," I mumbled.

"Listen," Derek continued, taking me aside. Mikhail's gaze followed us. I couldn't break our eye contact. "Mikhail and

I were talking yesterday. I think we need to alter the scene a little."

"Oh?" Out of the corner of my eye I could still see Mikhail watching us, his face still and observant.

"I know it's not in your contract, and I know I'm asking a lot here, but I think it'll work a lot better if Marcel actually kisses Sandrine's breast." He waited for the bomb to drop.

My mouth hung open. I felt cornered. I respected Derek's genius. I trusted his opinion; no fewer than four actresses had earned an Academy Award nomination through one of his films. But *kiss my breast?*

I looked at Mikhail. His expression was impossible to read. He walked over to us.

"Lydia?" Derek appeared concerned.

"Yup," I said, as Mikhail reached us and put his hand on the small of my back. The gesture was both protective and controlling at the same time. It had the perfect effect. I suddenly felt safe. If it had been anyone else—no way in hell!

"So will you try it?" Derek asked.

I looked at Mikhail again. He smiled and raised his left eyebrow ever so slightly. My eyes rested on his mouth. I imagined those full, wide lips on my actual, real, sensitive breast—not a prop, my *breast.*

"Oh, God," I whimpered. "Fine."

"That's our girl!" Derek slapped me on the shoulder. "Now remember, it's not binding. We don't have to use the scene. We'll shoot it both ways and see what works."

"Okay." I was down to monosyllables.

The three of us walked back to the staircase.

"Places everyone," Derek yelled. Everyone scrambled, leaving Mikhail and me on the set.

"So remember," Derek instructed, taking his place beside the cameraman. "You've just been forced to sit through an interminable dinner with the king. Marcel is furious with you, Sandrine, for entertaining the king's advances. You can't risk being caught with him or the gig is up. Ready?"

Derek waited a moment while I tried to concentrate myself into character. "Ready," I said.

"Okay, quiet everyone. And...rolling!"

"What in bloody hell was that?" Mikhail growled, grabbing me by the upper arm as I took my first step up the staircase.

"Get your paws off me! No man has, nor ever will, own me!" I squirmed away and went to take another step.

"This is not about ownership, and you know it!" He had me pinned against the wall, his mouth inches from mine. I could feel myself flitting in and out of character: brazen Sandrine one moment, breathless Lydia the next. I thought I detected Mikhail doing the same. We should have ended the scene and started again, but neither of us called it.

He went to kiss me. I dodged and turned my head to the side, as planned. He grabbed my bodice by the front laces with one hand and made me stare into his eyes. His knuckles pressed against my sternum, making the bodice constrict my breathing even more. I clutched at his hand.

"Don't you dare," I snarled. "If he catches us, it is done."

"So be it, then," Mikhail said, twisting the fistful of delicate silk so that the fabric gave.

I had expected my breasts to pop right out of the bodice. They didn't. The stiffness of the garment made it stay in place, my nipples still covered. Mikhail looked surprised, as well. We stared at each other, both of us clearly out of character. Then he slipped one hand into the bodice and cupped my breast, pressing me even farther against the cold wall with his thighs. I continued to stare at him. My heart was pounding. His eyes felt like knives. I was on the verge of calling for

Derek to cut. I knew it was Mikhail touching me, and not Marcel. I knew this was *us* playing the scene.

He ran his thumb gently, slowly over my nipple. I felt it spring to life under his touch. He angled the tip of his thumb so his nail grazed the erect nub, back and forth. We both knew that no one else could see this—this was not for the eventual viewer's pleasure. It was for mine. I leaned my head back and moaned, just as the script demanded. I was absolved of responsibility for my reaction.

Suddenly popping back into character, Mikhail squeezed my breast harder, tugging the bodice with his free hand. It slipped completely off, pinned between my hips and the wall.

"I don't care if you bed the fucking emperor himself," he said against my lips. "It will never change anything between *us*."

I still had a flimsy white batik shirt on, ripped down the middle, exposing my cleavage. Mikhail let go of my breast momentarily, seizing me by the shoulders. In one swift motion he pulled the shirt down around my waist, pinning my arms against my sides with the sleeves. I was completely topless to the waist. The wall against my back was freezing. I tried not to flinch. This felt so overwhelming, the last thing I wanted to do was start the scene all over again. I forced myself to stay with it.

"Stop this, Marcel." I tried to squirm away again, my voice hinting at the emotional torture of wanting something so badly you're ready to go to hell for it, but stopping yourself nonetheless.

We stumbled on the stairs. I turned around and tried to stand again, kicking at him as he easily pressed my breasts against the hard, cold stone steps. His weight nearly crushed me. Again I was on the verge of calling for Derek to cut, but didn't.

Mikhail wrapped his arms around my waist and turned me around so that I was facing him. The scene was supposed to be messy and turbulent. I began flailing my arms madly, managing to slap him, harder than I'd wanted, on the face. He grabbed my arms and pinned them to my sides, his torso now firmly wedged between my thighs. The voluminous gown twisted and bunched to the point where I could hardly move at all. We were both heaving and panting. This was quite the workout.

We stared at each other. The focus of my entire world had become condensed to Mikhail's eyes. I couldn't look away. It felt like drowning.

His mouth suddenly twitched, ever so slightly, into a mischievous half smile. I doubt the camera would have caught that look. But I knew what it meant. We were out of character again, playing ourselves. Then his mouth closed on my nipple.

The stone steps had been cold. The contrast with his warm mouth was shocking. He sucked and flicked his tongue against my erect nipple. He wasn't supposed to. And no one could see what his tongue was up to. Even without looking at him, I knew he was trying to hide his smile. A spiral of warmth spread from my nipple to my cunt. The costume was completely authentic, which meant loose pantaloons. I knew I was seeping all over them.

I arched beneath him. Weaving my hands in his hair, I pressed his head against me. He slipped one palm under my back and forced me to arch even more. I writhed as he took my breast farther into his mouth. I let out a low groan. I was dying for him to close his teeth on my nipple.

I wanted more—camera crew, bright lighting and ridiculous

costume be damned—but then Derek suddenly broke the spell.

"Okay, cut! That was awesome, you two," he said, walking over to us. Noise broke out again on the set as people started moving about.

Mikhail looked at me for a split second, during which I clearly saw how overwhelmed he was, as well. He looked a little stunned, actually. I took satisfaction in this.

I sat up on the step and covered my bare breasts with the thin shirt, holding it closed. At eye level with his crotch, I suddenly noticed what the mounds of fabric had obscured—Mikhail was completely aroused.

We made eye contact for another second. The amused, surprised look on my face said it all. He smiled and tried to adjust himself as discreetly as possible. I couldn't hold it in any longer and burst out laughing. His smile spread into a wide grin, as he scratched his eyebrow in embarrassment and turned away. I found the gesture endearing and charming; the man was human, after all.

"So we'll break and get your costume fixed up and try that again," Derek said, looking at me. "Except this time, really don't be afraid of one another, just—" he curled his fingers into taut claws "—just lay into each other."

"Only if you're trying to kill me," Mikhail mumbled under his breath.

"What?" Derek asked, his attention momentarily diverted by the cameraman on the stairs.

"Nothing. Sounds great," Mikhail said, holding out his hand out to help me up. I grabbed it gratefully.

"You sure you can handle it?" I teased as we walked away, looking pointedly at his crotch.

"Bring it on, you saucy wench," he replied with a smirk.

★ ★ ★

The next day was a free one for some of us. Mikhail found me at breakfast.

"A bunch of us are taking the Jeep and driving down to Collioure for the day. Are you coming?"

"Where's that?"

"It's a gorgeous little town on the Mediterranean. You can sunbathe topless," he proposed, a huge smile on his face.

My breasts had been in his mouth a total of seven times the day before—to the point of being slightly sore, Derek having demanded more and more fervor with every take.

"Haven't you had enough?"

"Not. Even. Close," Mikhail said against my ear. I noticed some of the crew eyeing us, but couldn't care less if tongues started wagging. I felt my cunt engorge with desire. *Two and a half more weeks of this and we* will *be ready to fuck each other for real, I thought.*

"When do we leave?"

Two hours later, we parked the Jeep in a drained canal near the beach and gathered up our stuff. There were five of us in total: Mikhail, myself, two of the cameramen and Lisa. It was a perfect June day, hot but not unbearable.

We found a spot just under the two-foot-high retaining wall. The charming, cobblestoned, terra-cotta-roofed town came right up to the small beach. Restaurants and cafés lined the sidewalk just behind us.

Mikhail was the first to strip down to his black Speedos.

"Oh my God," Lisa exclaimed, "I can't believe you *own* a pair of those! That is way too much information." She pretended to avert her eyes from the very prominent package displayed for all who cared to look.

"When in Rome." He shrugged casually, undeterred. "Do you even see anyone dressed in those horrendously baggy

American-style shorts? *No,*" he answered for her. "Nor will you."

I have to admit, as much as Americans make fun of the Speedo, Mikhail looked amazing. It was the first time I'd seen this much of his body; his costumes on set usually covered every inch of flesh except his face. He had a perfect swimmer's body: tall, lean and balanced in muscle tone. Not huge, but broad and substantial nonetheless. I immediately took off my summer dress and jumped up.

I saw him quickly scan my body in turn. This was the most he'd seen of me, as well. I was curious what would happen if he got a hard-on in that insignificant piece of stretchy fabric. *No better way to find out,* I thought, as I followed him into the water.

"Are you a good swimmer?" he asked as we waded into the sea.

"If we're planning on swimming to Croatia, then no."

"Just to that beach over there." He pointed to his right, not more than half a kilometer away.

The shoreline was rugged and dramatic. A huge medieval fortress rose straight out of the sea halfway to the other beach, framed by a serpentine walkway along the water's edge; giant rock outcroppings occasionally popped out of the waves. Looking toward the other beach I knew we'd be out of eyesight of the others within five minutes of swimming.

"Lead the way." I stood and waited with my hands on my hips. Mikhail dived in. I instantly followed.

We took it slowly, luxuriating in the feel of the cool water. When we rounded a three-meter-high rock, Mikhail grabbed me and pulled me up against it; we were at last out of view. He held on to the rough surface, his hands high above my head, while I wrapped my arms around his neck and just floated. I could already feel myself getting wet.

We stared at each other wordlessly. We both knew why we had separated from the group. This was the first time we were completely alone. He smoothed his wet, dark hair off his face and pinched droplets out of his eyes with one hand. I couldn't tear my gaze away from his mouth. I expected him to kiss me any second. Instead, he wrapped one hand around my torso and pulled the knot on my string bikini free; it floated up to the surface between us. He let go of the rock and dived under.

The shock of his hot mouth on my nipple sent seismic shivers through my body. He sucked and tugged on my nipple more roughly than he had on the set. Without him hanging on to the rock for support, we both slipped under the water.

With a limited air supply, we clutched at one another frantically until I had to resurface. He popped out, gasping for breath and laughing at the same time. We held eye contact and grew dreamy and intense again, our laughter dying down, our eyes clouding with desire.

He was hanging on to the rock behind us again with one arm. He slipped the other into the water. In the next second, I felt his hand cup my crotch. His eyes said it all. He looked ready to eat me alive.

I felt his fingers wrestle with the elastic on my bikini bottoms as he tried to push the tight fabric aside. Every accidental nudge of my clit with his fingers and knuckles made me jerk slightly, all my nerve endings ready to fire.

Finally, his hand cleared the fabric. He looked deep into my eyes as he plunged his fingers inside me, deep, and just held them there for a second. My instinct was to close my eyes and throw my head back. I kept staring into his eyes, though. I could feel the walls of my cunt close and contract tightly around his fingers as he began moving them—gently at first, then more insistently. The realization that Mikhail Sommerville was fingering me struck me at some point. I felt giddy.

Instinct took over. I put my hand under the water and placed it over his, forcing him to finger me even harder. He must have had at least three fingers inside me, creating a delicious pressure against the delicate walls of my cunt. I grabbed his wrist and forced him in deeper. *Screw this finger thing,* I thought at this point, *I want his cock inside me!*

"Want to continue this on solid ground?" he asked in a breathy voice, as though reading my mind.

"Oh, God, yeah."

He let go of the rock and swam out a few feet, treading water. My top had floated away by this point. I adjusted my bottoms and swam out to fetch it.

We were both desperate to reach land—and exhausted when we finally did. Heaving to get more air, I almost tripped over my own feet while wading out of the sea. Mikhail quickly grabbed my upper arm to steady me. The contact felt like a jolt of electricity.

Still panting, we fell onto the sand. Oblivious to the scattering of beachgoers, some with small children, we writhed like two coiled snakes until Mikhail was between my thighs. When we finally kissed, it was explosive. We tore into each other like there was no tomorrow. Our tongues thrust violently into one another's mouths, pushing the limits until I thought I would go insane. I pressed my cunt against his erection, adjusting my position until his cock ground against my clit with every movement, sending ripples of pleasure throughout my entire body. I was ready to strip and fuck right there on the beach, I wanted him that bad.

"Not here." Mikhail suddenly stopped and rolled off

me. "We're like sitting ducks for the paparazzi," he panted, recovering himself.

I didn't care if there were pictures of us on the cover of every tabloid. It would, no doubt, be great for *my* career. But I knew with Mikhail's messy divorce it would be a disaster for him. He never talked about his situation, not wanting to bring it on the set, but I could tell that Maxine's lawyers were putting him through the wringer.

"Let's go then," I said, smiling over at him. He grinned back, standing without a word.

The walk back to the others took us the long way, up and down the narrow, hilly streets. We tried to take the most secluded alleyways we could, bouncing from wall to wall as we devoured one another greedily like two stumbling drunks. Mikhail had to keep adjusting his erect cock so that it wouldn't pop right out of the top of his Speedo. At one point, I caught a glimpse of the head of his cock straining to get out. Not even thinking, I slid my index finger inside and gently circled its silky soft ridge. I was aching to take him in my mouth, fast and deep; I wanted to see his face in the throes of total, ecstatic surrender. It was understood that the second we were alone we were going to fuck each other into a senseless stupor.

As we rounded a corner, we found ourselves in a totally deserted, narrow alley. We looked at each other and smiled knowingly. This time I pinned *him* against the wall. As his back made contact with the bricks, I grabbed his hard-on through the fabric and squeezed. Mikhail sucked in his breath and groaned. I felt high, knowing I could elicit this kind of reaction from him. I was thrilled to note that it was quite the handful.

At the risk of getting caught by some unsuspecting tourist, I was about to whip his cock out and take it in my mouth, when Mikhail suddenly pushed me away from him so force-fully I hit the other brick wall.

"What ha—" I started to say, just as the flash of a camera went off, momentarily blinding me.

"Shit!" Mikhail swore as the man darted away.

He leaned against the wall and pinched the bridge of his nose.

"What part of that do you think he got?"

"We'll find out in three to four days, when the new tabloids come out," Mikhail said. "Fuck!" he exclaimed. "Her lawyers will have a heyday."

Sure enough, four days later, there were pictures of us all over *OK! Magazine, Hello!,* the *National Enquirer* and *In Touch.* They didn't get either the beach scene—not sure how they missed that one!—or his erect, Speedo-clad cock in my iron grip: we were at least a couple of feet apart, looking like deer in the headlights of an SUV. But they snapped tons of us walking—so close we could be Siamese twins—through Collioure, big grins on our faces. And they got Mikhail spreading sunscreen on me when we returned to the group.

"Fuck!" Mikhail swore, slapping a copy of *Hello* on the table as he joined me for lunch. We'd been lying low and avoiding each other ever since Collioure; everyone was now watching us so intensely, I felt naked all day long. "This can't happen again," he said, looking stressed and miserable. "Maxine's already taking me to the cleaners. I risk losing everything."

He was leaning back in his chair, his jaw tense and twitch-ing, his left hand on the table. At the risk of feeding the rumors further, I placed my palm gently on top of it. He looked at me and smiled grimly, sneaking his thumb up to rub my hand. I knew he was just as frustrated as I was; it made staying away from him more bearable just knowing that.

"Well," I said, quietly enough so that only he could hear, "at least we still get a go at each other on the set."

Predictably, with the next love scene that we shot, there was no need for Derek to urge us to "let the sexual fury come out," as he often termed it. After four days of nothing more than discreet glances and flirtatious subtext to all our conversations, Mikhail and I laid into each other so fiercely we both had bruises for days.

In this scene, Sandrine is the new queen. The king has just left to see to an important matter abroad. Oblivious to their history, the king makes Marcel Sandrine's personal guardian. Sandrine has been told that if she doesn't stop writing, queen or not, she'll be tried for witchcraft. Marcel has to convince her—or risk losing the only woman he's ever loved.

When I walked onto the set, I was shaking, knowing that in a matter of minutes I'd get to feel Mikhail's mouth on mine again.

Two wardrobe personnel were fixing something on his coat when I stepped through the door. Immobile, he turned his head slightly in my direction and made eye contact, his mouth curling into a wicked smile. For the previous four days, all I could think about was the feel of his fingers inside me. For the moment, his tongue would do.

The set was Sandrine's study. A massive wooden desk dominated the room, framed by floor-to-ceiling gilded bookcases all around.

"You okay?" Derek asked.

"Yeah, fine," I answered, forcing my eyes away from Mikhail. "Why?"

"You look..." he hesitated "...a little disturbed."

"No, no, I'm fine. Great."

He didn't appear convinced, but let it go. Wardrobe finished with Mikhail, who tugged on the sleeves of his coat and walked over to us. I had to let out a long, slow breath to steady myself, he looked so incredible. The costume was the typical long black overcoat, simple black trousers and a white shirt. His hair was raked casually off his face. He looked polished, yet reckless, sporting the same five o'clock shadow that was eventually to morph into a beard as his character went insane. I noticed that his walk changed when he was in costume; he looked more imposing, his stride longer, his body seeming to take up more space.

"I don't want to give you as much direction this time," Derek said to us. "I want to see what you instinctively do with this."

I nodded, trying to seem attentive. Mikhail stood right beside me. I felt as if I were being irradiated with his energy.

In flats, I barely cleared his chin. I couldn't resist tilting my head up and stealing a glance as Derek continued talking. Mikhail smiled, clearly aware that I was checking him out, but didn't look directly at me. My knees were already weak, and we hadn't even started.

"And how rough did you want this?" I heard him ask in his deep, melodic voice, snapping me out of my reverie. My stomach did a somersault. *Rough! Rough!* I wanted to scream. I'd been ready to claw the walls of my hotel room apart ever since Collioure.

"I don't want you decking one another or anything," Derek said. The three of us grinned. "But the scene is meant to be quite intense. Just go with it and we'll see how it turns out."

Derek cleared the space and made us take our positions.

I tried not to look at Mikhail for fear of completely losing character.

"Rolling!"

Mikhail began pacing about the room, his head downcast, his movements cagey and full of suppressed energy. I leaned against the desk, facing him, my arms crossed tightly across my chest.

"You have to stop, Sandrine!" He walked over to me and grabbed me by the shoulders, shaking me slightly.

"Fuck you!" I spat in his face, flinging his arms away from me and moving toward the window. "You above anyone else should know what the quill means to me! I will die if these thoughts—" I balled my hand into a fist and imitated small, successive punches to the head "—remain walled inside my brain, festering."

"Do you love your quill more than *this?*" He walked over to where I stood by the darkened window, grabbed my hand and forced me to seize his cock, staring into my eyes. I was stunned. This wasn't part of the scene. He was supposed to have said "more than *me.*" But Derek didn't say cut, so I went with it.

I bared my teeth and squeezed so hard I thought he'd faint. He didn't. In fact, his pupils—and his cock—both dilated with desire.

"What have I known of *this?*" I said, bringing my face as close to his as possible given the height difference, my hand still gripping his cock for dear life. I never wanted to let go. We were daring one another with our eyes to go further. We were so close I could feel his warm breath, coming in ragged bursts now, against my mouth. Three more inches and we'd be kissing—no, inhaling—one another.

"You bitch!" He pried my hand off. Lifting me clear of the ground, he easily covered the two meters to the desk, and laid me flat on it with a violent thud. "I was yours ten years ago! Look what you have done to me!"

This, also, wasn't in the script; we were taking some huge interpretive liberties here. I was surprised, but thrilled, and alive to the very tips of my toes. If a boyfriend ever tried this in private, charges would be laid. The set acted as a kind of buffer; I got all the thrill and none of the complicated reality.

I thrashed, bucked and kicked, holding nothing back. I wanted him to push the limits; I wanted to feel what it was like to be totally physically overpowered. I could sense my body silently daring him, urging him on. Every time he exerted more force in trying to handle me, I felt my cunt seep its juice all over my costume.

The contents of the desk went crashing to the floor as we struggled. Mikhail had my wrists in his hands as I flailed. I began to feel their circulation constrict, but I also knew he was holding back, afraid to inadvertently hurt me. I, on the other hand, was putting every fiber of muscle to work, and still couldn't manage to get off the desk. Mind you, the ridiculously heavy gown wasn't helping; I'd somehow whipped it into a straitjacket of a satin mess around my waist and legs.

Then, before I knew what was happening, Mikhail plunged one hand underneath all the mounds of satin, past the flowing pantaloons, past my engorged pussy lips, and straight inside.

"And what have I known of *this?*" he growled, not dropping a beat. "You have sold your cunt to the highest bidder and your soul to the devil." He withdrew his fingers an inch and pushed them back inside with such intensity I could hardly breathe.

I gasped and froze, staring at him in wide-eyed disbelief. He was actually daring to finger me right on the set!

Shocked, I checked my peripheral vision to gauge everyone's

reaction. No one had budged. I realized that with all the bunched fabric—Mikhail's arm was elbow deep in satin—and the way he had positioned himself between my thighs, no one could tell that he was actually inside me. I stared at him for a second, tacitly giving him the go-ahead, before I instinctively lay down and arched my back, my head against the desk.

He clearly knew what he was doing inside a woman's cunt; even under the pressure to remember his next line, Mikhail still curled his fingers upwards to hit my G-spot. Bright, clinical lights in my face or not, it felt incredible! Probably even more so because I was trying *not* to react too strongly and give the game away. Even if I'd wanted to, though, there wasn't much I could do without exposing us.

Torn between physical arousal and the terror of being found out, I alternated between low, guttural moans of pleasure and ineffectual attempts to free myself—exactly what the script called for.

Unfortunately, my mind had also gone blank with the first thrust. I didn't even know where we were in the scene, never mind recalling my line. The corner of Mikhail's mouth twitched up just a fraction into a smile. I could tell he was loving my utter and total uselessness.

"If you would rather die at the stake than give up your senseless rantings," he continued, bent over me on the desk, "then I might as well *take* what you have been withholding from me." He shoved his fingers in even deeper as he said the word *take,* upping the ante by rubbing my clit with his thumb. I didn't stand a chance. I could feel my brain slipping away. Every flick of his thumb sent electric jolts through my body. I was trying not to twitch too visibly. *How could they all not know?*

"I...I...Marcel, please," I begged, trying to shove him away, one hand pressed against his chest. I had to do something, fast! I knew Derek was going to yell "cut!" any second.

"So much to say on the page, all your passion reserved for a decrepit old king and your pen, while I have been dying a little for you each day," Mikhail said, not letting up one bit. *How was he managing to do this?*

His thumb continued to stroke and circle my clit. I could feel the sweet beginning of an orgasm deep in the pit of my stomach. I was aghast at the possibility of cumming in front of a dozen colleagues. The look in Mikhail's eyes told me how much fun he was having toying with me like this.

I squirmed more violently. Managing to plant one foot against his chest, I tensed my leg and gave him a powerful shove. Mikhail stumbled back, withdrawing his fingers from me so swiftly I gasped at the sensation against the delicate, wet walls of my cunt.

Spinning around, I grabbed a quill off the desk and brandished it like a knife, ready to strike.

"You want to kill me?" Mikhail growled, recovering. "Then do it!" He ripped his white shirt open partly down the front, grabbed my hand brandishing the sharp quill and made me bring it up against his chest. The sharp tip seemed to imbed itself slightly in his skin. My eyes flew up to his as a tiny spot of blood appeared beneath the black ink.

He took this instant to grab the quill out of my hand and throw it violently against the window.

"*This* is the only reality that matters," he said, shoving the two fingers that had been inside my cunt into my mouth.

I had just enough time to taste my own musky saltiness and note the look of total triumph in Mikhail's eyes, before he withdrew his fingers again, licked them himself like he would a melting Popsicle, and kissed me so hard I saw black spots dancing in front of my eyes.

"Okay! Cut!" Derek yelled.

Mikhail shoved his tongue quickly, desperately, into my mouth one final time, as though he hadn't heard Derek, before he went cool-as-a-cucumber blank.

The set was deathly silent. No one moved.

"Wow," Derek said quietly, rubbing his face with both of his hands, "I was starting to fear for your safety there."

People started moving about and the background noise steadily increased as we got ready for another take and camera angle.

I could feel my face burning up as I touched my cheek. I didn't dare look at Mikhail. Derek walked over to us, grabbed us both by the arms and dragged us over to the window, where we wouldn't be overheard.

"Okay, now tell me the truth." He stared intensely at Mikhail, then at me, his voice low and conspiratorial. "You actually did it, didn't you?"

My eyes went wide and instantly flew to Mikhail's. He met my look and smiled like a devilish child who just got away with a cookie. Putting his hands into his pockets, he angled his chin down and looked back at Derek unapologetically. I was mortified.

"No, no, it's fine." Derek put his hand on my shoulder and quickly reassured me, seeing the stricken look on my face. "Great, actually." He grinned at Mikhail, who raised and lowered his eyebrows rapidly, like a casual shrug of the shoulders, and glanced out the window, his smile deepening. "Good to know," Derek added finally, more to himself, before walking away. I should have guessed right at that moment what he was cooking up.

★ ★ ★

Three days before we were due to shoot our last love scene, Derek took Mikhail and me out for dinner to a small, unpretentious bistro in Perpignan.

Mikhail had just come back from a three-day trip to Paris, looking totally burned out. Apparently, Maxine's lawyers were threatening to take away his childhood London home. I'd noticed myself getting completely neurotic in his absence, lying awake at two o'clock in the morning, imagining him with someone else. After all, what did I really know about his life outside the set? He was intensely private to begin with, and we were still trying to avoid fueling the gossip train, by keeping our distance.

To my intense relief, his face broke into a huge grin the moment we saw each other again at lunch that same day.

"Lydia," he'd stated in greeting, his tone playful and seductive.

"Mikhail," I answered, staring up at him from under my lashes, trying not to give away how flustered I felt. The banality of our greeting belied, yet enhanced, the intense emotional dynamic between us.

"Hope you've been keeping busy in my absence," he said, grabbing a couple of croissants from a basket.

"You can say that." I'd masturbated myself to sleep the night before, imagining what it would be like to have him tie me to the bed and go down on me.

Sitting beside him in the bistro, his thigh touching mine, I found flashes of my fantasy come back to me. I saw his head descend slowly between my thighs, his hands curled around my legs to keep them spread apart. He looked at me for a second, his eyes hungry. I felt his hot breath against my pussy. His tongue slithered between my pussy lips and gently pushed a fraction of an inch inside the opening. I felt my clit throb and respond, aching for—

"I did have a reason for taking you both out tonight—" Derek broke into my fantasy "—other than to enjoy wonderful food together."

Mikhail and I exchanged a glance; he looked intrigued, I felt perplexed. A part of me was still terrified Derek would tell me I sucked, and that they needed to find someone else to play my part. I couldn't shake feeling like an impostor.

"There's no way to really sidle up to this question, so I'll just go ahead and ask." He paused for a moment, taking a sip of his wine, choosing his words carefully. "I was very impressed with the last love scene you both did. The passion was so palpable I'm sure you pitched more than a couple of tents—sorry to be crass." He took another sip of wine. "So, in short, I'd like you to consider actually making love in the final scene."

There it was. Hollywood's dirty little secret: on rare occasions, even really famous actors fuck for real on the set. When the rumors start to fly, like they did when *The Lover* came out, everyone always vehemently denies it.

My heart sped up. There was nothing on earth I wanted more than to have Mikhail's cock inside me. *But on a movie set?* Even with the set cleared, there would still be at least six people watching, the lights would be garish, Derek would be shouting orders. Sex was also a bit like dancing; you entered a trance and your true personality came out. Did I really want a group of strangers watching? Could I even let go enough to do my powerful attraction for Mikhail justice? If I was a lousy fuck under these circumstances, would he lose interest? Each question exploded into a million others; my head was reeling.

Then I looked at Mikhail and they all disappeared.

He leaned back in his chair, the arm closest to me draped across the back. Not surprisingly, he was the picture of equanimity. He spread his legs slightly and stared at me wordlessly. His eyes said it all—the ball was in my court.

"Of course I don't need to say this," Derek interjected, "but the set will be closed. I'll see what I can do about the lighting. We'll shoot everything else first and then I'll just let you two do it—I promise to keep my mouth shut for the whole take. And…" he looked at Mikhail conspiratorially "…naturally, given, um, physiological logistics, there will only be one take. If it doesn't work then we'll just let it go."

The reference to Mikhail possibly cumming inside me turned my knees to Jell-O. I imagined what his face might look like, how his cock would pulse inside me, how his thighs would instinctively contract, making him thrust deeper.

"I'm going to let you two talk it over for a minute while I go to the washroom." Derek stood up and left.

Even before Derek's back was fully turned, my eyes were already seeking Mikhail's.

"Have you ever done this before?" I asked tentatively.

He shifted his position. Resting his forearms on the table, he looked at me from under dark, enviably thick lashes. The way he gazed at me was always intense, a little intimidating, but even more so now.

One corner of his mouth jerked up slightly. "Have sex? Yes." His grin widened.

"You know that's not what I mean."

He took a sip of his wine. "What is your hesitation?"

"Why are you *not* hesitating? He's basically asking us to do porn. If your wife's lawyers get a whiff of this you can kiss your London home goodbye."

"No one will ever see me sliding inside you," he said in a low, seductive tone. I gasped, not expecting him to be so blunt. "It's more about the emotion than the money shot. I trust Derek," he continued. "He has a lot of integrity, and the others on the set blab at the risk of never working in the industry again."

Derek was taking his time. I looked away and gulped down the rest of my wine. "Convince me," I finally said, putting my glass down and looking squarely at Mikhail again, challenging him with my eyes.

His mouth slid into a sultry smile as he leaned in. "I can make you feel so good you'll forget your own name. Life's about adventure, right? Every time you see this movie you'll remember how amazing and alive you felt making love to me. How much will that be worth when you're ninety years old?"

Over the next two days, Derek, Mikhail and I rehearsed the scene on a closed set in between filming. Sandrine has been condemned to burn at the stake for witchcraft and treason. She's being held prisoner in her own bedroom. Marcel bursts in suddenly, barricading the door behind him as others clamor outside to stop him. Sandrine is in a thin nightdress, her hair loose and wild; clearly she's on the brink of insanity. Practically every inch of space is covered in loose sheets of paper; she's been writing furiously for two days. When she sees him, she breaks down, flying into his arms.

The day of filming, as I ate my breakfast, I noticed how differently the crew looked at me, speaking in hushed whispers and sidelong glances. I knew that they knew. I was relieved and grateful when Mikhail finally showed up. He grabbed his croissant and coffee and sat down beside me as though it was any other day. He really was a superb actor; this was why they paid him the big bucks. I couldn't pull off the same kind of unruffled, almost bored, composure to save my life.

He unfurled a newspaper, leaned back and sipped his espresso. I spread jam on my croissant, strengthened by his calm.

"Looks like Sarkozy's approval rating has dropped," he said, glancing up at me.

When our eyes met, I knew he didn't give a shit about French politics. The look in his eyes was impossible to define, but it made my insides feel warm and light. It was as though he was already reaching deep inside me. I felt him infuse every pore of my body. With every flicker of emotion in his eyes, I was spreading my legs wider, taking him in deeper; physical consummation was just a formality at this point.

"Ready?" he said matter-of-factly, after half an hour of ordinary breakfast conversation.

I could feel my body begin to shake imperceptibly from nerves, excitement, and being so turned on I wanted to scream. "Ready," I said just as casually, standing up to follow him out as though we were headed on a grocery errand, and not on our way to fuck in front of strangers.

We walked down to makeup and wardrobe together. The tension was so thick you could spread it on a cracker. Right before we parted, Mikhail put his hand on the small of my back.

"Lydia."

"Yeah?" I turned toward him, about to ascend the steps to the trailer.

"Relax and trust me," he whispered into my ear. I felt the flutter of arousal in the pit of my stomach and felt my pussy get ready for him. I didn't see him again until we were on the set.

"And, rolling!"

We'd already shot every other angle and done about twenty

PG-13 takes of the scene—underwear that's made of clear material in the back, and a flesh-toned patch covers the front—when Derek clears the set.

My extremities tingle. I can feel the adrenaline surge like an injection. I pace madly around the room, grabbing random pages off the floor, quickly scan them, then throw them away, my character clearly losing her marbles. A commotion happens just outside the heavy wooden door—people shout, the door rattles, Mikhail bursts in. I stand up, frozen in place, my eyes wide. Without looking at me, he bolts the door and drags the heavy desk in front of it. When he turns toward me, his breathing is labored, his body tense, and he seems to fill the room completely with his energy. He's grown a modest beard at this point. His hair is longer and almost as disheveled as mine. He stares at me with such intensity, I momentarily imagine he's going to eat me whole.

We stand cemented to the floor for five of the longest seconds of my life as the camera slowly moves on its tracks. We'd decided to try one uninterrupted take. I can see Derek and the other five remaining crew members out of the corner of my eye; I attempt to wipe them out of my awareness, concentrating on Mikhail as though he's the only one in the room.

Wordlessly, we cover the four meters separating us, colliding at the midpoint in an explosive kiss. My legs feel as if they're filled with helium; I don't know how I'm managing to move at all. I entwine my fingers in his hair. Mikhail encircles my waist in a viselike grip. He feels solid as a brick wall as he holds me. His mouth is warm as I hungrily push my tongue inside and circle and thrust; he does the same. Our lips become moist and slippery from our mixed saliva. We keep going back in for more, greedily lapping at one another. I can't help making incoherent moaning noises against his mouth.

I sense rather than witness his lips curling up slightly into a smile. He knows I'm lost, giving myself over to him, to us. *Finally!* every inch of my body wants to scream. A month of driving each other nuts comes to a head at last.

He pulls away, still holding on to my chin with his thumb and forefinger, forcing me to look into his eyes. I can practically hear him inside my brain, telling me in his deep, sensuous voice to lose myself, to ignore the fact that we're being watched, to let my body feel good. Nerve endings aren't familiar with the concept of "acting," after all.

Taking his hand away from my face, but still forcing me to keep eye contact, he undoes the laces on the front of my nightdress. I'm completely naked underneath, having removed the studio underwear during the break—and I know Mikhail is, as well.

The neckline is loose to begin with; when he pulls on either side of the front opening, the nightgown slips off in a delicate fluttering of fabric that pools at my feet. I stand naked in front of him. I can feel myself getting so wet I'm sure I'm dripping down my legs. My nipples harden just from the way he looks at them. His eyes rake quickly over every inch of exposed skin. I don't even need to note the evidence to know he's hard as a rock; I can see it in his eyes.

He flings his overcoat off and tears at the buttons on his shirt. I attempt to help, my fingers fumbling. He's shirtless in seconds, and smooth as marble, other than a treasure trail that invitingly disappears into his pants. Instinctively, my mouth descends on the satiny skin of his chest. I bite down when I reach one nipple. He inhales sharply. All I want to do is go down on my knees and pull his cock out and take it in my mouth as deep as I can. But, unfortunately, that *would* be porn; I try not to even think about it as I undo the string on his pants.

I know that any direct frontal of Mikhail's erect dick will be cut. I don't even try to angle my body in front of the camera to block the view. I pull his pants down and let my eyes drink him in. The sight of his engorged cock almost sends me over the edge. He stands there, shameless—confident, in fact. Out of the corner of my eye, I can see the crew getting agitated. I thought it would paralyze me to be watched like this. I'm stunned to observe the exact opposite—it adds to my arousal. I love that the cameramen can see how hard I've made Mikhail. I love knowing that they're all also staring at his bare cock, waiting to see what we'll do.

"Take me in your mouth," he groans softly, almost incoherently, against my lips. We're suddenly standing buck naked against each other, his cock sandwiched between our torsos.

Stunned, I inhale quickly and sharply against his open mouth. *"What?"* I heard him the first time—I just can't believe he said it.

"Do it," he murmurs, still kissing me.

"But—"

"Now."

Oh my God! I can't believe I'm even considering this! I stare up into his eyes. I suddenly grasp how kinky and wicked Mikhail really is—he's going to push this as far as he possibly can. I momentarily straddle the line between the safe and familiar, and the dangerous, dark place Mikhail is asking me to enter. I draw a sharp breath and drop on my knees. I can hear a couple of gasps of shock from behind me, but no one moves a muscle.

I take hold of his hard cock in my hand, squeezing down on the shaft, watching the head fill even more with blood. The skin's impossibly soft, like velvet. I open my mouth and slide down on him like a slippery glove, taking him in as far as he'll

go. I savor the feel of the head moving past my lips toward the
back of my throat. I withdraw all the way to the tip, lick long
and hard all around the head, and take him in deep again.
I hear someone choke with stunned disbelief; I grin against
Mikhail's cock for a split second. I repeat the motion a couple
more times, each time more abandoned, licking his cock like
a pro, before I pull away completely. I deliberately let a thin
string of saliva and precum linger between us as I stand up.

Mikhail grins, clearly exhilarated, his eyes swimming with
lust. I don't get a chance to do anything else, for in the next
instant he grabs me by the ass and lifts me up against his
body, making me wrap my legs around his waist. His cock is
now between his pubic bone and my pussy. With every step
he takes toward the bed I feel his dick press against my clit,
wedged between my pussy lips.

"Fair's fair," he says against my mouth as he lays me down
backward on the giant, four-poster bed.

Before I grasp what he's talking about, his head is between
my legs. I imagine the crew's a little confused about what
we've discussed with Derek, and what we're getting away
with—and I know Derek won't interrupt us. The ambigu-
ity lets us do anything. I don't fight Mikhail. He flattens
his tongue against the length of my pussy, almost cupping it
whole. I jolt against the bed, bending my head back, when
his tongue digs into my clit. His mouth feels so hot it's like
I'm being scalded—or maybe it's my cunt that's burning up.
His facial hair pricks my delicate skin; I relish the contrast
with his soft, wet mouth.

Mikhail circles and twists his tongue against my cunt in
long, lavish strokes. I let out a low, guttural moan, my arms
above my head now, hands raking and clutching at the bed-
cover. It feels so intense, I start to writhe and twist. Mikhail
grabs my legs and spreads them wide, increasing the pressure

of his tongue—now I know why they call it "eating out." He slips his tongue right inside and I think I'm going to go insane from the pleasure. He twists his tongue around against the inner walls of my pussy. I instinctively try to squeeze my thighs on his head like a vise, but he won't let me; digging his fingers into my thighs, he forcefully keeps them open.

Just when I think I can't bear any more, he stands up, grabs my waist with both his hands and turns me around. In the next instant, I feel his body flatten me against the bed. I'm bent over the edge, my toes touching the ground. He coils one hand around my hair at the nape of my neck and pulls slightly. Inserting one leg between mine, he spreads them farther. I'm breathless. I know he's about to slide his cock inside. I feel the head wait between my pussy lips for an instant.

Even as I concentrate on Mikhail, a part of me imagines what it must be like to be one of the crew, watching us fuck; it's almost as if I'm being fucked by seven people. The thought arouses me so much I try to buck against Mikhail to force him inside. He contracts and pushes in so quickly that I gasp. He fills me so completely, I can't tell where he ends and I begin— until he starts to move inside me. I've wanted this from the moment I laid eyes on him in the café. I voluntarily squeeze the inner walls of my cunt around his cock, increasing the delicious pressure and friction.

I keep squeezing my cunt around him as he slides in and out. I'm so ridiculously wet by this point, there's no resistance. Each thrust gets harder and harder. I'm dying to turn around and have him suck on my nipples, touch my clit as I ride him, grab me by the waist and pull me down on him. I've totally lost my rational brain at this point, and all I can think of is other ways Mikhail can bite, tug, spank and tease my flesh. And I love that they're watching every single stroke. I slide one knee up on the bed. I want them to see his cock going inside my pussy. I've never felt so scandalous, and I want to milk it for all it's worth. I want to shock them, make them all hard or wet. I want them to see my pussy dripping its juice all over his cock as he pulls out.

I want more. I reach behind me, grab his hand and make him squeeze my breast. It satisfies me for about two seconds, then I want even more. I grab his hand again and make him reach around my waist to my clit. I can almost feel him smile. With his index finger, he circles my clit while still fucking me from behind. The sensation of his cock deep inside, my burning clit and the knowledge that six people are watching us sends me right over the edge. My hand flies on top of his again, and I make him press so hard on my clit I'm sure I'm going to have bruises. I can't help screaming as I feel the spasms of orgasm rock me, blood pulsing back into the rest of my body again.

"My turn," he whispers against my ear, even I twitch with the last of the contractions.

He pulls out and turns me around to face him. I'm spent and languid, letting him do whatever he wants. I meet his smoldering eyes again. He slides a hand under my waist, lifting my ass slightly off the bed, and plunges his cock inside. I'm so wet after cumming that he can thrust as hard as he wants without hurting me. I start moving rhythmically against his thrusts, forcing him in even deeper.

He grins languorously for a second. He looks so sexy, I want to consume him. I start to moan loudly with every thrust. I want them to know how amazing it feels to have his cock inside me. "Oh, God! Fuck me!" I scream, my spine arched and my head thrown back against the bed. He complies. I know he's close to orgasm. I want to feel him explode inside me. And I know just what will throw him over the edge. I grab his left hand, the one the camera can't quite see, force him to look into my eyes, and guide his hand around toward my ass. I can tell that he instinctively understands what I want, what I know he wants. His grin widens lazily as he slides a finger inside my ass. It feels raunchy and wrong and wonderful all at the same time. He barely manages to move his finger in and out of my ass three times before he screams incoherently and cums deep inside me. He stifles his moan halfway through by sticking his tongue inside my mouth again. I kiss him back hungrily while his orgasm fades.

As I regain my ability to think, I already know that he was right—I can't wait to have the world watch me fuck him.

★ ★ ★ ★ ★

HER LORD AND MASTER

Jennifer Dale

PART ONE

MOLLY GRIPPED THE SILVER TRAY TIGHTLY AS SHE hurried down the hall. Though the food needed to arrive warm, it wouldn't do to spill the master's breakfast. She was newly come to Ashford Hall, and wanted to make a good impression. Fortunately, the door she sought was just ahead. Reaching her destination, she balanced the tray precariously with one hand and quietly rapped on the panel.

Through the wood she heard an indistinct bellow, then the door swung open. A handsome young man with blond hair and green eyes stood before her. Surely this couldn't be the master. Though he was impeccably dressed, he lacked the arrogance she'd already come to associate with the aristocracy. Molly surmised that this was his lordship's valet. He put his finger to his lips and then stepped back to allow her to enter the room.

The suite was a disaster. She nearly tripped over a pair of shining Hessian boots as she walked across the room, looking for a place to set the tray. Every available surface was covered with trunks and bandboxes, all of them overflowing with cravats, hose and other items of masculine clothing. As she stood there, bewildered, the valet tiptoed over to the enormous four-poster bed in the middle of the room.

"Breakfast, my lord," he whispered.

"Don' wan' any!" The reply came from a covered lump on the bed.

Molly just stood there holding her tray, unsure what to do. Finally, the valet came over and scooped a pile of clothing off a cherrywood writing desk, accidentally knocking an inkwell to the floor. Another loud bellow, this time quite clear, came from the bed.

"Plunkett! Quit that infernal racket!"

On the heels of this exclamation, two pillows came sailing across the room. The valet, burdened only by his master's clothing, was quick enough, or experienced enough, to step out of the way. Molly, however, was not so lucky. Both pillows crashed into the tray she held, sending tea and scones flying to the floor. The crash of breaking china seemed to further enrage the figure on the bed.

"By all the saints and sinners! Get out!"

Apparently deciding that discretion was the better part of valor, the valet beat a hasty retreat, still clutching his master's clothes. Molly froze for a moment, then knelt quietly and began picking the remnants of the master's breakfast off the floor. If she left a puddle of tea and porcelain, there'd be hell to pay from Mrs. Hutchins.

"Are you deaf, gel?"

Molly tried to ignore the commanding voice, and continued using her apron to mop up the tea.

"You must be deaf."

She took a deep breath, stood up and turned to face her master, who was now sitting up in bed, and nearly stumbled as her knees went weak. He was as beautiful as an angel—well, a fallen angel maybe, with his long dark hair and fiercely slanted eyebrows. Even from across the room, his flashing blue eyes seemed to bore a hole straight through her.

She summoned up her courage enough to reply, "No, my lord."

"Well, then, since we've established that Mrs. Hutchins has not taken to employing deaf-mutes in my household, I must assume that you are just stupid!"

"I beg your pardon, my lord."

"I said *'Get out!'*"

"Yes, my lord, but…"

He arched one of his perfect eyebrows. Molly swallowed nervously, then blurted, "Begging your pardon, my lord, but Mrs. Hutchins would turn me off if I left a mess in your lordship's room."

"Aren't you afraid I'll turn you off myself, gel?"

"Yes, my lord." She bowed her head, staring at her shoes, waiting…hoping he wouldn't sack her.

"Fine, fine, you may clean it up," he said, waving a hand idly at the mess.

"It'll just take me a moment, my lord, and then I'll bring you another tray," she told him.

"'S'truth, gel, I didn't even want the first one." He sat back in the bed and promptly banged his head on the wooden headboard. "Bloody hell!"

Molly thought privately that her new master was altogether too fond of cursing. *He swears like a tar,* she thought. In fact, Molly had yet to meet a sailor, swearing or otherwise. Though there was a smithy in the village who was well-known for his colorful cursing.

Still, the master hadn't sacked her, so who cared if he swore or not? She grabbed the pillows off the floor. Luckily, they had missed the strawberry jam, and there didn't seem to be any tea stains on them. She hurried over to the bed. "Here, my lord, please allow me."

He sat back up, and allowed her to tuck the pillows behind his head. The coverlet fell slightly as he moved, further exposing his broad shoulders and well-muscled chest. Molly felt a tingle between her legs as she stared at his perfect physique. When she adjusted the pillows, her breast accidentally brushed against his upper arm. A spark seemed to leap between them, and she quickly pulled back. But before she could step away, he grabbed her wrist. "How is it that I've not seen you before?" he asked.

"I have only been at Ashford Hall for a fortnight," she replied.

"Ah, that it explains it then. I've been in Scotland for a month," he said. "Shooting pheasants."

"Yes, my lord."

"What's your name, gel?"

"Molly, my lord."

"Well, Molly, I suppose, as your new master, I should officially welcome you to Ashford Hall," he said. There was no time to protest as he pulled her into his embrace and his mouth came down on hers. Molly had been kissed before by boys of the village, but the kisses of those callow youths could hardly compare to the kiss of an experienced rake like the master. He nearly took her breath away with the touch of his lips.

His arms tightened around her, and he pulled her more firmly onto his lap. He teased her bottom lip with his tongue, licking her and nipping her with his teeth, until she gasped. Then, quick as lightning, his tongue was in her mouth, twining hungrily with her own.

One of his hands slid down her back, to her hip, then continued along her leg, past her knee, to rest lightly on her stocking-clad ankle. She felt the warmth of his hand burning through the cotton stocking and into her skin like a brand. No man had ever touched her like this…actually, no man had ever touched her at all. So she was unprepared for the molten heat she felt as his hand stroked her ankle.

Just then, there was a knock at the door. Molly struggled against the muscled arms that held her, but it was like fighting against bands of iron. The master ignored both the knock and her resistance, and went on plundering her mouth with his tongue. The knock came again; finally, he pulled his lips away from hers.

"What is it?" he asked angrily.

"My lord," his valet called, "Mr. Lambert is downstairs. He has been cooling his heels in the drawing room for a quarter of an hour, my lord."

"Ballocks!"

This time Molly barely registered the cursing. The master looked down at her, his blue eyes sparkling like twin sapphires, and gave her a quick buss on the mouth. "We will have to continue this later, my dear. I have some urgent business with my solicitor to attend to."

Molly just stared up at the face of the dark angel, still too stunned to move, until the master set her on her feet again and gave her a quick pat on the ass. She jumped away and scurried toward the breakfast dishes still lying on the floor, but not before she got a full view of the master's splendid body as he rose, naked, from the bed. His shoulders were wider than even those of the swearing blacksmith from the village. Below them, his flat abdomen tapered to long, muscular legs, and nestled between them among dark curls was his thick cock. She blushed furiously at the sight of him. Nonchalantly, he strode over to a nearby chair, grabbed a silk dressing gown and donned it before saying, "Come in."

The door to the room swung open and the valet came in, a basin and towel in hand, as Molly was gathering the last of the mess from the floor. The master sat in a chair while his man prepared to shave him. She quickly scampered to the door, but couldn't help turning to ask, "Will there be anything else, my lord?"

"No, that will be all..." he replied, but then one eye dropped lazily in a wink "...for now."

Molly's cheeks were still hot and red as she rushed from the room and down the hall. She could scarcely believe what had just happened. She dreaded having to explain the broken china to Mrs. Hutchins. The cost would likely come out of her meager wages. But even worse than the shattered dishes was her shattered peace of mind. The master had kissed her! What was she to do? Maybe she was making too much of the incident. Maybe it had been just a welcoming gesture. She decided that it would be best to pretend it had never happened.

She hurried to the kitchen and scraped the leftover scones into the slops pail. Then she set the tray on the counter. Fortunately, there was no sign of the cook or Mrs. Hutchins. Still, Molly knew she would never be able to conceal her mishap. She washed the dishes, including the broken bits of crockery, and then dried and put away the still-intact pieces. The remains she wrapped up in a towel and set on the counter. She would explain the accident to Mrs. Hutchins, but the rest she would keep to herself.

By the time she crawled into her garret bed that evening, Molly had almost forgotten the events of the day. But that night her dreams were plagued with memories of brilliant sapphire eyes and fierce kisses.

Several days passed before she again encountered the master face-to-face. She was polishing the banister in the front hallway when he came in from riding. Holding her breath, she dipped him a curtsy as he approached, sure he wouldn't recognize her. Or that if he did, he wouldn't bother with her. She held the curtsy as he strode on past her, but then she felt his hand graze her hip. Still, he didn't stop. She sighed, her relief tinged with disappointment, as she heard him continue on up the stairs, and she resumed her polishing.

An hour or so later, she entered the library to continue her dusting and polishing. Of all the rooms in the house, she liked this one the most. Though she could barely read the stories contained in them, she loved the books and the rich leathery smell of their bindings; she didn't even mind climbing the tall ladders to reach the highest shelves. She was perched atop one of these ladders, dusting, when she heard someone enter the room. She turned slightly, and nearly fell off the ladder when she saw the master's brilliant blue eyes looking up at her. Thinking he wouldn't care to be disturbed, she started down the ladder.

"I beg your pardon, my lord. I'll come back later."

"No."

"My lord?"

"I shan't be disturbed in the least. Go ahead and do your chores."

"Yes, my lord."

Molly took a deep breath to steady herself, and set back to work. She ran her feather duster along the top shelf, and tried not to stare at the master as he browsed the shelves. It was hard not to look. He hadn't yet bothered to change his clothes from his ride. His dark hair was tousled and windblown, his Hessian boots were dusty, and his normally perfect and starched cravat was wilted. Strangely enough, she preferred this disheveled look to his normal sartorial splendor. It made him seem more human, more approachable. Not that she would ever dream of approaching him unless summoned.

It seemed, however, that the master had different ideas. While she worked, he came closer and closer to the base of the ladder. Before she knew it, he had mounted the first rung, his weight making it shift beneath her. She hoped he was only looking for a book. He took another step up the ladder. Her hopes were dashed when she felt his hand close on her ankle. Another step, and his hand crept higher beneath her skirts.

"I never got to finish welcoming you to Ashford Hall," he told her. "I think it is time we remedy that situation."

She knew she should flee, but he had her cornered, and he was the master. Truthfully, her desire to escape was weak. Secretly, she longed for the strange tingling sensations she felt whenever she saw him, or whenever she was near him. She wanted the warmth of his hands on her naked skin. So she stood there, staring at the books, and let him touch her.

She could feel his hard, lean body press against her as he climbed up the ladder. It inflamed her almost as much as the pressure of his hand on her leg. His fingers wandered up, stroking the curve of her calf and the sensitive spot behind her knee, before toying with the knot of her garter. When his hand moved higher across the bare skin of her inner thigh, brushing against the muslin of her undergarments, she thought she would swoon. Then, without so much as a word, he sought the slit in her drawers.

Her whole body shivered as the master's deft fingers parted her damp curls and found her clitoris. She nearly fell off the ladder when he stroked her there, but she soon relaxed under the gentle yet insistent pressure he brought to bear. Before long, her sex grew hot and wet as he rubbed slow circles against her flesh. He touched and teased her until her body was at a fever pitch. Then, he slowly slid one long finger into her snug sheath, eliciting a gasp from Molly.

He withdrew his digit from her tight passage, stroked her clit once again, then gradually slipped his finger back in. Over and over he probed the depths of her warmth. As she grew wetter, his pace increased, until he was thrusting his finger in and out of her cunny rapidly, while she struggled to keep her balance and her sanity. Soon, she could feel an unfamiliar need building within her body. She writhed against his hand as he continued to plunge his finger deep inside her. All her fears of toppling from the ladder were forgotten as she concentrated on the novel sensations he was causing.

Soon, her breath grew ragged and her heart raced as her body climbed toward fulfillment. Then, like the sun bursting through the clouds, something burst deep within her, and wave after wave of warm, golden pleasure swept over her. She grabbed at the top shelf to keep from falling from the ladder, but there was no need. His arm was around her, steadying her, as he buried his face in her skirts, while his other hand continued to stroke her, sending tremors through her body.

Finally, just when she thought she could stand it no longer, the stroking stopped. His hand slowly withdrew and she felt a trickle of moisture run down her thigh. Molly felt the ladder creak under his weight. Then, without saying another word to her, he was gone. She barely heard the click of the latch as the door closed behind him. Still she stood there, too shaken to move.

Nothing she'd ever experienced could compare to the pleasure she'd just been shown. Now she understood why some of the other serving girls stole away to meet their lovers behind the stables. Still, Molly knew that all pleasure had its price, and she was afraid what that price might be. Her job perhaps, or worse, her virtue. What could she do? She needed this job, yet if she ever wanted to marry well, she needed her virtue too. Losing either was not a happy proposition. She could only hope that the master would lose interest in her. In the meantime, she had work to do.

After finishing in the library, she went into the morning room to dust and polish. It was there that Mrs. Hutchins found her a quarter of an hour later.

"Molly?"

"Yes, ma'am."

"You are required in his lordship's room," the housekeeper informed her.

Molly's stomach fluttered at the mention of the master. "Is something amiss, ma'am?"

"Not precisely."

"May I ask what I'm to do then, ma'am?"

The housekeeper looked at her sadly and clucked her tongue. "Come sit down for a moment, Molly."

Molly was confused. Though Mrs. Hutchins was no termagant, she was strict. It wasn't like her to coddle her girls, and so such kindness made Molly wary. Still, she sat obediently, perched on the edge of a delicate chaise across from Mrs. Hutchins, who was seated on a nearby sofa.

"I came to this house when I was younger than you," the housekeeper began. "I was the tweenie. Then his lordship took note of me—that is the seventh viscount, not the current one. Soon, I was promoted to an upstairs maid, and after that I became the housekeeper."

Molly nodded, not sure what to say.

"Do you understand what I'm getting at, my girl?"

"Not really, ma'am."

Mrs. Hutchins sighed. "Ah, you are such an innocent." She leaned closer. "I was one of the viscount's light o' loves. At least until he was forced by his family to marry."

Molly gasped. "What about Mr. Hutchins?"

"There was no Mr. Hutchins until after the viscount was wed."

"But why are you telling me all this?"

"I thought that'd be clear to you, my girl. The master has decided he wants you to be his personal maid."

"What does that mean?"

"Don't be daft. It means he wants to bed you."

"He told you that?" Molly was shocked. It seemed that the master hadn't lost interest in her at all.

"Of course he didn't tell me right out," Mrs. Hutchins continued, "but I've been around the nobility long enough to know what he wants. If you have no interest in being his dollymop, just say so, and I'll make sure of it."

"Would you send me away?"

"I'd help you find another position."

"Do I have to decide right now?"

"The sooner the better. The choice won't change no matter how long you wait, and the master said he wanted to see you in his chambers right away."

"I can't decide, not like this."

"He'll be calling for you…"

Molly's heart beat wildly in her chest. This was exactly the choice she'd been dreading. On the one hand, she could spurn her master, saving her virginity for the man she would marry, whoever that might be, and lose her position in this house. On the other hand, she could succumb to the burning caresses of a man who stirred her blood, and in doing so, lose her last shreds of honor and dignity.

Again she wished that there was someone she could talk to, someone she could confide in. Mrs. Hutchins was being kind, but she'd made it plain what she thought Molly should do. And why not? It had worked out for her. Or had it? "Mrs. Hutchins, may I ask you something?" she queried.

"Of course, dear."

"The seventh viscount? Did you love him?"

Mrs. Hutchins looked as though she was about to cry. "With every fiber of my being, until the day he died." She turned away.

"And what about Mr. Hutchins?"

"Aye, I loved him, too. He was very good to me."

Molly knew she had her answer. She left the chaise and walked toward the door. "I'll be in the master's chamber." With that, she left the room and began the long climb up the staircase. She walked down the hall, then stood in front of the familiar door. With shaking hands and trembling knees, she knocked on the panel.

"Come in," said a deep, male voice. The master's voice.

Molly swung open the door and stepped inside. Her heart leaped at the sight of him, and she knew she'd made the right decision. How could she possible deny the desire that she'd felt for this man since she'd first seen him? To think that he wanted her in return, when he could have any number of fashionable ladies, was overwhelming.

He crossed the room, but made no further approach toward her. "I presume you've spoken with Mrs. Hutchins?" he asked.

She nodded, not trusting her tongue at that moment.

"And she explained things to you?"

Again she nodded.

"Well, then, you will attend me."

Molly felt a surge of panic. "Right here? Right now?" she blurted.

"Yes, I require a bath after my ride. Please see to it that

the tub is brought up and the water heated. Plunkett and the footmen will assist you."

Molly stood there dumbly, her face flushed with embarrassment. Obviously she'd mistaken his intentions. He only required a bath. Maybe Mrs. Hutchins was mistaken about his intentions, as well. Molly curtsied and hurried away to begin the preparations for his bath. Half an hour later, she was pouring the last steaming kettle of water into the tub, when the master walked in, clothed once again in his silken robe.

"Your bath is ready, my lord."

She waited to be dismissed, but he said nothing, just moved to the side of the tub and dropped his robe to the floor. Molly ducked her head, but it was too late. The vision of his perfect body was seared upon her mind. Before arriving at Ashford Hall she'd seen only one other man nude, but she was sure her young cousin was not so well built or so well endowed as the master. She heard the water lap against the sides of the tub as he settled into it. He did not dismiss her, so she remained frozen in place, head bowed. She heard him splashing about, but still he did not acknowledge her.

Finally, he spoke. "Come here."

Quietly, she stepped forward, head still downcast. "Yes, my lord."

"You will wash my back."

"Yes, my lord."

Nervously, she took the soap from his hand and knelt behind him. The soap smelled of sandalwood, she noted as she lathered it between her hands. His skin would smell of it, spicy and alluring. She tried to think of other things as she tentatively reached out to touch him, but it was impossible. His silken flesh was slick and warm beneath her fingers. Sweeping her hands over the broad planes of his back, she could feel his muscles bunch and tense beneath his skin. She lathered his shoulders and upper back, then lower as he leaned forward, allowing her further access. She ran her fingers along the knobs of his spine, just brushing the shallow cleft at the base, above his buttocks.

When his entire back was covered with foamy lather, she put the soap down on a nearby stool and reached for the dipper. Scooping up water, she rinsed his back, watching as the soapy rivulets cascaded across his sleek skin. Her muslin shift was soaked with water by the time she finished. She replaced the dipper on the stool, and stood. "Will that be all, my lord?"

"The soap, if you please," he said, leaning back in the tub. Trying not to look at his naked body, barely concealed by the sudsy bathwater, she once again took up the soap and started to pass it to the master. He grabbed her hand and pulled her down toward him. "The rest of me requires attention, as well," he said huskily.

Her startled eyes met his, and she felt a delicious shiver run through. Though she would never admit it, she longed to touch him again and feel the powerful muscles beneath his warm skin. She knelt. He placed her hand still holding the soap upon his chest, then released it. Then he tilted his head back and closed his eyes. With his gaze no longer upon her, Molly relaxed. She began to run the soap over his body, sliding it across his muscular chest and down along his rib cage.

As she explored his torso, she grew bolder, forsaking the soap and instead stroking her hand across the hard planes of his upper body, running her fingers through the dark springy hair that curled upon his chest. She slid her soap-slickened fingers over his flat nipples and felt them grow hard beneath her touch. Tentatively, her hand slid lower, feeling the rippling muscles of his abdomen, following the trail of dark hair that arrowed down beneath the water.

Abruptly, she stopped. She was feeling bold, but not that bold. As if aware of her hesitation, he sat up and looked at her, his eyes dark with desire. She had to glance away. He took her hand in one of his own slender, yet strong ones and tugged it downward.

"Touch me," he said.

Molly felt his cock spring to life as her fingers brushed against the length of him, and he drew in a sharp breath. Instinctively, her grasp closed around him. She marveled at the feel of him, wondered how he could be so hard, yet his skin be so soft. His hand, still wrapped around her own, began to move. He guided her in stroking his cock, sliding her palm along his hard length. Her own body began to tingle as she ran her hand over his swollen flesh.

She rubbed him gently beneath the water, until he squeezed her hand tighter around his cock. Her dress soon was soaked to the elbows as she continued to work at his hard, slippery shaft. His head tilted back against the tub, and his breathing came more rapidly. Before long, he groaned and thrust into her hand. She felt his cock jerk within her grip, and then he shuddered, cried out and was still. After a few frozen moments, his hand fell away from hers, and his cock grew limp.

With her body still tingling, Molly pulled away, but he didn't seem to notice. She knew her face was flushed, but whether from shame or desire, not even she could tell. Still, she knew her duty. She got up from aching knees, fetched a length of huckaback from the wardrobe and brought it over to the bathtub. The master lay slumped in the water, eyes still closed.

"My lord, the water grows cold."

"Mmm, yes," he replied, opening glazed eyes.

She held out the towel when he stood and stepped from the tub. As he rubbed the water from his skin, she turned away to pick up the robe that he had so carelessly discarded.

"Leave it," he commanded.

"My lord?" She turned to glance at him, then looked away again as he dropped the towel to the floor, as well. He moved closer, and she could feel the heat radiating from his naked body. His hand came up underneath her chin, tipping her face.

"Look at me!" She stared into pools of blue so deep she thought she might drown in them. "You always look away from me. Are you frightened, pretty Molly?"

"Yes, my lord." But that wasn't entirely the truth. She wasn't frightened of him, but of the feelings he awoke in her. She was frightened by her own desire.

He chuckled as though pleased. "You have nothing to be afraid of."

With light fingers, he tugged off her mobcap, loosening her hairpins and sending her tawny hair tumbling to her shoulders in riotous curls. Slowly, he lowered his lips to hers, while his fingers deftly unlaced her bodice. Mrs. Hutchins was right, after all, Molly thought to herself. The master meant to seduce her, and bed her. Within mere moments, her virtue would be gone, cast aside with her clothing. She hovered once more on the brink of indecision. Then his tongue delved into the warm depths of her mouth, and all caution was forgotten. *In for a penny, in for a pound,* she thought.

Giving in to desire, she rasied her hands to clasp his shoulders, his bare skin warm to her touch. Without breaking their kiss, he slipped her dress from her shoulders to puddle at her feet. His fingers then plucked the drawstring of her shift, loosening it until he could draw the filmy muslin down and away. Then he bent and removed her shoes, leaving her clad in only her drawers and stockings.

Grasping her shoulders, he walked her backward toward the bed, then pushed her down upon the coverlet. She sank into the bed from his weight, as he stretched out his naked body atop hers. She could feel his burgeoning erection nudge against her thigh, and the scratchy sensation of his hair against her skin. His mouth brushed softly against hers once more, before trailing along her neck, feathering her sensitive flesh with kisses. Molly moaned with pleasure, arching her body and baring her throat to his caress. Lower and lower his lips wandered, until his mouth greedily fastened on her breast, suckling her nipple until it was a hardened peak.

His hands were gentle as he drew her drawers down along her legs and tossed them to the floor, yet still she shivered beneath his touch. His hands stroked across her feverish skin, down across the swell of her belly, along the curve of her inner thigh, leaving desire in their wake, and his lips followed the trail that his hands blazed. His body shifted lower on the bed, his breath blew warm against her thigh. Molly nearly cried out as he threaded his fingers through her silken curls, arousing her passions to even greater heights.

With one hand, he spread her nether lips open wide. Before she realized what he was about, his dark head bent and his tongue licked across her clit, nearly bringing her off the bed. He continued to flick his tongue lightly against her, sending pleasure streaking through her with every touch. Her hands clenched the bedspread beneath her. Just when she thought she could take no more, he moved his mouth lower, thrusting his tongue into her, probing her inner depths. She moaned at this new sensation, and twined her hands in his thick hair. Then his tongue was replaced by one long finger, slowly easing into her. Another digit joined the first, a welcome invasion. As his fingers delved deep into her cunny, he dragged his tongue up from her entrance to lap once again at her clit. He nibbled lightly on the fleshy nubbin, eliciting soft cries from her.

Gradually, his strokes increased until she was once more on the cusp of that pleasure she'd experienced so recently at his hands. So it was with some disappointment that she felt him pull away from her. However, his absence was brief. He rose up above her, his hands braced on either side of her shoulders, and looked down at her, his eyes blazing with lust.

"Are you virgin?" he asked her.

"Aye, my lord," she replied, surprised.

"Then I am sorry for this." With that, he claimed her mouth in a tender kiss, and she tasted the flavor of her own musk upon his lips. Distracted, she felt him reach down with one hand and take his cock in hand, setting it at the entrance to her pussy. His manhood pushed bluntly against her, but still her body resisted him. He shifted his hips, and she felt the tip of his rod enter her waiting cunt. He paused, and then with a great thrust, his cock slid into her. She cried out and tried to move beneath him, to escape the burning pain that swept through her, but he had her pinned to the bed with his piercing cock.

"Shh, shh," he whispered in her ear. "Be still, and it will pass." He held himself motionless above her. Molly closed her eyes and tried not to whimper. Finally, she felt her body began to relax. He must have felt it, too, because he drew one of her stocking-clad legs up, draping it over his hip, which helped ease the pressure. Then he began to move within her body, his hips rocking against hers. He withdrew his rod until just the mere tip remained, rubbing against her tender flesh, then plunged it once more into her dripping cunny. Over and over, he drove his cock deeply into her, until she was in a frenzy of longing. She felt her body ascending to the heights of pleasure, felt the need for completion sweep over her.

She clutched desperately at his sweat-slick body, her nails digging into his flesh. Balancing his weight on one muscular arm, he slid his other hand down between their bodies and flicked a finger against her clit. His hand moved in a steady rhythm with his thrusting prick, sending her senses spiraling, until suddenly the moment of climax was upon her, turning her world upside down and leaving her breathless. She felt her inner muscles ripple as her release shuddered through her. With a moan, he thrust once, twice more, then withdrew his cock and spent his seed in a warm, sticky torrent upon her stomach. The resulting mess was unpleasant, but Molly was still quivering from her own explosion and so she barely noticed as he rolled off her and used a corner of the sheet to wipe both his cock and her abdomen.

He left her alone on the bed, while he picked up his discarded robe and walked into the dressing room without a single tender word. She heard the bell ring, summoning Plunkett to his side. Tears blossomed behind her eyes, but she blinked them away. She should know better. While the master would return her lust, he was unlikely ever to return her love. Even if he did come to hold her in some affection, he would never marry the likes of her. Her tender heart might long for romance, but her pragmatic head knew better. Resignedly, she climbed out of the bed and rescued her clothing from the floor. Quickly, she dressed and made herself presentable. When she was suitably attired, she began to clear the bathing paraphernalia from the room.

And thus began her affair with her lord and master.

PART TWO

AFTER BECOMING THE VISCOUNT'S *CHÈRE AMIE,*
Molly found her duties remained much the same, but her attentions were focused solely on the master. Her first task in the morning was to creep quietly into his room and tend the fire. Most mornings he awoke sporting a cockstand, and so usually her next chore was to relieve his needs. After that she brought hot water for his morning ablutions. If this included a bath, she would often assist him, instead of his valet. Then she helped serve him breakfast.

During the day, she made his bed, cleaned and dusted his chambers, as well as the library where he conducted much of his business, and generally waited on him hand and foot. She brought him his tea and even did his mending. But her chief duty was pleasing him in bed or wherever else he might fancy—the drawing room, the music room, once even the kitchen, after the rest of the household was asleep.

But most often, the library was the location of their trysts, out of convenience, since that was where he spent most of his time while indoors. And Molly knew it was convenience, rather than affection that drew him to her, just as she knew he had a mistress in London. There were no whispered words of love when he took her, but she soon came to enjoy the pleasure his body provided. Too, she enjoyed the cachet that her favored status gave her with the other servants. Some of the other maids whispered and called her a bawd behind her back, but Molly knew they were just jealous. They'd have done the same thing in her place and been grateful for it. And though he never said so, Molly knew the master was fond of her. Why, once, after a trip to the village, he'd given her a length of ribbon for her hair. "Green," he'd said, "to match your eyes."

Time of day didn't seem to matter to the master, either. He was in the habit of taking her whenever the desire struck him. It was a wonder she ever got any work done at all. One time, he came upon her unexpectedly while she was in the upstairs hall sorting linens. He pushed her roughly into the linen cupboard, pinning her body against the wall. Fondling her bubbies with one hand, he used the other to unbutton the fall of his trousers, revealing his well-primed cock. He then rucked her skirt above her knees, and found the opening of her drawers. With little warning he hoisted her high, wrapping her legs around his waist, and impaled her on his engorged prick. She was tossed about like a rag doll as he slammed into her, driving her back against the wall with each thrust of his powerful body before exploding into her with a cry.

It was one of the few times he spent himself within her body. Usually he was careful to withdraw before spewing his seed, or to use a French letter. Molly was thankful he showed her that courtesy, at least. She knew if she caught his by-blow, she'd be turned off for sure.

He also showed her ways of fornication that wouldn't result

in offspring at all, such as when he taught her to "play the bagpipe."

They were sitting in the library, in his favorite chair, while he dandled her upon his knee. His face was buried in her bared bosom, nibbling at her breasts, while his hand stole up her skirts to stroke her inner thigh.

"I think it's time I introduce you to fellatio," he said offhandedly.

"Who, my lord?" she asked naively.

He chuckled. "Fellatio is not a *who,* but a *what.* You know when I kiss you here?" He brushed his hand across her mons, causing her to shiver. "Well, you shall learn to do the same for me. Come, I'll show you." He set her on her feet, then stood up and rearranged himself in the chair, leaning back.

"Kneel," he commanded her.

She knelt at his feet and watched as he unbuttoned the fall of his trousers. Already erect, his thick, stiff cock stood out quite impressively from a thatch of dark curls. She reached out to touch him, wrapping her hands around him, drawing the skin down, knowing what he liked. His shaft was hard and velvety smooth beneath her hand

"Yes, that's it, my dear. Now, kiss my cock," he demanded in a husky voice.

Molly slid forward and lowered her head to his body. She inhaled the familiar scent of sandalwood and musk that rose from his skin, and felt her pulse accelerate. Cautiously, Molly stuck out her tongue and touched it to the head of his cock. He tasted slightly, but pleasantly, of salt.

"You call that a kiss, my girl?"

Molly licked her lips, wetting them nervously, before placing her mouth once more on the engorged, purplish head of his cock.

"That's much better. Now, have you ever had a stick of

penny candy?" he asked. Molly nodded. "Well, then, pretend my prick is a confection. You must suck it and lick it like a sweet."

Obediently, Molly tried to do as she was told, only to wring a gasp from him.

"Gently, gently," he told her.

She slid her mouth down on him again, and was rewarded this time with a moan, before sliding back up along the hard length of him. Encouraged, she continued, gliding her warm, wet mouth down around his shaft, trying to take in as much of his cock as possible. He moaned again, and thrust his fingers into her hair, drawing her down on him. She gagged, unaccustomed to the feel of his cock pressing at the back of her throat. Thankfully, he quickly released her, and she was able to breathe once more.

At his urging, she continued licking and sucking his cock, gaining confidence and experience as she went. Her untutored mouth explored his shaft, guided by his gasps and moans, while her hands stroked and caressed his ballocks. Her tongue twirled around his shaft, tasting the salty-sweetness of his skin, until once again he thrust his hands deeply into her hair. She raised her eyes to look at him, only to find his head thrown back in ecstasy, his eyes closed tight. With a hoarse cry, he spurted into her mouth, filling her throat with his warm, salty seed. Instinctively, she swallowed, and swallowed, until he at last shuddered and was still.

She pulled away, resting her cheek upon his leg while he idly stroked her hair. She basked in the unusual show of emotion, knowing she had greatly pleased him despite her ignorance. In this, as in all other aspects of carnal knowledge, she was an apt pupil. After all, her only security lay in continuing to please her master. If he ever tired of their dalliance, then where would she be?

Though she would scarcely admit it, even to herself, Molly knew that she would never refuse a request of this man. Not because he controlled her employment, but because he controlled her heart and soul. Whatever he asked, it would be his. Secretly, Molly had come to love not only her master, but every torment he visited upon her, and there were many.

London life had left the master with a taste for debauchery. One of his favorite activities was to tie her arms and legs to the posters of his enormous bed using his cravats, a practice that drove Plunkett, his exacting valet, to distraction. Once he'd secured her, the master took great pleasure in bedeviling her, stroking and suckling her breasts until she writhed beneath his touch. Over and over, he would bring her to the brink of climax with his hands and mouth, only to back away, leaving her unfulfilled, until she cried and begged for release. Only then would he consent to fuck her, usually hard and fast, bringing them both to screaming relief.

Though he was often aloof and always demanding, Molly had to admit her master was rarely cruel. She could only recall one time he'd truly hurt her. He'd come home from a neighbor's, three sheets to the wind and furious about his losses at the whist table. Though it was late, he summoned her and more brandy to his chamber. When she tried to gently dissuade him from drinking more, he threw her forcefully onto the bed. Pinning her down with his strong body, he pushed her night rail up to her waist, baring her arse.

Taking his riding crop in hand, he slashed it across her buttocks, causing her to cry out. Although his position atop her, not to mention his inebriation, caused most of his strokes to land wide of the mark, it still hurt. Matters improved only a little when, tossing the crop to the floor, he began to use his bare hand on her. Mashing her face into the coverlet, where she could barely breathe, much less cry out, he spanked her arse until it was red and throbbing, leaving welts all over her buttocks.

Then, gradually, his touch changed in nature. Instead of smacking her arse, he was now stroking it. His hands slid soothingly over her tingling flesh, and his weight shifted off her body. He ran his hand down the cleft of her buttocks to where her nether lips glistened, and dipped his fingers in the moisture he found there. Then he stroked upward, rubbing her juices across her bunghole. After he repeated this action several times, her arse was slick with her own honey. Still, she was caught off guard when he slipped a finger into it, probing her body. She felt a strange stirring deep within as he wiggled his finger into her channel, and a sudden relief when he withdrew his hand. The relief was only momentary.

He spread her still-tingling cheeks with both hands, and then she felt the blunt tip of his cock positioned at the entrance to her arse. With a grunt, he shoved his way into her. Molly felt a sharp stinging pain as the head of his thick cock penetrated. He paused only a moment, barely allowing her to adjust to his presence, before easing his way inch by inch into her channel. She moaned, strangely aroused, as he sank himself to the hilt. Still, she wasn't nearly ready when he began to thrust into her.

Seemingly oblivious to her discomfiture, he buggered her soundly. At first it was painful, his thick cock stretching her with every stroke, but as he continued rocking his hips against her, she found herself thrusting back against him. But before she attain any sense of satisfaction, he began to make a harsh, grunting noise. He thrust hard, and Molly felt his warm seed shoot into her arse. After spending himself, he withdrew with a sigh. Then he rolled off her, wiped his cock on her night rail, and passed out facedown on the bed, drunk as…well, a lord. All in all, it was not his finest moment.

Thankfully, when he woke the next morning, his lordship had no memory of the previous night, so Molly was able to pretend it had never happened, except for the slight welts she carried for a few days.

Most of the time, though, Lord Ashford was an agreeable master. He asked only for her obedience and her passion, and she was happy to give him both. Until a stranger arrived at Ashford Hall. And changed her life forever.

PART THREE

MOLLY WAS IN THE SERVANTS' HALL WHEN THERE came a ringing from the library. She eagerly answered the summons of the bell, expecting a midday tryst, only to find the master in conversation with his steward and an attractive stranger.

"My lord, the new game laws—" the steward was saying. He broke off as she entered the room and dipped the men a brief curtsy.

"A tea tray, Molly," requested Lord Ashford.

"Yes, my lord."

On the way to the kitchen she wondered about the visitor. Who was he? Why was he here? True, her master had many interests, and there were many visitors to Ashford Hall, but usually they were familiar faces.

A mere quarter of an hour later, she carried the tea tray into the library and set it down on the master's desk. As she fixed his lordship a plate of his favorite tidbits, she covertly gazed at the stranger. Where the master's looks were all dark and flashing, this stranger's appearance could only be described

as brown. He had short, wavy brown hair, long brown side-
burns, velvety brown eyes, and his skin was a golden bronze.
His clothes appeared well made, though not of the finest
quality. His linen was plain, yet clean. Clearly he was not of
the gentry, but his manner marked him as well-bred. Molly's
curiosity was aroused, and so, she found to her surprise, was
her body.

When she handed the visitor his cup of tea, her fingers
brushed against his, sending an unexpected frisson of desire
through her. Then he smiled at her, and her heart leaped in
her chest. He might not be as sinfully beautiful as her master,
but there was something about this stranger that stirred her
senses.

By dinnertime her curiosity, if not her body's hunger, had
been satisfied. The servant's grapevine had told her all she
needed to know about the newcomer, including his name,
Will Adams. Apparently the master had met him while in
Scotland, on the estate where he was an assistant gamekeeper.
According to Mrs. Hutchins, he came highly recommended
and was to replace Old Jarvis, the gamekeeper, who was being
pensioned off due to age. Adams would occupy a room in the
servants' quarters until the repairs to the gamekeeper's cottage
were complete.

Since he was occupied most of the day with his new duties,
Molly rarely encountered Mr. Adams before the evening meal.
At supper, however, he was always there, smiling at her from
across the table. His ready smile was enough to send her
stomach somersaulting, but she was careful not to do more
than smile back politely. After only a few days, she began to
look forward to dinner. When they met on the stairs or in the
hall, he was unfailingly polite, but it seemed as though there
was something beyond mere courtesy in his behavior toward

her. In fact, it wasn't long before the other servants began to comment on his marked attention to her.

Molly knew that soon one of them would reveal her secret, and then Mr. Adams would want no more to do with her. The thought depressed her more than she would have thought possible.

Late one evening, as she mounted the stairs to retire, Molly was shocked to find Mr. Adams watching her from the shadows at the top of the steps. In the glow of her lantern, his face was dark and sensual.

She nodded to him, and went to brush past, but he stepped in front of her.

"Molly, have I given you cause to dislike me?" he asked.

"No, Mr. Adams," she replied.

He loomed over her, backing her up against the wall with his sheer presence. "Good, I was afraid I had offended you in some way." He braced his hand on the wall next to her head, his body uncomfortably close to hers. She could smell the scent of earth and forest that clung to his skin.

He bent his head to hers. "You're very bonny," he whispered in her ear, his thick Scottish burr sending shivers up her spine. His soft, warm lips brushed her throat in the sensitive spot just below her ear, and she felt her knees go weak.

"I belong to my master!" she blurted out.

He pulled back, startled by her outburst.

"You cannot mean…" His voice trailed off sadly. "Well, then I can only say that his lordship's taste in women is as fine as his taste in everything else. Leave it to him to find a diamond among the coal."

Molly blushed at the compliment. She knew she was pretty—after all, hadn't the master chosen her for her looks?— but Mr. Adams made her feel beautiful.

"I am heartily sorry to have bothered you," he said, stepping back to let her pass.

Molly felt like crying. She finished climbing the steps to her garret room. How could she feel so keenly the loss of something she'd never had?

Following their encounter in the hallway, Mr. Adams avoided Molly for a few days. However, on Sunday, she was surprised to find him at her elbow, ready to assist her into the wagon bound for church. She couldn't help but admire his long, lean form as he mounted his horse for the ride into the village.

All throughout the sermon, Molly couldn't help but steal glances at Mr. Adams, seated in the pew opposite her. He really was very handsome. She saw that she was not the only young lady in the congregation who cast longing looks in his direction. However, Mr. Adams seemed to take no notice. After the service, many of the same young women thronged around him, but Mr. Adams excused himself and caught up to her.

"Molly, would you do me the honor of walking home with me? I wish to speak with you."

"That would be most improper, Mr. Adams." In public, Molly always tried to protect the little reputation she had left.

"Jane and Ralph shall walk with us." He indicated the couple that stood under a nearby tree. She didn't know them well. Jane was the daughter of a tenant farmer on the estate; Ralph one of Lord Ashford's grooms. Molly could tell from the looks that passed between them that they would be poor chaperones, oblivious to anything but each other.

"I've already asked Mrs. Hutchins," Mr. Adams told her, whisking away her next objection.

"What about your horse?"

"Romulus? I will hitch him to the wagon. He'll be happy to walk home without me."

He'd obviously planned this ahead of time, and Molly was flattered. "Well, then Mr. Adams, since you seem to have thought of everything, I will walk with you."

Eagerly, he took her arm and escorted her over to greet the other couple. Leaving her to exchange pleasantries, he tended to his horse, and then the foursome set off toward Ashford Park. The walk was not a long one, and the day was glorious, and Molly soon found herself enjoying the outing. Jane and Ralph were obviously in love, and they spent most of the journey mooning over each other. Mr. Adams kept up a steady stream of conversation, skillfully eliciting opinions from Molly that she didn't even know she had. Whatever it was he wished to say to her, it must have been of little importance, for he never mentioned it. Instead, he spoke wistfully of his home in Scotland, speaking so eloquently that she could almost see the heather-covered hills. For a man of his station, Molly thought he was extremely well-read.

She soon discovered that, like Jane, he was the child of a tenant farmer, and was the youngest of five siblings.

"How came you to be educated then?"

"The countess was a great disciple of Mrs. Shelley's. She set up a school for the tenants' children. Then throughout my apprenticeship, I begged and borrowed what books I could from a generous curate. Now that I am earning my own wages, I vow I shall spend a pound a year on books alone."

"I would love to be able to read," Molly admitted. "I know most of my letters, but..."

"I could teach you."

"Mr. Adams..."

"Will. My friends call me Will."

She smiled shyly at him. "Will, then. I would like it very

much if you would teach me to read." They agreed to meet the following Sunday to begin her lessons.

Before long, they had reached the turnoff to Ashford Hall. Here, Jane and Ralph begged to take their leave. Ralph would escort Jane home along the lane, while Molly and Will would cut across the park. Molly knew it was improper, but she couldn't begrudge the young lovers a few moments alone. It was unlikely that anyone would see her with Will, and it wasn't as though she had any virtue left to guard.

They set off through the light woods that bordered the estate. Will, of course, was quite familiar with the terrain, and guided her expertly through the trees. They came to a clearing, and on the other side Molly could see Ashford Hall, rising majestically to the sky, its gray stone facade tinted pink by the fading light.

"I hadn't realized it was so late. I must get back," she exclaimed.

"Molly, I must speak to you. I understand that you are not at liberty to entertain me as a suitor, but perhaps that will change. I am quite attracted to you. Please give me some hope that you feel the same."

"Will, it is as you say. I am not in a position to feel anything toward you. Now, I really must go."

"Say that you'll still meet me on Sunday."

"I'll still meet you on Sunday," she called over her shoulder as she ran for home, leaving him standing there in the twilight.

All week long, Molly couldn't wait for Sunday, though she wasn't sure if that was because she was going to see Will, or because she was going to learn how to read. Finally, the Sabbath came.

Once more, the oblivious Jane and Ralph were enlisted as chaperones. Will had secured a picnic lunch, and led them to a small meadow on the edge of the Park's woodland. After finishing a hearty meal of ham, bread and cheese, washed down with a fine cider, Jane and Ralph decided to go for a stroll through the woods. Molly had no doubts what their "stroll" would entail.

She was content to sit on the blanket Will had provided and look out over the golden meadow while he reclined next to her, his hand propped beneath his head, and finished his cider.

"Are you ready?" he asked her finally.

"Oh, yes."

Will rolled over and got a book out the basket. Then he flopped over on his back and patted the blanket next to him. Molly scooted over next to him.

"Lie down here with me," he said.

"I don't think that's a very good idea."

"I can hardly teach you to read when you're up there and I'm down here," he told her with a grin. Reluctantly, Molly lay down on the blanket next to him, her head resting in the crook of his arm.

"Open the book."

At first Molly found it hard to concentrate on the letters with his body lying so close to hers, but soon she was absorbed in trying to make out the unfamiliar words. Will was patient and encouraging, and with his help she was finally able to finish a passage. She laid down the book with a great sense of satisfaction.

"Good girl."

"I couldn't have done it without your help."

"I guess I deserve a reward then," he told her with a gleam in his eye.

Molly could read his intentions, but she couldn't summon up the strength to object as he rolled over, taking her in his arms, and pressed his lips to hers. Her arms came up around him, pulling him close. She could feel the warmth of his sun-kissed skin beneath the linen of his shirt.

For once in her life, Molly longed to be free. Free from guilt, free from care, free from obedience and duty. For just a moment, in Will's arms, she could taste that freedom. Throwing caution to the winds, she slid her hand down to cup his burgeoning erection. He nudged against her palm. His mouth left hers to nibble down her neck, inflaming her further.

He pulled away, bracing himself on one arm, and looked down at her, his eyes glazed with lust, before once again crushing his mouth to hers. Then he reached up under her skirts to languidly stroke her sex. His fingers flicked over her clit before dipping down to slip gently into her cunny, causing her to moan. She was already hot and wet and panting with need. He withdrew his hand, and slowly licked his fingers as she watched, appalled and yet fascinated.

"I need to be inside you."

Molly agreed. Her hands went to the waistband of his breeches, unbuttoning the fall, and pushing them low on his hips. His rigid cock sprang into her palm, the tip already wet with his juices. She couldn't help but make a comparison. Will's cock was much longer than Lord Ashford's, though not as thick. She had no doubt it would fill her nicely. As he pushed her skirts up, she spread her legs wider, welcoming the invasion of his cock. She felt its head brush against her clit, then he slid into her smoothly, until he was seated to his ballocks.

Slowly, he drew back, and then sheathed himself once more in her heat. With his hands braced on either side of her head, he held his weight from her, their bodies joined only at the hips. Over and over he stroked into her, until her body grew taut as a bow, aching for release from the glorious torment he was inflicting upon her. Then her muscles tightened and a wave of pleasure flowed over her, dragging Will in its wake, until he too climaxed, calling out her name. She held him tight and wished the moment would never end, but all too soon, the heat of the afternoon sun and the scratchiness of the blanket beneath her reminded Molly of the world around her. Reluctantly, she and Will parted with a kiss, and straightened their clothes. By the time Jane and Ralph returned from their stroll, everything was packed and ready to go.

In the days that followed, she and Will stole every moment they could in shadowed hallways and empty rooms to exchange kisses and furtive embraces, though she knew it couldn't last. Luckily for her, the master was away on business in London.

She was both regretful and relieved when she found he hadn't stayed away long.

The master walked into the library, surprising Molly while she stood at the desk, feather duster in hand and an open book in front of her. She had chosen a slim volume with plenty of pictures, but still she was struggling to decipher the letters on the page.

"What are you doing?" he asked, as she turned to face him.

"Sorry, my lord, I was just looking at the book. I…"

He moved over to the desk and picked up the volume. *"The Tale of Robin Hood."* He tossed it back onto the desk. "I would have thought it better suited to the nursery."

She moved to put the book back in its rightful place, when he stopped her with a hand on her wrist. "You may have the book, Molly."

"My lord?"

"You may have the book. It obviously pleases you, and is of little consequence to me."

"Oh, thank you, my lord." Molly was so excited that she threw her arms around his neck. Then, realizing what she'd done, she blushed and jerked back. He caught her around the waist before she could pull away, and kissed her soundly. "If I'd known you would show such enthusiasm, I would have given you a book long ago," he told her with unusual good humor. Then he kissed her again more forcefully, backing her against the sofa.

Her legs hit the damask-covered cushion and she sank onto it, while his mouth continued to devour hers. His kisses were different from Will's—hungrier, more rapacious. Will's kisses made her feel loved and cherished; the master's kisses made her feel wanton and wicked. How could two men have such different approaches to the same act? She resolved not to think about Will; it felt too much like betrayal. Truth be told, after a few minutes of heady kisses, she could barely think at all.

The master pulled down the neckline of her dress, exposing her breasts. Her arms came up to twine around his neck, and she nearly hit him with the forgotten duster. He reached up to take the object from her grip, and gave it a curious look. Molly thought he might toss it across the room, but instead he drew the feathers lightly along her throat, tickling her with their silky strands. The duster was made of ostrich feathers mounted on an ivory handle worn smooth with age, and the feathers were as soft as a kitten's fur. The master ran it over the delicate skin of one exposed breast, then the other, tickling her and leaving a tingling sensation in its wake. He ran it across her nipples, a barely there caress, before lowering his mouth to suckle her. His mouth closed around one nipple, licking and sucking at it until it hardened into a rosy peak, before moving on to the other. All the while, the wispy touch of the duster danced along her neck and shoulders, tickling her skin and causing her to shiver. Just when she thought she could stand no more, the master's mouth and hands stilled.

He scooted lower on the couch and suddenly threw her skirts over her head, baring her lower body to his gaze. Slowly, he drew her thin muslin drawers down, his fingers stroking along her legs as he went. After discarding her drawers and dropping a kiss on her belly, he nudged one knee between her thighs, then the other, spreading her legs wide. He draped one stocking-clad leg over the back of the sofa, exposing her pussy, which ached to be filled. But he was intent on teasing her further. Taking the duster once more in hand, he played the feathers along the top of one thigh, the soft wisps dancing across her skin. Over and over, he teased her with the feathery touch, until every inch of exposed flesh was prickling and tingling. She stifled a giggle when he played the feathers across the tender skin of her stomach, but when he brushed them across her clit Molly thought she would swoon.

However, that gentle touch was not repeated; instead, Molly felt something smooth and slightly cool rub against her. She shivered, and looked down to find that the master had reversed his grip on the duster, and was rolling the handle against her clit. It was an unusual, but not unpleasant sensation. It grew more pleasant as he drew the smooth, bulbous tip of the handle along the folds of her pussy, then back up, causing a rush of moisture between her legs. Molly sensed what was coming, and so she was not overly surprised when the master slowly began to work the tip of the ivory handle into her pussy.

The feeling was unfamiliar. The ivory was slightly cooler than the warmth of a human body, and unlike a cock, there was no flexibility or give to the hard handle. Still, the sensation she was feeling was pleasurable. Because the handle was thinner than anything she'd felt before, it slid into her waiting cunny easily. It was also longer, she found, when the master began to slowly thrust it in and out of her body. She felt it against the back of her womb as he drove it deep into her pussy. The strokes gradually grew harder and faster, the handle pistoning between her legs, leaving her gasping, until finally she reached the apogee of her pleasure. She cried out as the master thrust the makeshift cock into her one last time, her body convulsing around it.

Slowly, he withdrew it, took a handkerchief from his pocket and wiped the handle clean. Then he straightened her clothes and brushed her lips lightly with a kiss.

"Enjoy the book," he told her as he strode out of the library, leaving her more confused than ever.

All that week, Molly practiced reading from her new book as much as possible, but it wasn't until Sunday that she got to share it with Will. When she told him it was a gift from the master, although she left out most of the details, Will still grew very upset.

"It's not fair," he said jealously. "He gives you a book, and you are in awe. If I could, I would give you everything… books, pretty dresses, a house, children, *my name*."

"Surely you don't mean that, Will."

"I don't care if you are ruined, I want to marry you."

"You do?"

"I love you," he told her.

"I love you, too." Molly was surprised to hear the words on her lips, but she knew as soon as she said it that it was true. Will was good, and kind, and true, and she loved him. But she also loved her master…how could this be? Still, there was no future with the master. She knew her place in his world and it was not at his side as a wife. Will was her future.

He grabbed her hand, saying, "Come with me. The cottage

is mine now. Old Jarvis is pensioned off and gone to live in the village with his daughter."

The tidy gamekeeper's cottage lay just off the main drive, with the bulk of Ashford Park beyond it to the north. A small stone wall enclosed a garden desperately in need of tending, and behind the house, Molly could see a henhouse also in need of repairs. Will kept her hand in his, excited as a small child on Christmas morning, and led her through the place, extolling its virtues. The holland covers had already been removed, and Molly could see the worn, yet still sturdy furniture. The house was small, but cozy. There were just four rooms, a parlor and the kitchen downstairs, and two upstairs. It was to the larger of these two bedrooms that Will eventually led her.

"This is where we will lie together as man and wife someday," he told her, gesturing at the huge featherbed.

"You are already the husband of my heart," she replied.

"Then lie with me here," he whispered. He shrugged out of his long, brown greatcoat, before removing her bonnet and her dew-damp redingote, laying them carefully over a chair. He removed his tall, scuffed brown boots, while she slipped off her shoes and stockings. Next, he removed his jacket, waistcoat and shirt, and placed them upon the chair. Clad in only his trousers, he advanced on her, and drawing his hand along her cheek, kissed her softly on the lips. She responded to his kiss with a gentle kiss of her own.

He drew his hands slowly along her shoulders, then spun her about, facing the bed. His hands went to the laces of her bodice, unfastening them, while his lips returned to nuzzle her neck. He slid her dress off her shoulders, then loosened the drawstring of her muslin shift. Meanwhile, his lips never left her neck, licking and nibbling at the sensitive skin there. With a flick of his wrist, her shift billowed to the floor, followed by her undergarments.

She stood naked before him, and she could feel his erection nudging her buttocks as she pressed back against him. His hands came up to fondle her breasts, his fingers plucking at her nipples until they were drawn into hard peaks. One hand slid to her waist, the other to the nape of her neck, where he toyed with her tawny curls, before sending his fingers skittering along her spine.

Gently, but firmly, he bent her at the waist, and pushed her lightly onto the waist-high bed. Molly was surprised, but unalarmed. Her master's tutelage had taught her to be unafraid of new and undiscovered pleasures. Her cheek against the counterpane, Molly looked over her shoulder to see her lover unbutton and then discard his trousers and drawers.

In all their hurried and stolen moments, she'd never seen Will fully unclothed before. Gads, but he was beautiful. He was not as broad-shouldered as the master, but was every bit as well-formed. Skin bronzed by the sun lay over the whipcord muscles of his arms and chest. His stomach was flat and chiseled, his hips narrow, tapering down to long, lean limbs. Even his bare feet were beautiful.

He stepped behind her, and once more ran a finger along her spine, along the seam of her buttocks, and then across her waiting cleft. Molly wiggled against his hand, letting him feel her warmth and wetness. She watched over her shoulder as he reared back and, grabbing his engorged cock, guided it into her slick passage.

His hands went to her hips, pulling her back as he thrust himself deep inside her. Molly sighed with pleasure as Will slid slowly out of her, then thrust back in hard, driving into her cunny. He soon set up a slow, steady rhythm of thrusts that had her moaning and pushing back against his hips, unable to get enough of his long, hard cock.

Her hands clenched the counterpane as she felt her climax drawing close. She could feel the sheen of sweat on Will's body each time his skin slapped against hers. As he plunged into her warm depths, again and again, she felt herself hovering on the brink. Then, with a warm rush, her muscles clenched tight around his cock, sending Will into an orgasm of his own. He stiffened, cried out and managed to thrust deeply into her one last time, before collapsing against her.

Molly couldn't move. Will's cheek was damp against her back, and his weight pressed her into the bed, but she didn't seem to mind. Finally, he rolled to the side, dragging her with him, burying his face in her neck as they both flopped onto the mattress.

He stroked her damp skin as he snuggled up to her and talked to her of the future. He spoke of the repairs he would make to the cottage, creating a snug home for her, and the laughing children they would raise there...a half dozen at least. Molly knew it was wishful thinking. The future would bring what it would, and in the meantime, they should grab at all the present had to offer.

With that in mind, Molly began to return Will's caress. She ran her hand across the wide, muscled planes of his chest, making lazy circles around his flat nipples, before dancing her fingers down along his flat stomach to his resurging manhood. She stroked his cock, rubbing her thumb against the sensitive tip until he grew hard in her hand.

He pulled her down to him for a kiss, her naked body slanted across his. His palms caressed her backside as he dragged her leg over his, aligning their bodies. "Ride me," he told her in a husky voice. Molly quickly grasped his meaning and sat up to straddle his body. He reached up to fondle her breasts, rubbing the pads of his thumbs against the sensitive nipples until they were ruched. She took his hard cock in hand and guided it within her aching passage.

Both of them gasped with pleasure as Molly sank down onto the instrument of his desire, seating him deep within her womb. Then she began to ride him, arching her back and grinding her pelvis against his hips. At first her movements were slow and easy, as she reveled in the new sensation; she had never been with the master in this manner. He always dominated her instead. Now, she was in control and enjoying every minute of it.

The best part was the look on Will's face as she rocked against him. Knowing that he was at her mercy, enjoying himself at her whim, filled her with a sense of power. Will was able to relinquish control to her, and control was something she'd rarely had before. He thought of her as a partner, an equal, and she knew that this was one of the many reasons why she loved him.

She couldn't deny that another one of the reasons was the pleasure she took in his body, a pleasure that was rising even now. She leaned forward to capture his mouth, bracing her arms on either side of his head, and thrust her hips forward. Will moaned against her lips. She began to rock her hips quickly, her sweat-slick skin gliding across his. He grabbed her hips and thrust upward, and was soon matching her stroke for stroke. Molly felt the approaching flutters of an orgasm and felt Will's body tense beneath hers. With a grimace, he came, his seed shooting into her in a warm explosion. At that, Molly was undone. Her body convulsed in a spasm of pleasure that left her collapsed, limp and panting against his hard chest.

As they lay there entwined, with Will stroking her hair and murmuring sweet words of love in her ear, Molly was paralyzed with bliss. *If only this moment could never end,* she thought, but of course all moments must, and all too soon.

The afternoon was drawing to a close by the time they'd gotten properly dressed, and Molly made her way back to the house with a heavy heart. Now that Will was moved into the gamekeeper's cottage, she knew she would see less of him. But perhaps that would be a good thing. Perhaps then, she wouldn't feel so guilty about betraying her master with Will, and vice versa. Molly sighed. She knew she was walking a dangerous tightrope, and she could only hope that somehow, someway, she would find a way across. Little did she know that her prayers would soon be answered.

A few days after her last encounter with Will, Molly was in the parlor when she heard a loud commotion from the front hall. Along with several of the other servants, she rushed in to see Will and three of the grooms carrying the master into the house. Lord Ashford was white as a sheet and apparently unconscious.

"What's going on?" demanded the butler, Mr. Cutter.

"I found him along the stream," Will said. "I fear he's badly hurt."

The butler immediately sent one of the footmen to fetch Dr. Miles, while Will and the other servants, including Plunkett, carried Lord Ashford up the stairs to his bedchamber, with Mrs. Hutchins and Molly close on their heels.

A torturous half hour later, the doctor arrived, only to find that his patient had yet to regain consciousness. Immediately, he asked Will for his particulars of the accident.

"I was walking Remus, my mastiff, alongside the stream as I often do, when I noticed a bay horse limping along. Sure that it belonged to Lord Ashford, I looked for him nearby. Then, my dog caught scent of something. Upon following him, I came to the berm, where I found Lord Ashford lying

Jennifer Dale

upon the ground, barely conscious. I'd wager that his horse threw him. I did not stop to check his injuries, just brought him here as quickly as I could."

After hearing this explanation, the doctor began his examination of the patient. Thankfully, his lordship remained unconscious. Finally, the doctor rose and declared, "His lordship has broken his leg and has a severe concussion. We must address the first injury immediately, as for the second, we can only hope for the best." He issued instructions to Mrs. Hutchins and Molly to bring hot water and bandages, and he sent one of the footmen to find something to use as splints.

Returning to the room, Molly found it hard to watch as the doctor cut away the master's boot, revealing swollen, mottled flesh. Then the doctor washed his hands and examined the leg further.

"Good news, there appears to be no breakage of the skin." The doctor next instructed Will, Plunkett and the footman to hold down his lordship's body while he set the broken limb. As he tugged on the leg, his lordship came awake, screaming with pain. Molly heard the grinding of bone on bone, and then, thankfully, the master once again passed out. He remained blissfully unaware as the physician finished setting and binding the leg.

"Who will be responsible for his care?" Dr. Miles asked, as he prepared to leave. Molly and Plunkett both stepped forward.

"You must wake him every hour," the doctor said. "You must not give him anything for the pain, until we have determined that the blow to his head has not damaged his faculties. Once he is able to stay awake for several hours at a time, you may give him some of this." He handed a small vial to Molly. "A drop, as needed, will suffice. I will return tomorrow to check on his lordship."

Molly spent a harrowing night tending to the master. However, it was well worth it; by the next morning he was seemingly out of danger and quite lucid. When the doctor arrived to examine him, Lord Ashford was able to relate the details of the accident more fully.

"I was riding my horse down by the stream. When Jupiter went to jump the berm, he landed awkwardly and fell, crushing my leg beneath him. I must have hit my head on a rock and passed out then, because I don't remember anything else until Adams came to rescue me. I remember him hoisting me up, then blackness, until I woke up this morning."

"It's a good sign that you remember the accident," the doctor said. "A clear memory is one indicator that there should be no lasting effect from your blow to the head. However, should you have any trouble with your memory or vision, or any dizzy spells, you must send for me immediately. As for your leg, you must let it heal for at least a month. I will come once a week to look in on you."

After the doctor departed, Lord Ashford called for Adams. At his behest, Molly escorted Will into the master's room, where Lord Ashford lay recuperating.

"Adams," his lordship said. "It seems I owe you my life."

"Nay," said Will, "nothing so serious as that. Someone else would have found you, had I not."

"Still, I am in your debt. How can I ever repay you?"

"Molly," Will blurted out, surprising her and, from the look on his face, the master, as well. "I would have Molly to be my wife."

The master looked over at her where she sat next to his bed, her head bowed, so as not to reveal her turmoil at this unexpected development.

"May I speak freely, my lord?" Will asked.

His lordship nodded.

Will continued, "I know that she is your paramour, and I do not care. The fact is, my lord, that even if you love her, you can never marry her. I do love her, and *can* marry her. I can give her a respectable home and children, and will do so gladly if you will give me your blessing."

"You speak the truth," said his lordship, quietly. "What say you, Molly?"

"You are my lord and master," she replied, "and I shall defer to your wishes, but I must confess that I am not opposed to Mr. Adams' suit."

Thankfully, the master did not appear to be too distressed by her confession, or too curious about the sudden romance between her and Will. Instead he looked thoughtful. Finally, he spoke. "I do give my consent, but on two conditions. First, you may not marry until I am able to attend the wedding, and second, you must swear to take good care of her."

"I swear," Will promised. "Thank you, my lord. You have made me the happiest of men. I shall go immediately to the vicar and ask him to post the banns." Nodding to his lordship, Will strode from the room, leaving Molly alone with her master.

After a long silence, Lord Ashford spoke. "You care for him," he said.

She nodded. "I have not known him long, but he is a good man."

The master was silent a moment longer, then he said quietly, "In all this time, I have never asked if you care for me."

For the first time in her experience, he sounded uncertain, and vulnerable.

"My lord…" she began.

"Anthony."

"What?"

"My given name is Anthony. I have never heard it from your lips. I would do so, before I lose you forever."

Molly's heart thudded in her chest. If she had ever doubted that he cared for her, her doubts were now erased. Tears burned her eyes.

"Anthony," she said softly, her voice thick with unshed tears. "I think that I have loved you from the moment I saw you." Only now did Molly truly understand what Mrs. Hutchins had told her those many months ago. The love she felt for Will was not the love she felt for Lord Ashford, but both were real and true.

This seemed to satisfy the master, since he gave her a sad smile and nodded, before dismissing her. As she left the room, Molly looked back with love on the lips that had so often kissed hers, the arms that had held her, the body that she'd so often felt pressed against hers. She would never forget his lordship—or the passion he'd taught her. She would take that gift, along with her precious book, into her marriage.

Four weeks later, on the day of her wedding, his lordship gave her another gift, a purse containing five hundred pounds. Then he watched, along with all the servants and half the village, as Molly stood before the vicar and pledged her vows to Will, promising to love, cherish and obey him for all time, as her husband, her lord and the master of her heart.

★ ★ ★ ★ ★

MIRROR, MIRROR

Amanda McIntyre

CHAPTER ONE

"HOW MUCH DID HE PAY YOU?" I ENJOYED watching this one dress. He had a slow methodical style, much like having sex with him. His dark eyes twinkled in the twilight of the afternoon as he fastened the cuff of his dress shirt. My heart ached, but more than that, my body ached to have him just once more.

"Does it matter? Was it good for you?" His boyish smile produced a sexy dimple on his firm jaw.

I stretched luxuriously beneath the smooth white hotel sheets and returned a savory smile. "It was perfect, darling. I just hope that it was worth every cent he gave you." I sat up and leaned back against the tufted headboard, not bothering to cover my nakedness.

He chuckled. I chuckled in return. Oh, don't get me wrong, I'm not paranoid. Despite my age, I keep myself fit. My body has always been a sense of pride for me. It's so much easier to find good clothes. Having had the good fortune to marry late in life, to a man twice-before married and, like me, not interested in having a family, allows me to enjoy a tight, firm body as well as my dear husband's wealth.

My afternoon lover sauntered to the edge of the bed, his shirt unbuttoned, revealing his tan, chiseled and smooth chest. The man could have been a navy SEAL with his physique. He wouldn't tell me his name, and I knew it was better this way, just like the others before him.

"You were fantastic," he whispered, leaning toward me to offer a soft kiss of approval.

"I know," I whispered back as I curled my hand around his neck, tufting his wayward dark hair with my fingers. I loved the way it curled up at the end of his collar. His kiss was sweet and thorough, producing a throbbing between my legs that screamed with need. I wanted the warmth of his young, firm body drilling deep into me, his breath hot against my shoulder, muffling his exquisite determination.

He pulled away and slid a strand of my hair over my ear. His deep brown eyes, the color of fresh, hot espresso, stared into mine.

"You're one of the best, sweetheart."

"True, but I bet you say that to all your clients." I held his sexy gaze, perhaps to challenge him, perhaps because I wanted to keep my pride. It was no secret to either of us that my husband paid him to service me, because he couldn't get it up himself.

The first few months of wedded bliss had been like a Ken and Barbie dream date come true. We traveled to exotic places, dined in the moonlight on white sandy beaches. He showered me with trinkets and baubles in appreciation. Yes, the sex was hot, a trifle stilted, but satisfying. His age and the meds for his high blood pressure had some effect on his performance, but he was and still is a man of innovation. His gifts of diamonds and flowers soon gave way to an array of toys that he used with great skill to satisfy me when he wasn't able to.

But as time wore on, I could not help but begin to note the detached, vacant look in his eyes when we made love.

I held tight to my charmed life.

I didn't think about it much until after his freak boat accident, a year after we'd married. It occurred when he was entered in a boat race while vacationing in the Mediterranean. It left him a quadriplegic, but still a very wealthy man.

My gaze was drawn to lover number seventeen as he slipped his watch over his wrist. He was one of those men you'd look twice at on the street, or in a restaurant. He exuded a youthful confidence, a calm sense of being comfortable in his own skin, which, by the way, looked exceedingly good on him. For a brief moment I pretended that we really knew each other, but the truth was, I didn't even know his name. That was part of the bargain.

"Not true. I don't say that to all of them." He grinned as he pushed from the bed and resumed dressing.

I slid from beneath the sheets and toyed with the idea of showering, wondering if he might be enticed to stay if I offered. Instead, I decided to wait, not wanting to wash his heavenly, masculine scent from my skin just yet. I turned purposely to watch him as he tucked his crisp, charcoal-gray dress shirt into his tailor-made pants. I had to give him credit. He was a professional, and dressed the part very well. His silver ring, likely a college fraternity keepsake, glinted in the light streaming through the window. The man had magnificent hands. My body tingled even now with the memory of them gliding with exquisite precision over my flesh.

"You look as delicious dressed as undressed, darling." I smiled and crossed my arms casually over my full breasts, still tender from his teasing. I had no shame in standing before him without a stitch. Given the slightest signal that he might be interested, I would gladly have offered myself to his pleasure again.

"Has he got you on the schedule for next week?"

He cleared his throat, but refused to meet my eyes. I knew something was up and that likely it wasn't what I'd hoped it was.

"I'm sorry, but this is the last time."

"You aren't serious?" My God, in comparison to all the men my husband had paraded in my direction in the past six months, this man was an Adonis. Exceptional, grade A, off-the-charts sex. I couldn't just let him leave. Not like this, not without knowing why. My eyes darted to the mirror and I saw a flicker of desperation cross my face. I turned my focus back to him.

I knelt on the bed facing him, my knees not so discreetly parted, straightening my shoulders for the desired effect, hoping that would persuade him.

"Just like that? Was it so bad?" I pouted and looked through hooded lids at him.

He shook his head slowly, pausing as he closed his zipper, and raked a hand through his unruly hair. I loved that about his hair. It was sexy and tousled as if he'd just gotten out of bed, which he had. And I wanted him back there where I could muss it again, hold it tight in my fists as my climax shook my body. The thought made me wet and I eased my hand between my legs, my nipples tightening as I held his gaze.

"You do know that we're good together, don't you?" I stroked my slick folds, gliding my other hand deliciously slowly over my breast.

The Adam's apple in his throat bobbed delightfully with his hard swallow.

"I've...I should...go," he choked out, but his eyes were fixed on the languid stroke of my fingers.

"Are you absolutely sure you have to run off so quickly?"

I sighed through my parted lips, aroused by my own hand and the hungry look in his eyes. It was a decadent sensation, this control I possessed.

"He...said until four." He jerked his gaze from my pussy to check his watch. I could see his will crumbling. It was 4:05.

I offered him a soft moan for good measure.

"Shit," he growled, and in two strides jerked me up from the bed and slammed me gently against the wall, his mouth boring down on mine until I had to shove at his shoulders to breathe.

"Go for it," I whispered with a smile, unbuttoning the shirt he'd so dutifully fastened seconds before. His body trembled next to mine, his fever clear as he yanked his belt free and flung it over his shoulder. He wasted no time dismissing his pants and briefs in one motion, then picked me up by the hips and braced me against the wall.

I sighed blissfully when he entered me, grinding against me, adjusting my hips until we fit tightly together.

Saddled on his perfect cock, I curled my arms over his shoulders and hooked my ankles at his waist. My breasts pressed to his hard body. I leaned forward and softly bit his shoulder as he began to move within me.

Lovers dancing a tango old as time.

He tucked his face against the curve of my neck and, with the grace of his slow-easy style, proceeded to take me to the edge of oblivion. A piece of my heart broke free of the pure, sexual ecstasy and for a brief moment I pretended we were together, for always. He was hard and slick, and smelled like a lover's dream. Where my husband had managed to find him was anybody's guess. More than once that afternoon I'd imagined him working in a fine men's clothing store, or seated behind the executive desk of a successful company.

The fantasy of our being a couple lasted less than the time it took for us to crash hard and fast into one another, our bodies jerking in primal rhythm to satisfy the ancient urge. The ferocity of his breathing mingled with his deep chuckle.

"My God, you're fantastic," I uttered through the shuddering aftermath of my climax. He lowered me to the floor and rested his forehead to mine.

"You're right, we *are* good together." His eyes rose to mine then and in them I saw a look of regret.

Reality was a bitch. There was so much more that I wanted to say, but I dared not risk it, not now and likely not ever. My husband was a very powerful man despite his disabilities.

"Perfection, love. You better go now." I dipped beneath his arm before he had the chance to kiss me again. I got lost in his kisses.

I slipped on my peach-colored satin robe and this time kept my eyes lowered as he dressed. I couldn't chance the piece of my heart—however infinitesimal it might be—to have any feeling toward him.

It wasn't part of our agreement.

He dressed facing away from me and we spoke no more. I didn't even look up until I heard the door shut quietly behind him. I walked to the oversize mirror and studied my reflection. With great calm, I picked up my hairbrush and stroked it through my short brown hair. There were just a few strands of silver showing my age, but nothing so noticeable a good hairdresser couldn't fix.

Yes, I was still a viable, passionate woman and I could rival any of the twentysomething divas I often lunched with, and who often looked to me as a "seasoned" woman for advice.

What a strong and wonderful marriage I had. Wasn't I the lucky one?

I wondered how many others like me existed out there. One or two? Ten or twenty? It wasn't exactly a topic you might bring up at an afternoon charity tea.

We, whose lives, mastered by passion, are caught somewhere in a vortex comprised of need and circumstance. We agree to whatever is necessary to derive a moment of pleasure in an otherwise cold and sterile world, and be able to enjoy the good life.

The phone by the bed rang and I knew it was Paul. I picked up the remote receiver, my throat still dry from the mind-boggling sex. I grabbed the bottle of champagne, praying there was a little left. All that was left of the ice was chilled water. There was enough for one glass, maybe two.

"Did you enjoy yourself, my dear?"

I'd become a pro at disassociation. "Why, of course—didn't it appear so?" My response was short, rather snappish, and I reeled in that part of me that remembered the look of regret on my lover's face. With careful precision I steadied the bottle as I poured the golden nectar into my glass. I glanced up, my eye catching my lover's glass still on the nightstand.

"You looked lovely, as always, Charlie."

The soft tone in his voice caught my heart unaware as it did always, and what's more, he knew it would. I closed my eyes, draining the glass as I held the receiver a few inches from my ear.

"Was he as...proficient as the others?"

I hated the part where he insisted on analyzing every moment, but I played along. After all, the man I'd just let ravish me all afternoon was off the scale in terms of "proficient."

"He was," I agreed, setting my glass on the dresser, readying to pour another glass. I wanted to embrace the bubbly haze of the champagne and enjoy the afterglow a bit more. Maybe I was being selfish.

"He won't be back, you know. I can keep them just so long, and then they get on with their lives. This one mentioned a fiancée, I believe."

Two pricks in the same moment, one on the phone and one to my heart.

"I thought it must be something like that. He told me it was his last time." I licked my lips and stared into the mirror. I was careful not to say too much, give him too much praise. Yet if I showed any displeasure, I wasn't sure what my husband might do.

My reflection stared back at me, my eyes still bright from sex, my cheeks flushed from arousal. But I could see his face, his ice-blue eyes peering at me, dissecting my every nuance.

My gut twisted, but I fought hard to keep my expression objective, almost apathetic, but not quite.

Paul could read me like a book, and if he had an inkling that I might have actually had some feeling for this man, or any of them, he'd sever our agreement, and then where would I be?

"Will I see you at home soon, then?"

My eye caught the champagne bottle, condensation running in rivulets down its side, leaving a pool on the dresser. "In a little while. I'd like to shower first."

"Understandable."

There was a brief silence.

"I'll have Jenkins waiting downstairs, whenever you're ready."

"Fine, thank you." The words stuck in my throat, mixed with the bile forming there. I hung up, refusing to look again in the mirror.

CHAPTER TWO

"I WANT YOU TO WEAR THE PEARLS THIS TIME."

It was a cloudy day, causing me to have to turn on the lamp beside the bed. I stood transfixed at the bedside, studying the long strand of pale pink pearls that lay across the satin coverlet. I picked them up and let them dangle from my fingertips. They were quite beautiful, really, glimmering in the soft glow of the lamplight.

"Any particular reason?" I asked, speaking into the phone's receiver. A gentle knock on the door pulled my attention for a moment.

"You'll think of something, dear. You always do. For me, Charlie—wear them for me."

My dear husband's health was beginning to deteriorate, and with it, I feared, his mental state. It wasn't enough that he paid other men to have sex with me, or that I succumbed to every one of his odd demands. Now he was giving me props. Before, he'd let me handle things on my own. But this—this made me feel cheap for some reason.

"Fine," I replied, not wishing to deliberate the new concept. I slipped them over my head, and they hung past my hips.

I swallowed the remaining champagne and poured two glasses, carrying them to the smooth gray stone foyer. I opened the door and there, dressed in an impeccable Armani suit, was the human equivalent of a fine Italian race car. Polished, perfect and very sleek. The Italian prize offered an equally perfect smile.

"Charlie?" His accent breathed my name softly, making the *Ch* sound like *Sh*.

His dark, hungry gaze took me in from head to foot. He leaned against the door frame with the casual flair of a man who did this every day.

"That's me, and you must be...?" I handed him the flute and waited, wondering if my question would trip him up. I couldn't help teasing; sometimes it broke the ice.

He grinned, his teeth white and even, bright against his beautiful olive skin, but he did not answer. Instead, he plucked the glass from my hand and sauntered past me, his head on a swivel as he scoured the suite.

"See anything you like?" I eased the door shut and leaned against it. A wicked desire rose up my spine as I imagined the tight ass hidden by that jacket. I had to give my husband credit for finding men who looked exceptionally good in quality clothes.

He grinned over his shoulder and took a sip of the champagne.

"Would you perhaps like to take a few moments to get to know each other?" He looked past me to the original Monet hanging on the wall in the entry. Chances were he had no desire to know anything about me any more than I wanted to know more about him.

"Let's not waste any time, shall we?"

He tipped his glass toward me. "Whatever the lady wants, the lady gets." His smooth baritone accent slid over my flesh as he sauntered toward me. He removed his jacket and folded it carefully, laying it over the stark-white leather couch.

I tipped my head and offered a pleasant smile.

"Here, my lovely lady? Or would you prefer to escort me to your bedroom?"

It wouldn't matter, of course, to my husband. His surveillance included every room on hidden camera. The poor men were the only ones who didn't know that their performances were being closely watched and rated by the man who'd solicited their services.

For me.

"What do you prefer?" I swallowed my drink and placed the flute on the front hall table. I met him halfway, brushing close by him so I could inhale his cologne, let it begin to intoxicate my senses, mingle with the heady champagne. It was easier if I could imagine what type of man he might be like under different circumstances.

He drew me against his chest, reaching around my waist, where he began slowly drawing my blouse from my sensible gray pinstripe pencil skirt. Today I'd worn the four-inch stiletto heels. I kept my focus on the rain as it smacked against the picture windows. The view was exceptional, of course, careening high above the other rooftops of the city, an unobstructed view of the horizon. Only the best for my husband.

His hand slid beneath my blouse, his smooth fingers tentative as he unfastened the clasp at the front of my bra. The pearls caught beneath his hand, gliding over my flesh in an admittedly erotic and delightful way.

I glanced beneath hooded lids to the gold, gilded antique mirror above the fireplace and smiled. It was genuine.

My Italian storm gathered quickly, removing my clothes first, and then his, with methodical precision, until we both stood naked in the dusky light of the pelting thunderstorm, with the exception of my heels and pearls, of course.

"Turn around," he urged, holding the pearls as I faced away from him. The pearls tapped against my spine, cool and smooth to the touch. My body curved instinctively into his as he pressed against my back, providing a preview of his magnificent size against my bottom. He was a maestro with his hands, commanding my breasts to attention, strumming my clit until I ached.

"Duro e veloce," he whispered as he leaned me forward to grasp the back of the couch. The fireplace across the room loomed dark and empty, and the thought occurred to me that a warm fire would have been a nice touch on such a rainy day.

A gasp rose from my mouth as I sensed the small pearls, wrapped around his fingers, sliding between my legs. He glided them over my swollen lips, seducing, coaxing, driving me crazy with need. I glanced up in my euphoric haze to see his reflection behind me in the mirror. He was a fine-looking man, finely tuned, and his powerful biceps sported a series of artistic tattoos that curled over one shoulder. His chest was without hair, just as Paul knew I liked, and his rock-hard abs made me fantasize gripping them later as I rode him to exhaustion.

What he did with those pearls was beyond phenomenal. The dominating expression on his face created a greater arousal as he continued his ministrations, dipping the slick, round beads deeper between my folds. My fingers curled into the leather, my knuckles turning white as I swayed my hips slightly to enjoy the sensation. Lost in the ecstasy and the delightful champagne haze, I hardly thought of Paul at all. Forgetting everything, I just wanted this moment to go on forever

My Italian stallion, without warning, grabbed my hips and drove into me with such force that I had to cling to the couch to keep from toppling over. I watched in the mirror, seeing my body jerk with each ferocious thrust. The muscles of his neck bulged with his clenched teeth, and his fingers dug into the soft flesh of my hips.

The pearls slid over my rib cage, dangling in my peripheral vision; they, too, jerked as he rocked my body to his.

I came in a shattering climax, hot and fast, not at all like my last lover. The man with the slow hands and gentle, espresso eyes.

My current lover's climax finished with a crescendo and a primal howl, as though he'd mated with a she-wolf in the wild.

"Magnifico!" he cried out in jubilation, and proceeded to swat my butt in triumph. Had it not been for his cleverness with the pearls, I would have thrown him out after that alone, regardless of Paul's agreement. As it was, I discovered when I held the dominant role, he was quite an enjoyable lover. After he left, I poured another glass of champagne and curled up in my robe on the couch, reminiscing on the afternoon. I had a sense that perhaps I'd taught him a thing or two about pleasuring a woman.

I sipped my drink and waited for the phone to ring. After a few minutes, I stepped to the mirror over the fireplace and straightened my hair. I realized with a quiet surprise that I still wore the pearls.

There was no way to reach him. That was part of the

agreement. He would always call me, and if he didn't, I was to return home, where he would meet me later.

Apparently this was one of those times.

I dropped my robe and the pearls onto the bed and turned toward the bathroom door.

The phone rang.

Startled at first, I started to put on my robe, but the phone rang insistently again and I simply reached to the nightstand and answered.

"How was Italian cuisine, my love?"

I folded my arm under my breasts and turned to the dresser. "The pearls worked nicely, thank you."

"I thought they made a nice touch."

"I'm going to take a quick shower, then—"

"Leave the door open."

"The door?"

"The bathroom door, Charlie. You know I love to watch you in the shower."

I thought he'd gone home. I couldn't let him see my dissatisfaction at the idea. I was beginning to feel as though I could not take a breath without him watching me.

"Sure, Paul, if you like."

"Yes…yes, I really do like to watch the water run down your body, Charlie. I imagine the showers we used to take together. Do you remember those, Charlie?" He sighed, but the sound was tired.

God help me, pity rose in my heart for him. My poor husband—his mind alert, but his body lifeless. "I do. They were the best." Tears pricked at the backs of my eyes. Those memories seemed like a hundred years ago.

"I'll leave the door open, Paul."

There was a click and I snapped off the receiver and walked

into the bathroom, easing open the door as I glanced at the dresser mirror reflected in the vanity mirror.

Was my life going to be like this forever?

CHAPTER THREE

Three months later

THE DAY WAS PERFECT, AS PERFECT AS THE CITY could get, and I chose to have lunch on the café sidewalk instead of being cooped up inside. I was to meet a friend who'd just returned from Saint-Tropez. I was dying to go there myself. I could stand to soak up a little sun and sea air. Maybe I'd approach Paul about a quick trip, or maybe he'd allow me to go alone.

I took a sip of my mimosa and pondered the thought. No, it was doubtful he'd let me out of his sight for that long.

It had been a while since the Italian fling. Paul had grown increasingly quiet, often skulking around the house and spending more time in the main computer center he so loved.

I let him have his fun. After all, what more could I offer him than his deepest desires? Affection had been a stranger in our marriage ever since the accident. He hated me to mother him; he said it made him feel less of a man. I obliged his request, but at the same time began to notice his possessive streak strengthening with each day.

Before I left for lunch today he'd insisted that Jenkins drive me and wait while I had lunch. When I expressed the thought that I might do a little shopping, he went into a tirade, and I finally succumbed to having the driver park discreetly down the block and wait for me.

I was beginning to feel more like a prisoner than his wife, and I wasn't sure who I could talk to about it.

"Hey, Charlie."

Misty Vancouver plopped into the café chair across from me. At thirty, she was married to Jeff Vancouver, president and CEO of the up-and-coming Vancouver International. Suffice it to say, Misty lived the charmed life.

"Ooh," she squealed with delight, "I need one of those. Waiter?" She waved her dainty French-tipped nails at him and grinned widely when he smiled at her. "Could I please have one of these? And heavy on the juice."

He bowed, but his eyes never left Misty's face.

I eyed her youthful figure wrapped in a designer sundress. She wore her frosted blond hair straight, where it fell in abandon to her bronzed, slim shoulders. Her smile turned to me as she shoved her sunglasses atop her head. She was exquisitely tanned, looked happy—dazzling, to be exact—and I hated her instantly.

"You two have got to get away to the beach." She shut her eyes and tipped her head back, reveling in her memory. "The white sand, the water, the sultry nights, God, it's pure paradise. Oh, and they have this massive yacht you can charter now—"

She stopped short, her eyes round with her horrified expression. "Oh, God, Charlie, I'm sorry. I forgot that Paul doesn't like the water anymore."

I smiled and shrugged, pretending my ambivalence to her remark. "He does stay at home a lot more now."

"Really, I'm sorry."

The waiter brought Misty's drink and, I noted, eyed her with the same admiration. She returned his approval with a sweet smile. I waited as she watched him walk away in his tight-fitting black dress pants. At least if they had a fling, it would be discreet, and likely because they both wanted it.

"So you had a good time, then?" I swallowed a good half of my mimosa and held it up to our waiter across the way. He came as quickly to my rescue, but without the same attention he paid Misty.

"It was very nice. But we had to cut the week a day short so Jeff could get back to some *bigwig* meeting."

"Don't you hate that?" I smirked, wondering if Jeff had a disgruntled mistress demanding his attention. Maybe not; maybe I was becoming too cynical. I laughed to myself and caught Misty's curious gaze.

"I suppose you're used to that sort of thing. I mean used to be." Her tiny catlike claws came out of her diamond-clad, manicured, perfect fingers.

I raised my brow and my drink. "It's a part of the territory, my dear, and the sooner you learn to accept it the better."

She eased back in her chair and crossed her long, tanned legs. Our waiter took note of that, too.

"What can I get for you two special ladies today?" He spoke directly to Misty, who had the decency to blush.

"I'll have the baked salmon, with wild rice and a salad—no onions, please. Oh, and dressing on the side," I offered, not shifting my relaxed stance in my chair. I watched with pleasant satisfaction how the splash of grenadine filtered through the drink.

He nodded and scribbled on his notepad, not once looking

at me. Misty perused the selections more than a dozen times, it seemed, before finally smacking the menu down. She offered the waiter a sweet, dazzling smile. Pure innocence, no doubt not wearing panties at all.

"What do you recommend?"

Good Lord.

"That depends on what you're in the mood for," he countered, shifting to focus on her with his body language. I considered shoving everything off the table so they could just have a go of it right then and there.

"Well, maybe you could surprise me with *your* favorite dish?"

She was openly flirting with him. This was getting hard to stomach.

I sipped my drink and let my mind wander from the vocal seduction going on between the two of them. I supposed it was one thing to have a choice who you had an affair with, rather than who your husband handpicked to have an affair with you.

I spied a men's clothing shop on the corner across the street from the restaurant, and made a mental note to stop in quickly and pick up a nice tie or perhaps a new sweater for Paul. His birthday was coming up and a tie might come in handy—if not for him, perhaps for me.

"So what's new with you and Paul?"

The waiter was gone and Misty turned her attention back to the fact that someone was seated across from her. "Nothing much, really. We pretty much have our daily routine down now."

She sighed as though I'd just told her I was the Queen of England.

"I wish Jeff and I were as comfortable with each other as you and Paul. You two have been through so much and yet have managed to remain so strong. I wish I knew your secret. Some days, I wonder if our marriage could survive anything so serious."

The poor girl would faint dead away if I told her the secret of our marital success. Then again, maybe she wouldn't. Misty impressed me as the type that could ease into the role I played without much discomfiture. Still, she wasn't the one I could talk to frankly about my situation. She loved to talk too much, and she and Jeff were heavy into the social scene.

"Well—" I lifted my second mimosa to her "—you never really know what you're capable of until it happens."

"Boy, that's true." Her gaze wandered off and I knew she was searching for her handsome young waiter friend.

"Jeff working late tonight?" Yeah, it was a baited question.

"Hmm? Oh, yes, but I have a million things to do. All that laundry from the trip, catching up on bills, you know the menial stuff."

"Right." I smiled. I guessed what Jeff didn't know wouldn't hurt him, and perhaps even if he did, it wouldn't faze him. The craze of open marriage seemed to be an up-and-coming lifestyle for the very well-to-do. I figured by suppertime, Misty would be ushering our waiter into her bedroom to help her with a few menial tasks.

Our food was set before us and, sure enough, Misty didn't think I saw when she slipped a folded bill into our waiter's hand. What denomination I wasn't sure, but I knew it contained a phone number.

I guess pleasure is a marketable commodity.

CHAPTER FOUR

IT COULDN'T BE HIM. I STEPPED AROUND A TALL shelving unit stacked with every color of dress shirt known to man. I nearly sent toppling a freestanding rack of specially priced clearance polo shirts.

I kept my sunglasses on, and fortunately, my wide-brimmed hat shielded me from being recognized. I knew I should leave, but my feet felt glued in place. I turned and stared at an array of ties, fumbling through them without an ounce of thought to color, design, or anything past the sweat of my palms.

I quickly slid my hand over my shift and swallowed hard. I couldn't remember the last time a man had made me so visibly nervous, and I'd been naked with this one. If indeed, I was correct and it was—

I turned to sneak a peek and my heart stopped as I met his radiating smile.

"How can I help you today?"

My Lord, he smelled so good. The scent made the back of my knees weak with the memories it produced. He hadn't yet recognized me, apparently. I toyed with the idea of turning around and leaving and just letting him wonder the rest of his life what he'd done to offend me as a customer.

But I couldn't be so rude. And yes, I knew it was just an excuse.

I removed my glasses and tipped my gaze to meet his.

"Charlie?" he whispered, as though I'd been a dream of his long ago set aside.

"Funny how life happens, isn't it? I pictured this might be what you did for a living. You have impeccable taste in clothes." I smiled, though my gut churned like a schoolgirl braving that pivotal chat with the untouchable best-looking boy at school.

"How did you find me?" He glanced around to make sure no customers were within earshot.

I could see clearly how he would feel so awkward. I'm sure it wasn't every day that the lover who paid for your services walked into your store.

"Don't worry, I didn't track you down. I happened to be having lunch across the street and decided to come in and find a gift for my husband. It's his birthday next week. I was thinking of a tie."

My hand ran down the edge of the ties hanging on display. He reached up, checking the store once more, before his fingers lightly hovered over mine.

"Did you have a particular color in mind?"

He eased closer in the narrow aisle, his focus on the ties and not me, but my body sensed his interest as a metal rod senses lightning.

"Nothing in particular. He doesn't wear them often."

His expression was curious as his gaze dropped briefly to mine. "So it's whatever color you like?" He licked his lips and boldly held my gaze.

"Pretty much, I guess." I offered him a smile, though I fought the idea that it was like Misty to flirt with him. At least he and I shared a past, and I had missed him, almost to a desperate state. There'd been a few impromptu times when Paul had demanded I use my toys, so he could watch. Nevertheless, when I closed my eyes, I saw the face of the man standing before me, and it aroused me as much then as it did now.

I knew Jenkins was outside in the limo and would be expecting me. "Which would hold up the best...with time?"

A sexy grin appeared and quickly disappeared. He cleared his throat. And scanned the area around us before he spoke. "That, too, depends on the frequency of the use."

"Really?" I wrapped the end of a cobalt-blue plaid tie around my wrist and looked up at him. "What do you think? Does this color look good against my skin?"

He closed his eyes and took a deep breath. "Maybe you'd like to look at a few in the mirror against a dress shirt?"

"Yours?" I slid him a smile. I'd never been more thrilled for warm weather, no stockings and sandal dressing.

"Step this way. The mirrors are here, way in the back near the dressing rooms."

He did not touch me, but led the way to the back of the store where there were no customers milling about the rows and rows of suits.

"I'm going to be busy modeling a few suits for this customer, Stan. Can you watch things up front for a few moments?"

I raised my brow and caught his eye in the mirror. Fortunately, Stan didn't. Odd that I still didn't know this man's name.

"Sure thing, Cade. I'll get started marking down those shirts."

Cade. The name fit him well, almost as exceptionally as did his suit, a deep charcoal-gray with a perfectly matched blue shirt. His hand yanked off the tie he was wearing, and his gaze bounced to mine before he tossed it on a nearby chair.

He ushered me to a set of doors hidden by a bay of mirrors, took a quick look over his shoulder and grabbed my hand, pulling me into the dressing room. He locked the door as he faced me, wasting no time as he cupped my face in his hands, capturing my mouth in a kiss that left no question what was to come.

My hat and purse thudded to the floor as my fingers threaded through the hair at the base of his neck. It was a desperate kiss, primal, needy at first, turning slow and seductive after a moment or two. I celebrated the taste of his lips, the way he sampled my mouth like a man dying of thirst.

I brushed his jacket off his broad shoulders, reveling in the strength still so fresh in my mind. With the patience of a virgin I busied myself with carefully turning each button as he fumbled with my dress. It fell to my feet as I continued to undress him.

"I've thought of no one else since that day with you," he whispered. His breath punctuated with a breath mint blew close to my face. His kiss, just as I remembered, was divine, insanely slow, as though he wanted to taste every part of me. I was clad in simple lingerie, not expecting, of course, to meet up with anyone, and never, God forbid, on my own.

"I missed you. I thought you were getting married," I breathed between kisses. I took his fabulous hands and kissed them, running their tips over my lips, noting with delight that he wore no ring, at least not yet. I bit the end of his finger playfully.

His hands left mine and drifted over my lace-covered breasts, leaving fire in their wake. He kissed my stomach as he drew my panties to my ankles, pausing as I stepped from them. My panties were soaked with my honeyed arousal. The minute he had acknowledged the tension between us, the need for him had throbbed like a dull ache between my legs.

He knelt, lifted my leg over his shoulder and leaned forward, kissing my dark curls, rubbing his jaw, shadowed with a hint of a beard, along my thigh.

"Sweet, sweet woman," he whispered.

I turned my face to the ceiling, holding his head like a precious gift as he made love to me with his skillful tongue. When I could no longer hold back, I came in a rush, my fingers entwined in his dark hair, gripping fiercely to keep from screaming in ecstasy.

He smiled up at me and licked his lips.

"I love the name Cade." His name rolled from my mouth, breathless from my shuddering climax. It sounded so right, so natural. Cade and Charlie.

He stood then and peeled off his shirt, and I held my palms to the wall, enjoying the simple, masculine beauty of his body. He reached for his belt, I touched his hand, and with understanding he allowed me to kneel before him and do to him what he'd done to me.

I pressed my hand to his crotch, giving rise to his masculine hardness. He felt heavy and thick, tailor-made just for me. I already knew how we fit; I already knew he'd adjust to the right to gain deeper penetration. It was as though we'd had sex for years together.

His hands smoothed over my hair as I took him into my mouth, drawing my lips slowly over his silky tip, delighted to lick the dew from his head. He stood, legs apart in front of me, not masking the sighs evoked by my ministrations with teeth and tongue.

"You're still on birth control?" he whispered, taking my hands and pulling me up against his chest.

I nodded once before he kissed me hard and backed me to the wall. He lifted me, easing me onto his erection, and I smiled as he shifted to the right, and felt him slide deep inside my core. We stood for a moment just like that, not moving, just relishing our joining.

He held his forehead to mine. I still wore my bra and nothing else. He wore only a pair of black dress socks. My heart tugged at our reflection in the mirror. Here we were, secret lovers in a stolen moment of passion. It was so sweet, so completely forbidden, and yet neither of us could deny our need.

"You smell so sexy," he murmured, nuzzling his mouth under my chin. His biceps bulged as he braced me around his hips and offered languid kisses over my shoulder and face.

"I could stay this way forever, Charlie. I don't know what I'm going to do." His mouth closed over mine in a kiss that spoke more of commitment than fast, thoughtless sex.

"What about your fiancée?"

"There isn't one." He lowered his face to my shoulder and left soft kisses there. I should have been ecstatic, really, but the absence of a fiancée left him single and me still married.

"What happened?" I shifted my back against the wall and hooked my ankles around his waist, angling to draw our bodies closer. His hands held my hips as he began to move inside me.

"There never was a fiancée, Charlie. Your husband told me to tell you that." He withdrew and pushed deep, the slick friction between us providing a sensuous treat. My body began to tighten again, my breasts to tingle. I pushed my shoulders back, shoving my aching breasts into his face.

He did not skip his rhythm as his mouth closed over the lace of my hardened nipple, teasing it between his teeth, pulling it gently until I opened my mouth with a tiny scream.

"Shhh," he cautioned with a deep chuckle, and kissed me long and hard as he pumped into me with unbridled need, tearing a shattering climax from my body. As I released myself, squeezing my pelvis to milk his thrusts, seconds later he toppled over, his hot seed shooting into me.

Savoring the moment, I kept my arms around his neck and buried my face in his shoulder. It was a stupid thing to do, and if Paul ever found out, this man might lose more than his job.

"Why would he do that?" I leaned back and held Cade's gaze even as our bodies parted from one another.

He shook his head. "I don't know. I thought maybe you could tell me." He slipped on his boxer briefs, and it was hard not to stare at his magnificent body and remember where we were.

Of course, Cade didn't know of the many lovers my husband had hired as a guise to pleasure me, but really for his own amusement. "He can be very controlling at times." If I left it at that, perhaps he wouldn't ask any more. Perhaps we could move on and let this be the last time we saw each other. My stomach churned with the idea of telling him that he wasn't the only man my husband paid to have sex with me.

He held up my dress as I slipped into it. His hands ran down my bare arms.

"I want to see you again, but I have to tell you something and I hope it makes more sense to you than it does to me."

Cade's warm brown eyes searched my face. Nothing much made sense to me at the moment, except that I was beginning to regret what I'd just done. And regret was not part of who Charlie was.

"He called me about a week ago and hired me to keep an eye on you."

I stared at him. What in the world was Paul up to? "Keep an eye on me? Why? Why would he call you?"

The flashback of my expression the day Cade left me at the hotel sprang like a nightmare into my mind. Had Paul seen it?

Cade shrugged. "I have no clue. He just said that he felt he could trust me. He thought maybe you might be seeing another man."

I laughed and quickly covered my mouth, realizing we were still locked in the men's dressing room together. The statement was so absurd that at first I could only stare at him. It was clear now that Paul had me where he wanted me. He'd seen the look in my eye, known what I felt with Cade.

I had to get out of there. I pulled on my panties and stuck my feet in my sandals. For all I knew these mirrors were part of his voyeuristic web. I hoped I hadn't already endangered Cade by this chance encounter. "I need a tie." I spoke hurriedly, gathering my purse and hat. I fumbled with the doorknob, frantic to open it, to get away from the mirror and the small room. Cade gripped my shoulders.

"Charlie, wait, what's going on? My God, you're trembling. What is it? You can tell me." He tried to turn me toward him, but I held tight to the door.

I couldn't face him. The darkness of my agreement with my husband, of whoring myself to other men for his pleasure in the name of love, made me want to vomit. "I can't. Just leave it at that, okay? I can't."

"Charlie, has he hurt you? Has he threatened you in some way? There are people…agencies who can help with this kind of thing. Let me help you."

His comfort scared me, made me wish for things that could

never be mine. I forced myself to think he couldn't afford to keep a woman like me, not on a clothier's paycheck.

I forced my sunglasses onto my face and straightened my shoulders. "Don't try to contact me, and if my husband asks, you must tell him that I came in, but be sure to say that I only talked about him. Tell him I behaved as coldly toward you as if we were strangers."

"We aren't strangers, Charlie. You know that," Cade whispered softly against the back of my head.

"Leave me alone. Forget this ever happened—forget we ever met." I jerked open the door and scanned the area before stepping out into the open space in front of the bay of mirrors. I caught my reflection, seeing the fear on my face.

Don't you cry. I gave my image a stern, silent warning. *Make it clean. Make it believable.*

"Thank you for your help. I'll be sure to put in a good word for you to your boss."

Cade stared at me from the door to the dressing room. His shirt, disheveled, hung loose over his dress pants. He was still barefoot.

I left him, made my purchase and climbed into the limo without looking back.

"Everything satisfactory, Ms. Charlie?" Jenkins glanced up at me through the rearview mirror.

I couldn't trust him. At the moment I couldn't trust anyone. I had to figure out what I was going to do. If I divorced Paul, would he use the tapes to prove I was cheating on him? By the time I was able to get proof of his myriad of technical equipment, he'd have it all torn down. Whatever I chose to do or not do, it needed to be carefully thought out.

"I found a nice tie for Paul's birthday, but I think the mimosas I had at lunch have given me an unbearable headache. Please drop me at the suite. I'll stay in town this evening."

"Shall I notify Mr. Paul, then?"

"No, I'll contact him when I get there."

"Very good, Ms. Charlie."

"YOU'RE SURE YOU DON'T WANT ME TO COME into town?" Paul's voice soothed like a cool compress through the receiver. I knew if he did, I'd not have a moment of peace.

"Not tonight, sweetheart." I nearly choked on the words. "I just need to sleep. I'm sure by morning I'll be fine."

"Okay, then. Sweet dreams, dear. I'll keep watch over you while you sleep."

His offer sent a shudder down my spine. "No, Paul, I've covered the mirrors. Tonight I don't want to think about anything but sleep, do you understand?"

"No, you're up there all alone and the surveillance helps keep an eye on things. It's more for your protection than anything. I'll activate the cameras—"

"Don't, Paul. I'm on the thirty-third floor. No one can reach me up here."

"Except me, of course."

"Except you, of course," I said placatingly. My head was throbbing in earnest now.

"You're sure you're okay? I can send Jenkins with something for—"

"Paul, please just give me some private time. I promise to call if I need anything, really."

"Promise?"

"Absolutely," I lied. I'd sooner choke on my own spit than ask this weasel for anything, but I couldn't afford not to have a plan, and it had to be infallible.

"All right, then. I'll call you in the morning to arrange for the car to come around. When you get home, I'll have the cook fix us a nice breakfast, with mimosas. You like mimosas, don't you, Charlie?"

I sat down on the edge of the bed, holding my hand to my forehead. "Yeah, I do, but the couple I had at lunch today really threw me. They must have made them with exceptional champagne."

"Nothing but the best for *my* girl," he cooed.

The tone of his voice caused me to blink. It wasn't possible. How could he have known where I would be for lunch? What was he doing to me?

A panic rose in my gut. What if that waiter knew? What if Paul had paid him to put something in my drink? "I need to go lie down, Paul."

"Sure, sweetheart. I'll see you tomorrow."

The receiver clicked and the sound of it echoed in my ear. I stared at the receiver. He hadn't told me, as he always did without fail, how much he adored me.

Something wasn't right.

I showered, closing the door, and later slipped into my sweatpants and hoodie that I used for workouts. The hot shower had helped to clear my head, but my stomach still roiled. Scrounging through the cupboards, I found some chamomile tea, nuked a hot cup and curled up on the couch, staring out at the darkening sky.

I've no idea how long I sat there, letting my life play like a movie in my head. The first time I'd met Paul; how he never wanted me to bring up the topic of his other wives; how he was selfish, admitted openly that he didn't want kids. He wanted to give me everything my heart desired. And he'd kept true to his word.

I hugged myself and leaned my head against the back of the couch. The room grew dark as I stared through the picture window at the neon lights of the city beginning to dot the skyline.

A sound startled me, pulling my attention to the dim shadows near the front door. There in the dimness I saw the silhouette of a man standing in the foyer, watching me. Without thought, I leaped over the couch and grabbed the floor lamp, flicking the switch in the process, momentarily blinding the intruder.

"This apartment has surveillance cameras crawling all over it. You'd be wise to leave now before the alarms go off."

"The alarms aren't going to go off, Charlie. And you've done a remarkable job of covering all the mirrors. That's where the cameras are hidden, aren't they?"

At the sound of Cade's voice, I let the lamp slide from my fingers and returned it to the floor. "What are you doing here? How did you get in?"

He was dressed in black clothing from head to foot. Only his handsome face was exposed.

"I'm pretty handy with alarm systems as well as locks, Charlie. I figured this one out the afternoon we spent together. It really wasn't that difficult."

My mind reeled with confusion.

His eyes narrowed, studying me for a moment. "I suppose

you'd like an explanation?" he offered, sauntering down the
two steps into the living room. He headed for one of two
leather chairs flanking the French provincial fireplace. Cade
eased down into the seat and crossed his leg over his knee,
as if he had all the time in the world. He worked at pressing
the fingers of his leather gloves tighter on his hand.

I stared at those leather-encased hands, remembering how
they had felt a few hours earlier caressing my body.

"You see, when your husband hired me the first time, I
had to guess that any man who had enough money to hire a
guy to have sex with his wife was a man who would likely
strike a bargain to get her back."

My brain went numb as I stared at Cade. My sweet, gentle
lover with soft brown eyes—those dark orbs that now glinted
as they held me captive. "I don't understand." I thought I was
going to be sick.

"The idea hadn't occurred to me until this afternoon, really.
After he approached me a second time, the seed began to form
in my head. And shortly after you left today, the whole plan
fell into place. I just needed to fill in the details, and hopefully
the rest will be as easy."

"The rest?" I swallowed hard, forcing the bile back down
my throat.

"It's fairly simple, really. I kidnap the wife, demand the
ransom, collect it, but unfortunately, they'll never find your
body. Eventually the case will be closed."

"You plan to kill me? You planned this all along?" My
throat was parched with fear. I looked around the room,
searching for a weapon…anything to defend myself. However,
the furnishings were sparse on purpose. It helped to create an
ambience of anonymity for Paul's videos.

"Oh, no, not all along, Charlie. I just realized it's the only
way, don't you see? Now, are you going to come quietly, or

are we going to get the police up here, where they are sure to find all those incriminating tapes your husband has?"

My eyes welled. He knew all about the others. But what about the tape with him and me on it? "They'll check the tapes after I'm gone, and they'll find the one of you and me that afternoon."

His grin sparkled in the low light of the room. He held up a video case, waving it in his hand. "That one will be with his wife."

"You think you've thought this through, don't you? You've no idea how possessive my husband can be. How powerful his connections are."

"It's infallible."

I stared at him and wondered if he was as clever as he thought he was. Still, he was right. I had no option but to go along with his plan. "Fine, just let me get my things."

He grabbed my arm as I walked past him. "You won't need them where you're going. Come on, Charlie."

I jerked my arm from his grasp.

"Look, I'm sorry it has to be this way, but you'd do the same in a heartbeat. You know you would."

In the dark shadows of the night, Cade did not detect the flicker of regret in my eyes.

CHAPTER SIX

"MADEMOISELLE?" A SHADOW FELL OVER MY FACE and I shaded my eyes against the brilliant sun. My thoughts had drifted to dreams of my lover's sighs as he cherished my body, a temple to his pleasure, an offering to our mutual lust.

I looked up beneath my sun hat at the face of reality. A beautiful skin bronzed by a tropical sun I allowed only on my limbs, never my face.

My lover took my hand and brought it to his lips. "You slept well last night?"

"Yes, thanks to you." I smiled.

"You realize there was no other way to save you, but to trap him like that."

"Of course, darling. It just took me some time to put it all together. I have my vulnerable side, he played on it, and you recognized that and took control of the situation. You take such good care of me."

I shut my eyes briefly as a warm tropical breeze caressed my near-naked flesh. I'd worn little more than next-to-nothing bikinis for the better part of the past month. I could spend my life here, quite content, just as we were at this moment.

"You seemed to enjoy last night?"

I peeped open an eye, smiled at him and swung my legs over the side of the hammock. He was a handsome man and the time spent in the sun had given color to his face. His once-dark hair, now threaded with silver streaks, held continental allure. Holding his gaze, I padded across the red-brick patio dusted with the silky white sand from the beach beyond. With great care to let him view the backside of my pearl-and-crochet thong, I sat in his lap, nestled my bottom into his crotch and took his face in my hands, kissing him passionately.

"Yeah, I like that, Charlie. I like that a lot," he whispered, staring into my eyes.

"Darling, did Jenkins get to the car before the authorities found it?"

He nodded toward the breakfast table, where the morning paper lay. Beside it was the black videotape.

"Paul, promise me that you'll destroy this one—it's not one of my favorites." I stroked my husband's cheek, imagining his hand on my breast. He was physically unable to, of course, but I knew, as always, he would make sure that if I wanted a hand to touch me, he'd have a tantalizing lover for me by sunset.

"I'll see to it, sweetheart. Whatever you want." He lifted his chin for another kiss.

I kissed him again and glanced down at the headline: Man Arrested in Kidnapping/Extortion Plot of Wife of Erich Technologies Tycoon.

Cade had let his greed surpass his desire. It was too bad, because I had so enjoyed being with him. However, Paul had warned me of the risks. He'd said there might be men who couldn't see the gift they'd been given, having just one day with me. He was right. Paul was always right.

The warm tropical sun shone down, warming my skin, reminding me of the first time I'd met Paul, on this very beach in Saint-Tropez. We'd made love all night on our private stretch of beach. He'd told me repeatedly how he'd always watch out for me.

I lifted my leg over his hip, straddling his wheelchair. A padded metal brace held his head erect; white straps, made of softest chamois, kept his shoulders back, his body from toppling out of the chair. His form, though lifeless, was exercised daily by a private therapist, but it wasn't enough for Paul. He needed to remember what it was like to make love to me, and every time he watched as my body gave way to ecstasy, in his mind and in his heart, he came, too. How could I deny him this one simple pleasure?

It had all come clear to me after Cade explained his plan. He was more interested in the money. Even if he had planned to run away with me, it was still all about the money. With Paul, it wasn't about the money. It was about me.

I was glad for the chip Paul had planted in my cell phone, which I'd carried in the pocket of my jogging suit that night.

I brushed an errant wisp of hair from his forehead and leaned forward, purposely pressing my breasts against his chest, hoping he might feel something. "Did I show you the tie I bought for your birthday?"

His smile turned to a sexy grin, his eyes bright with arousal. "No, but I'd love to see you wearing it."

★ ★ ★ ★ ★

REASON ENOUGH

Megan Hart

IT WASN'T THE SORT OF QUESTION I COULD answer at once, without hesitation. It took me hours to pick out which bath mats to put in our new bathroom. How on earth could I decide in one split second if I should agree to have a baby?

"Yes? No?" Dan nudged his chin into the curve of my shoulder and neck from behind as his arms slipped around my waist. It made washing the dishes difficult, so I let the greasy pot in my hands slide back beneath the soapy water, and leaned against him. "Maybe?"

"Where did this come from?" I asked—practically, I thought.

Dan's hands moved up and down my waist and crept below the hem of my shirt to link over my belly. "I was just thinking about it, that's all."

"Hmm." I turned to face him, my own hands going behind me to grip the edge of the sink. "A baby is a big responsibility."

He grinned.

"Dan..." I had nothing to say, really. No real protest.

"Never mind, Elle." He kissed me. "It's just something I thought about, that's all. When you mentioned the pills."

I'd had a hangnail gone awry. My doctor had prescribed antibiotics to help get rid of the infection. Antibiotics can interfere with the effectiveness of birth control pills. I'd offered to use my mouth on Dan instead of making love.

"I thought you'd like a blow job." I heard the slightly cool tone of my voice and imagined the slightly cool expression on my face, to match. "I mean, you usually do."

Against me, on the places where our bodies touched, I imagined heat growing. He pushed his hips forward a little bit to nudge a definite bulge against my stomach. He kissed me again, our mouths opening, and his hands gripped tighter on my waist.

"You know I do," Dan murmured against my lips.

"Here? In the kitchen?" I raised a brow, but kept from my mouth the smile threatening to tip it. "How shocking."

"Shock me."

We'd been in the new house, our first together, only for a few months. We hadn't yet made love in every room—though not for lack of effort. I let my hand slide to his belt buckle. I tugged it open, moving his body as I did.

Dan let out a small grunt. "Use your mouth on me, right here."

It would kill my knees, that tile floor, but I didn't protest. I liked sucking Dan's cock. He thought he was lucky. I was the lucky one, though. Lucky I'd found him, and that he loved me.

Luckier I loved him back.

I pushed him, not too gently, until he took a couple steps back. I unzipped his dark trousers, his work clothes, and pulled them over his hips. I went to my knees as I pushed the cloth past his thighs and down to his ankles. His cock tented the front of his soft boxer briefs, and I got rid of those, too.

I looked at him for a minute with my hand on the base of his prick. I licked my mouth to wet my lips, and Dan's hands slid into my hair. Not pulling, not pushing. He was waiting for me to move. He could be patient if he had to be. If I made him.

I tilted my head to take him in as deep as I could. The groan of his response thrilled me. Sucking Dan was about him, but it affected me, too. My nipples tightened. My clit rubbed against my panties, and I reached with the hand not holding Dan to pull my skirt up my thighs. My knees protested the cold, hard tile without the cushion of my skirt, but I ignored the sensation. My fingers crept under the skirt to touch, just once, the silk between my legs.

"Yes," Dan said. "Touch yourself."

I didn't answer, my mouth occupied with other tasks. I sucked him a little harder, my lips closing over the head of his cock and meeting. Like a kiss. A second later, the pause so brief it was hardly there, my mouth opened again and I took him down the back of my throat. Up again, this time with one hand following and the other rubbing the front of my panties.

Dan's fingers slid deeper into my hair, and he pulled out the spring clip I'd used to keep it up. Dark lengths tumbled around my shoulders. I smelled the shampoo I'd used that morning when I'd bound it up, still damp. He finger-combed it, careful not to pull too hard as my head moved under his hands.

His breath hitched, in and out, faster. It wouldn't take long for him to come. The question was, how long would it take me?

I closed my eyes. The kitchen went away. So did my job,

the bills I meant to pay later, the message on the answering
machine from my mother. The discomfort in my knees and
jaw vanished, too.

My world became the taste and smell of my husband, and
my hand between my legs. I rubbed faster over my panties,
my clit a tight, hard bump under my fingers. I sucked Dan's
cock a little harder, a little faster, losing my rhythm once or
twice when my own pleasure made me sloppy.

"I'm going to come, baby." Dan's regular voice was often
enough to get my hormones jumping, but the way he sounded
just before he came was the trigger on my cunt's pistol. He
spoke. I shot off.

I teased myself with rapid flicks of my fingertip on my
silk-covered clit. A harder touch would send me over faster,
but it felt so good I didn't want it to end. Pleasure built. My
muscles tightened. I couldn't breathe. I had to breathe.

With a low moan, Dan bucked his hips forward. His taste
flooded me. His hands tightened in my hair and I swallowed,
hard, so I could find the breath to moan.

I pressed my palm between my legs as my body shook. I'd
become a fist, closed tight, but now I opened wide. I shuddered and swallowed again. Dan pulled back.

I blinked as my orgasm subsided, and looked up at him.
Sweat fell at that moment from his face onto mine, onto my
lips, and I licked it away. Dan reached to help me up with a
hand beneath my elbow, and I groaned at the creak of my
joints.

He pulled me close and kissed me, then hugged me, my
face against his chest. "You are so good at that. You know
that?"

I smiled against the familiar, fresh scent of his shirt. A shirt
I had washed and dried and hung in his closet. The closet in
the house we shared.

"I know," I told him, just to hear him laugh.

He hugged me tighter, and we laughed together. The phone rang. I knew who it would be, and though I didn't really want to answer it, I knew my mother would keep calling until I did. I looked up at him.

"I love you," I said, and meant it.

"I love you, too," Dan answered, and didn't talk about babies again that night.

"Hot," my brother said in a no-nonsense tone. "Don't touch!"

The little girl reaching for the canister of fireplace matches pulled back her hand and gave Chad a reproachful look. But she didn't reach again, just turned her attention to the stack of magazines on the coffee table.

"Sorry," I said. "I should've put those away. We're not baby-proof, I guess."

My younger brother laughed and shrugged. "The princess needs to learn. Don't worry about it, Elle."

The little girl—my niece! I had a niece? How had that happened? I was an aunt. My baby brother had fallen in love and adopted a child and had a life.

"What?" he asked as I shook my head in wonder. "No, Leah. Don't tear Aunt Elle's magazines. C'mere to Daddy."

He held out his hands and the girl made her way around the coffee table to take her place on his lap. She grinned, self-satisfied, and looked every bit the princess her daddies believed her to be.

"I just almost can't believe this," I told him, knowing he'd understand. "You're a daddy! Chaddie, it's just incredible."

He beamed. My brother looked better than I'd ever seen him. He'd gotten slimmer, and impossibly taller. He'd cut his hair, and it emphasized the leaner lines of his face. He'd gotten older.

Hell. We both had. I shouldn't have been so surprised. I looked in the mirror often enough, after all.

Chad kissed the soft, round cheek of his daughter and stroked the length of her black curls. She settled contentedly against him and kicked her chubby legs. He let her crawl off his lap to sit on my couch.

"She'll crash in about fifteen minutes," he said confidently, though to my eyes Leah looked about as far away from sleep as a kid could get. "Then we'll really catch up."

I watched my niece gnaw on the edge of one of my expensive, dry-clean-only pillows, and bit my tongue against the words that would have made me sound like my mother. "I'll go make some coffee, okay?"

"Sure." My brother grinned, though the force of his love was directed at his daughter now, and not so much at me.

I didn't mind, I told myself in the kitchen as I ground beans and measured them into the brand-new, complicated coffeemaker Dan had bought when we moved in. I still wasn't entirely sure how to work it.

I didn't mind that my brother was happy. I was, in fact, nearly overwhelmed with happiness on his behalf. We'd grown up in a house fairly devoid of joy, and I'd been an adult before I'd even begun to allow myself to believe I wouldn't be pretty miserable for my entire life. Instead, he'd met Luke. I'd met Dan. We'd both managed to escape the past and make a present; I had no reason to believe we wouldn't both create a joyful future, too.

Hell, I'd even forged a relationship, of sorts, with my mother. Chad hadn't managed that yet, though I hoped the fact he and Luke had moved back to Pennsylvania from California with the only grandchild my mother could claim would change that.

It absolutely wasn't that I was jealous of my brother.

"Coffee—" I bit off the words when I saw Chad put a finger to his lips. Leah, sprawled on top of the cushions and covered with her blanket, had indeed fallen asleep. He made a barrier with more pillows to keep her from rolling off, and gestured to me.

We broke our silence in my new kitchen, with all its new appliances and dishes and pictures on the walls. Chad took the coffee from me with a grateful gasp and drank back half his cup in a large gulp.

"God," he said. "I swear to you I'm living on caffeine now. She's finally starting to sleep through the night, but it's been a hellish six months. The pediatrician says at twenty-two months she should be sleeping through with no problem, but she's having adjustment issues."

I liked to sleep. Really, really liked it. Was pretty unfunctional without enough sleep, as a matter of fact.

"So, has she said anything about us?" Chad didn't waste time. He got up to pour himself more coffee, and helped himself to a muffin from my fridge. Only the slope of his shoulders gave away his tension.

"Oh, Chaddie, do you want to know?"

He turned. "Yes, Ella. I want to know."

He'd used my old name, the one my mother still insisted on using. Point taken. "She asked if I'd seen her. Meaning Leah. I said yes. She wanted to know...."

The words lodged in my throat. I shouldn't be embarrassed to repeat them. Chad was the one who'd always called my mother The Dragon Lady, after all. He wouldn't be surprised, but he would be hurt. I didn't want to hurt my brother, not even by proxy.

"What?"

I sighed. "She wanted to know how dark she was."

Chad's expression went so carefully blank I knew he was furious. "Uh-huh. What did you tell her?"

"I told her," I said, "to stop being so damn ridiculous."

He smiled. "Did you?"

"I did. I can't make excuses for her, Chad, but you know how she is."

"It's bad enough I'm gay, I know. But that I have a black daughter…God. What will the neighbors say?" Chad grimaced and slugged back more coffee. "And she wonders why I don't come home."

"At least she's asked you to," I pointed out, drinking my own coffee. "At least she's not pretending you don't exist."

He made a derisive noise. "If she doesn't accept Luke or Leah, then she still doesn't really accept me. End of story. She can kiss my ass."

I knew his partner's name, of course, and his daughter's, but hearing them together that way made me giggle. "Luke and Leah."

"What about them?" He must have heard it, too, the sound of two names that paired brought to mind one of the most easily recognized film references from the past thirty years. "Very funny!"

But he was laughing, and my kitchen filled with giggles and chortles we tried to stifle so as not to wake his child. All our best efforts went to ruin in the next minute, because I heard the front door open and a booming voice carry down the hall.

"I'm hooome!"

Leah's thin, high wail followed a moment later. Chad was already off his chair and I went after him. We were too late, both to shush Dan and to quiet Leah.

"Hey, there, little girl," Dan was murmuring, the child in his arms already when I came down the hall and into the living room. Leah looked up at him with wide eyes, but no more tears.

My heart melted.

That night I brushed my teeth, washed my face, smoothed cream into my skin. Every step of my bedtime ritual was the same as it had always been, steps to be counted without even thinking of them. A routine that provided some small measure of comfort in its perpetual sameness, no matter what had happened during the day. Yet when I lifted the white plastic case containing my birth control pills, I didn't simply pop one out of the silver foil and swallow it with a swig of water the way I always did.

I thought about punching out the pill, letting it drop into the sink and running the water to flush it away down the pipes into darkness. That one, small pill that had been my womb's only protection since the day Dan and I had stopped using condoms. I'd trusted my life to those small white discs of compressed hormones.

In the end, I swallowed the pill. I also took the last dose of antibiotics, because even though my infected finger had cleared up days ago, the instructions on the pill bottle had said to finish the medication. I wasn't then and doubt I ever will be the sort of woman to throw caution to the wind and ignore even something as simple as a doctor's prescription.

I thought about it, though, as I pulled my nightgown over bare skin and tugged back the blankets to get into bed beside my husband. He'd been reading a paperback novel with a lurid cover, but now his chin had dropped to his chest. The series of small, puffing breaths that always announced his falling asleep had begun. His glasses had slipped to the end of his nose.

He woke when I removed the narrow wire frames and set them on the nightstand. His breath gusted hot against my chest and his arms went around me.

"What a nice view," he murmured into my cleavage.

It had been more than a week since we'd made love in any traditional fashion, if you could call whatever love we'd ever made traditional. It was the longest I'd gone without him inside me since we'd been married. For a couple who fucked more often than we exercised, this had been an eye-opener.

Dan looked pleased when I straddled him, and even more so when I undid the row of tiny pearl buttons at the front of my gown. His hands slid up my sides to cup my bare breasts and push them together. I shivered when his tongue flickered out to taste me. My pulse instantly sped up.

He nuzzled his face against my skin, then used his mouth to pull gently on my nipples. One, the other, then back to the first. Underneath me, nestled along my cunt and ass, his cock got hard. The soft flannel of his pajama bottoms rubbed my bare skin. I wanted to rock my body against it, but held still.

"Take this off." He didn't wait for me to comply, but lifted my nightgown over my hips as I tugged it over my head.

The tips of my breasts brushed his bare chest as I leaned forward to kiss him. His lips parted at once. Greedy. Hungry. I kissed him hard and threaded my fingers through his hair. I tipped his head back to gain access to his throat, where I nipped and sucked until he groaned and his cock pulsed beneath me.

I was naked, and Dan was still partially dressed, but I felt no disadvantage. If there was power being played, I was the one in control. If I'd had any ideas about drawing this out, they fled when his hand slipped between us and his thumb settled on my clit. It wasn't that I hadn't had any orgasms in the past ten days, but I hadn't had any with Dan inside me, and I could no longer wait.

He made the noise I loved when I lifted myself to grasp his cock and guide myself onto it. I was already so slick with wanting there was no resistance when I slid all the way down. His eyes closed for a second as he arched to push himself deeper.

We stayed that way without moving, our breath coming faster. My heart had started to pound. His thumb pressed again on my clit and a spasm of pleasure rocked me. I moaned.

His eyes opened. "Fuck, Elle, I love that sound."

I laughed and moved on him; the laugh stuttered into a groan as he made small circles on my clitoris. He knew just how to touch me. I sat up, my hands on his chest for support, and rocked on his prick.

We took our time. In this position he couldn't thrust too hard, too fast or too deep. I could set the pace, but I had to do the work, too, and with my clit pressing his thumb every time I moved, I was content to go slow.

If marriage had made any sort of change in our lovemaking it was that we did it more often in the dark now. In bed, the way I imagined most "normal" couples did. I hadn't turned off the bedside lamp, though, and I was glad for the light to show me Dan's face. I loved the way his eyes crinkled at the corners, and the beads of sweat that formed at his hairline and turned his sandy hair the color of wet sand. I loved the way his blue-green eyes darkened as his pupils dilated with arousal.

I loved everything about this man, not just each piece but how they all fit to make the whole of him. I'd bound my life with his and never regretted it. So why, then, did I fear so much sharing one more piece of myself?

I wanted him inside me harder, faster, deeper. I leaned

forward to kiss him and he pumped upward. I no longer needed the help of his hand. My clit rubbed his belly as he thrust, and I cried out into his mouth as I started to come. My cunt clenched on his erection and he grunted. His hands gripped my sides, sliding on my sweat-slick skin. I tasted salt on his mouth.

I wanted to close my eyes when I came, but I kept them open so I could see his face. His mouth tightened. He thrust so hard he moved my entire body. He blinked, his gaze going faraway, and knowing he was so close sent another thrill of climax jittering through me.

"Elle," Dan panted. "Is it okay?"

"It's great, baby," I murmured. Sex makes even the silliest sentences all right.

He shook his head a little, still thrusting. "No, baby. Is it okay?"

He hadn't meant my orgasm. He'd meant his. I hadn't made him use a condom, and I still had the antibiotics in my system. I loved him a hundred times more for his concern.

"It's absolutely okay."

It was like I gave him permission, because that's when his body tensed and he let out a long, low groan. His cock throbbed inside me and he thrust upward once more before clutching me to him and kissing my mouth.

I couldn't feel him spurt inside me, but I imagined I did. In my head the army of small, swimming sperm surged upward through the welcoming territory of my womb, seeking their target. Would one find its goal tonight?

Had we made a child?

And if we had, would it really be all right?

Nobody in her right mind would have ever asked me to help plan a baby shower, but Marcy's sister Linda didn't know

me. Or maybe she wasn't in her right mind. At any rate, as
Marcy's self-proclaimed best friend, I'd been strongly encouraged to help her sister with organizing this party.

It was supposed to be a surprise, but getting Marcy out of
the house and to the restaurant where dozens of her friends
and family waited was harder than I'd expected.

"I'm a whale," she complained from her place on the couch.
"A frigging whale, Elle. I'm not going out of the house like
this. I can't buy shoes. My feet are way too swollen."

"It's BOGO at Neiman Marcus." I had no shame. I also
had fifty people and a buffet lunch waiting for us. "Buy One,
Get One! C'mon. Get your lazy ass off that couch."

"I'm not lazy," Marcy said reprovingly. "I'm knocked
up."

"Shoes," I said sternly.

"Fine. Bitch," she said and held out her hand. "Help me
up."

I wanted to laugh. I wanted to run away. I most definitely
did not want to be the woman sprawled on the couch with a
belly so big she wouldn't be able to see the shoes I was sup-
posedly bullying her into buying. I tugged her to her feet.
In the car I had to help her buckle her seat belt, and we both
laughed until I felt sick to my stomach.

I also didn't want to be the woman weeping at the sight
of her friends shouting "Surprise." Marcy's tears didn't seem
to embarrass her, but little did. I, however, would've been
mortified to break down like that in public. It would have
been like wetting my pants, or throwing up on myself. I never
wanted to be that woman with such a precarious hold on her
emotions. Not ever.

"You're quiet." Marcy, plate laden with cake and pasta
salad, wore a hat festooned with ribbons and bows from the

packages she'd spent forty minutes unwrapping. "Everything okay?"

"Absolutely." I smiled. "You made out like a bandit."

"I love you," Marcy said suddenly. Tears welled in her eyes again.

I've never been a hugger, but there wasn't any graceful way to avoid her embrace. "Oh, Marce. Hush."

"This was the b-b-best…" She sniffled and then dug into her cake. "You're the best friend ever!"

"I just helped, that's all."

"Thank you," Marcy said. "I mean it, Elle. I'm so… Thank you."

"You're welcome," I told her, because there wasn't much else to say.

Marcy was pulled away by some other friends who wanted to take her picture, and I was left alone for a moment to look around at the heaps of baby items she'd received. Diapers, wipes, blankets, tiny little outfits in pale colors and decorated with ducks and bunnies… Only a few months ago she and I had gone shopping for sexy lingerie, and now her entire life had changed. Her entire focus had turned toward the stranger in her belly.

She didn't notice when I slipped out.

I drove for a while before going home, just trying to clear my head. When I pulled into my driveway and saw a familiar car parked in front of my house, I wished I'd driven a lot longer.

My mother rarely visited us, but when she did she never called first. I think she knew if I had warning I'd probably make excuses about why she couldn't come over. Since my father's death, her life had changed a lot and so had our relationship, but it would never be the sort to write about on a greeting card.

My mother might not view me as the perfect daughter, but she loved Dan. This brought me no end of amusement and surprise, because she'd been set on hating him at the start. I never knew what changed her mind, aside from the fact I didn't see how anyone could not love Dan. Still, my mother wasn't known for loving anyone, and every time I saw her smile at him I couldn't help wondering when she was going to sink the knife in his gut.

Dan, on the other hand, had no doubts about his ability to charm my mother. I watched them through the kitchen door before I went in. He poured her coffee and offered her the creamer. He was talking about something, his hands waving, and she watched him, nodding. I might have been jealous if I really wanted her to like me as much as she liked him, but thankfully, I'd managed to get past yearning for that.

"…rip out the floor and put in hardwood."

Ah. He was telling her about his grand plans to renovate the house. Dan talked a lot about what he wanted to do. I talked a lot about how much it would cost. We usually found a compromise.

"Elle." My mother looked up from her coffee. "You're home."

I bit my tongue on the sarcastic "duh" that wanted to come out. "Hi, Mom."

Dan came to kiss and hug me. "How was the shower?"

"Fine." I wanted some coffee and helped myself.

"Shower? What shower?"

"My friend Marcy is having a baby," I said.

"How lucky for her mother," my mother said. "She must be thrilled to become a grandmother."

Dead silence filled the kitchen. I glanced at Dan, but he was getting ready to flee. My husband is a smart man.

"Mom," I said mildly, turning with my cup in my hand. "You're a grandma, too."

"I've got some…stuff…to do…in the place…." Dan exited the kitchen before my mother could reply.

"I need a cigarette," she said. "Come outside with me."

I'd learned to pick my battles. I went outside. My mother lit up at once, smoking and looking out over our small backyard. I waited for her to talk.

"He sent me a picture of her."

"Her name is Leah, Mom. She's adorable."

My mother glanced at me sideways and blew twin streams of smoke from her nose. "I know you think I'm being awful. But I just can't, Ella. I just…"

"Oh, why not?" I asked, weary of her drama. "Because she's black? Because he's gay? What the hell is your problem, Mother, really?"

"Because I'm not sure how to be a grandmother!" she cried in a thin, high voice nothing like her usual one. Her hand shook as she stabbed out her cigarette and lit another.

I couldn't speak at first, not until I'd swallowed some coffee. "I thought you wanted to be a grandma. God knows you keep dropping hints about it."

"It would be different with you."

"How would it be different?" I demanded.

My mother looked at me. "You are my daughter. It's different with a mother and a daughter, that's all."

I hardly thought our relationship qualified, but I didn't say that. Sometimes the things we most want to say are the ones that should never be said. "She's just a little girl, Mom. All you have to do is…all you have to do is love her."

I was horrified at the way my throat closed on those words and at the burning of tears in my eyes. "Just love her."

We stared at each other for what felt like a very long time

while my mother's cigarette burned to ash in her fingers, unsmoked.

"I don't know if I can." Her words came out low and soft and naked. "I just don't know if I can."

Honestly, I wasn't sure she could, either.

"You should try."

How had the tables turned? How had I become the one who knew what should be done and how to do it? How had my mother become the child needing to be taught?

"Maybe we could...go see them together," she said after another long, long minute. "Would you go with me?"

She had asked, not demanded. I couldn't remember if she'd ever asked me to do anything in my entire life. And though we never touched, I reached for my mother's hand.

"Yes," I told her. "I'll go with you."

My period had come and gone. I stared at the plastic compact in my hand. Today I was supposed to take the first of this month's pills. I hadn't decided if I was going to.

"Elle, are you coming?"

"Just a minute." I punched the pill from the foil but didn't swallow it.

I'd just finished my nightly shower, and as usual, the mirror had steamed over. My hair hung in wet tendrils on my cheeks. The towel I'd tucked around my chest hit me only at midthigh and wasn't much in favor of staying on. When Dan poked his head into the bathroom and I turned to face him, it slipped down.

"Nice view." He grinned.

I grabbed it with the hand not clutching the pill. "Ha ha."

He came in, naked and unconcerned with his nudity. He

reached for the towel and yanked it with a grin. We tussled over it. I didn't fight too hard. I was naked in a minute.

Dan put his hand between my legs as he looked into my eyes. "Hello."

"You," I said, "are a perv."

His brows raised. "Why? Because all I can think about right now is eating that sweet pussy until you scream?"

His dirty talk made me giggle, even though it turned me on, too. "I hear you talking, but I don't see you on your knees."

He dropped at once, so fast I let out a startled cry. He kissed me, hot breath stealing over my flesh and parting my legs. I took a step back until my rear hit the countertop.

"Is this better?" he murmured against my flesh.

Whatever witty comment I'd planned got lost as his tongue came out to taste me. I put a hand on his head, my fingers threading through his hair. It had grown long, needed a cutting, but it was perfect for grabbing.

He opened my thighs with his hands and found my clit with his lips and tongue. I could see his cock in his fist if I tilted my head just right, but I found it hard to concentrate on anything but the pleasure sweeping through me. I settled for putting my other hand on his shoulder and letting the smooth rise and fall tell me how fast and hard he was stroking.

My head tipped back as I lost myself in the sensation of his hot, wet mouth on my hot, wet cunt. When he added a finger, then two, inside me, I cried out. It sometimes took me too long to come this way, and sometimes I didn't like it at all, but not tonight. Tonight it was all I could do not to ride his face and hand…well, I'll admit it. I did.

His soft moans and the steady, slick sound of his cock pumping in his fist encouraged me. He licked me and I rocked my hips to press my clit closer on his tongue.

I was going to come. He was going to come. Best of all, there was absolutely, positively no way I was going to get pregnant this way.

He got there before I did. He let out that certain groan-moan-sigh I knew so well. I smelled him, that familiar scent. My orgasm ripped through me and the world spun. I took a breath, then another, gasping.

When I opened my eyes, Dan was looking up at me with a cat-got-the-cream grin. He rose to his feet and kissed me. I put my arms around him, hugging him tight.

"I love you," he said, and kissed my mouth again before turning on the shower. I heard him whistling a jaunty tune as he stepped under the spray, and I envied him the nature that made everything so swiftly eased.

I turned to the mirror again and saw my flushed face before the steam once again covered the glass. I'd had my fingers closed tight and the sting in my palm made me open them. The pill still lay within, half-dissolved, and I stared at it before I brought my hand to my mouth and licked it clean.

When my father was alive, my mother had thrown a gala Christmas party every year. We children had been banished upstairs while the grown-ups ate and drank and smoked and played cards. It was a party for adults, never us. I remembered peeking through the banister to watch my mother, dressed as always in a perfectly matching outfit, her hair and makeup immaculate. The perfect hostess. I had grown up thinking that was what a woman should be. What a mother should be.

I wasn't anything like my mother.

This party, too, was nothing like the parties my mother had organized with such precision. As Dan pulled into my brother's driveway, a cluster of children in party hats stampeded around the house. My mother let out a distinctive, sniffing sigh. Whatever caustic comment had risen to her lips stayed locked behind them, though. She said nothing as she got out of the car and stood, staring at the house.

My former neighbor, Mrs. Pease, had given me the heavy crockery bowl on my lap before she moved in with her son, but though she'd tried to teach me her best recipes, Dan had been the one to fill it with his Macaroni Salad à la Dan. He took the bowl so I could get out of the car, too, and he stole a kiss while he was at it.

"Relax," he murmured in my ear. "It will be fine."

From the backyard came the noise of chatter and music. I smelled burgers grilling, and my stomach rumbled. My mother clutched a small tray of cookies with both hands. She'd baked them herself, but if I knew my mother it had been out of a sense of social propriety rather than any sort of ooey-gooey, fuzzy feelings. She'd no more have shown up at a party empty-handed than she would have spit on the sidewalk. Yet now she clutched that tray so hard her knuckles were white.

"Mom?"

She turned to look at me. Her lips had pressed into the thin, grim line I'd seen so often. "Let's get this over with."

I wanted to shake her then, I really did. Dan's touch on my arm turned me toward him. His smile made me forget I had an evil side.

Dan looked at her. "Let's go around back, okay?"

She nodded just once and moved forward with a series of jerky steps unlike her usual graceful ones. He shot me a glance over his shoulder as I followed. Dan touched my mother's shoulder gently.

"Why don't you let me take the tray?"

I thought she'd say no, but after a second she nodded. "Yes.

I think...Ella, would you show me the restroom, please. I think I'd like to freshen up."

Another look from Dan stayed my retort. "Sure. We'll go in the front."

Again, she nodded. Dan took the cookies and headed around the back while I took my mother through the front door and into the kitchen, where I dropped off the bowl of macaroni salad and showed her the powder room.

My brother's house was newer than mine, and in a suburban neighborhood rather than in the heart of Harrisburg. The previous owner had been a big fan of country decor. The apple-and-rooster border on the walls of the kitchen and attached den didn't quite match the modern leather and wood furniture Chad and Luke had brought from California. Toys had been tossed into a series of brightly colored plastic bins along the far wall, and those didn't match, either.

Through the sliding glass doors I could see the deck where my brother's partner reigned in his chef's hat and apron over the grill. Dan was shaking Chad's hand and taking a beer. A few women mingled, but mostly men chased after the hordes of children swarming the jungle gym and trampoline and wreaking havoc on the grass.

"Ella, my God," my mother said as she came out of the bathroom. She'd refreshed her lipstick and powder, and brushed her hair. I even caught the fresh scent of perfume. Any earlier hesitation had vanished beneath the cosmetics she wore as a shield. "Did you know there are...kittens...in that bathroom?"

She said it as though they'd decorated the bathroom with photographs of severed limbs. I'd seen that bathroom. Severed limbs would have been less disturbing. "Yes."

"Kittens in a washtub!" Clearly, she was appalled.

"It came with the house, Mom."

"Well," she said with a familiar sniff, "I know your brother has better taste than that."

The sliding glass door opened and Chad stepped through, blinking as he came from bright into dim. "Hey."

Her chin lifted a bit. "Chad."

Their embrace was so stiff I felt awkward just watching it. The hug he gave me was much more natural. I felt my mother watching us, but when I looked at her I couldn't tell what she was thinking about the fact her children were more comfortable with each other than either of us was with her. Maybe she wasn't thinking anything. Maybe I was the one who always thought too much.

The door slid open again, letting in the smell of grilling meat and the cries of children. Luke came in bearing a platter of burgers, which he set on the counter. Dan followed on his heels, Leah a squirming bundle in his arms.

"Mrs. Kavanagh." Luke, who stood over six feet tall and had arms the size of my thighs, made no move to hug her. "Glad you could come."

The kitchen was suddenly much smaller than it had been five minutes before as we all eyed each other. Dan put Leah down and took a second to straighten her frilly white dress. She wore lacy socks, too, and white patent leather shoes. Her daddies thought she was their princess and had dressed her as one.

My mother didn't move. Didn't look. Her expression remained rigid. Tension strangled us all into silence.

Leah toddled over to my mother and grabbed her around the knees. She tilted her little face up and up. She grinned. "Gammy."

Nobody gasped, not physically, but I heard the sound of surprise echo through the kitchen just the same.

My mother looked down at the small girl clutching her legs and wrinkling her skirt.

"Gammy," Leah said again. "Up, Gammy."

She lifted her arms as if it were the most natural thing in the world to ask for and receive. And my mother, who hadn't even yet told her friends about the child her son had adopted, bent and lifted her up as though she had no other choice. She had held all of us that way, I thought. My brothers and I. When we were small.

"She knows me?" my mother said.

"We've shown her your picture," Chad said, as though he were challenging her. "She's very bright."

For another instant we all hung there. Luke and Dan might have imagined they knew what they were waiting for, but they would never know my mother the way Chad and I did. I don't know what my brother waited for, but I waited for her to ruin this.

"Well," my mother said to Leah. "Aren't you just the smartest girl? Aren't you, just?"

If relief washed over me in a wave, it must have been a veritable tsunami for my brother. After that, there were guests to feed, children to chase. Chad and Luke knew how to throw a party, and if it didn't have the glitter of those long-ago Christmas galas, there was one major improvement, in that I'd been invited to attend.

Later, Dan found me sitting in a lawn chair on a patch of grass as yet undiscovered by children. I had a plate overloaded with food, but I'd already eaten myself full. He took it from me and sat in the empty chair next to mine to dig in.

"Great party, huh?" He waved his fork toward the house.

"Yes." I watched him eat with the fondness women have for

men whose manners on a stranger would have earned scorn. "You have schmutz all over your mouth."

He leaned forward as though he meant to kiss me and laughed, withdrawing, when I wrinkled my nose. He wiped his mouth with a paper napkin. "Better?"

"Yes." I looked toward the deck, where my mother sat with Leah sleeping on her lap.

Dan watched me looking. "Nice, huh?"

"Unexpected."

He put the plate on the grass and leaned back in his chair with a contented sigh, hands laced over his belly. "You don't give her enough credit."

I raised a brow at him. We'd had this discussion before. He was lucky that he couldn't really imagine what it was like not to have a doting, affectionate mother. His own would have been a parody of sitcom moms if she hadn't been so utterly sincere in her motherhood.

"Babies change people, Elle."

"Uh-huh." I swirled some ice in my plastic cup.

I watched my mother stare into the face of the sleeping child. Had she ever looked at me that way? Yes, I thought. Long ago, she had. No matter what had come between us, and it had been a lot of very awful things, she had looked at me like that. My mother had loved me.

"You ready to get out of here?" Dan stood and gathered up the garbage.

I was. As much as I loved my brother, the cacophony of the party had given me a headache. I hugged and kissed him and Luke goodbye. We said nothing about my mother with our voices, but our eyes said enough.

When I went to kiss my niece goodbye, she barely stirred.

"She's worn-out." My mother stroked the soft black curls. "Too much party for a little girl."

"We're leaving, Mom."

She looked up at me. Her face was softer than I'd ever seen it. "Your brother will drive me home. You go on ahead."

"You're sure?"

She looked again at Leah, whose small pink lips had pursed in sleep. "I can't wake this baby, can I?"

It would have been too weird to hug or kiss her goodbye, so I didn't. I left her holding the grandchild she'd been so sure she couldn't love. In the car, I let out a laugh.

"Strange, strange, strange," I said.

"You knew she'd be okay, Elle." Dan had more faith in me than I had in myself, but that was only one of the many reasons I loved him.

At home, I groaned when he came up behind me to slip his arms around my waist as I stood in front of the full-length mirror in our bedroom. "I'm going to explode."

He rubbed the taut curve of my too full belly. "I can help you work it off."

"Oh, sure. Just roll me onto the bed like that girl from the Willy Wonka movie."

"Veruca Salt?"

I laughed. "No. The one who ate the pill that changed her into a blueberry."

Dan turned me sideways to look at us both in the mirror. "You're not blue."

"But I am round. God, why did I eat so much?"

"You were making sure you had enough sustenance to get you through the night?" He waggled his brows.

I rolled my eyes. "Riiight."

His hands, though, were working their usual magic. He moved them up and down my sides, over my hips. Over my belly, which most definitely could benefit from a few hundred sit-ups. Between my legs.

"I like you curvier." Dan's fingers played along my inner thigh and a little higher.

"You haven't ever known me as anything but curvy!" The light, tantalizing touch forced my voice into a seductive breathiness. "You have no basis of comparison."

"You've been thinner." Dan's other hand ran up my side to cup my breast. "When I met you. Just before we got married. Last year when you were deciding whether or not to quit your job."

My feminine sensibility demanded I be affronted, even though I knew he was right. "Gee, thanks for reminding me."

He pulled me closer, so our naked bodies touched. He looked deep into my eyes. "I like you better with a few extra pounds on you. It's not bullshit."

I was only slightly mollified. "Why on earth do you like me better when I'm fatter?"

"Curvier," he corrected. He dipped his head to kiss the swell of my breasts, then to suckle each nipple.

My breath quickened. His hand moved between my legs, finding my heat and slickness. He suckled a little harder, and my pulse skipped in all my secret places.

Dan kissed his way up to my shoulder, then my neck, then at last to my mouth. His cock got hard between us. Even with a few extra pounds on my belly I had no trouble feeling that. When he pulled me toward the bed, I didn't protest.

We lay on soft, smooth sheets that warmed quickly beneath us. He kissed me endlessly while his hand moved between my legs. He dipped a finger inside me and drew it up to slide along my clitoris. He knew just how to touch me, over and over, until I went boneless under him.

"Get on your hands and knees," he told me. He had a knack

for knowing just what I wanted without me ever having to say it.

I did, and clutched the pillow as he moved behind me. Dan stroked his cock along the edge of my cunt, wetting himself before he pushed inside me. He did it slowly, half an inch at a time, until I pushed back to force him inside me all the way.

We both moaned. His hands gripped my hips. I imagined how I must look in front of him, how the line and knobs of my spine would stand out as my back curved. I buried my face in the pillow and lifted my ass in the air, changing the angle so he could go deeper.

Dan went deeper. There were times when I felt he'd never fill me entirely, times when I counted my empty spaces and knew they'd always stay that way. There were times when this mattered to me, very much, and times I secretly despaired... But there were more times like this, when those small and secret empty places became insignificant.

He stroked deep inside me, and I opened my body to take him all the way. His thrusts got faster. He leaned forward, the heat of him all along my back, and reached around to press his hand to my clit.

I was close enough that he didn't need to do much stroking. The force of each thrust moved my body against his hand. Pleasure built bit by bit as he fucked into me. It lasted forever.

Sometimes I came fast and hard, but now I rode on waves of slow, steady climax. My orgasm built, receded and built again. My body tightened as we moved together, as Dan thrust faster. Heat flooded me and I bit down on the pillow to hold back my cries.

Our bodies slapped. I was so wet I felt slick heat sliding down my thighs. I breathed in the soft scent of fabric softener and the linen spray I used on the pillows; when I turned my head the heavy, familiar musk aroma of our fucking surrounded and overwhelmed me. I gulped in air saturated with our lovemaking. I wanted to drink it, eat it. I wanted to survive solely on the touch and taste and smell of the man behind me, and the pleasure sending me whirling into mindlessness.

"Count them." Dan's voice, thick with desire, trailed off into a groan. "Count them for me."

My longtime habit of counting in my head had diminished over the months we'd been married, but when he told me to now, I didn't hesitate. "One," I gasped as my first orgasm burst over me. "Two," I groaned a minute later as the second burst inside me.

And later, not much later, "Three!"

Three was the most I could manage. I shuddered with the last climax. My fingers dug furrows in the sheets. Dan thrust once more inside me and came with a shout that made me smile.

He paused for a minute before moving in and out of me a couple more times, then withdrew and collapsed beside me on the bed. A gush of hot fluid surged down my thighs, and I let out a cry as I clamped my legs together.

He laughed. "Sorry."

He wasn't, but I didn't care. "Feh. Hazards of the sport."

I rolled onto my back, making sure to position myself on his side of the bed with a grin he didn't notice at first. When he did, he rolled onto his side to put his hand on my belly. He nuzzled into my shoulder.

"You're going to make me sleep on the wet spot?"

"Absolutely," I said with a sigh of utter satisfaction. Already my eyes were trying to flutter closed, and I stifled a yawn with the back of my hand.

Dan snorted softly. "Nice."

His palm made hypnotic circles on my stomach. I would have to get up in a minute to use the bathroom, to brush my teeth. Take a shower. But for now it was too nice, lying here with him, for me to move.

I put my hand over his to stop it from moving. I thought about Marcy, the swell of her giant belly in front of her like something belonging to another person. It was another person. She'd complained vociferously about getting fat, but I'd never really believed she meant it. She'd always said it with a hint of smug satisfaction, her hands on the mound of her stomach, holding it as though it were a prize.

"Do you really like me curvier?"

I'd been ready to fall into sleep, but Dan was almost there. "Mmm," he muttered.

"Why?" I whispered as I threaded my hands through his hair. I didn't really expect or need an answer. No matter what Dan said, I was going to love and hate my body in equal turns.

"It means you're happier," he mumbled against my skin, and fell silent.

It wasn't what I'd expected him to say, but I knew he was right. I waited until he started snoring before I slipped from his grasp and went to the bathroom to run the shower. I washed away the evidence of our lovemaking, but slowly, letting the hot shower soothe aching muscles and relax me even more.

I did some of my best thinking in the shower, and the day had given me much to think about. What Dan had said was true. I had been thinner before, with hollowed cheeks and hip bones jutting from my skin, mountains on either side of the valley of my belly. I'd been able to count my ribs and see the delicate bones of my wrists. Now my flesh curved smoothly, without wrinkles, over all of me, and though I was nowhere near overweight, there was also no way to deny the difference. And I was happier—that was also true.

I was happy with Dan, our marriage, our life. Our house. My job, which had been precariously balanced a few months ago, had worked out in my favor. With my brother back in the area and my relationship with my mother on steadier ground, I had a glimmer of a family life, not to mention that Dan's mom and dad had embraced me as the daughter they'd never had. I had friends, health, success.

And I cried, thinking of all of it, and how easy it would be to lose it all, and of how terrified I was of that happening.

Tears disturb and confuse men, but women know the relief they can bring. I didn't cry because I couldn't deal with my life, but because I could. The hot water hid the sound of my sobs and washed the tears from my cheeks before I could even taste them. I cried for a solid ten or fifteen minutes, and when I was done, I turned the water to icy-cold needles that stabbed me but refreshed me at the same time.

Stepping out onto the bath mat, I didn't criticize my flesh, or obsess over the jiggle of my thighs. I scrubbed my face and combed the tangles from my hair and I slathered cream on every inch of bare skin I could reach, but I didn't worry if there was more bare skin to cover than had been available a few months ago.

I turned sideways to look at my stomach in the mirror. It curved, but nowhere nearly as much as it would if I were pregnant. I put my hands on it, imagining the bulge. Thinking of how my breasts would weigh so heavily. What on earth would that feel like?

Dan hadn't been bugging me about the baby decision, but he hadn't forgotten it, either. I'd seen him with Leah. I knew he wanted our child—children! I knew he believed we would be good parents. That we would love a baby.

He knew he could do it. He believed I could. I was the one uncertain of that.

My mother hadn't been sure she could love the offspring of a stranger, even though Leah had become her son's daughter as fully as if he'd created her. I wasn't so foolish as to think one afternoon could change everything overnight, but I also couldn't forget the look on my mother's face as she'd looked down at my niece.

My mother had loved her children. If I wanted to be entirely charitable, I could postulate that she still did, no matter how difficult it was to see that love. And if my mother had been able to do it, if she could do it now with my brother's child, well…maybe I could do it, too.

It wasn't until the next night that I realized I'd forgotten to take my pill the night before. I stared at the small foil package and the extra pill with some befuddlement. I couldn't recall ever forgetting a pill, not in all the years I'd taken them.

I knew the importance of taking them both, doubling up to prevent them from failing, but when my fingers made to punch out both pills, they hesitated. What if I didn't take the one I'd missed, but just kept on with the week as though I'd taken it?

I could have calculated the risk easily enough, if I'd had the statistics in front of me. I was very good with numbers. All I did instead was to pop the regular pill in my mouth and toss the other down the drain.

"Everything okay?" Dan looked at me from over the edge of his book. He'd started another garishly covered paperback, but he put it aside with his finger marking his place when I crossed to sit on his side of the bed.

"Yes." I took the book from him and settled it on his nightstand.

"Ah." Dan took off his glasses and put his hands behind his head. "You've come to ravish me."

"I have." We smiled. I ran a finger down his chest to where the sheets covered him. When I pulled them aside, I shook my head in mock scolding. "This doesn't help."

He looked at the soft cotton pajama bottoms. "Take them off."

I stood. "You take them off."

He grinned and hooked his thumbs in the sides, but I held up my hand. "No. Not like that."

I took a seat in the rocking chair and gestured at him to stand up. "I want to watch you."

The pajamas were already tenting when he got out of bed. "Do you want me to put on some music?"

"No." I kept my face stern even though I felt like giggling. I didn't want to laugh; it would ruin the mood.

Dan stood in front of me, thumbs hooked in his waistband. "You want me to just strip 'em off, or what?"

"Surprise me." I parted my legs so the hem of my short nightgown rode up. I was naked beneath.

I loved the way his eyes gleamed and the way his tongue sneaked out to swipe across his lips. Dan didn't have to worry about extra curves. He had been blessed with good genes. Now he eyed me, one hip cocked.

I inched my hem higher and ran a hand over the soft patch of hair between my legs. I wasn't stroking myself. Not yet. But there was definitely the promise I might start.

He had such a playful side. It was sexy. Now, watching me, he ran his hands over his chest. Up and down, then over his belly. He traced the lines of muscle in his abs and the indentations of his ribs. He licked the fingertips on both hands and circled his nipples. It should have been silly, but my throat tightened.

He didn't do a bump and grind. It was more like a slow, easy exploration of his body. He kept his gaze locked on mine the whole time, too. My hand slid again, and this time found my clit. I moved my finger in small circles as I watched him touch himself the way I wanted to be touching him.

He turned around to slide the waist of his pajamas down just far enough for me to see the small patch of hair at the base of his spine. I loved to lick that spot. He loved me to lick it. He eased the elastic a little lower, then lower again, to reveal the crack of his ass. He tossed me a look over his shoulder and turned, pulling the waistband up again.

"Tease," I murmured.

He laughed softly and pushed the cloth down in front until the first fluff of his pubic hair showed. He'd offered once to shave down there, but I'd protested. Now he just kept himself trimmed. I held my breath as he pushed the pants lower, lower….

"You are a tease!" I told him when he let go and the elastic snapped back up around his hips.

"You told me to surprise you." He hooked his thumbs into the fabric but didn't pull it off.

I couldn't deny it. Instead, I parted my legs wider and gave him a full glimpse of my body. I slipped my fingers down low enough to find slippery fluid. He licked his mouth again.

"I love to watch you touch yourself," he said.

"Let me see you do the same," I breathed.

Dan put a hand over the bulge in his pants. He stroked himself a few times through the cloth. Then he reached inside and stroked again. His face tightened and he bit his lower lip a little.

"No fair!" I said.

Dan's laugh came out a little strangled. "Fine."

He pushed his pajamas down, finally, and stepped out of them. He gripped his erection as he kicked away the bottoms. When he stroked down, slowly, I couldn't decide where to look: at his face, taut with desire, or at his cock, so deliciously hard.

My body responded. My breath came faster, my pulse sped up, my clit grew harder beneath my fingertips. The smooth, curved wood beneath my bare ass had warmed, and I slid on it as I set the chair to rocking.

We'd fucked on this chair, more than once, and I thought of that now. Of how Dan's prick felt inside me as we rocked, of how good it felt when my clitoris rubbed his stomach. How easy it was to thrust and move with the chair helping us.

Dan's hand worked up and down on his erection. I did love watching him. There was something singular in him jerking himself, and in watching how he moved his hand to bring himself the most pleasure. He added a twist to his wrist as he stroked the head of his cock. I caught a glimpse of precome glistening as he stroked. He stood with his feet spread apart to anchor himself, and it was easy to imagine myself on my knees in front of him.

I knew how he'd taste and the sound he'd make when I closed my lips over his penis. I didn't, though. I watched him stroke himself, instead, as I brought myself closer and closer to climax.

We could have finished that way, watching each other. But when my cunt gave its first spasm, hovering on the edge of coming, I pulled my hand away. I wanted to squirm on the chair. I wanted to push my cunt against the air, or squeeze my thighs together, keeping myself from tipping into orgasm, but only barely.

"Dan," I said.

That was all it took. He crossed to me in two strides. I almost came when he pulled me to my feet. The world tipped a little as pleasure swooped over me, but I breathed deep and managed to hold it off. Dan took my place on the chair and pulled me onto his lap. I slid onto his prick, my clit against his belly, our mouths locked. I cried out, the sound lost against his lips. He fucked upward as his hands cupped my ass.

I was already coming. My body jerked. My fingers dug into his shoulders. He thrust harder as the chair rocked. The floor squeaked. He said my name. My orgasm became all-encompassing, immense, enormous. The world. The universe. Pleasure overtook me.

Dan yelled when he came. His final thrust lifted me up, and when we settled the chair kept rocking, though we'd stopped. He put his arms around me, tight. I felt him throb inside me as my cunt fluttered in climax. I couldn't always feel it, and tonight it seemed especially appropriate that I could.

I thought of him spurting inside me. Dan's body had made sperm—small, wriggling and invisible—that even now were swimming mightily up the convulsing corridor of my vagina to seek the cavern of my womb. Would it welcome them? Had my body created an egg, waiting, even now, to be conquered? It wasn't likely, but neither was it impossible. Many women who'd counted themselves "safe" had ended up getting pregnant.

Dan had buried his face against my chest with a happy sigh. His hair tickled my nose. Our bodies glued together, sticky from sweat, as the chair rocked to a stop. I didn't move, too content to bother.

We didn't have secrets anymore, and I was glad for that. Even so, I didn't tell him I'd forgotten and then deliberately not taken my pill. I wasn't sure there'd be a point in telling him we may or may not have made a baby.

"I love you." Dan kissed my collarbone.

"I love you, too." So easy to say it, now.

Easier to mean it, too.

"Fuck me with a barbed-wire dildo!" Marcy's voice echoed through the tiled hall, and nobody blinked an eye. "Where the fuck is Wayne?"

"I've left a message with his secretary, on his voice mail and on his cell," I told her. "He'll be here."

Marcy let out a low, guttural groan. Sweat had plastered her hair to her forehead. Dark circles shadowed her eyes, and the corners of her mouth had cracked a little. She gripped my arm with fingers like talons, but I didn't dare wince. I wasn't the one getting ready to push a bowling ball out of my body.

We'd been walking for an hour as she labored. Marcy had called me when her efforts to get in touch with her husband had failed. She'd driven herself to Harrisburg Hospital and I'd met her there, not because I had any burning desire to watch my friend give birth, but because she had nobody else.

Funny how Marcy hadn't considered me her last resort, though. She'd hugged me fiercely when I got there and chattered on and on in a bright, happy voice as we got her settled in. It took me twenty minutes of listening to her babble for me to realize Marcy was terrified.

Her water hadn't broken yet, so she'd been encouraged to walk up and down the halls to help with her labor. The first half an hour had been fine. She'd been upbeat, if still a little manic, but as time wore on and the contractions got harder and Wayne was nowhere to be found, Marcy had ceased with the little Susie Sunshine act.

"Goddamn him," she said. "I fucking told him to keep his motherfucking phone charged…. Fuck!" She clutched her belly and stopped, hunching. She breathed in a series of rapid, whistling breaths while I stood by, helpless to do anything but watch.

"He'll be here," I repeated. *Please God,* I prayed. *Let him get here. Soon.*

When the contraction stopped, the tears started. Marcy turned to me with a desperate look. "Thank you for being with me, Elle. Thank you."

Guilt stabbed me. "Of course I'd be here for you, Marcy. You know that."

She gripped my hand as another contraction rolled over her. Her lips thinned to pale lines in her face. "Fucking hell!"

Marcy wasn't the only woman in labor. I could hear the burble of television sets in some of the labor and delivery rooms, and an occasional grunt or cry. There were women giving birth all over the place here. The air was thick with the odor of blood and fear and joy; my stomach kept trying to turn and I wouldn't let it.

"I'm so glad you're here." Marcy gripped the wooden hand-rail along the wall. "You're always so together, Elle. You're always so calm."

I was anything but calm, but hell, Marcy was expecting me to be something for her and I could give her that, at least. "It's all going to be okay."

She nodded and then looked up at me, her face a mask of surprise. I didn't know why until a second later, when the rapid patter of liquid hitting the tile floor caught my attention. We both looked down, though I doubted Marcy could see past her belly.

"My water just broke!"

"It's okay." I gripped her hand. "Let's get you into your room."

It all happened very fast after that. Nurses and midwives showed up to do their jobs. Wayne, tie askew and hair windblown, arrived with a story about traffic and dead cell batteries. Marcy forgave him at once. The looks on their faces when he held her hand and kissed it was like something from a movie.

Wayne's eyes rolling up in the back of his head and him hitting the tile floor with the sound of a pumpkin breaking open was somewhat less glamorous.

I'd been edging my way out of the room at that point, preferring to leave them to their privacy, but when Wayne hit the ground Marcy shrieked my name, and I found myself at her side in a second.

"He's okay," I told her. Two orderlies got him to his feet and into a chair, where he promptly put his head between his knees.

"Get ready to push," the midwife said. "Elle, can you hold her leg for her?"

Did I have a choice? I positioned myself beside the table with Marcy's knee lodged firmly in the stirrup of my hands as I kept it pulled back to help her push. She screamed. Wayne looked up, face pale but determined, and got to his feet. They slapped a gown and gloves on him as fast as a pit crew changing the tires on a race car. The midwife cooed soothing phrases I didn't hear.

And Marcy's baby was born.

I saw the head, crowning, the sleek dark hair wet and the skull pulsing. She pushed again, in silence this time. The baby slid forth in a gush of blood and liquid, the smell of it ripe and indescribable. Wayne held out his hands and his son slid into the welcoming cradle of his arms. He was crying. So was the baby, and Marcy.

So was I.

Ten minutes later she held him, dried and buffed and wrapped in a blanket, to her breast. She didn't care who saw her nakedness, or that strangers were wiping her body clean, or that she needed three stitches to repair a tear.

"Look, oh, look," she said in a voice full of wonder. "How beautiful he is."

And he was.

My phone buzzed in my pocket as I washed my hands at the sink of the main restroom on the labor and delivery floor. I'd left Marcy and Wayne to share their son without witness. They hadn't even noticed me leaving.

"Elle?" Dan's voice sounded strained. "Where are you?"

"I'm at Harrisburg Hospital." Elation made my own voice shake. "Marcy just had her baby. Where are you?"

He was silent so long I thought we'd lost the connection. When he spoke again, he didn't sound like my Dan, the man who always made everything all right for me.

"I'm at the hospital, too," he said. "My dad just had a stroke."

Dotty Stewart wrung her handkerchief in her hands over and over until the fabric twisted. Then she'd let it unwind, only to twist it again. She didn't hold herself the way my mother would have. Dotty didn't care how she looked to anyone else just then.

"Have you called your brother?" she asked. "Did you call Sam?"

"I tried. I left a message." Dan's voice was still strained, but he'd pulled himself together for his mom.

"Oh, I wish Sam were here," his mother said, before she went to sit again by her husband's side.

I don't think she meant it to be hurtful. If Dotty had favorites I'd never seen evidence of it. Then again, I'd only met his brother very briefly at our wedding. Dan and his brother got along fine with distance between them. Though they'd never said it, I got the impression Sam's moving to New York hadn't exactly made him the favorite son.

Dan paced in the waiting room and drank cup after cup of black coffee. His mother kept up her vigil by Morty's side. I would have held Dan's hand, if he'd wanted, but instead I sat and watched him traverse the linoleum floor. I'd have gone in his father's room with him, too, when they came to get him, but he shook his head a little.

"You don't have to come."

"If you need me, Dan, I'll be there." He'd been there for me when my father had died. I'd needed him to be. I reached for him and pulled him close for a kiss, both of us ignoring the nurse sent to fetch him.

"It might be uncomfortable for you." He spoke in a low voice against the side of my neck. His arms tightened.

I thought what he meant was that it might be uncomfortable for him to have me there. To see him upset, maybe even crying. I held him a little closer.

"If you need me, I'm here."

He nodded and gripped my hands. He looked into my eyes. "I know you are."

I'd never had to be strong for him before. It wasn't as hard as I thought it might be. Together we went to listen to what the doctors had to say.

It wasn't entirely good, but it wasn't all bad. His dad had suffered a stroke, but a mild one. He was expected to regain consciousness within a few hours, and they didn't think there'd been much damage to his brain. It meant another few hours of waiting, though, during which we visited the cafeteria and Dan tried calling his brother again. We waited another hour in the small hospital room before Morty opened his eyes. Dotty had stepped out to use the bathroom. Dan had heard from his brother and was even now out in the corridor talking to him.

"Heya," Morty said, and licked his lips. He gestured at me to come closer. "Heya, girlie."

"Hi, Morty." I took his hand, which felt like it was covered with onionskin. "How are you feeling?"

"Not so good, not so good." He coughed a little, but the monitors didn't beep erratically and I didn't think I needed to holler for a nurse. "How're you?"

I hadn't known Morty that long, really. A couple years. But he'd been more of a father to me than my own had been for a long time. My throat closed as I squeezed his hand ever so gently. I didn't want to lose him, and yet my grief would be so much less than Dan's.

"I'm okay, Morty. I should go get Dotty."

He shook his head a bit. I'd always seen a lot of Morty in Dan, but now I saw a bit of Dan in Morty. "Not yet. Sit here with me for a minute."

I did, without letting go of his hand. We didn't speak for a few seconds. Morty looked as though he wanted to say something important, and my heart beat faster as I anticipated some sort of last words. It wasn't my place to hear them, if this were his final speech.

"You're good for my boy."

"He's good for me."

Morty smiled. His fingers twitched in mine, not quite a squeeze but a valiant effort. "Me and Dot, we always wanted a girl. She couldn't have another, you know. After Sam. We tried, but she lost 'em. Finally, the doctor just said no more. You'll kill yourself. So that was that."

I hadn't known. "I'm sorry."

"Don't be." Morty shook his head a little again. His grin was a ghost of its normal brightness, but still there. I could so easily see how Dan would look in another thirty years. "We got our daughter, didn't we?"

I smiled. "Thanks."

"Our Sam, now, he might not ever settle down. But Danny, he's a smart one." Morty shifted in the bed and looked a little pained. Alarmed, I made to move, but he shook his head yet again. "Now, it's not my way to push."

Not compared to my mother, that was for sure.

"But it surely would make me happy...me and Dotty both, you know..."

"If we had a baby?" I said quietly, leaning forward, though there was nobody to overhear us.

"Yes." Morty's eyes gleamed.

I leaned even closer, conspiring. "I think we're working on it."

He laughed, and the laugh trailed away into a weak cough. "Good. Does Danny know that?"

"He was there," I said, which wasn't quite the right answer, but made him laugh again. I'd never have said such a ribald thing to my mother, but Dan's dad was different.

"Good," he said again and closed his eyes for so long I was afraid he wouldn't open them. Then, "Good."

"C'mon. You've had a very long day." I bent over the bath and turned on the faucets. We had a nice, big tub put in by the previous owners. They'd obviously been obsessed with the bathroom, since it was the only room in the house to have been completely renovated. I added some lavender-scented oil. "You need this."

"I need to get to bed...." But he was only protesting for show as I unbuckled his belt and helped him out of his clothes.

I put him into the bath and scrubbed him with some body

wash and a loofah. Water splashed over the edges of the tub and wet my clothes, but I kept at it, washing and kneading him until he closed his eyes and gave himself up to my ministrations. When I was done, I helped him out, dried him off and took him to bed.

I slid in, naked, beside him. He was warm from the hot water and my skin was a little cool, but he didn't object when I put my arm over his chest and my leg over his thighs. I kissed his shoulder.

Sometimes we said more with silence than with all our words.

When I kissed my way down his arm and across to his belly, he sighed. When I kissed lower, Dan's belly vibrated under my lips. My hand found his cock and I stroked him erect in a minute. He put his hand on top of my head, though, when I went to move lower.

"Elle."

I looked up at him. "Shh. I love you. Let me do this."

He smiled a little. "I need this, too?"

I nodded. "You want me to do this."

He'd said those same words to me in the past, and he'd been right. The way I was right now. Sex has many uses I would never pretend to know or want to know, but I did know the comfort losing oneself in pleasure could bring.

I made love to him with my hands and tongue for a while until he shivered. Then I climbed on top of him. He groaned as he slid inside me; that simple sound sent a pulse of arousal through me. I always got turned on at the sounds he made.

I'd meant to do this for him, not for me, but he slid a hand between us and I wasn't going to complain. We moved together, slow at first, then faster. I thought he might come right away, and that would have been fine, but Dan looked at me, watching my face as he used his thumb to provide steady pressure on my clit. When I gasped, he smiled.

"I want to watch you come," he whispered. "Let me see it."

I did a minute after that.

He thrust inside me a few more times before his face tightened and he gasped out my name. Then he gathered me to him and held me tight. He kissed me.

"I love you," he said. "God, I love you so much."

"I love you, too," I whispered, holding him as hard as I could. I didn't want to let go, not when he needed me to hold on.

I thought he might cry, but he didn't. His breathing slowed. Our bodies cooled. I pulled the blankets over us and snuggled into his side. I didn't sleep, but I listened to him sleeping.

I knew I should get up, take a shower. Brush my teeth.

Take my pill.

Instead I lay there listening to the sound of my husband breathing, and I held on to him with all I had inside me. I'd worried I didn't have enough for him, but time had shown me I was wrong.

I didn't get out of bed.

It wasn't my conversation with Morty that had changed my mind about having a child, or watching my mother with my niece, or my niece herself. It wasn't watching the miracle of Marcy's son being born, either.

All of those were reasons. Good reasons. But it was the man beside me who'd proved to me that love was worth everything. That my life, my heart, had room in it for more love than I ever thought possible.

There were dozens of reasons to agree to have a child, but as far as I was concerned, just then, with his breath on my face and the warmth of his skin on mine, there was only one that mattered. Love.

That was reason enough.

★ ★ ★ ★ ★

THE FLOWER ARRANGEMENT

Adelaide Cole

I CAME INTO THE RIGGS HOUSEHOLD IN THE winter of 1903, when I was seventeen years old. I'd done nicely selling flowers in the London markets for a year, but a cold, wet summer had wreaked havoc on all the farmers, and I couldn't buy any decent blooms to sell. The big sellers snatched them up and left the rest of us with naught. Sachets of dried lavender and hyssop hardly paid the rent. I resorted to dirty char work, which paid little. I could barely pay for my room and certainly had no money to heat it. Then my luck changed. I had sold roses and sweet pea in Covent Garden Market with a girl named Margaret, and it was thanks to her that I found a new undertaking. Margaret had been hired to cook for a household, and she brought me there.

After Margaret left Covent Garden we still had a pint together sometimes. She knew that I was on my own, and she thought me a hardworking girl, which I was, and she knew I needed a better wage. In fact, I considered my industriousness my best quality, alongside pretty brown curls, of course. She gave me a stellar reference when Missus Riggs began looking for a live-in house servant. I am forever grateful. Being taken into that household changed my fortune.

I hadn't wanted to return to the countryside, where I had some family. A village was no place for an independent girl. I would be expected to marry, and that would be that. I simply knew I would lose all the pleasures and freedoms of my life. I'd likely be treated as a maid, but without the earnings!

I was happy in London. The working girls in the city markets were a delight, and we were truly family to one another. The city wasn't without its perils, and some surely fell to those hazards, but I was careful in every way. I had lost my mother to pneumonia, and my brother had left the city to apprentice as a stonemason. Our father had abandoned us many years before. I suffered losses to be sure, but on the other hand I was free to decide my life quite by myself. I could make my own successes—and failures!—and I had only myself to answer to. I needn't worry about a family reputation, or of pleasing others.

I tried to be careful and clever, as a girl had to be in order to avoid the dangers and pitfalls of the city. I'd seen other girls led into drink and drugs, disease, begging and even prostitution. I was determined to stay independent and childless. I wanted a better life, and I needed to secure savings for my goal: a flower shop of my own. The world was opening up to women, and I knew I had a chance.

I had advantages. I was pretty. I had big green eyes and a lovely ivory skin tone. I had a good, round bosom, which I took advantage of for flower selling. And my beauty wasn't just good for my livelihood, but for fun, as well! Like my girlfriends, I loved a romp with the lads. I enjoyed lifting my skirts for a hot, wet fuck with a handsome boy.

Delicious! We working girls could do such things. We didn't have family reputations to concern ourselves with, but we had to have our wits about us in every way. Who knew that my job in the Riggs household would combine two of my talents: flowers and a good fuck.

So I was introduced to the household by Margaret. Missus Riggs was involved in charitable causes about town, and she needed to have the house kept up. Her three small children were looked after by the nanny, Olive. We three working girls shared a room beside the kitchen, which suited us nicely. Our small space was warm and clean and I had nothing to complain about. Margaret and Olive were chatty, and the household was a friendly place and there was enough to eat. We were lucky, indeed. I cleaned, did the washing, ran errands, served meals and dealt with the tradesmen. It was a lovely house on a quiet, tree-lined street, and I dreamed of living like that one day. I knew I could if I applied myself and worked hard.

Master Riggs was an officer in the Royal Navy. He had served abroad and now was stationed in London. I saw him occasionally, as he came and went, and when I served the meals. He cut a powerful figure in uniform, and was a hand-some man. I liked to sneak a look at him. His starched white shirts emphasized his strong shoulders, and I could see the shape of his slim ass under his trousers. He had deep blue eyes and thick, dark hair. But in any case, I answered to Margaret or the Missus, and my path crossed little with his.

Doing chores, I imagined running my hands over hard muscles…his hands squeezing my ass…his full lips on mine… undoing his trousers and taking his hard cock into my mouth. I would draw a deep breath, squeeze my pulsing cunt between my thighs and beat a rug very hard to relieve myself of such frustration.

"What energy you have, my girl!" said Margaret, standing at the kitchen window, seeing me return inside with freshly beaten carpets.

Sometimes, on an evening out, I would stop by one of my lads in a pub in the market. I'd twirl a soft, brown curl with my finger and run my tongue over my open lips just enough to encourage a romp in his room. We would roll about, his sweaty flesh pressed to mine. I imagined it was Master Riggs caressing and squeezing my tits...and that it was his cock diving into the warm, pink flesh of my pussy.

The devil makes work of idle hands, and over the months those excursions allowed me to stay out of any trouble and concentrate on my tasks. And I wasn't just drawn to Master Riggs, but also had to keep myself from the handsome trades-men who came and went. A simple effort with the fat butcher and the scrawny milkman, but by the summertime it was not so easy to leave off the virile carpenter who was around the yard for days on end, with his shirt off and the hot sun making sweat glisten off firm, undulating muscle.

"Why did you close the curtains, Emma?" Cook asked, looking at me as though I were mad. "It's not even midday. Besides, summer sun is fleeting."

"Sorry, Margaret," I replied. "I was dusting there. I must have forgotten to open them again," I replied. Why, indeed? I could hardly tell her that the sight of the olive-toned flesh of the half-naked tradesman in the yard was making me lose my breath, could I?

Time passed like that, and I was proud of my work. By the time autumn turned to winter I was given more responsibility and a raise in my salary from the missus. I saved my earnings and envisioned a day when I might have my shop. The idea even began to regularly occupy my thoughts. My own shop! Such independence!

One gray and wet autumn afternoon I was sweeping the floors and polishing woodwork in the Master's study when he came in. "Good afternoon, sir," I said, continuing my work.

"Yes...good day, Emma..." he replied in a preoccupied way. He stood in the doorway, seeming to look at his own feet on the red Persian carpet. My heart began to beat hard as I felt his presence. The sounds amplified in my head, of the rain hitting the windowpanes and of my heart beating. *Silly girl,* I thought, *he's taking no notice of you. No need for such theatrics!* I continued my chores.

Then I heard the door close and the key turn in the lock. I stole a quick glance and saw that he was still there. Indeed, he was preoccupied with something. He went to his desk. Where was everyone? I wondered. In fact, the Missus was at the dressmaker's, and Cook would have been occupied at that hour with lunch preparations. The children were at the park with Nanny. I realized that Master Riggs and I were quite alone.

But when I gathered my things to leave, I turned and found him looking straight into my eyes. Our gazes locked together for the first time ever, but he was quite silent. "Uh..." I stammered, "C-can I do something for you, sir?"

"Draw the curtains, Emma, if you would," he replied, betraying nothing. My cunt began to pulsate and I swallowed hard.

"Yes, sir," I replied. I went to the window. Outside, the rain still poured. I drew the curtains closed. Pale light was all that remained in the room.

"Emma," he said quietly, "will you sit down?" He motioned to a nearby chair. I sat in it, holding his gaze. "I'm led to understand that you are an ambitious girl." He seemed to want a reply. He stood calmly but straight, with his hands in his pockets.

"Yes, sir… I suppose that could be said of me…" I answered breathlessly. My heartbeat still reverberated in my chest.

"You know you're a lovely looking girl, don't you…?" His voice was low and intoxicating. "And you must know you've a comely figure, as well. I've watched you for some time."

He stopped, but I didn't know what, if anything, to say.

"How would you respond if I asked you to open your dress…?"

I felt the blood rush into my pussy. My nostrils flared with excitement, but I felt that I needed to keep my wits about me. "Sir…I might comply, sir…" My head swam. Was this some sort of trap? Was my job in jeopardy if I refused? Would he think me wanton if I did as he suggested? *But I wanted him!* I didn't know how to answer, or what to do.

"Then would you open your dress, please?" We held eye contact as my fingers unbuttoned my bodice. He could see that he had his willing partner.

"Open wider," he said. He moved behind me. He slipped his hands inside my dress, to my bare shoulders. He pushed my gown off my shoulders, exposing me, then slid his hands down to cup my breasts. Slowly, even calmly, he lifted the round weight of them, squeezed them gently, pinched my nipples and palmed them with open hands. I caught my breath, but tried to keep from moaning aloud. Then he began to speak.

"So you're ambitious," he breathed softly in my ear. "I think ambition is a worthy attribute and ought to be rewarded along with hard work. And I'm told you are indeed very industrious, as well. Would you raise your skirts and open your legs…?" he whispered. I pulled my skirts up till they sat high on my thighs. "Push your knickers down and open your legs…"

I raised my ass off the chair just enough to push my kickers down, then I kicked them to the floor. I spread my thighs.

"I'll bet you have a beautiful pussy," he said calmly, sotto voce. His hands left my breasts. One palm grazed my thigh, and the other skimmed the dark hair on my pussy, petting it like a cat. I moaned out loud. His fingers ran lightly from my ass to the top of my aching, hungry cunt. His finger slipped stealthily through the slippery, wet folds of my sex.

"Sir…" I said quite pointlessly. His other hand returned to my tits, and he pinched my nipples and rolled them between his thumb and fingers. My body warmed and quivered.

He continued speaking quietly. My senses could barely process both the sensations on my flesh and the words coming in my ears. "I have a business proposition for you, Emma." He paused. "An opportunity to fulfill an ambition, which I'm told might include opening a small flower shop." My head swam with the feel of his fingers rolling my red, erect nipple, and his other hand fingering my pussy. "And I might have something I need, as well…." His voice trailed off.

"And here's what I need now…" His hands left me as he moved around in front of me. "Undo my trousers," he said. His crotch was at my face. His thigh brushed my nipples. I clumsily unbuttoned his trousers, and his hard cock strained against the fabric. I didn't wait for instructions. I took his sex out, and it was like the stamen of a flower about to burst with seed. I looked up at him and he looked at me, breathing hard. He ran his fingers through my curls and pushed my head to him. I took his cock in my mouth and pumped it, making it wet with my spit. I licked it like a sweet from the shaft to the head. He moaned. I licked his balls and ran my hands along those thighs that I'd fantasized about for so many months.

"Down on your hands and knees," he whispered urgently. I came off the chair and dropped to all fours. In a moment he was behind me. He pushed my skirts up to my waist. My pussy wetness dripped out of me. He held my hips and I felt the head of his big sex slip through my opening and slide into me, firing every nerve in its path. My cunt exploded in waves of pleasure deep inside. I panted and cried out, but his hand covered my mouth. "Shhh!" He moaned low and fucked me, pumping my cunt. My body shivered in ecstasy.

His arm encircled my hip, and his other hand ferociously kneaded my tits. Then he pulled himself out of me, held me to him and groaned as he came in my skirts. After a moment, he caught his breath. "We don't want you in the family way, do we?" he panted.

We were both spent. He let go of my waist and got up, wiping his brow and buttoning his trousers. Disheveled and sweaty, I picked myself up and sat in the chair as he gathered himself.

Finally, he spoke again. "So then let's talk about an arrangement, my dear." *An arrangement?* I thought.

"You're clearly a respectable girl," he said with a coy wink, "if a bit wicked...." His voice subdued and more serious, he continued, "Of course, this would be an entirely secret proposition...and a benefit to us both. We can 'meet.'" He said the word with a sly smile. "And over time you'd be in a financial position to leave us for a more independent venture."

A domestic prostitute? I thought to myself, horrified at the concept, and it came out of my mouth. "But I'm no whore, sir!"

"Oh, my," he said with an indignant tone. "I wouldn't have one under my roof, dear... It's an *arrangement,*" he repeated. "The terms of the deal are secrecy and great care. You don't seem like you mind the 'work' too much—" he said this with a smile "—and you can view it as a financial dividend." He put his hand in his pocket and removed some pound notes. He placed a generous sum on the desk. "Do we have a deal, Emma?"

I looked at him and replied as demurely as I could muster, "Why, yes, sir. I believe we do."

"Then good day, dear," he said, and turned to the door. He unlocked it and left. In the hallway he took his hat and coat, and I heard the front door open and close with a bang that shook the brass knocker. I straightened myself and went downstairs to the kitchen.

"Margaret," I said to the cook, "I forgot to run to the butcher's this morning. Do you mind if I fetch the roast now? Would it be a bother for you to serve lunch?"

"Not a bother, dear," Margaret said, not even looking up from her turnips. "You go right ahead."

I took my coat and cape and left, more than happy to have a reason to walk in the fresh air and clear my mind of the strangest event I could ever have imagined!

In the weeks and months that followed I went about my work and didn't utter a word to a soul. Nobody in the house suspected, nor should they if I were to keep my job. It was surely a prosperous adventure for me, a pleasurable one for Master Riggs. Earning the money for my own shop and all the while frolicking around the house with this gentleman? An offer I could not have refused!

Springtime arrived and I asked the Missus if I could take over the flower and bedding plants from the gardener. Missus Riggs may not have known how I was earning my extra pay, but she knew I had it in my head to open a flower shop, so she let me at the garden. That spring I planted purple iris, primrose, daffodil and wallflower. When the summer came, I did orange marigold, blue geranium, pink meadowsweet and mullein. My buttercups did nicely, as did the red campion, honeysuckle and lily. I learned which seeds did better in certain soils, and which needed more sun or less.

My flowers and posies now regularly sat in vases on the

Missus's tables. Cook helped me improve my reading, and I learned about flowers and plants from botanical books. And I couldn't have been bored, since every so often I'd be surprised by a visit from Master Riggs.

He took me where he liked, though he was always careful of two things: that no one should find us, and that he shouldn't make me pregnant. But still, he often surprised me with an adventuresome appetite. One afternoon, he brought home another gentleman. I didn't think a thing of it until he summoned me. "Emma!" he called, and he rang the bell in his study.

"Yes, sir," I said, and noticed a gentleman with him. I took their hats and coats and went to leave.

"Then return, please," he said.

I half wondered...

And when I returned, the Master did indeed turn the key in the study door. "How would you like to earn a bit extra for your pot, dear?" he asked. I was taken aback. I didn't know quite what he was wanting, but at the same time his friend was a fine-looking man, and I couldn't refuse a little well-paid adventure. What a wicked girl! "Sirs..." I replied, not wanting to refuse, but not wanting to appear as if I anticipated any pleasure out of what might transpire.

The gentleman glanced at Master Riggs as if for permission, then looked at me. "Let me see your titties, my girl..." I also looked at Master Riggs, but he revealed nothing. I gazed at them both as I undid my bodice and opened my clothes, freeing round breasts and hard, pink nipples.

"Mmm..." The gentleman moaned immediately. He stepped right to me and turned me around so that I faced the desk. There, he bent me over the Master's desk, pushed up my skirts and plunged his cock right into me. He held my shoulder and fairly slammed into my pussy. My breasts bounced and slapped against me, and he grabbed them as though they were pieces of ripe fruit. Master Riggs enjoyed the whole sight. He worked his sex with his hand till he came with a moan in a handkerchief.

The gentleman pulled himself out of me and his hot, white cream spilled over my ass and down my thighs. "What a girl!" he said, and he smacked my bottom hard with his hand.

"Ouch!" I cried, and he laughed. And though I liked a quick fuck also, his manner didn't please me and I was satisfied when he was gone. I was paid very well for that time, and was glad for it.

When I wasn't working I began to spend time at Kew Gardens, where I learned more about trees, bedding plants and flowers. At the Riggses', I even planted herbs in pots in Cook's kitchen. And since the small glass conservatory had become a bit of a fashion in London, Missus Riggs had one built. I worked on roses, violets, irises and other plants out of season. Margaret was glad to see my kitchen herbs moved out of her windows and into the glass house.

And as I began branching out with my interests and ambitions, so, apparently, did Master Riggs. One afternoon, he told me that the Missus required me to fetch a dress from a seamstress she didn't normally do business with. I had no reason to doubt the veracity of his request, as I was often sent out for various household errands. He gave me the address and told me I was to go immediately. He had a carriage for me, which wasn't odd since I had far to go.

It was well out of the Riggses' neighborhood, but still a respectable corner of the city. I rang the bell and was seen into a lovely apartment. A well-dressed woman came to the door. "You're Emma, from the Riggs household? I'm Miss Hazel," she said.

I replied, and she escorted me in, and asked me to wait

while she put Mrs. Riggs's order together. I sat down in the drawing room and waited patiently.

It couldn't have been more than a quarter hour later when the doorbell rang. I imagined a seamstress's flat would be very busy, with people coming and going throughout the day. But who came into the room but Master Riggs himself!

"Hello," he said calmly. He took off his own hat and coat and put them over a chair as if he was quite familiar with the flat.

"M–Master Riggs…!" I stuttered. "Whatever are you doing here?"

"Oh, I had an errand myself in this neighborhood. I thought I would escort you back home," he replied, and sat down. It was odd, I thought, but not outlandish. We sat in comfortable silence for some minutes. Eventually the dressmaker returned from down a corridor.

"Emma, come now, please," Miss Hazel said. I followed her down the corridor into a bright, sunlit workroom. A dressmaker's dummy stood near a window, and fabric lay everywhere. On a table were dress pins, measuring tape and all sorts of tailoring tools.

A package wrapped in brown paper sat on a corner of a table, marked "Riggs," which I took to be the Missus's. I was about to pick it up when the seamstress said, "Listen, dear, would you do me a favor? Before you take your mistress's dress, would you be a dear and try something on for me? I have a client about your size, and instead of calling her here for a fitting when I've only just basted, you could try this on and save us all much bother."

This request seemed odd, but I simply wasn't in a position to refuse a reasonable request. But I was beginning to have some doubts…

"Happy to help, ma'am," I offered.

"There's the fitting room." She pointed to a smaller room off the workroom. She handed me a gown filled with basting stitches. I undressed with some trepidation and donned the dress. When it was on I called to her, and she did indeed fit it on me for some minutes, under the arms, around the waist, measuring the length. I felt badly for having had suspicions, and when she sent me to take it off I was thinking of what I needed to do when we returned to the house. I had been polishing silver when I was called to this errand. I needed to finish the silver before midafternoon, and the dressmaker's reminded me that I had mending of tablecloths to do.

But my thoughts were interrupted by Master Riggs's voice in the workroom. "Emma, will you come out?"

"But I'm not yet dressed, sir," I replied.

"Yes, I realize as much," he said.

The rascal! He did it again! Was this woman even our Missus's dressmaker? Who else was here I didn't know about?

"Sir, I'm only half-dressed," I said. He opened the door to the fitting room and led me out by the hand. The dressmaker wasn't in the room at all. He held my hand and led me out of the workroom, across the hall and into another room. There, I saw the dressmaker, also in her underthings, on a big bed. She was smiling, and apparently waiting.

Master Riggs closed the door behind us. So it was a ruse, I thought. How wicked and strange. I certainly hadn't imagined a thing like this. "A surprise for us, Emma, and some special payment for a very special errand...."

"Come here, dear," said the dressmaker in the calmest tone of voice I'd ever heard. "Let's all take a spot of sherry." And she motioned to a tray with a bottle of tawny port and glasses.

Master Riggs poured three glasses. He handed them to us

and took one for himself. "Here's to new adventures, ladies…."
We all drank.

It was a lovely port, indeed, like a liquid red gem. I felt a
bit relaxed and it sparked a little flame in my pussy, as wine
always did.

"Arthur tells me you've got a real knack for gardening, is
that true?" the seamstress asked, taking a sip. My, she was
clever, I thought. I truly loved to talk about my flowers.

"Yes, well, I certainly hope so, ma'am. I read as much as
I can, and I experiment with bulbs and seeds. Every time I
learn something new about a plant I just have more questions.
And the Master's new conservatory has given me whole new
varieties of plants to work with…" I stopped, thinking I was
running on overexcitedly. But she continued, and beckoned
with her hand for Master Riggs to pour again. Mmm, it was
delicious, this sherry.

"Do you mean to apprentice with a florist, eventually?"

"Why, yes, ma'am," I told her, realizing as I spoke that she
had the loveliest hazel-colored eyes I'd ever seen. "My aim is
indeed to secure such a position, if I can find it."

"Well," she said, gazing into my eyes as she spoke, "I know
some people in gardening, and many shop owners. I myself
apprenticed with a milliner in Chelsea when I was younger.
I'll ask around for you, my dear."

By this time the port had gone not just to my head but
through my whole body. Master Riggs had been quiet till
then, but when I glanced at him I saw he'd removed his jacket,
collar and tie. I'd never seen him appear so relaxed, and it
made me feel that way, as well.

Miss Hazel sat up from where she was reclining, reached
over and gently touched my curls. "Undo this…." She began
removing pins from my hair, and brown curls tumbled down
over my shoulders. "You have such lovely hair," she said,

combing her fingers through it. And then she pulled my head swiftly but gently toward her and kissed my lips.

I froze for a moment, but then instinctively returned her kiss. I'd never touched such soft, giving lips. I wanted more, and she could feel it. She licked my lips gently, then pushed her soft tongue slowly inside my mouth.

The port swam through my body, and I could have kissed her for hours. Soft kisses, then urgent, passionate kisses where our tongues met in a sea of softness and sensation. She stopped for a moment and took her glass of port, tipping it first to her lips and then to mine. We both drank, and then kissed again, tasting our mouths and the sweet, ruby port. *Heaven!* I almost swooned.

I touched her hair, and it was soft as lamb's ears' leaves. Her skin smelled of lavender. I was drunk as much with her as with the port. She pulled me to her and we pressed together. She opened my shift and then opened her own. Our naked breasts brushed each other, our nipples touched. Her breasts were round, her brown nipples erect. I was heady with these new sensations.

She pushed me down onto the bed and put her mouth to my nipple. I moaned as she sucked and bit me. Then her hands roamed over my tits, and I took her breasts, hanging in orbs over me, and kneaded them, pulling her nipples, rolling them with my palms. *Where was Master Riggs?* I half wondered, not really caring. I didn't care if he watched or didn't, I was so heady with this steamy seamstress.

And as I thought of him his body was suddenly on the bed with us. Miss Hazel made room for him and I felt his hands pulling my knickers down. As Miss Hazel and I kissed and sucked and caressed, I felt him parting my thighs and moving over me. He slid his fingers into me, and I was wet with port and excitement. He pushed his sex into me and all my nerves burst like pistons in a steam engine. I shuddered and cried, and as he kept pumping I shuddered again. What a ride!

He pulled out of me, and Miss Hazel and he moved to each other, where she bent and took him in her mouth. *That beautiful mouth,* I thought. And I bent down, too, and we shared our mouths and Master Riggs's hard cock. When she came off him we kissed with passion again, our lips and tongues inseparable. I tasted port and felt Master Riggs dribbling it between our mouths. Every taste was delicious, whether it was her mouth, or his hard, craving cock.

Then her mouth left mine and she lowered herself; her lovely orbs bubbled out of her muslin shift. She opened my thighs with her hands. Her fingers parted the folds of my cunt as if they were the petals of a rose. And then her red, round mouth was on my sex! Her soft tongue brushed the length of the crimson folds of my pussy, and I thought I would take flight with pleasure. While she licked and sucked the hidden bulb inside my cunt folds, I shook and moaned. Master Riggs moved again and mounted Miss Hazel from behind, and I raised myself on my elbows to look. What a sight, his big sex between the perfect white globes of her ass.

He slid himself in and out, in and out, and she purred and moaned, her eyes closed as she licked me and slid her fingers in and out of me. We were a purring machine of pleasure, we three. I'd never imagined such a thing. Then she came and came in moans and cries, and when it was done he took his member out of her and worked his cock with his own hand until he spurted his white seed over her ass, spreading it over her skin with his other hand.

We were all spent and happy. Miss Hazel drew herself up to me and kissed me again. "Let's pour a little glass to an afternoon of nice surprises, shall we?" And Master poured glasses. The port was still lovely to taste, as I hadn't been so

drunk as to have felt poorly. Our underclothes were in disar-
ray, and Master Riggs had nothing on but his shirt, which
hung open. I had never seen him as naked, and he was a nice
thing to look at with his tawny, muscular chest.

"Oh, my dear," Miss Hazel said as she swept up some of
my disheveled hair with her hand. "You are a sight. Did you
think you'd have such an errand for your employer? Arthur,
take some money out of my drawer and let's sweeten her pot
of honey." She motioned to a desk drawer and Master Riggs
went to it and took out some pound notes, counting them.

"I am serious, Emma," she said as Master Riggs handed
her the money. "I'll be happy to help you find an apprenticeship."

"Well, I would be most grateful, ma'am," I said.

Master Riggs smiled at me proudly, as if I was a successful junior protégée."You're a clever girl," he said, beaming.
"You'll do well for yourself."

"I'll make us all a strong cup of tea," Miss Hazel said as she
got up off the bed and put on a covering. "We've all got work
to do today! Can't waste our whole day puttering about." She
laughed. She left the room, and Master Riggs began to dress.
I realized that he had been in the bedroom, waiting for such
a mischievous event while Miss Hazel was fitting her client's
dress on me. I was excited to think such a plan had been laid,
in secret, about me. Alone, across the hall in the dressing
room, where I had left my clothes, I mulled over the images
of what had transpired. Such an adventure! I thought, and
smiled to myself.

After a cup of tea, Master Riggs indeed took the package
with his name, and we left in a carriage. "Sir, is Miss Hazel
really your seamstress? I've been sent to a dressmaker's often,
and never to her," I said.

"Yes, she does my things, not my wife's. You've always

reminded me a bit of her, you're both independent girls with an adventurous streak, eh?" He laughed, giving me a little poke with his elbow. And then he reached into his jacket and gave me a pile of notes. My eyes widened, for I'd never received such a handsome sum. Just as well, I thought, since I was taken by surprise after all!

Life continued for some months until one day Master Riggs announced that his friend, Miss Hazel, had indeed found an apprenticeship for me at a large conservatory outside the city. That position took me out of London and so I left behind my sensual adventures with Master Riggs.

Two years later I entered a horticultural college for women and used my earnings to pay my tuition. However could I *not* be grateful to Master Riggs, who helped me along my garden path? Today, I'm the assistant to the head gardener at an important conservatory; and I spend my time designing the gardens, a kind of job I didn't even know existed when I was seventeen. I didn't open a shop after all, though I may wish to do so one day. I never did tell a soul about how I went from selling bunches and sachets from a basket on my arm to where I am today, altogether happy and independent. And I think it will always remain one secret in my own garden of secrets.

★ ★ ★ ★ ★

naughty bits 2, the highly anticipated sequel to the successful debut volume from the editors of Spice Briefs, delivers nine new unapologetically raunchy and romantic tales that promise to spark the libido. In this collection of first-rate short erotic literature, lusty selections by such provocative authors as Megan Hart, Lillian Feisty, Saskia Walker and Portia Da Costa will pique, tease and satisfy any appetite, and prove that good things do come in small packages.

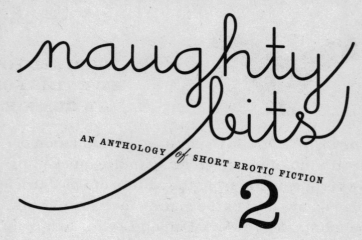

naughty bits

AN ANTHOLOGY *of* SHORT EROTIC FICTION

2

on sale now wherever books are sold!

Since launching in 2007, Spice Briefs has become the hot eBook destination for the sauciest erotic fiction on the Web. *Want more of what we've got?* *Visit* www.SpiceBriefs.com.

Spice

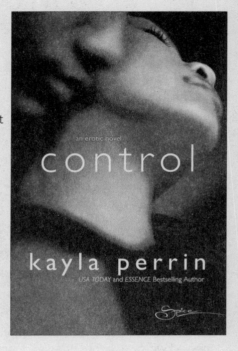

A Hell's Eight erotic adventure from national bestselling author

SARAH McCARTY

Before his trade became his name, "Tracker" Ochoa was a scrawny Mestizo runaway. Now as fearsome as he once was frightened, he's joined the notorious Hell's Eight… and they have a job for him.

He must rescue kidnapped heiress Ari Blake and deliver her safely to the Hell's Eight compound—by any means necessary. Turns out that includes marrying her if he means to escort her and her infant daughter across the Texas Territory. Tracker hadn't bargained on a wife— especially such a fair, blue-eyed beauty. But the pleasures of the marriage bed more than make up for the surprise.

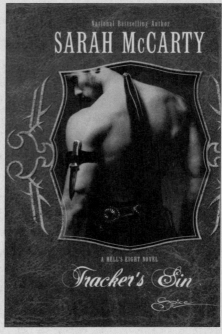

Tracker's well-muscled bronze skin and dark, dangerous eyes are far more exciting than any of Ari's former debutante dreams. In the light of day, though, his deep scars and brooding intensity terrify her. But he's her husband and she's at his mercy. With the frontier against them and mercenary bandits at their heels, Ari fears she'll never feel safe again.

Tracker, too, remembers what fear feels like. Though he burns to protect Ari, to keep her for himself always, he knows that money, history—and especially the truth—can tear them apart.

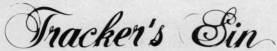

"If you like your historicals packed with emotion, excitement and heat, you can never go wrong with a book by Sarah McCarty."—*Romance Junkies*

Available wherever books are sold!

www.Spice-Books.com

ALISON's WONDERLAND

ALISON TYLER

Over the past fifteen years, Alison Tyler has curated some of the genre's most sizzling collections of erotic fiction, proving herself to be the ultimate naughty librarian. With *Alison's Wonderland,* she has compiled a treasury of naughty tales based on fable and fairy tale, myth and legend: some ubiquitous, some obscure—all of them delightfully dirty.

From a perverse prince to a vampire-esque Sleeping Beauty, the stars of these reimagined tales are—like the original protagonists—chafing at unfulfilled desire. From Cinderella to Sisyphus, mermaids to werewolves, this realm of fantasy is limitless and so *very* satisfying.

Penned by such erotica luminaries as Shanna Germain, Rachel Kramer Bussel, N.T. Morley, Elspeth Potter, T.C. Calligari, D.L. King, Portia Da Costa and Tsaurah Litzsky, these bawdy bedtime stories are sure to bring you (and a friend) to your own happily-ever-after.

"Alison Tyler has introduced readers to some of the hottest contemporary erotica around."—*Clean Sheets*

www.Spice-Books.com

SAT60545TR

the LOVERS
Eden Bradley

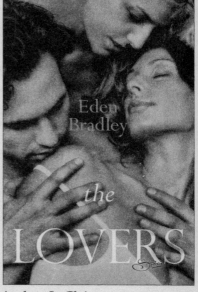

I had long dreamed of having a single experience that would change me forever. Who knew the one to change me would be a woman? But the story doesn't end there. No, that in itself is a whole new beginning.

It seemed ideal—two months at a charming writers' retreat, surrounded by kindred souls. But Bettina Boothe wasn't prepared for just how long eight weeks truly was. Or that in the process she would have to open up and reveal the most secret places in her body and soul.

Fortunately, her fellow authors do not share Bettina's self-consciousness and begin to draw her out of her self-imposed shell. One in particular—Audrey LeClaire—seems to ooze confidence and self-assuredness. Dark and petite, Audrey possesses a potent sensuality that draws the men *and* women in the workshop to her like flies to honey. Bettina is just as vulnerable, finding herself overwhelmed by a very unexpected attraction to Audrey, who makes Bettina her special project.

But when Jack Curran arrives at the retreat, everything changes. Jack is tall, beautiful, masculine. A writer of dark thrillers, he is as mysterious and alluring as his books. He and Audrey are obviously an item, but they eagerly welcome Bettina into their bed. Suddenly Bettina finds herself swept up in a maelstrom of lust, obsession and jealousy, torn between her need for two very different people in a love triangle where she will either be cherished…or consumed.

Available wherever books are sold!